The Nightman's Odyssey

THE NIGHTMAN'S ODYSSEY

Corridors of Eternity
Book 1

Tony-Paul de Vissage

EPIC
PUBLISHING

This book is a work of fiction. Names, characters, places, events, and dialogues are drawn from the author's imagination or are used fictitiously. Any resemblance to actual events, locales, or persons, living or dead, is coincidental.

The Nighttman's Odyssey © 2011-2023 Tony-Paul de Vissage
Cover art © 2023 Rebecca Frank
Edited by Lily Luchesi

Epic Publishing supports the right to free expression and the value of copyright. The purpose of copyright is to encourage writers and artists to produce creative works that enrich our culture.

The scanning, uploading, and distribution of this book without permission is a theft of the author's intellectual property. If you would like permission to use material from this book (other than for review purposes), please contact publisher@epic-publishing.com.

Epic Publiblishing
370 Castle Shannon Blvd., #10366
Pittsburgh, PA 15234
www.epic-publishing.com

Original publication 2011 by Class Act Books, under the title *The Nightman Cometh*

First publication by Epic Publishing 2023

ISBN 978-1-7346486-6-9

Epic Publishing is an imprint of Mighty, LLC.
The Epic Publishing name and logo are trademarks of Mighty, LLC.

The publisher is not responsible for websites (or their content) which are not owned by the publisher.

*For Blake Slack, whom I have watched grow up Online.
Mon tres meilleurs voeux.*

Time . . . something a vampire has in abundance . . . time to enjoy the pleasures of Immortality . . . and time to contemplate his mistakes.

I learned that the hard way . . . for Time brings with it one thing: the desire for the company of another being.

One doesn't have to be human to feel alone, to suffer the grief of loss or the need for companionship and love. That which once was a man can still harbor gentle emotions though he denies them. He may unconsciously seek forgiveness though he never says the word aloud.

Chapter 1

Antoinette
Limousin, France
May 21, 1249

"*Hail, Mary, full of Grace, the Lord is with thee . . . Holy Mother, Pray for us now and at the time of our deaths . . .*"

Even as he muttered the prayer, Damién cursed himself as a hypocrite and a liar.

The priests teach Man is a Sinner from his first breath, cursed by our Primal Parents and born into willful disobedience against the Lord, and therefore should welcome death and its reward of heaven with open arms.

Damién suffered the double guilt of his disbelief and of keeping that doubt secret.

To him, Death was the end, not a beginning or even a continuation, and he was sorely afraid he would be confronting that ending very soon.

It was a reasonable fear, he told himself. Everyone feared death, though some might accept it more readily than others.

He tried to rationalize his terror. His life was too valuable; his death would leave the Domaine de La

Croix without an heir, but that was a mere shading of the truth.

Damién didn't care who died as long as it wasn't himself. As far as he was concerned, Heaven was a lie fed to ignorant peasants to hide a stark reality discovered only too late... that death was Oblivion... a fall into bottomless darkness with no resurrection in sight, a snuffing of breath, heartbeat, and thought.

Damién didn't want that oblivion, he wanted to continue his existence... to be with his Antoinette... to live and love with her... not become food for some hungry worm waiting even now to grub in his grave.

He was a child of his Time, pampered and spoiled, accustomed to getting what he wanted. At this particular moment, what he wished most was to live to enjoy the woman he loved. Nevertheless, in this instance, what he desired was being cruelly withheld.

This time, Damién wasn't going to get his way.

His traitorous mouth continued praying as he'd been taught, spewing words more and more desperate... *Sweet Jesu, don't let us die... protect us from this scourge... I call upon St. Jude Libraeus, Saint of the Impossible, Patron of Desperate Situations, have mercy, and bring about this miracle, I beg you... St Christopher, have mercy, I invoke your protection against this plague... Dear Lord, Holy Savior help me!*

Desperation and panic mingled with unmanly tears, streaming down his clean-shaven cheeks.

St. Damién, Patron of Physicians, and my namesake, steal the power from this plague, prevent it from infecting us so my Antoinette and I may survive... oh God, I don't want to die...

For over a year, the *Great Mortality* had been in France—a year and fifteen days, to be exact—and in Limousin less than a month. If ever a Scourge from God had been placed upon Mankind, this was it.

Nevertheless, no one dared question. All accepted as something deserved, for being human, if for no other reason. Sinners condemned by the mere fact of their existence to suffer and die.

And be swept away into nothingness. If Damién's doubts had previously hovered secretly in his mind, the falling of this pestilence upon the people of Limousin—*his* people—confirmed them with a vengeance.

Doctors attempted treatment, and he asked himself, *Why? If we are already condemned, why bother? Why go through such useless motions?*

And if a few survived? Did that mean those were so saintly as to be allowed to live, or were they simply now doubly condemned, and the dead to be envied as destined for that much-touted salvation?

He was well aware such thoughts were heretical and could consign him to flames much worse than the plague fires should he dare speak them aloud, so he held his own counsel and his ever-growing anger.

Who would he speak them to, anyway? His friend Armand? His betrothed Antoinette? Neither was allowed near his father's estate, as he was forbidden theirs. Some nonsense about isolation making one safer.

He doubted that.

If the pestilence is miasma-borne on the wind as the physicians think, how can hiding ourselves away protect us? The wind was everywhere; even if a man climbed the highest peak or sank himself into the deepest well, that ebbing and flowing stream of air would find him.

All seclusion did was prevent his having the solace

of friendship or love.

His desperate supplication ended, he got to his feet.

Now for something more important. Going to his Antoinette.

Crossing himself once more, he returned his rosary to his belt-purse and started down the aisle to the entrance only to stop as the doors swung open. A body blocked his path, a bulky silhouette against the late evening sun.

"*Père* Gervais?" Damién put up a hand, shading his eyes from the direct glare. Under its shield, he could make out the priest's features ... eyes reddened, face pale and streaked ... with tears?

Thinking the Father was manifesting some new phase of the plague, he took a step backward as Gervais came toward him.

Damn it, if he's infected, I'll kill him before I let him touch me, priest or not.

"Damién ... my son ..." The words were muffled by a filled throat, so low he barely heard. One hand extended, clutching something inside.

A folded piece of vellum. A letter.

"Wh-what is it?" Damién's own hand went to his side, remembering too late he'd left his sword and belt-dagger hanging from his saddle, obeying the priest's command not to bring weapons into the Lord's House. He stepped back, holding up his hands, warding him away.

The priest stopped. Lowering the upraised hand, he took a deep breath and collected himself.

"I'm sorry, my son. Truly I am." A tear trickled down his cheek, making a new track across the others.

"What do you mean?"

"I've just come from *Château de Chevigny* ..."

"*Non.*" If the priest was called, that meant only one thing.

Gervais said nothing else, merely held out the letter. When Damién snatched it from him, he let his hand drop to his side, like a dead thing, like those in the *château* would soon be. He stood without speaking, watching the young man rip away the seal and unfold the single sheet, closing his eyes as Damién's frantic ones scanned the words placing a death sentence on all his hopes.

Damién, ma cher,

I am stricken. In spite of your prayers, the Scourge is visited upon me. My maman has already been taken and I fear I will be next. As I breathe my last, I will think of you and of the life we might have had.

I pray we meet again in Heaven.

Toujours je t'aime,
Your Antoinette.

"It can't be. I saw her just yesterday." He didn't add it had been through the bars of the *château's* gates. He waved the sheet. "This letter is a lie!"

"'Tis no lie, my lord." Gervais dared come close enough to place a hopefully calming hand on his shoulder. "I was called to the *château* early this morning. I gave Lady Antoinette her Last Rites and she, in turn, asked me to deliver that letter to you."

With the swiftness the Plague carried away its victims, it had become the custom to call in the priest as soon as symptoms manifested.

Silently, he accepted Gervais' words. His Antoinette was going to die. Instead of coming a blushing bride to his marriage bed, she would be consigned—a rotting, blood-weeping corpse—to the plague fires.

Nevertheless, he said again, "Lies," as if repeating it would make it so. "Just as everything else is a lie . . . even the Scriptures we've been taught all our lives."

"Lord Damién!" Gervais staggered as if he'd been struck. Clutching the rosary around his neck, he sucked in the strength to say, "Listen to yourself. You speak blasphemy." He looked upward, clasping the length of beads. "Father, forgive him. 'Tis his grief speaking."

"Grief? Aye, I've grief. A great one. I'm losing the woman I love, damn it! And I can't even tell her goodbye. I have to receive her last words in a *letter*." He spoke the word as if it also held pestilence.

He wouldn't even be allowed to attend the funeral, for there would be none, only the plague wagon, coming with its tolling bell. Come to carry his Antonette to the fire.

"She'll be placed in the de Chevigny crypt. She won't be burned."

He hadn't realized he spoke aloud until Gervais said that.

"It doesn't matter. She'll still be dead. Dead—and not my wife." Damién flung the letter to the floor. Turning away so the priest might not see, he allowed tears to flow.

Grief mixed with his anger. Crying because God had failed him, tears for someone lost before she was gained.

"Why is it happening, Father? I prayed . . . most devoutly . . . every day since the Plague came to La Croix. Why didn't the Heavenly Father answer my prayers?" He began to sob in earnest, hands pressed to his face.

"Perhaps . . ." Gervais was at a loss for words. He left that single one fade into silence.

"Perhaps . . . *what?*"

Damién's expression startled the priest. Briefly, he appeared furious rather than grief-stricken.

"Perhaps God was too busy? Perhaps he doesn't care? *Perhaps he doesn't really exist?*" He spat the sentence viciously. "Why not tell the truth for once, Father?"

He was raving now, fury building with each word.

"That all this—" Waving his arms to take in the now-empty pews. "—is a farce . . . a falsehood to make us accept dying without a struggle. Those of us fool enough to believe such deceits."

The priest didn't answer.

Because there isn't an answer, and he knows it. Damién dropped his hands, looking at the guilty missive, lying where he'd thrown it. He lifted his foot, grinding the paper against the floor with his boot-heel.

He wanted to destroy it all, smash and grind to dust every stone of this monument to the lies fed to them all their lives. He began to shake, the fury inside struggling to force itself free.

"My lord, please." Gervais was still attempting consolation, reaching out to touch a trembling shoulder. "Come. Perhaps Confession will salve your doubts, or . . . let us talk . . ."

"Confession? Aye, I'll confess." Damién jerked away from the priest's grasp. Clasping his hands together, he held them out, grip so tight their tremor was visible. "Father, don't forgive me for I have knowingly sinned . . . and I . . . don't . . . care."

His words were a sarcastic twisting of those he'd spoken devoutly so many times.

"I've long questioned everything and doubted it all. That doubt makes me now ignore the *Matins* and the *Angelus* . . . and I haven't believed in that garbage you spout to us for a long, long time, either."

His hand clenched into a fist, raising it with such a violent movement the priest shrank back.

"Do you know why I really come here to pray each day? Would you like to know a *real* truth? My prayers for our survival are a test to God. If we are saved, I'll believe, if not . . ." He laughed, and the sound was so bitter, *Père* Gervais felt his heart break. Damién raised the fist higher, looking upward as if he'd threaten Heaven. "Well, we aren't saved, are we?"

The fury took over. He rushed toward the priest who scrambled aside.

"We aren't saved! And never will be."

Next to the door stood the baptismal fount, placed there until needed at the pulpit, so heavy it took two men to carry it. With the strength of the furious, he seized it, flinging it aside. It crashed against the wall, the marble basin cracking, carved wooden base in splinters. Water splashed, trickling across the floor.

"God's been tested and found wanting." He whirled, singling out something else to destroy.

A pew was lifted, heaved toward a window. The precious stained glass shattered outward in a spray of colored fragments; the broken bench lodged within the frame. Other furniture was upended, thrown against the wall, smashed against pillars holding up the roof. Fragments of wood-dust floated to the floor.

Damién ran down the aisle toward the altar.

"No! My Lord, please. Don't do more desecration." Gervais caught his arm, was dragged by his fury, sandaled feet skidding on the stone floor. "Don't condemn yourself even more."

He was slung aside, sprawling against the base of a still-standing pew as Damién's arm swept a row of candles to the floor. Melted wax splashed and sputtered. Flames guttered, dimmed, then rose as fire leaped from one fallen candle to another.

What have I done? For the briefest moment, Damién stared, appalled, at the destruction. In the next, he didn't care. To the sound of *Père* Gervais' cries for help as the flames spread to the tapestries and the wooden images behind the altar, he ran for the door.

His horse was tied to a hitching-ring set to one side, attached to a picket driven into the earth. Untying the reins, he flung himself into the saddle, jerking the animal's head toward *Château de Chevigny*.

***

The plague wagon lumbered by, pulled by two slow-moving oxen. Walking beside, its masked and hooded driver didn't look up, tugging on the bridle of the nearest animal, moving it along. It didn't hurry; the cart crept with the rhythmic slowness of a funeral *cortege*, though nowhere near as solemn nor regal, plodding hooves keeping time to the dull clanging of the bell the attendant swung back and forth as he followed the wagon.

Bodies were piled high, heaved in without regard for how they landed or even if actually dead. In an attempt to contain the pestilence, a heavily waxed cloth had been tossed over the unwieldy pile of corpses and fastened to the cart's sides by lengths of rope. The reek of corruption, of pus and blood, vomit and rot seeped from under its edges.

Some of the corpses had been dead for days before being discovered, the last of their households. Thus having no one to bring them out for the wagoneer to gather. Others were tossed from windows, retrieved from the dirt and thrown onto the ever-growing pile. Only a few were carried out by family members and given up with tears and wails of grief.

Pulling his horse to a dust-stirring halt, Damién slid from its back and stopped. Even in his fury, he didn't dare cross the path of a plague-wagon. Standing with head bowed, one hand clasped to nose and mouth to prevent inhaling death-laden air as the cart passed, his other hand raised to make the Sign of the Cross before he caught himself.

No, no more of that foolishness.

A wagon wheel struck a rock, wobbling. The canvas lifted, then settled again. A body shifted, one arm falling out of the cart, swinging inches above the road, fingers stiff and curved as if clawing at the dirt. Its skin was speckled and splotched, swollen with open sores from which yellow ichors still leaked. A few drops struck the soil, spattering puffs of dust. Did he hear a faint moan, see a slight tremor of that wasted arm hanging through the staves?

And this will happen to my Antoinette. He didn't believe she'd be placed in the family vault.

All bodies were burned.

It was Law. *Now.*

Antoinette, chérie, mon amour . . .

As Damién had told *Père* Gervais, his last sight of his beloved had been the day before. It had been three weeks since Damién was allowed admittance to the *château*. Every day, he came to the gate, standing like a beggar waiting to be given the alms that were a sight of his Antoinette. For twenty-one days, he rode to the church to beg God and the Holy Mother to protect them, then to the *château* to speak with her.

***

She always met him at the gates where they talked but never touched. This time, she stopped a good ten yards away, hands clasped to her bosom.

"Go away, Damién. The mayor has ordered our gates locked to all but the physician."

"The mayor? Antoinette, the mayor died weeks ago. How can a dead man give orders?"

"The Council then . . . someone . . . I don't know. You see the guards." Her voice rose in a desperate shrill as she waved a hand at the armed soldiers standing to each side of the gate. She was shouting to make herself heard across the distance.

At that moment, the wind—that death-carrying air—swirled around her, then dipped, ruffling the edges of her wimple, fluttering the half-sleeves draped around her elbows. There was a sudden brilliant flash, sun reflecting off the band of her betrothal ring. Damién had chosen it himself, presenting it to Antoinette only three weeks before.

"I'm not leaving, Antoinette." With his fist, he beat

the gate's stone pylon. "I came here to see you and I will, if I have to climb these walls."

At that, one of the guards raised his lance, and Antoinette gave a short, quick cry. "Please, my love. Don't endanger yourself any more than you already have."

"My Lady?" Marie—Antoinette's old nurse, now her *chaperon*—stood a few feet away, giving her a modicum of privacy, if being in the open yelling into the wind could be considered *private*. She plucked at the blue wool sleeve. "We must go. Your father will miss you."

"Don't," Damién begged. He leaned against the gate, wrapping a hand around one of the upright iron shafts. It felt hard and cold to his skin, grains of rust from years of rain and weather, flaked onto his palm. "Stay and talk to me. If this is the only way I may see you . . ."

Marie continued tugging Antoinette's arm, turning her inexorably away. She allowed the old woman to lead her down the footpath toward the *château*. After walking a few feet, she broke away and turned back. Pressing her fingers to her lips, she hurled a kiss into the air, then whirled and began to run, leaving the old woman shuffling after her.

Damién was certain he felt the kiss strike his cheek. *Please God the wind brings none of the pestilence with it.*

He watched until Antoinette reached the *château's* looming bulk and disappeared inside. Continuing to lean his forehead against the roughness of the iron pickets, he pressed against the cold metal, letting it abrade his skin until the sun slid behind the trees and shadows lengthened.

At last, one of the guards spoke. "My lord, you should go."

Only then did he turn away, walking back to where

he'd tied his horse to the low-hanging branch of a yew tree.

Yew, symbol of darkness and death. He shivered, hoping it wasn't one more sign.

* * *

The horse raised its head, nickering and snorting slightly.

Why are the animals not affected?

Some died but it was mostly because their owners succumbed and there was no one to feed them. Starvation, not plague, killed animals.

Why does it only strike their masters? Does God favor a dumb animal over an intelligent man because He knows it won't question Him?

The gate creaked as one of the guards swung it open. While he'd been distracted by the wagon and his own thoughts, the doctor left the *château*.

Damién waited until the physician was outside before he waylaid him. "*Docteur le sangsue*, tell me, how is she? How is my Antoinette?"

He was desperate, begging the man not to say exactly what he said.

"I'm sorry, Your Lordship. 'Tis a fast-moving case, faster than most." His sigh was irritated, more at being inconvenienced by Damién stopping him from leaving than holding any regret or sympathy.

Damién's resentment flared. *He sounds as if he truly doesn't care. You bastard. The vicomte's your patron. You owe him your best skill.*

"I doubt she'll last another day." It was said flatly with

no concern for his feelings.

Without another word, the doctor walked away. Damién kept pace with him, though far enough from the robed figure they didn't touch.

"You shouldn't have come here. By leaving the safety of your estate, you place yourself in danger."

Safety? Hah. How can that stupid man call my home safe when eight of our serfs already show the first signs?

Damién wanted to backhand the fool, pick him up and heave him into one of the pits where his many patients now lay waiting consignment to purifying fire.

If one's home's so damned safe, how did Antoinette and her mother, who rarely left its confines, become ill at all? Does he believe he's safe at this distance? Fool, he wanted to shout. *You're no more protected than the rest of us. Doctors die of the same things as their patients all the time.*

Didn't the churchyard have a special section for the illustrious medical men who'd succumbed while treating others? Though now, of course, there were no new graves. There was no room; the cemetery yard of *Village de La Croix* was filled, the holy soil itself contaminated.

Thus, the dead, whether noble or common, *marquis* or serf, were now taken to a pit on the edge of town and burned, relinquished to cleansing fire. And when that one was filled with too many ashes, another was dug, and when it filled, another...

What's the use?

He said none of it. Just nodded numbly, bowed to the physician, and stumbled back to his own horse, grazing a few feet away.

Will arguing save Antoinette?

If that were so, he'd have been her salvation and his

own the moment the first soul was stricken.

Catching up his reins, Damién swung into the saddle and left the doctor standing there.

He tried not to think as the horse broke into a canter before being kicked into a head-long gallop. Didn't *want* to think, but memories of Antoinette, of what had already happened, and what might have been, crowded his mind.

Only three weeks before, they'd still been unafraid to come together in fellowship, mingling for celebration; in this case, the betrothal of the son of the *Marquis* de La Croix to the daughter of his old friend, the *Vicomte* de Chevigny.

* * *

It was an arranged marriage, of course. Blue bloods didn't dare do otherwise. But the two young people had known each other all their lives, and were convinced they were, indeed, in love. Shy glances—at first a novelty for the lusty Damién— timid clasping of hands, sitting side-by-side on a small couch laughingly called a *loveseat,* all under the supervision of old Marie or sometimes their parents, was the closest they came to intimacy.

Damién was willing to play that game. He had other ways of seducing. Through the written word, he wooed his Antoinette, being more indiscreet and sometimes so frank on paper it brought a blush to his own cheeks. In secret correspondence carried by servants, he told the girl he loved her, would worship her once they were wed. When she came to his marriage bed, he would show her the delights of heaven in uniting her body with his.

My dagger waits for your slender sheath, my beloved. I tremble to show you the power your love gives me . . . I pant in expectation for the night I may caress your naked flesh and show you what is truly meant by Paradise . . .

Armand had made suitably doubtful noises, of course, then laughing threats of what he'd do if Damién ever was unfaithful to his sister.

"I vow I've misgivings of wanting such a libertine as *le Seigneur* La Croix even looking at my *petite soeur,* must less bedding her, you scoundrel."

All in jest, of course. His companion in the pursuit of carnal delights was as happy as he that soon they would be brothers by marriage.

Damién was thinking all these thoughts at the betrothal celebration, and if Antoinette's blushes were any indication whenever her eyes met his, so was she. When everyone's attention was elsewhere, he dared look at her and slowly ran his tongue along his lower lip, then flick it quickly in her direction. Her blush told him she understood that gesture's general inference if not completely its meaning.

Oh, to be alone with you for even an hour, ma petite.

After toasts from both their fathers, Damién presented her with his ring, a single cabochon of red jasper, symbol of love. Holding her left hand gently on his open palm, because closing his fingers around it was forbidden at this point, he slid it onto the thumb of her left hand—*"In the Name of the Father"*—then onto her forefinger—*"the Son"*—and middle finger—*"and the Holy Spirit"*—before placing it on her fourth finger—*"I ask you to become my wife."*

Overcome by the emotion of the moment, and the look of love on his darling's face, he dared raise her hand

and press his lips to the ring. To the gasps of those present at his effrontery in performing such an intimate act before them, he turned over her hand and kissed her palm also, touching the tip of his tongue to its center. When he released her, Antoinette clasped the hand against her breast, fingers curled into a fist as if to protect the kiss inside.

"Well! You must forgive my son for allowing his emotions to get the best of him."

The *marquis* touched Damién's shoulder, fingers tightening as he nearly jerked his son away from the girl, making him stand beside him again. He gave him a quick shake before releasing him.

"You see he truly loves your daughter, François." In an aside to Damién, he hissed, "For the Lord's sake, control yourself, *mon fils*."

The *vicomte* had been sympathetic, though protective, nodding he understood. It was well-known he and his wife were very much in love in spite of having had an arranged marriage also. That gesture stated he tolerated Damién's rashness though it must go no further. Not before the wedding, anyway.

Damién didn't care. He told himself he'd be patient for the night he and his bride would be alone and naked in their marriage bed. Nevertheless, he thought of it . . . relished that image in his mind . . . dreamed of it to the point of several times releasing himself during the night. His Antoinette, pale and bare . . . their flesh brushing and uniting. He'd be gentle but passionate . . . loving but considerate of her untouched state.

Damién himself was no virgin. At twenty-four, he and Armand, like most young men of their class, had rid themselves of that useless condition as soon as they'd seen the first curl of groin-hair. Once that was done, no female was safe; they'd cut a swath through village girls and serving maids—taking maidenheads by the score—as well as serfs and willing tavern wenches who liked it hot and fast and occasionally cruel. There were very few virgins left in Village de La Croix thanks to Damién and Armand de Chevigny, they were so skillful and ruthless in their lures and pursuits.

Village fathers protested . . . to the priests, the magisters . . . to no avail. The two young lechers were simply following established custom, and *les autorités* saw no wrong in that. It was expected young nobles should sate their burgeoning lusts with lower-class females and thus protect the gentler-bred ones.

Like Antoinette . . .

In a fit of love, or lust, or something in between, Damién declared to her he had found his *anam cara*—his soul-mate—and once they joined as husband and wife, he'd never seek any other female again. For at least a month, anyway.

As far as their not being alone, tonight was no different; for the rest of the evening, they used their eyes and soulful glances to communicate across the dining table, each look stating quite clearly *soon, my love . . . soon . . .*

And then the Pestilence struck . . .

***

Where the hell am I? His mind was so befuddled with his blasphemous thoughts, Damién hadn't paid attention to where he rode. He'd simply let the horse have its head.

They broke from the forest and found themselves in a man-made clearing, butts and limbless poles of trees stacked clumsily about. As his horse stopped, the wind shifted, bringing a scent of decay and burnt flesh . . . telling Damién their location.

The plague pits.

In his distraction, he'd unconsciously guided his mount directly to the last place he might wish to be. Not that he could see much of it at the moment. While he was riding alone in that self-induced fugue, the sun's last rays long ago winked out through the trees' shielding branches.

He was alone. In the dark. At the edge of a charnel pit.

I must get out of here.

Damién pressed a rein against the horse's neck, urging him to turn. The animal balked, instead giving a chesty nicker. He touched ribs with his heels, pulled on the reins. The creature refused to move, legs stiffening. This time, the sound it made was a protest, sounding almost . . . *frightened?*

'Tis the scent of death here. How could anything living not be affected? Nothing to do but lead it, then.

He slid from the saddle, walking to the horse's head. Gripping the bridle at the bit, he stroked the fine Barbary muzzle, whispering some soothing nonsense. Raising his head, he did something he hadn't intended.

He looked out across the pit.

Nothing could've prepared him for that sight. Not the woodcuts of Hell in the family Bible, nor the threats of damnation *Père* Gervaise heaped upon them at services . . . not even his own most secret nightmares.

The hole was nearly twelve feet deep. It must have taken laborers a goodly time to dig it. Dirt lay in high heaps around the sides, silhouetted like low mountains in the dimness. It extended a fair fifty feet, more a *gorge* than a pit but to Damién's horror-struck eyes, it appeared a valley into Hell.

How many bodies can this hold?

A good number of La Croix's population, to be sure, for beyond it was a mound of the same size, piled high with tamped dirt and beyond that another, testimony to the number already buried here.

In this one, the bodies were still uncovered, a fresh layer, though the wagoneer and his helper would be back soon, pouring lamp oil over the corpses and tossing lighted faggots to send these unfortunates to their Reward.

As the bodies burned, those under them, already reduced to human charcoal and cinders, would burn again, transformed into even finer ashes rising with the smoke to float away on the winds. When the pit could hold no more, it would be covered over by that waiting dirt.

Sometimes the flames would leap so high, they could see them at the *château*, tinting the sky a lurid red. *Like the flames of Hell, Maman* would murmur and cross herself.

Damién pushed thoughts of his mother from his mind. He didn't want to think of her.

The horse snuffled again, an odd, little choking deep in its chest. That brought Damién out of his grisly reverie. He patted the dark neck.

"Quiet, now. 'Tis all—"

What's that? Whatever else he was going to say died away as he saw something move.

At the far side of the pit, it seemed to have simply appeared. He'd swear it wasn't there a moment ago. A dark, hunched, unwieldy shape, picking its clumsy way among the bodies.

A survivor? Some poor soul not yet dead, awakening to find himself covered by his friends and neighbors' corpses? Now stumbling over them in half-mad terror?

The shape halted, bent as if peering at one of the bodies, and reached out. Its hand dropped and the dark form moved on. It went a few more feet, then hesitated again. This time, it seized a body, wrenching it from under another. It embraced the corpse it held.

Is it actually kissing its neck? Damién felt his throat clog in revulsion.

The body was tossed aside, disgust in the movement. It fell with a liquid thud. The thing moved on, peering this way and that, searching for something it didn't find, coming closer to where Damién stood above it.

The horse threw back its head, short, sharp squeals bursting from its throat. It struggled to back away, pulling the reins from Damién's hands. As he recaptured them, the creature below him raised its head.

Holy Mother.

Its eyes glowed, red as coals . . . and they looked straight at him.

The wind swirled into the pit. It stirred the thing's cloak, making it flutter away from the thin body. For a moment, it looked like . . .

Wings.

Lord God, save us. They are *wings.* Unfurling, great dark sails dwarfed the creature's body, flapping as if preparing to take it airborne.

The horse moved again, backing frantically, Damién following. It reared, and he felt the burn of leather across his palm as the reins were jerked out of his hand. He made a futile grab for the flying straps, but the animal whirled on hind legs, galloping into the safety of the trees.

There was a sound behind him. Something landing with a *thump*. Damién spun around.

The creature stood before him, eyes still glowing. He swore he saw flames flickering within them. It collapsed its wings; once more they were merely clumsy shreds of cloth. It took a step toward him. Hands curved into claws reached out.

Damién didn't run. He knew the creature's identity, and that there was no chance he could escape. The priests told of such night-demons and of their incredible speed and powers greater than any mortal's.

What had they said of ways to overcome them? He couldn't remember.

The thing gathered itself for a leap. It would be on him before he could run . . .

. . . and was.

He barely had time to reach into the pouch at his waist, fingers scrabbling for the rosary tucked there.

Thank God I didn't toss it away. He thought of that irony as the creature launched itself. Damién thrust out his arm, crucifix dangling from the string of beads wrapped around his hand.

The creature ran directly into it. With a scream, it recoiled, falling backward so quick it appeared to have been tossed by the holy object.

Perhaps it had.

It fell on its back in the dirt and Damién was upon it, pressing the cross into its chest through the filthy rags, one knee on its belly, holding it down.

It gasped and struggled, a smell of rot and filth floating upward from the rags. Under the edges of the crucifix, flesh sizzled and blackened.

Damién swallowed and fought the urge to gag. He forced himself to touch the creature, catching one flailing wrist and pinning it to the ground. He was surprised by how light it felt, at the frailty of the body beneath his. He thought if he pressed harder with his knee, it might actually crush that bony chest and go through.

It stopped fighting. The eyes blinked, the red glow faded, and it lay still.

Has it died? Have I crushed the hellish life from it?

When it spoke, he was startled.

"If you're going to destroy me, go ahead. Oblivion is better than the existence I now suffer." The sound was deep and hoarse, rusty, like a gate hinge grown solid with age being wrenched open.

"What do you know of oblivion?" Damién asked. "You're *le sans mort,* aren't you?"

There was a faint nod. Another wafting of that frightful smell. Damién swallowed, gulping back his disgust.

"*Oui,* I'm *le sans mort* but what good does immortality do me?"

He couldn't believe the whine in the creature's voice. It might be *sans mort,* an undead one, but it sounded so . . . human. So full of self-pity.

"What pleasure is there in feeding on corpses?"

"Why bother?" Damién surprised himself by laughing. "There's an entire village only a short distance . . ."

"A *dying* village. No one has the strength to invite me in. I can't get to them, so I hunt among the dead, disgusting as that may be. Bah!" He made a spitting motion.

Damién shrank back without releasing his hold on the

bony wrist.

"Blood thick and drying... solid in their veins... and if I find one still holding a spark of life... 'Tis too mixed with pus to be palatable." He shook his head. "Go on. Destroy me. I no longer care."

By now, Damién had gotten a good look at the *sans mort*. It startled him, for he'd expected a distorted, inhuman face, thin, twisted, disfigured... like those in the woodcuts.

The creature's face was thin, to be sure, as was his body. Not exactly human but close enough to believe it had once been so. High cheekbones, thin lips... almost aristocratic in their luminous paleness... Emaciated but with an odd beauty. It snarled slightly—or was it a laugh?—revealing thin, needle-sharp fangs, gleaming in the dim light.

That sent a chill through Damién, thinking of those fang-points sinking into his own flesh. There was a second sensation. A brief pang of a thought... a desperate idea.

"Perhaps I will and perhaps not."

"What does that mean?" The *sans mort's* brow wrinkled.

"It means, I also am in a dilemma, *M'sieu le Sans mort*. And I may have a way out for both of us. I'll give you a choice. You can listen to what I have to say or—"

He didn't finish, merely applied pressure to the cross.

There was a faint *sizzle* as he pressed it against the creature's chest. As long as the crucifix touched it, the *sans mort* would be unable to move. He'd have plenty of time to release the cross, leaving it immobilized, and find a stick or tree limb to drive through its heart. Then, he'd catch his horse, get his sword, and hack off its head... or not, if it was agreeable to his proposal.

"I'm listening," the creature wheezed. "You have a captive audience, I'm afraid."

It had a sense of irony, even when faced with its own destruction?

Damién took a deep breath. "Take me. Make me as you are, and I'll let you go."

"What?"

He couldn't have believed any face, mortal or otherwise, could've shown such surprise. Damién repeated what he'd said.

"I shouldn't argue, but may I ask . . . why would you wish that?"

"I don't want to die of the plague, and that's inevitable. Make me as you and I'll be immortal. You can't be harmed by human illness, can you?"

Doubt slithered through Damién, momentarily quashing his plan. What if the creature could be infected?

Then I'm certain to die, lying against him as I am. He felt his skin cringe, his whole body wanting to jerk away. He forced himself to stay still.

"I'm well beyond the reach of any human malady," *le sans mort* growled.

"Make me as you, and I'll give you a *château* full of living bodies, and all the blood you can drink." Callously, he offered his servants, the serfs, and his family to the creature in exchange for his own survival.

Surprisingly, the thing hesitated.

"Think of it . . . freedom to enter whenever you wish . . . good, rich, red blood . . . no more scavenging . . ." Damién startled himself by the fervor in his words. "You said you don't enjoy being a ghoul. Why continue when I offer you exactly what you need?"

"You have a point, and not just the one on the end of that damned thing burning into my chest." The creature coughed, swallowed, and nodded. The movement made a dry rustling in its flesh. "Very well, I accept."

One last doubt niggled. "How do I know I can trust you? Mayhap I let you go and you'll simply kill me."

"And do myself out of an estateful of meals? I'm *sans mort*, not stupid. Besides," it looked thoughtful, "it would be good to have a *compagnon de nuit*. I've been alone a very long time."

Its tongue, pale and long, thrust out, raking across its lower lip.

"You look a tempting morsel. I could enjoy you in more ways than one."

That sent a shiver through Damién. *Whatever that means, I'll worry about it later. For now . . .*

Nodding, he removed the cross and stood up.

Like a ragged shadow, the creature rose with him. Wings rustled and flapped. It made a leg, bent with remarkable grace, one hand gesturing delicately. The bow of a man at court.

Can this creature have once been a noble?

"Geraint LeMaitre." It was a travesty of a formal introduction. "And whom do I have the honor of addressing?"

"Damién La Croix, *fils de le Marquis* La Croix." In case the creature had no idea of its location, he added, "Village de La Croix is a short distance from here. In Limousin."

"Ah," LeMaitre nodded. "I wondered the name of this place. 'Tis so different from Paris. *Oui*, I've come a long way in my wanderings," he said to Damién's surprised look.

"It doesn't matter where you're from, just that you're here."

"You can get rid of that." LeMaitre gestured.

Damién looked down at the rosary.

"Soon, you'll have no need of it."

"*Oui*," he agreed. He tossed it into the pit. With the other hand, he unbuttoned the neck of his tunic . . . businesslike, making certain his hands didn't tremble. "Let's get on with it."

"With pleasure." LeMatire took a step forward, placing a hand on Damién's shoulder. Bony fingers brushed his forehead . . . and stopped.

The thin face turned toward the trees. Damién followed the red gaze. A faint gleam peeked through the branches.

"I can't. Not now. Morning comes."

"Then hurry." Damién caught the hand on his shoulder, gripping the wrist, preventing him from pulling away. Now that he'd come this far, he had to finish.

If I must wait, I may not again have the courage.

"The sun won't be up for minutes yet."

"*Non*. This takes time. There's ritual involved. It must be done properly, or you won't rise . . . and that would defeat your purpose, *n'est pas c'ainsi?*"

Stepping back, LeMaitre pulled his arm from Damién's grasp. He looked at the trees again, speaking quickly.

"Go home. I'll come to you tomorrow night. You have my word."

"Let me give you directions . . ."

"No need." LeMaitre took his hand, leaning forward.

For a moment, Damién thought he was bowing over it. Then, he felt the sting, saw a welling of blood, and the *sans mort's* tongue snake out and lick it away. It was wet but cold as a sliver of ice. He shivered.

"I'll find you by the call of your blood." LeMaitre raised his head, breathing deeply. "Ahhh . . . you're truly delicious, my young *chevalier*. I'm going to enjoy quenching my thirst at your well."

With that, he disappeared, body breaking into fragments, dissolving bit-by-bit into dust until nothing but a vague man-shape hovered in the air. Then the wind swept it away, tossing the transparent shards upward as the sun broke through the trees.

Staggering, Damién rubbed his eyes.

He was alone in the early morning sunshine, standing at the edge of the charnel pit, bleak and stark and stinking in the pale light.

I've been here all night? Did I imagine it all? Or . . .

The back of his hand stung. Looking down, he saw a long, red scratch across his knuckles. He remembered LeMaitre's tongue slithering across his skin, and the sensuous shudder it produced. He thought of the coming night, wondering what the ritual involved and found he was looking forward to that with as much fear and expectation as to his coming immortality.

* * *

His arrival home was met with exclamations of joy and concern; his mother anxious, his father worried.

"Damién, *ma bébé*, you were gone so long." Mathilde La Croix didn't hide her fear. "I was afraid. You shouldn't tarry outside after dark."

Outside. That's what they called anywhere not within the shelter of the estate's walls. *Outside.* As if it were another country.

Perhaps it is. The Country of the Dead. And he'd soon be escaping it.

"Your *maman's* right, my son," Pierre La Croix spoke, making his words gruff to hide his own alarm. "The countryside's no place to be now, what with looters and scavengers about."

Oh, Papa. You can't imagine what kind of scavengers are out there. But I do. I've met one of them and made him a bargain he couldn't refuse.

"My apologies, *Papa*. I . . . received upsetting news while at prayer."

Upsetting? Aye. If nothing else, I've probably damned myself with my destruction of the church.

He was surprised news of it hadn't gotten back to the *château*. Perhaps *Père* Gervais had perished in the blaze. Briefly, he hoped not. A second later, he didn't care.

"Upsetting news?" his father repeated. "What could be more upsetting than what is already happening?"

"*Père* Gervais was called to *Château de Chevigny* last night . . ." He couldn't go on, stopped and looked away.

"Antoinette?" his mother asked softly, and Damién nodded. Mathilde reached for his father's hand; for a moment they were silent, watching him. Finally, she said, "*Ma cher*, I'm so sorry. May *le Bon Dieu* receive her unblemished spirit. But that doesn't explain why you delayed so long in returning home."

Anger burst within him though he forced himself not to show it.

Foolish woman, he wanted to shout at her. *The woman I love is dying. Do you think I want to hear such trite words as those you just spoke? As for my returning home . . . What is here for me now?*

"I wished to think." To prepare them for what would soon come, he began his lie. "Besides, I don't feel well."

"*Non.* Are you feverish?" Before he could stop her, she pressed the back of her hand to his cheek.

He wanted to slap it away and scream, *Don't touch me.* Instead, he caught her wrist.

"Don't, *Maman*, I beg you." Releasing her, he took a breath and spoke the rest of his deception, well-rehearsed on his way home. Holding out a hand as if to ward them away. "Papa, I fear I'm stricken."

They both recoiled, his mother looking at her hand as if it now offended her. She held it away from her body like an unclean thing. Her face held horror. Because of his words, or what she'd done?

"Perhaps you're mistaken," his father suggested, voice quavering. At the thought of losing his heir or simply of losing his only child? "You're overwrought after learning of Antoinette. A betrothed's death is a terrible thing. You're tired from the long ride."

I've made that ride every day for almost a month. Why should today tire me any worse? Their stupidity was infuriating.

"Perhaps . . ." He backed away, toward the stairs. "I'll retire to my chambers."

"I'll send for *Père* Gervais . . ." His father's voice became weaker. "Just in case."

"*Non.*" Damién stopped. "Don't send for a priest . . . nor *le docteur.*" He couldn't bear to see either of those hypocrites again. "Not yet anyway. Merely tell everyone to stay away."

Neither spoke as he went to the high, winding staircase leading to the second story and the family bedchambers. At the foot of the stairs, he looked back.

For one last glimpse at his parents, he told himself. One last look through human eyes at the two who gave him life.

Soon, I'll have another parent. Soon, LeMaitre will be my sire.

Père Gervais had used that word to describe a *sans mort* who made another like himself. He wondered how much of what the priest said was true and how much as false as the Scriptures he quoted.

Soon, I'll find out.

With that thought, it was as if he were seeing the *marquis* and his wife with another's eyes. He'd always thought his father so strong and certain of himself, his mother sturdy and calm; now Pierre looked shaken and weak. *Old.* And Mathilde trembled with fear.

Damién's cold detachment wavered.

"*Maman* . . ."

Holding out his arms, he ran back to her, flinging himself at her small body. He felt her recoil slightly, then enfold him in her arms, clasping him against her heart as she had when he was an infant and had bad dreams. His father's embrace encircled them both. Briefly, he was enclosed in warmth and love.

One last time . . .

"Shh. Shh, *ma petit* . . ." his mother whispered. "It'll be all right. If it happens, we'll be together again in Heaven."

That did it. Damién stiffened and pulled away. He forced himself to swallow his anger at her parroting that lie, instead whispered, "If . . . Papa, if I am to die, please promise me one thing..."

"Anything, child." At that moment, he imagined his father would've agreed to the massacre of the entire household.

"Don't burn my body. Please let me lie in the tomb with our ancestors." Damién met his father's eyes as he spoke. Begging.

That seemed to shake his father more than anything else said. He went white, looked away, and slowly nodded.

"You have my word, *mon fils*. I'll lay you in the tomb myself. And if the magister says otherwise... I'll kill him." He spoke with grim determination.

"Thank you..." He let his words trail off in a grateful whisper, then released them and backed away.

As he left his mother's embrace, her arms stayed held out as if reaching for him. He forced a concerned note into his next words.

"Please. Go. Bathe in rosemary water. Mix in ginger flakes and chamomile leaves. Dr. Rousseau has said 'tis possibly a preventative in washing away the miasma if it clings."

Turning, he ran up the stairs. His mother's anguished wail followed him.

* * *

In his chamber, Damién undressed, carefully folding the clothes he had worn and draping them over a chair.

Won't need these anymore. In a few hours, a winding-cloth will be my only garment.

He remembered the filthy rags wrapped around LeMaitre's shrunken body. The awful smell. That wasn't particularly inviting, to be clad in shreds of fabric, smelling of rot for eternity.

Damién had always been more than particular about keeping his body clean. Sometimes Armand teased him about that.

Does one smell offensive to one's-self? Perhaps LeMaitre hadn't been buried in a shroud but some of his own clothes, wearing them until they fell apart. He supposed he'd learn that soon enough also, but what to wear was the least thing to consider now.

Naked, he walked to the mullioned double doors opening onto the balcony, flinging them open.

I'll watch the sun travel the sky, see it set for the last time. Until that moment, he'd not thought of that. *I'll never see the sun again, nor feel its warmth upon my skin . . .*

By now, it was noon, and the sun was directly overhead, beating down on a day so bright it hurt his eyes as he stood on the balcony looking out over the estate. Miles and miles of green meadows dotted with clover and wildflowers, plowed fields waiting for plantings never to happen, and woods of dark pine, yew, and hemlock.

Will it look different by moonlight? Do sans mort *eyes see more . . . or less?*

A sudden shudder ran through him. Damién told himself it was a *frisson* from standing naked in the open air. He hurried back inside.

His bed was made, the covers turned back. The goosedown mattress was soft as a cloud, enveloping him warmly as he lay upon it.

Will I be able to accept a cold granite slab beneath my body?

Pulling up the sheets and quilt, he thought of the things LeMaitre had said. The fabric felt smooth and sensual to his bare skin. Strange, how he'd never noticed that before. It made him want to run his hands over his body, explore his flesh with his fingertips and seek its intimate places.

Can the sans mort love? Why did I not ask these things? What have I condemned myself to?

He forced his hands to lay still atop the coverlet, commanded his mind to think of nothing. Outside, he heard hushed whispers, muted footsteps. The servants, going about their tasks, were ordered not to come near his room. He hoped his father kept his promise.

Damién closed his eyes and waited for the sun to go down . . .

***

He must have fallen asleep.

There was a sound from the balcony. The faint brushing of a bare foot on the planking. A whisper of wings.

Damién opened his eyes.

He'd forgotten to light a lamp and the room was dark. Only moonlight shining through the open doors gave any light, and not much of that, for the body in the doorway—shrunken and hunched as it was—blocked the light and kept it from entering.

A twisted shadow moved across the floor. Wings flapped slightly. A wave of that awful smell drifted to him.

"You've come." He couldn't control the tremor in his voice as he raised himself on one elbow.

"Did you doubt it?" A deep, croaking chuckle accompanied the question. "Or have you changed your mind, Damién La Croix?"

Damién shook his head. He couldn't speak, didn't dare.

"Then bid me enter, *chevalier.*"

"Come . . ." Briefly, his words crowded his throat, threatening to choke him. He took a deep breath, saying the greeting with which his father always welcomed guests into their home. "Come in, Geraint LeMaitre. And may your stay here be a pleasant one."

"Oh, it will, Damién. It will." LeMaitre crossed the threshold, and everything changed.

He could feel it, the very air in the room was different now, heavier, difficult to breathe. There seemed to be no sound, as if the moment that emaciated, naked sole touched the rich nap of the carpet something within the *château* died.

LeMaitre cocked his head as if listening.

Does he also sense it?

There was a crackling as his wings collapsed, melding with the fragments of fabric clinging to his back.

He was beside the bed before Damién realized he'd moved.

Will I be able to do that, also?

Hands touched his bare shoulders, light as his mother's own touch.

Maman . . . Damién thrust thought of her aside.

"Well, my young *chevalier*. Shall we begin?" There was so much eagerness in the *sans mort's* voice it made him tremble. "Are you ready?"

Damién nodded, unable to speak.

"You come to me of your own free will?" the rusty whisper persisted. "Accepting the consequences of our coming together?"

"*Oui.*" He choked out the answer, couldn't raise his voice above a whisper.

"Then give yourself to me, Damién La Croix." LeMaitre's voice sank even lower.

He could barely hear it, a mere murmur, tickling his ears, floating around him like the softest breeze.

Damién started to sit up. He was pushed backward onto the pillow, lying to look up into LeMaitre's gaunt and sunken features. A thin hand plucked the coverlet from his fingers, flinging quilt and sheets to the foot of the bed so he lay, exposed and naked to the *sans mort's* eyes.

He felt a single wish to cover himself and shrink from that glowing gaze. It died as swiftly as it came. Damién continued staring at those burning orbs, felt himself being drawn in, consumed in their fire.

The *sans mort* shrugged. Rags disappeared; naked skin exposed to the moonlight. He was emaciated to near bones, every rib visible, belly nonexistent, navel a dark hole in a pale stretch of flesh. His shanks so starved, Damién could've closed his hand around them, fingers meeting, and what hung between those thin thighs . . . a thing so shrunken and shriveled and hairless it was a travesty of Man's proudest possession.

Above everything was that wan, white, still-aristocratic face with its straggling fall of hair. And those red, red eyes . . .

I don't want this! He gave one last thought of protest before LeMaitre touched his forehead and he was helpless,

Fingers slid to his temples, his cheeks, clasping his face with one hand as the other caressed his jaw and chin.

"So young . . . *mon petit chevalier* . . . so handsome . . . so full of the life you wish to share with me . . ."

The hands traveled down his throat, brushing his collarbones as if defining their shape and strength. Fingers walked his chest. There was a faint *snick* . . . claws flicked out, tangled in curls, combing through thick, dark hair, encircled his nipples. They pressed inward, moving round and round, massaging those nubs of flesh.

Damién stirred, an unexpected stab of desire coursing through him.

"Please . . ."

"Shhh." Before he could protest, the hands ceased their insinuating caress, moving downward. They slid over his belly, invaded his navel. A burning lust-tinged wave followed that hot, deep probing, aiming itself at his groin.

Oh, God . . . that brought a swift pain around his heart. *No, never again think that Name, never say it. Ever.*

He tossed it away with any other thought, closing his eyes as the hands slid lower. Fingers delved and explored the curls at his root, combing them as that on his chest. In horror, Damién felt himself responding. Heat coiled around his shaft, his member tightening, engorging itself to rise.

His stones were seized, claws scratching gently, trailing his length to rake around and around the crown. Shame flared as he felt liquid trickle.

I'm wet, as if ready to make love. Is that what's going to happen? He stifled a whimper, felt his resolve waver, then strengthen. A single tear dripped from one eye.

"*Non.*"

The hand withdrew. It wiped away the tear.

Damién opened his eyes.

LeMaitre smiled. It was the most beautiful expression

Damién had ever seen, even with the sparkle of fangs. Like a fallen angel's—ethereal, pale as moonshine itself, nearly luminous in the dimness.

"Come, *chevalier*... into the dark with me."

The *sans mort's* body covered his, lying full-length upon him. Cold, so cold... like a living slab of marble molded to his own warm flesh... Damién shivered as LeMaitre kissed him on both cheeks, then ran his tongue down the side of his face to his throat, lapping gently. It should have been rough as a cat's, but it was smooth, slick, and cold. It licked a circle against the vein pounding just under his jaw, withdrew...

His hands were seized. Fingers entwined, the *sans mort* forced them above his head, pinned them there. LeMaitre paused, inhaled and...

... groaned, a sound too much like lust to be ignored.

"*Sweet, Unspoken Name!* I can hear it. Flooding your veins... You smell so delicious, my young *chevalier*... I can't wait..."

The stab of fangs into the vein was a shock. Damién gasped, stiffening to fight, pushing against the body pinning him down.

As the hands holding his tightened, he heard LeMaitre inhale again, felt his blood flowing, not through his veins but into the waiting mouth and with it such a flood of desire, he wanted nothing but to stay that way forever... pressed against the cold body atop his, becoming one with him through that blood. Again and again, that sucking movement, as the currents of his life-giving fluid flowed out of him and into the *sans mort*.

LeMaitre raised himself. Biting at his own wrist, he held it against Damién's lips, the blood filling his mouth.

He swallowed, felt it slide, thick and cold down his throat.

The body upon his was getting heavier . . . flesh firming around bones filling with marrow, the shrunken organ thickening, pressing against his own hardened rod, rigid as iron now.

The room was shockingly bright—*where did all the light come from?* At the edges of his vision, darkness mingled with sparks of silver, growing larger and brighter. There was a ringing in his ears, thousands of bells and tinkling chimes, high-pitched keening . . .

Damién gave a single convulsive shiver of desire and pleasure as the clamor rose to a deafening pitch and the darkness covered everything . . .

***

Someone was weeping. Loud wracking sobs ripped from the heart. He wished they'd stop.

How can I sleep with that racket going on?

He prepared to open his eyes, roll over and demand that whoever it was *shut up!* when someone spoke.

"Oh, my son, my child. Pierre, you should have called for *le docteur* as I asked."

Maman? Crying for me?

Everything came flooding into his memory.

"Mathilde, how could I know?" His father had never sounded so shaken. "I-I thought him merely grieving from learning of Antoinette. H-he . . . he.." He rallied, defensively. "He showed no signs of the Plague. He still doesn't."

". . . and you didn't send for the priest, either." His

mother wasn't listening, continuing to sob her accusations. "Our son died unshriven. His soul now resides in Purgatory."

Non, Maman, my soul's in Hell, but my body's here and still alive.

"Come, Mathilde. You mustn't touch him. You might become . . ."

"Infected? I'm probably infected already, Pierre." She gave a broken, ironic laugh. "We all are . . . and I'm glad, for that means I'll soon be with my *bébé* again."

Oh, ma mere, *you and I will never meet in any form in the Afterlife.*

"We must leave him to the women now, to prepare him."

"You won't let them take him to the pits, Pierre. You promised."

"I intend to keep that promise. Damién will lie in the tomb with our ancestors. Now, come . . ."

His father's voice died away as the door opened and shut. Damién relaxed and drifted back into slumber.

***

He was being bathed, a rough cloth rubbing in large circular motions down his chest. It was such a stirring, sensual movement, he nearly made a purr of satisfaction deep in his throat before he caught himself. The motion continued down his belly, lightly along the length of his member, over his legs to his toes. A similar movement began on his face and arms.

Two women, servants no doubt, ordered to prepare his body for the tomb.

The movement stopped, soft pats of cloth, drying away the dampness. Something liquid sprinkled upon his flesh. The flat of fingers and palm rubbing it in. They were anointing his body with an aromatic oil of some kind, massaging it into arms, chest, legs. A dry, rustling, the scent of clover and sweet shrub. Dried flower petals added to the mix. More stroking, rubbing, until his skin absorbed oil and flowers.

His shoulders were lifted, his head falling forward; one holding his upper body upright while the other wrapped something around them. The winding sheet; he felt it encircle his chest, around and around, pinning his arms to his sides, moving to his waist.

There was a brief desire to struggle. *How can I move if I'm wrapped so?*

A hand touched his face, lifting his head. His hair was brushed back from his forehead. He was lowered again to the bed, his legs lifted . . .

Once more, Damién fell into sleep.

* * *

When next Damién opened his eyes, it was night again, and the room was in darkness except for a single candle burning by the bedside.

It highlighted the figure of a woman sitting a few feet away. He recognized her.

Adéle, his mother's maid, elected—involuntarily, no doubt—to sit with his corpse until it could be carried to the tomb. Her head was bowed over her rosary, lips moving silently.

Praying for my soul?

He should've been grateful; all he felt was irritation at such a futile gesture. She didn't see as he tried to raise a hand before realizing it was still tightly bound to his side, didn't hear the muted rustle of the winding sheet as he struggled against it. A surprising sensation coiled through his body and with it a barely audible internal growl.

Hunger.

He was famished. He tried to speak. No sound came out as he realized he hadn't drawn a breath since awakening. Apparently, breathing was no longer requisite . . . except to make a sound. Inhaling deeply, he expelled the air in a long whisper.

"Aaahhh-delll . . ."

Her head came up. Wide, frightened eyes met his.

"Master Damién?" She was out of the chair, staggering backward, the rosary thrust before her, the same gesture he had made to entrap LeMaitre.

He almost laughed as he thought of that, but now, he was also affected by the holy thing. He could feel its power radiating over him in stinging golden tendrils, even from that far away. He inhaled so quickly he nearly choked.

Mustn't let it show. If I appear weak, 'tis natural at this moment.

"A-Adéle . . . what has happened?" It wasn't difficult to feign confusion. His brain was awhirl. He struggled against the confining sheet, trying to kick, making his body bounce on the bed. "I can't move . . . What's going on?"

"Calm yourself, master. Please." Fear forgotten, she rushed forward, dropping the beads into the pocket of her apron. "Merciful God, we thought you dead."

"Dead?" He winced at that Name before he could

stop, hoping she thought it merely a grimace of confusion.

"Your mother found you cold and not breathing—or so we thought. The *marquis* ordered you prepared for burial . . . as he promised you."

"Well, I'm not dead, as you can see." He began his struggles once more, managing to somehow lunge himself upright. "Here, get me out of this thing. Quickly."

"Yes, Master." She came closer and Damién was assailed by the most delicious scent.

Hell's demons, what's that smell? So heady and robust. It made his mouth water, his hunger grow. He could feel saliva gushing from under his tongue, threatening to overflow his mouth.

Adéle plucked at the sheet's edge, tucked in at his throat.

'Tis coming from her. Now he recognized the scent. *Blood.* Good, rich, peasant blood. His father fed his servants and serfs well. He wanted them to be healthy so they could work hard.

As she unwound the sheet from his shoulders and chest, the heady fragrance of the liquid flowing through her veins wrapped itself around him as tightly as the cloth had. Damién leaned forward, letting his head drop to her shoulder.

She'll think me simply weakened.

Drool seeped from his open mouth, dripping onto her sleeve. He could see the vein in her neck, exposed by the heavy linen wimple wrapped around her head, beating rapidly with remnants of her surprise still lingering and her haste to get her master's son out of his shroud.

One hand was freed. He raised it, flexing his fingers.

They felt stiff and heavy. The other hand slid out of the binding cloth. Another rumble within his belly. His body screaming for nourishment, for some of that rich flow.

I'm so hungry . . . I must feed . . .

Adéle continued unwrapping the fabric down his body. She was at his waist now, didn't protest or even look up when he put his hands on her shoulders.

"Adéle." She continued working the fabric. He repeated her name a little sharper. "Adéle!"

"Master?" She paused, looking up, met his eyes, and was lost. "M-master . . ."

The word died away in a whimper. She tried to pull away.

Damién lunged for her throat and that pulsing vein. He pressed his mouth against it, felt the warm beating within, for the briefest moment, caressed it with his tongue. Then, he bit.

Weak as he was, she was even weaker. There was no struggle at all.

Blood flowed. Not enough. That puny trickle didn't fill his needs. He bit deeper, felt his teeth click against each other, then ripped outward. Spat out the patch of flesh, turning to cover the gaping tear with his mouth as blood splashed and spurted . . . onto his face and chest . . . into his mouth. He drank in long, loud gulps like a man perished, as the body in his hands went limp, only his grasp of her shoulders keeping her upright.

When he raised his head with a long-sated sigh, Adéle was as light in his hands as one of the feather pillows. She'd been a plump woman but now her body was a mere husk, dry as chaff. He let it fall to the floor.

It barely made a sound as he collapsed on the bed,

wiping his mouth.

Ahhh, it's so good.

Holding out his arms, he licked the blood off his hands, sticking his fingers into his mouth—like a child lapping away syrup—and sucking them dry.

As he leaned over to finish freeing his body from the sheet, there was movement at the window.

LeMaitre stood there, a very changed being from the emaciated stick-thin creature of the night before. Still naked, but body filled-in and handsome. His flesh was pale as alabaster, hair like floss in the moonlight, long and luxuriant, that on his chest and groin a thick, silver brush.

"You're awake." The *sans mort* glided into the room. "I was afraid I'd failed. 'Tis been some time since I turned anyone. Good to see I haven't forgotten how."

Damién tossed the sheet away, sliding from the bed. Immediately, LeMaitre was at his side, moving with that incredible swiftness.

"What's that?" He studied Adéle's body. "You've made a kill? Already?"

"I-I was hungry . . ." Damién's voice held the whine of a chastised child. Had he done wrong? "She smelled so good."

"Nevertheless, I'm supposed to guide you in your first days, my son. I should've been here to instruct you, but . . ." LeMaitre chided himself. "'Tis so long since I'd really fed, and your blood was so filling . . . I was soothed and didn't want to wake."

"I didn't have any trouble." He smiled and his lower lip stung suddenly. Damién touched a fingertip to his left canine, looking at the drop of blood welling on it.

I don't need guidance. I know what I must do, he thought,

rebelliously.

"Did you enjoy it?" LeMaitre, caught his hand, licking away a lingering smear. He took Damién's forefinger into his mouth, sucking roughly and growled, "Mmm. She *was* delicious, wasn't she?"

"Oh, yesss . . . it wasss . . . wasss . . . ssso . . . good . . ." The words were a sensual hiss. Damién's tongue swiped around his lips, searching for more of the maid's blood.

"*Bon.* And now, for your christening, my fledgling, my child." LeMaitre caught his hands, clasping them tightly. He kissed both cheeks, then his mouth, then that long, sinuous tongue flicked out, lapping at a spot of blood on his chin.

Catching Damién's face between his hands, he began to clean it. Licking away the blood, LeMaitre knelt before his new creation, cleaning the remaining gore and spatter from his body, while Damién accepted the sensation of that tongue upon his flesh, reveling in the excitement and desire rising within him at his sire's touch.

When LeMaitre got again to his feet, wiping at his mouth with one pale hand, his cock was erect and totally arouse, its tightened flesh brilliant crimson with the blood surging through it.

"Time for that later." A cold hand pressed down on his cock. Instantly, it relaxed. "For now . . . Where's your clothes press? You'll wish to dress for . . . dinner . . ." That last word was delivered with a crooked smile. "Won't you?"

Without speaking, Damién looked at the clothes he'd taken off the night before. They still lay on the chair where he'd left them, unseen and ignored by those entering his chambers. He picked them up, pulling them on. LeMaitre didn't speak again until he'd tied the points of his hosen to his belt.

"Are there garments for me also?"

"But of course..." Damién was contrite. He'd clothed himself while his master stood there still naked. He waved a hand at the wardrobe. "We're of a size. Select whatever you wish, my sire."

LeMaitre dressed with the same speed as he moved, and in a few moments, stood before Damién in hose, shirt, jerkin and doublet, the image of a noble who could grace the *Cour de le Roi*. Laughing, he tossed that luminous hair and made another bow as elegant as the one he'd given Damién the night before.

Now, it no longer seemed out of place.

"*Merci*, my son. 'Tis centuries since I've worn anything so elegant. I vow it feels uncomfortable." He ran a hand along his sleeve, fingers caressing the fabric. "But I'll adjust." He clapped a hand on Damién's shoulder. "Come, child. Introduce me to your household."

Stepping over Adéle's corpse, Damién opened the door.

* * *

The next hours were a panorama of bloody violence. They attacked the first servant they saw—one appointed to make final rounds of the *château* before retiring for the night—bearing him to the floor under their combined weight. Too startled to cry out, he fought briefly, then collapsed as the rapid loss of blood made him swoon. Already having fed, Damién finished first, raising his head to watch LeMaitre's heaving shoulders as he continued to drink.

"That was good." His master stated, wiping his mouth with the back of his hand and lapping away the blood on his palm.

A sound from downstairs floated toward them. His head jerked in that direction, like an animal hearing prey. "There's more?"

"All you wish." Damién got to his feet, reaching for his sire's hand. "Come."

"There's something to be done first."

"What's that?"

What can be more important than feeding this ravenous hunger I now feel? His guts twisted viciously.

"You invited me into your chambers, but you don't own this *château*."

"True, 'tis my father's. *He's* the *marquis*," Damién agreed. "So?"

"So . . . think it out, my fledgling." Briefly, LeMaitre looked as his old tutor often had when Damién professed difficulty in solving some mathematical problem. "'Twould be more convenient if *you* were master here."

He didn't have to consider it. Without hesitation, Damién led LeMaitre to his parents' bedchamber door.

Once before it, a last vestige of filial love struggled free. He pictured them lying side by side, peaceful, dreaming. Perhaps his mother had cried herself to sleep. She might even now have tearstains on her cheeks. And his father . . . Pierre loved him, he knew, though he ofttimes withheld showing his affection, considering it unmanly to be so demonstrative.

"N-*non* . . . I-I can't . . ."

"Of course not." The hand touching his shoulder

held understanding. "I'll do it." LeMaitre caressed his own belly. "After all, I've a tremendous void to be filled. You stay here, my son."

He swung around, striking the door, battering it as if frantic.

"Master! Please, wake up."

"Who's there?" There was movement inside. Footsteps coming to the door. It opened. His father, robe thrown over his nakedness, peering out sleepily. "What is it? Who are you?"

"That's not important." LeMaitre's voice underwent a change, became cultured, courteous. "I must speak with you, my lord. About your son. Please."

Damién's father did what he never expected. He swung open the door. And saw Damién standing there.

"Damién? What miracle is this?"

The joy on his face stabbed Damién's heart.

"No miracle, sir," LeMaitre answered for him. "May we come in?"

"O-of course," Pierre turned to lead the way into his sitting room, calling, "Mathilde, wake up. I've wonderful news."

LeMaitre followed, kicking the door shut behind him. Damién twisted the handle.

Locked out. He leaned against the frame, claws scraping at the polished wood, listening to the screams coming from within. The growls and roars as they died to liquid gurgles, and then, the soft, slow, sucking . . .

. . . and he cried, the last time there would be tears for a long, long time . . . for now Damién *did* consider himself damned.

. . . *I've killed my parents, murdered them. LeMaitre may have done the deed, but I brought him here. I gave him permission . . .*

When the *sans mort* opened the door, pushing him back and stepping into the corridor, he helped him clean himself, as LeMaitre had done to him only a short time before. When he raised his head from lapping the last smear of blood from the velvet doublet, he took his master's hand.

"Come."

"Wait." LeMaitre held back, saying, as Damién turned an inquisitive gaze on him, "We won't kill them all. We'll need some. Which do you wish to survive?"

In a few words, Damién made his choices . . . Charles, his *valet* . . . Simone, one of the housemaids whom he'd always lusted after and could never convince to submit . . . Bernard, the butler . . . All chosen coldly within seconds for their value and no other reason. LeMaitre questioned some of his choices, adding a suggestion now and then, and telling him how to proceed.

"Take just enough to make them swoon. When they revive, they'll be *fascinez*—enthralled—and will do as you bid. We're speaking of just the house servants, of course. We can decide on those living on the grounds, later. Ah, Damién!"

In a sudden spasm of gruesome joy, the *sans mort* seized him by the shoulders and hugged him tightly.

"'Twas a lucky night for both of us when you strayed into my path." He pushed him away. "Now, shall we go?"

The upper floors were strangely quiet, but that was as they should be. After all, it was night and everyone would be abed, that one unfortunate houseman to the contrary. The son of the *château* had just died; they would keep a respectful silence because of that if for no other reason.

A grim smile twisted his mouth. *Would they be even quiet-*

er if they knew the master and his wife no longer lived, also?

Damién led LeMaitre to the servants' quarters housed above his own. On one side, Charles' room, his father's valet, the butler . . . on the other Adéle's room. Above those were the house servants, and in the attic story, the cook, the scullery and other kitchen maids . . .

Outside Charles' door, Damién paused, drawing a deep breath, savoring the scent of his valet's blood as it wafted through the paneling. He reached for the door handle.

"Can we enter?" LeMaitre laid a detaining hand on his arm. Damién shot him a questioning look. "Without being bidden?"

"These rooms belong to me now. I need no permission to enter any room in this *château*. You are my guest."

To prove his words, he didn't turn the handle but released it, and kicked the door in instead.

As he should've expected, Charles wasn't alone. His *valet* was as lascivious as he where lower servants were concerned. Even with a death in the house, he couldn't control his desires. He lay on the bed, one of the upstairs maids cuddled in his arms. Briefly, his snores still sounded before the crashing of the door against the wall sank in.

Both stirred; the woman pushed herself away from Charles and sat up. The *valet* rolled over and stared.

"M-master? How—" He fumbled at the lamp on the bedside table, turning up the flame.

They were both naked, flesh gleaming in the firelight. Blood rushed beneath the skin, making it even brighter as both realized the man standing before them was supposedly dead. Fear replaced confusion, making hearts pound and liquid flow and thrum as they understood what this meant.

Charles jumped from the bed as Damién flung himself across the darkened chamber. He'd never thought how delicious the *valet's* blood would be. How all those late nights at taverns where he'd joined his master in downing tankard after tankard and stuffing himself with rich meat was preparing him to be a feast himself.

Slow . . . he cautioned *. . . not too much . . . you'll need him . . .*

As he felt Charles become a limp weight in his hands, he jerked his mouth away, dropping the unconscious body. That paltry sip made no change in his hunger. It simply made him want more.

The woman cowered, petrified. There was a brief hesitation as he looked at LeMaitre. The *sans mort* nodded.

"She's all yours, my son. I'll take the next one."

He turned on the woman. She was so frightened she hadn't moved, merely huddled in the bed making wordless little sounds and clutching the coverlet against her breast like a useless shield. She shook her head, giving stupid little chokings as he lurched toward her.

His leap carried him over the bed and onto her body, pinning her to the mattress. Holding her immobile in a dreadful travesty of the carnal act, he drove his fangs into her throat. No gentle puncture this time, only a frantic, desperate stabbing of those sharp points into soft flesh.

Kicking frantically, she fought before fear made her faint, going limp in his hands. In a few minutes, Damién inhaled the life from her.

Flinging her body aside, he crawled from the bed. She struck the headboard and bounced, falling half-on, half-off the bed. Her head hung above the floor, ripped throat dripping blood onto the carpet. He could hear the soft *drip* . . . *drip* . . . as it soaked into the thick nap.

He was panting as he got to his feet, breathing deeply, listening to the blood dribble from his hands and face to the floor.

LeMaitre took his hand and led him away. He looked back at Charles, still unmoving.

"He'll be out for a while yet. We'll be finished before he awakens."

The next hours were a wash of crimson . . . Bodies being ripped apart, slashed throats spouting fountains of red froth . . . Men and women—and children, too . . . screaming and begging for their lives . . . the air a single shrill scream of terror, and hunger-maddened, gore-smeared faces and fangs locked in a feeding-frenzy.

It was past midnight before they were sated.

***

Replete for the moment, Damién lay naked amid the reek of blood and corpses in the charnal house once the La Croix family salon.

When Charles awoke from his swoon and staggered downstairs, still groggy from lack of blood, he was ordered to find the other *fascinez* and have them round up the surviving servants. It had been too easy; they were all stunned by the sudden attack.

He and LeMaitre chose several more, then sent the rest to the little cell block at the back of the family wine cellar, a place once used to hold servants awaiting punishment. There, they could await their master's hunger, while Charles and the others stood guard outside the salon door as Damién and his sire completed their evening's feast.

A hand raised above the bodies, touched his ankle, slithering through the blood to his thigh, reaching for his stones. They caressed and grasped. He slid to his feet, kicking a body out of the way to stand as he caught the woman's wrist and hauled her upright.

Simone, the tease. Naked and blood-smeared also.

When she realized she'd been spared, she couldn't show her gratitude fast enough, ripping off her clothes and offering herself to him. More to ensure her continued survival, Damién didn't doubt, but he didn't care about the reason, all he wanted was her body.

He'd made her pay for all the times he'd pursued and been rejected. Forcing her to her knees, he'd shoved his still-erect member into her mouth, laughing as she gagged and choked. That quickly changed to gasps and moans of pleasure as she recovered and began to fondle and suck. No need to be silent in his enjoyment as he'd had to when seducing maidservants in his bedchamber.

Now, his mother could no longer hear.

Damién screamed as he came, the roar ripping out of his throat as cruelly as the gush of his seed into Simone's waiting mouth sent it dripping onto her chin and from there to her naked breasts. The sound died away to faint groans as she milked him dry . . .

That answered his question of whether *sans mort* could know women in ways other than through the blood. It also brought a surprise. He'd been wrung of his seed but he was still erect.

He flung himself upon Simone, thrusting into her, again and again until she bled. While she lay whimpering in pain and desire, he licked away the crimson smears upon her thighs and sat back with a sigh, then flung himself upon the bodies of his previous victims and rested.

Throughout it all, LeMaitre sprawled on a nearby couch, watching . . . smiling . . . approving his fledgling's actions . . . enjoying the spectacle . . .

"Go." Damién thrust the woman away, speaking through her protests. "I don't want you anymore, Simone. Out of my sight."

She burst into tears, rushing from the room. Damién shrugged and turned away, saying to LeMaitre, "I must go."

"Where?" The *sans mort* sat up, one leg sliding off the couch to land on a corpse beneath it. He toed it out of the way, making a place for that elegant, pale foot.

"To my Antoinette."

There was a faint pang of remorse that he'd not thought of her at all during the bloodletting, and especially not while he was coupling so wildly with the now-rejected Simone. Still, what did his beloved have to do with what he had ever done with other women?

"She's dying, master. I must go to her and save her."

"If she's stricken, you may be too late, you realize that."

"If I am, my sacrifice will be for nothing, for 'twas for her I did this."

Damién now painted himself as self-sacrificing. He'd died only for Antoinette. Not for himself. *Liar.*

"What must I do, master? How do I turn her?"

"Drain her. Totally."

The words were so cold, so unfeeling, he was shaken, even now.

"While you do so, she must think of *surviving. Life*

above all else. The will to live will bring her across the Veil . . . if she's strong enough."

"You mean, there's a chance she won't . . ." He refused to finish the question.

"Things may always go amiss, when dealing with mortals, my child. Accept that now." LeMaitre glanced at the windows. "Sunrise is still a few hours off. I must return to my hiding place before then. If she lives, if she agrees to follow you, I'd like to meet her before I go into *Unsleep* this night."

"'Tis a long way to *Château de Chevigny.*" Damién had another thought. "Do I now have wings like yours?"

In answer, Geraint got to his feet, walking behind his fledgling. Without speaking, he seized Damién's shoulders, pressed a knee into the small of his back and twisted his hands. There was a wet, ripping sound and the *sans mort* leaped out of the way as the flesh between Damién's shoulder blades split and two damp and twisted wings uncoiled. In a moment, they were completely unfurled.

"Best clothe yourself. The air's cold at night."

Damién was helped into his braies and stocks, his shirt slit up the back allowing his wings to come through.

Geraint returned to the couch as Damién ran to the balcony and flung himself off it.

* * *

Getting to the *château* took less time through the air.

Damién dropped soundlessly onto Antoinette's balcony. The doors were open and that made his heart sink. *Does this mean there is no further need to protect my beloved from the miasma? Did she die while I was slaughtering my household?*

From where he stood, the room appeared empty. No servants sitting with a corpse. None tending to an invalid, either. He could see the bed but not whether it held anyone, the heavy hangings making too many shadows. He took a step across the threshold and was stopped as suddenly as if he'd run into a wall of glass.

What the Hell? Then he remembered; he'd never been allowed into Antoinette's bedchamber. Such a thing wasn't done even between betrotheds. She would have to invite him in. *If she's dead . . .*

"'Toinette. Sweetheart?" he called to her.

To his relief, there was movement within the bed, something pale turning toward the sound of his voice. He willed his wings to collapse; with a silken whisper, they obeyed. He felt the flaps of flesh on his back close over them.

"Damién? Is it you?"

Her dear voice had never sounded so sweet as in that moment.

"*Oui, mon précieux.*"

Hurry, we're wasting time. Ask me in. What if she refuses? What if her chasteness prevents her from bringing me inside?

"You shouldn't be here. Why have you come?" She didn't raise her voice above a whisper, but he heard its quaver, as clearly as if she shouted.

"How could I stay away? They told me you were dying."

"I-I am." The tremble in her voice shook him as well as her bravery in admitting it. "And now, you're . . ."

"I don't care for myself. Antoinette, may I come in?"

She hesitated, nodded. He didn't move, willing her to say it aloud.

"Please, Damién. Come in. I've no wish to be alone. Not now. No matter if 'tisn't proper. What does propriety mean to the dead?"

That made his heart sing. *She's begun to question also? Even this late?*

He stepped into the room and again hesitated. There was another, stronger barrier, keeping him from entering. He could feel it, sending out its invisible stabs of holy fire. The crucifix around her neck. Like Adéle's rosary.

Taking a deep breath, Damién ran to Antoinette, forcing himself to ignore the pain encircling him as he took her in his arms.

"You don't have to die." He kissed the pale lips, ignoring the bloody streaks on her face and arms, the foul odor of death from the eruptions leaking pus onto the coverlet. Carefully, he avoided pressing her body to his. "You can live, and we can be together."

"I know, my love." She misunderstood. "We'll be together. In Heaven."

That trash again.

"*Non*, that's not what I mean. You can live. *Now*."

"They've found a cure?" Hope gleamed. "What? How?"

"No cure, *chérie*, but a way to escape the Plague and live forever."

"Damién . . ." She pulled away. "You talk in riddles. There's only one way to live forever. Through belief in our Lord Christ and his Salvation."

"There's another way, my darling." He had to speak quickly, get it over with. The pain was getting worse. Soon, he was certain he might burst into flames. "'Toinette, I died tonight. If you survive until morning, you'll be told of my death."

"B-but how . . ." She stared at him as if he'd gone mad. Even he admitted it sounded that way. "What are you saying?"

"Hush. Just listen. Will you do something for me?"

She nodded. She was scowling, confused, but her love held her still compliant.

"Take off your cross. I wish to kiss you again and it . . ." He affected shyness, looking away. ". . . I feel odd doing so while you wear that."

She didn't argue, but unclasped the chain and dropped it on the table. A bloodied cloth lay there. To wipe her brow, no doubt. Damién pushed it over the cross.

Immediately, the pain ceased.

"Now then . . ." He sat beside her on the bed and told her all that had happened the night before.

As he spoke, her confusion and fear faded away, replaced with a new emotion . . . *hope*.

". . . and you wish me to follow you into the dark?" She grasped his invitation quickly enough, and to his surprise, accepted it calmly. There was a faint shrug, a *moue* of cynicism he'd been unaware his Antoinette would ever possess, and a surprising eagerness. "Why not? If it saves me from the charnel pit. I love you, Damién. I'll gladly give my soul to stay with you. What must I do?"

"Only two things, my darling." He'd expected protests, his having to further convince her. This quick capitulation was startling but would make it easier. "Accept and wish to live. I'll do the rest."

She sat up, sliding her feet over the side of the bed. She was wearing a sleeping shift, something Damién and Armand, in their blatant masculinity, had refused to utilize.

At sight of her breasts half-shadowed by the fine fabric, even befouled with the plague's deadly smears, Damién felt his desire and his hunger spring to life.

Ma petite . . . How small she was, how delicate. *Can her body hold enough to quench my thirst and make her mine?* He wanted the pleasure of tasting that pure, sweet, blood. *I'm so hungry and she'll be so delicious. It isn't only hunger, it can't be. She's my Antoinette, my beloved, my wife.*

As he reached for her, she shied away, hands coming up. One final moment of doubt, fighting that last vestige of the priests' teachings? She reached to the table, fingers scrabbling for the crucifix on its golden chain.

"Put it down. Put . . . it . . . down."

She didn't move, and he made his voice soft, a whisper spoken between loving lips, forcing himself to be calm so she wouldn't be afraid.

"Put down that ornament, beloved. Think of me. Of our being together. What joy we'll have through the centuries. Think of living, *amour*, of survival and nothing else."

The cross slid from her grasp. It fell to the floor, bouncing under the bed.

Damién darted forward, lifting her. Her flesh was so sweet, so thin against his tongue. He could almost taste the blood through the skin, though it pulsed slowly. He licked away the dried befoulment, let his tongue linger as if searching for the right spot. He drove in his fangs. Blood spurted onto the front of the white nightgown, a crimson rosette . . .

Damién drank in one long, continuous swallow, then stepped back, leaving her lying on the bed, still living. Though barely breathing, she didn't want to let him go, hands clutching at his sleeves. He had to pull himself from her arms.

Desire won out over hunger now. He had to possess Antoinette before he took her through the Veil. Take that precious maidenhead while she lived, not later. She mustn't be chaste through eternity.

She gave a quick, whispery sigh, and coughed, spattering blood. He didn't bother to undress, simply threw himself back upon her, pushing aside his doublet and shirt, parting the front of his stocks.

His cock burgeoned forth like the weapon it was.

My sword into your sheath.

The irony of those words he'd written to her came back to him. He hadn't intended them this way.

"Antoinette, look at me."

She opened her eyes. They met his and he was shocked by the naked, blazing desire in them.

My precious, we will be so good together.

Damién kissed her, tongue claiming her mouth as his body claimed hers. He felt her maidenhead tear, his cock plunged deeper.

She screamed and bit. Blood flowed from their lips, dripping to the spot where their bodies joined, his stiffened dagger, her naked mound soaked in their blood. Damién pulled his bleeding tongue from her mouth, seeing her convulsive swallow as his blood slid down her throat.

He began to thrust against her as he sank his fangs again into her neck.

Antoinette died as he came.

Afterward, he laid her gently on the bed, smoothing the bloodied shift and sat beside her.

How long does it take? How long must I wait before she rises? LeMaitre had doubted his own ability to turn someone.

What if the will to live isn't enough? What if I'm too much of a novice to do it properly? Sunrise will come soon. Will I have to leave her?

While he sat there, visions appeared before him. Scenes of himself with Antoinette, accompanied by their parents as they rode and hunted. He and Armand laughing in their depredations among the womenfolk of *Village de La Croix*.

Armand.

Until that moment, he hadn't thought of the man who would've been his brother-in-law. He couldn't leave Armand behind to become dust. He'd take him with them, also, save him as he had Antoinette.

With a kiss to his beloved's cold cheek, Damién went in search of his friend.

* * *

The way into Armand's room was easier than Antoinette's; when much younger, he stood many times below his friend's window and watched while Armand climbed out to join him in some misadventure. Now, he landed on the balcony. He could see his childhood friend inside, kneeling at his *prie-dieu*.

Damién's anger rose. *After all we discussed, after the way he agreed with me, he still clings to that hope?*

Hastily, he tapped on the glass. Armand looked up, staring at the figure on the other side of the balcony door. Damién knocked again, harder this time. His friend crossed himself, rose and ran to the door.

"Damién, is it you? My God, we received a message saying you had died." He caught Damién's arm, pulling him inside. "Come in. Sit down. We haven't told Antoinette yet. What happened?"

"There's no need to tell 'Toinette, Armand. She knows." He didn't try to form any gentle way to say what was on his mind. "She's dead now."

"Did you get to see her before . . . Damién, are you a fool? I know you loved my sister but to expose yourself to the plague to come to her . . . Good God."

"Stop saying that." Damién pulled away, turning his back. "Don't speak that Name."

That so startled Armand he fell silent. Damién looked back at him.

"Armand, the Plague is the last of my worries right now. My friend . . ." Hands went to his shoulders. "The message was the truth. I *did* die."

"Is that some mad joke?" Armand pulled away. "If so, it holds no humor. Especially not now."

"No joke. Just truth."

"How can you be here, talking to me if you're dead? Damién, have you taken leave of your senses?"

"Armand, shut up and listen. I don't have much time. Two nights ago, I met a *sans mort*." He wasn't going to bother with a lengthy explanation. That could come later. "Now I'm like he. So is your sister. I want you to come with us."

Armand continued to stare, shocked into total silence.

"Armand?" Damién shook him. "Say something."

That broke the spell. "You're a creature of the night? One of the damned? Damién . . ." He took a loud convulsive swallow. "You wish me to give up my soul and join you?"

"I wish you to continue to *live*," he corrected. "To be

immune to any plague or human sickness, to look forward to living forever."

There was still doubt on his friend's face.

"Armand, you and Antoinette are the two people I love most in the world. How could I leave you to this horrible existence that ends so quickly? Say *yes*. Come with us."

He was going to agree, Damién could tell.

He went on, "Think of it, Armand. Of the long life awaiting you. The women. The adventures we can have. No worry about illness or dying . . . ever."

"What do I have to do?"

He would've shouted for joy if he'd had the time.

"Submit to me. Simply bow to my will, acknowledge me as your master. 'Tis merely a formality. Afterward, it'll mean nothing. We'll be as we always were. Friends . . . comrades . . . *Brothers*."

Armand still looked doubtful. Damién never thought he'd see such indecision on his friend's face.

"Should I pray first? Ask God to forgive me?" He gestured to the *prie-dieu*.

"If you have to do that, you're not worthy of immortality." Damién put as much contempt into his answer as possible. "Turn your back on that foolishness. Remember what we discussed so many times? All our doubts? Armand, the sun will rise soon. I don't have time for disputation."

There was a bare nod.

"Good. Now . . ." It would have to be quick. He could already feel the pull of the sun though it was still below the horizon. "Close your eyes, my friend, and think of living. How much you wish to survive. Keep that desire foremost in your mind."

He didn't wait for Armand to obey, simply lunged, sinking his fangs into the bared throat. The movement bore them both onto the bed, and whether it was fright or a mere reflex, his friend fought him. They'd always been equally matched, whether in fencing or wrestling or any other sport, but Damién's strength was more than five mortals' now.

He quickly overpowered his friend, weight holding him immobile as he gulped down the blood pumping from Armand's veins, heavy, spicy with wine, thick and delicious.

He drank and Armand's struggles became weaker and slower and . . .

. . . stopped . . .

With a single jerk, his friend lay still. Damién inhaled one last swallow and slid off Armand's body. As he had with Antoinette, he settled him upon the bed. Then he flew back to his beloved's room.

* * *

Antoinette still lay cold and unmoving, and when he saw the first faint streaks touching the sky above the trees, he reluctantly made himself return to the *château*.

LeMaitre was waiting for him.

"You're alone? Were you too late?"

"I don't know what happened. I did as you told me. She . . . neither awakened."

"Neither?"

"Her brother. I couldn't leave him behind."

"Perhaps their Faith was stronger than their will to live."

"You mean, they'd rather go to Heaven than be with

me?" That thought infuriated him.

"Calm yourself." LeMaitre's hand was on his shoulder as he looked at the rapidly brightening sky. "If they were exposed to the plague, perhaps they were too weak to respond quickly. Tonight, we'll go to the pit, see if they are there. I must go now. Sunrise is here."

Left alone, Damién ordered Charles and the others to clear the corpses from the house. "Toss them over the wall for the plague wagon . . . .and Charles?"

The *valet* turned back to look at him out of dead eyes, uncaring of anything but the desire to obey.

"Throw my parents out first, as befits their rank."

As he returned to his bed and composed himself for the dreamless darkness of *Unsleep*, Damién caught himself repeating over and over, *Please let Antoinette and Armand be waiting for me at the pit. Please.*

He wondered who he was praying to.

* * *

The following night was a joyous reunion. Surprisingly, it was Armand who awoke first.

They stood at the edge of the pit, watching as he staggered toward them. They helped him climb out, then he and Damién embraced as if seeing each other after a long separation. When he released Armand to introduce him to Geraint, he bowed courteously, then took a deep breath and forced the stale air from his lungs.

"Let's find my sister and get out of here. This place stinks."

That sounded more like his old friend.

That night, they returned to *Château de Chevigny*. It was

a repeat of the events at *Château de La Croix* with the exception of the killing of their parents. *La comtesse* was already dead. The *vicomte* died while Damién was turning his children. Letting a few survive as *fascinez*, they ordered the rest herded to *Château de La Croix* where they joined the others in the dungeon.

Damién's home was now their headquarters, their haven from which they flew each night to seek their prey and returned at sunrise to sleep.

And so began the second Scourge to be visited upon the people of Limousin . . .

* * *

Château La Croix
1449

When Damién awoke that night, Antoinette wasn't beside him. Having shared blood, she stated as far as she was concerned, they were husband and wife, and she'd slept in his bed since being brought to the *château*.

Armand had a chamber close by. His casket and Antoinette's were stored in an empty room; of them all, only Geraint slept in a coffin, it having been fetched by two of the *fascinez* from its hiding place, while Damién's own, victim of termites and dry rot, still lay in the abandoned carpenter's shed after its hasty construction the day of his death.

For the peasants, the previous night had been a festival of blood and terror, the latest in two centuries of fear.

The Plague was now a mere memory, but *les sans mort* were still very present, reaping a harvest of blood in Village de La Croix and further into Limousin. They had descended upon the town, swooping and carrying off villagers, draining them while in the air and dropping the bodies to dive and seize more. Again and again, until they were gorged, appetites sated.

The *château* was silent when they returned. The old servants had long ago perished, only the *fascinez* remained and they were long abed.

Gorged with good rich blood, they slept long and hard, and Damién was surprised to find Antoinette gone when he woke. Staggering from the bed, still heavy with *Unsleep*, he left the chamber in search of her. Sounds coming from LeMaitre's room took him in that direction.

He heard a woman's voice.

Was his master amusing himself with Simone? Damién hadn't touched her since the moment he'd sent her crying from the *salon*. Unlike his former expectation of enjoying his wife for a short time before straying, with Antoinette as his Undead lover, he found he needed no one else, and thus gave his sire free rein over any female within biting distance.

The woman spoke again, but it wasn't Simone. That voice sounded uncomfortably familiar.

Ear to the door, Damién listened in disbelief as he recognized Antoinette's tones. Her voice had changed when she crossed over. It was no longer soft and quiet but ofttimes shrill and strident. It was *stronger*. Her laugh now held an ironic, lascivious twist.

"'Twas too easy." Again, that luscious, wicked trill.

"Silent, *amour*. We don't want Damién to hear." His master's voice also held laughter.

"He's asleep. He glutted himself last night on that parlor maid. He won't wake for hours."

Was that contempt in his beloved's voice? *It couldn't be.*

"Let's not speak of Damién. 'Tis enough I have to tolerate him when he's awake, even if he is my fledgling. *Unspeakable Name*, I wish you were mine, my darling. When I saw you crawling out of that pit . . ."

"I think, my love, you must do something about Damién," Antoinette's whisper echoed around him. "And soon."

"I agree. I'd like to rid myself of him once and for all."

"After all, we no longer need him, now that I'm *la Marquise.*"

There were no more words after that though Damién stood for a long time, ears straining. Only moans and whispers and liquid sounds as bedclothes swished and the bedstead creaked. Sickened, he turned away, hurrying back to his own room and feigning heavy sleep when Antoinette returned.

He could smell LeMaitre's scent upon her.

Why did I not notice it before? Was it because I was too in love to sense such a thing?

It took all his control to pretend he knew nothing. Throughout the entire night, he smiled and acted as if he were ignorant of their *affaire.* Ignoring the glances they swapped and the little *double-entendres* they shared, he asked himself why he hadn't heard or seen all that until now?

He didn't share his betrayal with Armand, fearing his friend might try to stop him, but clung to the knowledge of his betrayal like a drowning man to a floating log. Damién made revenge his one thought, his only desire.

Whatever loyalty he'd felt for LeMaitre transformed itself to hatred; his love, his passion for Antoinette became ashes in the hot coals of his wish for vengeance . . . and he knew what he must do.

He pretended everything was as it had been and hated himself for what he planned to do. Still, he would do it. To protect himself.

While the household was silent, when he felt the fingers of the sun plucking at the heavy draperies over the windows, he forced himself out of the bed.

With the dawn, it was difficult to stay awake. *Unsleep* was an irresistible pull on the body, as insatiable as the *Thirst* when it came upon him. It took an effort, but he let his anger keep him strong. Making certain Antoinette was deep in *Unsleep's* grasp, he left the room, hurrying to his master's.

He didn't knock, simply pushed open the door and walked in. It was dark but he needed no light. He could see as clearly as if a thousand candles blazed . . . the bedstead, its sheets and quilts tossed about from their last tumbling, the heavy scent of sex in the air, and LeMaitre's coffin on trestles in front of the fireplace.

The lid lay on the floor. Damién walked over, looking down at his sire. In *Unsleep*, LeMaitre reverted to his previous condition of emaciated dessication, looking like the miserable *sans mort* of that first night.

He sleeps in a coffin but fucks my beloved in the bed I supplied. Damién forced himself not to feel pity.

Sliding his arms under LeMaitre's body, he lifted it from the coffin. In spite of its dried-out appearance, it was heavy, filled as it was with the life's-blood of Limousin's citizens.

He carried it back to his room, dropping it carelessly onto the floor in front of the balcony door. In spite of his rough handling, LeMaitre didn't awaken.

That's something to remember. Perhaps I should station a nightguard outside my chamber. Damién turned to his own bed.

Antoinette hadn't roused, either. He had only the slightest hesitation, taking in that beautiful profile, the alabaster of her skin glowing in the darkness, remembering the passion of their first nights and the way possessing her body filled his own with raging happiness. Damién shuddered slightly and lifted his beloved's body from their bed.

Adieu, faithless bitch. I offered you my love and you ground it into the dust. Pay for that now.

He lay her next to LeMaitre, then walked to the balcony door. Outside, the sun was above the trees. He could feel its pull, as strong as that of *Unsleep* but more holy, more deadly. He reached for the curtain-cord.

"Damién, what is this?"

Unspeakable Name! Not Armand. Not now. Why is he awake?

"Something woke me, and I felt a *prescience*. I thought to warn you." He gestured at the bodies of his sister and LeMaitre, sprawled on the floor. "What are you doing?"

"She betrayed me. She's been lying with my sire while pretending love to me."

Perhaps this is best. That he knows now. If he tries to stop me . . . Armand, you're my friend, but I won't give up my revenge.

"They were going to destroy me."

He waited for the outrage, for Armand to protest and attempt to protect his sister.

His friend did neither. Instead, he simply contemplated the bodies before looking back at Damién.

"Bringing her across changed her." His voice was sad. "I saw it immediately but didn't speak. I know how much you love—*loved*—her and I didn't want to disenchant you. You've seen how cruel she is, how she enjoys inflicting pain. We were that way before we died, Damién, so 'tis nothing new for us, but Antoinette? I can only guess she hide her maliciousness and being turned brought it out." He sighed as if in surrender, then turned his back on the pair on the floor. "Do what you must. my brother. This creature isn't the woman we both loved."

Taking a step into the shadows, he waited with face averted as Damién pulled the cord opening the curtains.

Brilliant, golden sunshine flooded the room. In the shadows, Armand shivered at its warmth and Damién crowded against him, making certain he was out of its reach.

The two bodies were surrounded by the fiery glow. Then . . .

There was a sudden crackle, like a flame catching a bit of tinder. Clothing and flesh smoldered. Small flames appeared. The carpeting burst into flames and Antoinette and LeMaitre along with it . . . .

. . . and they awoke, searing pain dragging them from *Unsleep* . . .

Armand didn't look around, though he shivered at the sound. Damién forced himself to watch, wanting to witness their destruction.

It didn't take long. Briefly, they writhed within the flames. LeMaitre struggled to crawl into the shadows, Antoinette following, but it was too late. They were too far ablaze.

He managed to get to his knees, pulling her with him. Her blackened arms came off in his hands, her body falling back into the blaze. The flames rushed upward, consumed them both, then died away into smoking embers.

On the floor lay a pile of ash.

Damién pulled the curtains shut.

"Go back to your room, Armand. Finish your sleep." His friend started to look back. Damién pushed him toward the door. "Don't look. Just go."

Silently, Armand obeyed.

Damién avoided the burned ruin on the floor. Skirting it, he returned to the bed. Smoothing the sheets, he erased the imprint made by Antoinette's body. He'd thought he might experience sadness. Instead, all he felt was a deep hollowness, as if something inside him had been removed.

He lay down and composed himself for sleep.

When he awoke again, it was evening.

He and Armand gathered the ashes. Standing on the balcony, they tossed them into the air and watched the night wind bear them away.

The next night, the villagers, at last roused to fight after that last atrocity, attacked the *château*. Charles and the other *fascinez* were killed in the onslaught. Damién and Armand barely had time to gather some of their native soil and make their escape.

Damién's last sight of his ancestral home was of flames rising into the air as they winged their way south.

Thus ended my life and death at Château de La Croix.

I lost my life and my Antoinette. I never regretted what I had done, neither giving up my mortal existence so I might become eternal with my beloved, nor destroying her for her infidelity. I consoled myself with the thought if such deviousness existed within her while she lived, she would've eventually betrayed me in our brief existence on Earth and her temporal punishment would have been much more lengthy and less swift. My justice to her and LeMaitre held more leniency.

As I was driven from my home by those damned peasants, I wondered if perhaps 'twas best that I now leave that place. It held too many memories of what would never be. I allowed myself one moment of regret, then turned my thoughts to the future.

A new and plague-free world awaited me. It was mine to conquer, and somewhere in it, I was certain, existed a woman I could love as much as I had loved my Antoinette. A woman who would be faithful.

I'd find her and be happy again.

Chapter 2

Konstancza
Sebeş, Transylvania
November 4, 1462

They attacked the little town shortly after sunset, when few of its inhabitants were awake. It had taken no great feat of military accomplishment. Damién and his men simply flew over the gates, killing any who were about, the *domnul's* men following them.

The first casualty was a woman emerging from a shop, a late-night shopper, basket on one arm, baby balanced in the other. She looked up in time to see the winged figure bearing down on her, its mouth open, curved fangs glittering in the lamplight.

She was knocked off her feet by the impact as its arms closed about her, the child flung from her arms to be trampled by one of the Transylvanian's sellswords, its blood spattering the charger's hooves. Deadly canines sliced into her throat, biting so deeply they gnashed against each other in the soft flesh, then ripped the pulsing artery in half, her scream dying in a blood-choked gurgle.

Her death-sound brought the shopkeeper to his doorway as the vampire dropped her body in a heap on the stoop, blood spurting from the wound for the few remaining seconds her heart continued beating.

By now, those men capable of defending the town were roused, rushing into the street with swords and spears. Some were fully clothed, others wore only their nightshirts, standing barefoot on the snowy cobbles. Young boys and less able greybeards, armed with staves, walking sticks, even fire pokers, joined them.

"'Ware the canes!" Damién warned, voice rising above the din. Striking at the right angle, even a twig could be as deadly as a stake when wielded by a mortal fighting for his life.

It was a mad babble of neighing horses and the shouts of fighting men, punctuated by women screaming, children shrieking. Bodies crowded into the little square as horsemen and armed townspeople came together in a momentary bloody clash.

Damién's *garde de nuit* swarmed above them, darting down, seizing a hapless victim, flying aloft to deliver a deadly bite, then dropping the body among those still fighting. There was a wild thrashing of horses' hooves. One animal reared and slipped, legs striking out as it regained its footing, knocking a man to the ground and trampling him before he could scramble away, nearly hitting a vampire lunging into the fray.

"Control your horse, you Romanian fool!" Wings flapping frantically, he lifted himself above and away from the wild-eyed beast as its rider struggled with the reins. Spinning in mid-air, he aimed for another victim.

Nearby, someone slashed out with his sword, impaling a diving *garde* unable to stop his downward flight. Wings flapping, his body slid down the blade, striking the hilt. The townsman heaved backward with all his strength, slinging the creature into the street where the sword rose and fell again. The vampire's head bounced over the cobbles and into the crowd, crushed under their feet while its body spasmed, wings jerking wildly before it lay still.

Someone caught at a charger's bridle, twisting upward. Thrown off balance, the animal fell to the ground, its rider pinned beneath it. Two men leaped upon him, one beating at him with a staff while the other wrenched the sword from his hand and drive it through his chest.

Above it all, the *vampiri* rose and swooped, seizing their victims, biting deep and deadly and tossing the bodies upon the stones to melt the snow with still-warm blood.

By this time, foot soldiers were rushing into the houses, attacking those still abed. A few awakened in time to leap from their beds, looking frantically about for something to use in defense as the invaders fell upon them. Others never woke, slain as they slept.

In spite of the surprise of the attack, the townspeople defended themselves well. The invaders suffered casualties, to be sure—even the *garde de nuit* lost their share—but not enough to matter, and too quickly, it was over.

The sudden silence accompanying the defeat was shocking.

In the quiet only one sound was heard, the clop of the *domnul's* horse's hooves as the conqueror, he whom they called the *Son of the Dragon*, rode into the village square. Expressionless, Vlad Drakula surveyed the bodies of the slain, noting those of his men as well as Damién's *garde*, then gave orders for the houses to be searched.

While some of the men performed that chore, others

dragged the corpses into the square, piling them in heaps. The rest formed ranks and watched.

One by one, the surviving *garde* floated to earth, joining their mortal comrades-in-arms.

"I want a body count," Drakula ordered. "*Le Chevalier* says there were three hundred and forty souls here. I would be assured today we sent that many to heaven."

A flapping of wings sounded behind him, but he didn't turn, simply waited as Damién landed at his side. His hand closed on his sword, gripping it so tightly he was certain it would show the marks of his fingers.

"Will you use that against me, *domnul*?" came the soft, taunting question. "Do you hire men to fight, then kill them when the way they obey your orders repulses you?"

The prince didn't answer, merely turned his head, looking at him.

"What would you have me do with the bodies of your . . . men?" His hesitation stated plainly he doubted he should call these vile creatures of the dark *men*, though they once had been.

"You'll burn them also," Damién nodded to the rapidly growing hill of bodies.

The *domnul* raised an eyebrow. "You'd consign your brethren to the flames?"

"Each of us is aware what follows the True Death, my lord. Destruction by fire is our expectation for willingly accepting this accursed state. 'Tis our reward." He gave Drakula a sardonic smile. "We're already damned, *domnul*. This way, the path to Hell is quickly taken."

Thinking he would never understand how men calling themselves Christians would voluntarily damn themselves, Drakula gestured. Two of his soldiers hastily dragged the bodies to join the others while a third found the smashed remains of the bodiless head and gingerly reunited it with the trunk, the stave still protruding from its heart.

They tossed them onto the hill of corpses and ran back to join their comrades, crossing themselves while Damién and the others hastily turned their heads and shielded their eyes. Some of the soldiers wiped their hands on the tails of their *gambesons* as though they'd touched filth. The one carrying the head barely managed to keep from vomiting. Only his fear of the punishment his prince would exact upon him prevented him from allowing his belly to spew its contents.

Someone thrust a torch into the pile of bodies.

The flame flickered, then flared as clothing smoldered. In a few moments, the blaze spread from body to body, leaping from one hill of corpses to another until the entire square was a ring of light, the stench of burning flesh, hair, and cloth rising above it. Some of the buildings were also burning, ignited by sparks from the pyres of its inhabitants, as well as the torches the soldiers tossed into them.

A sudden shriek came from inside a house.

Two of Drakula's soldiers burst through the open doorway. One held the wrist of a young woman, dragging her with him in his hurried return to his master. She was dressed in a flimsy night rail, hair in a sleep-frazzled braid over one shoulder. Though she stumbled and fell, she was pulled on relentlessly, knees scraping the stones before she regained her footing.

The other soldier dragged two younger girls in his wake, all three struggling and sobbing.

"Please . . . let us go!"

"Sweet Lord." Socza Jacza, the prince's lieutenant, breathed a bare whisper. Before he realized what he was doing, he crossed himself, his other hand touching the crucifix resting against his breastplate. Hastily, he released it as he saw *Le Chevalier* shield his eyes.

Drakula didn't speak as the three were hauled into the square, the soldiers stopping before their general with hasty salutes.

"Sir... Look what we found hiding in a closet."

General Ragoczy turned his dark gaze upon the three. "Did I say spare anyone? Kill them."

"No!" The oldest wrested herself free of her captors and threw herself at Drakula.

She tripped, found herself caught by a strong pair of hands, looked up into blue eyes in a blood-stained face, his body hidden by bloody armor.

In that moment, Damién felt a tension greater than the frenzy floating about them, a desire having nothing to do with death. Wresting her hands from his, she turned to the prince, falling to her knees beside his horse. She grasped his ankle, pressing her forehead against it.

Startled by the movement near its hooves, the horse shied slightly, nearly knocking her down. Once again Damién reached out, only to stop as Drakula brought the animal under control.

"Please." She looked up at him through a tangle of pale hair. "My lord, spare us."

Drakula looked at Ragoczy.

"'Twould be a pity to slay them, my general." As the young man took a deep breath to protest, he added, "Especially since your men haven't had a woman for many months now." He looked down at the girl, meeting eyes wide with horror. "Let them be useful. Give them to the men."

Ragoczy caught the girl by the waist, dragging her away from the horse. She screamed, fighting against her captor while her sisters beat against the soldier's back with their fists.

"*Domnul* . . ." The call was soft and sibilant as a serpent's hiss.

"You disapprove, *Chevalier*?" Drakula didn't look at Damién. "Surely one who rips out men's throats can't condemn my actions."

"I neither condone nor condemn, sire." Damién's reply was still quiet. "How can I, when my men and I are being paid as well as the others, but in a different coin?"

Behind them, what started as a murmur of voices was now a chorus of shouts and laughter as the men crowded around the three women. The soldier shoved the oldest toward the first line of men.

She stumbled on the snowy cobblestones and slid into the nearest pair of arms, nails raking his face as they closed around her.

"Let me go."

"Bitch!" He caught her wrist, twisting the arm behind her. One hand wound itself into the neck of her night rail, ripping downward, and she cried out as the night air rushed against her bare skin.

Laughing, the soldier pressed his face against her breasts, mouth open, tongue licking over them while the girl beat at his shoulders. Somehow, she managed to pull free, lost her balance, and careened against another. Before she could escape, a mail-gloved fist backhanded her across her jaw, knocking her senseless. Wrapping his arms around her, he called out something and lifted her off the ground. Two of his companions seized her bare ankles, throwing the hem of the sleeping shift over her head.

Beside the prince, Damién drew in his breath in a sharp hiss.

As the girl kicked, the soldier settled between her thrashing legs, fumbling under his quilted leather *gambeson* to loose his belt and drop his stocks. He was already aroused by her struggles, caught his straining member in his fist and aimed it between her thighs, then stopped.

He said something softly, free hand brushing up the girl's belly, laughing slightly as her skin quivered under his touch. Without warning, he thrust forward, nearly falling, and his companions moved with him, wrapping the girl's legs tightly around his waist and holding them.

Her body bucked as the soldier plunged into her. The men's laughter drowned her screams, their breath forming a frosty cloud over the heaving bodies.

Nearby, one of her sisters was sprawled in the snow, a soldier full-length upon her, metal skirt hiked up, mail trousers around his knees. Driving her slight nakedness against the snow-covered stones, his body held her immobile while the gathering men urged him on.

The youngest had been thrown against the side of the building that had been her home, one of Damién's men pressed against her, her little body hidden by his open wings as he sank his teeth into her neck. There was a brief interval of frantic thrusting, then the vampire gasped in release, catching at the girl's hips to steady himself as he raised his head. Panting, he pushed away the hands holding her ankles and staggered from between the now-lax legs. One hand wiped blood from his mouth as he stooped to seize his stocks with the other and refasten them.

Her body slid to the ground. Another soldier took his place, snatched her up, and pinned her against the cold bricks again.

Behind them, a Transylvanian rose from the oldest girl's body, settling his garments as he gestured for a comrade to come forward. Through it all, she continued to scream, a seemingly endless wailing, echoed weakly by the other two. By the time a third soldier replaced the second, her cries faded to a low moaning, barely audible above the grunts of those satisfying themselves and the calls of the waiting.

There was a noise behind the prince, a rapid whirring of wings. Out of the corner of his eye, he saw dark movement and when he turned his head, the *Chevalier* was gone. Rising above the soldiers, Damién swooped in a dead fall to the center of the crowd.

Briefly, the winged body was blotted out by those of Drakula's men. There was the sound of argument, a shout of protest, then Damién beat his way free, armor gleaming in the firelight, a woman's naked body in his arms.

Ah. The prince's smile was cruel and cold. *Briefly, the wench will think she's been rescued.*

He had no doubt soon enough she would welcome the death that would have come once the *strigoi* finished with her.

* * *

Six months before, Vlad Tepes, *Voivode* of *Tara Romaneasc* and Prince of Wallachia and Transylvania, accepted a most unusual group of mercenaries into his army.

It happened late one night as the prince allowed himself a rare moment of relaxation in his private study. He was examining a gilded and bejeweled cross, a gift from the local priest for his contributions to the church, rumored to be the *Voivode's* attempts to buy his way into heaven. It was a lovely thing, hand-crafted and precious, and he was trying to determine where it should be kept.

There was a sound at the window but he paid it no mind. *Doubtless some bird striking the outward-opening shutters.*

When the sound came again, he gave the window a negligent glance—and stiffened as he saw someone standing before it, an extremely pale young man about the same age as himself. He was dressed in a split-skirted riding coat and thigh boots, the heavy ringlets resting on his shoulders as dark and lustrous as the prince's own.

His unexpected visitor closed the window.

"How did you get in here?" Vlad demanded, placing the cross on the desk. "How did you get past my guard?"

Not giving the stranger a chance to answer, he bellowed for the sentry and when he appeared, turned on him so violently, the young man cringed.

"Were you asleep at your post?" He gestured at the stranger watching the exchange with sardonic amusement. "You dared allow someone to make his way into my private chamber?"

"Sire . . . I-I wasn't asleep, I swear . . . no one came past me . . ." The soldier knew what his punishment would be if he couldn't convince his prince he had been wide awake and saw no one. Already he could feel the tender flesh of his backside shrinking from the impaler's lance.

"Liar! This castle is built on a precipice over the Arges. No one can access it except through *that* door." He gestured at the door through which the guard himself had come.

"Your Highness . . ." The call from behind him was soft but commanding.

Vlad turned to look at the stranger who had taken several steps into the room.

"Your guard tells the truth. He neither slept, nor did I come past him to enter this room. Send him on his way and be thankful you have such alert men guarding you."

With a desultory gesture, Vlad dismissed the sentry who gratefully ran for the haven of his post, breathing a prayer of thanks to God—and the stranger—for his salvation.

"Explain yourself." The prince turned back to the stranger. "How did you get in here? Did you fly?"

"As a matter of fact, I did." At the *voivode's* look of disbelief, he went on, "You shouldn't leave your windows unshuttered, sire."

Vlad chose to ignore his statement, knowing full well no human had wings. If the stranger had somehow managed to scale the castle walls, he might be someone to reckon with. In a disdainful tone, he asked, "What do you want . . . that you brave my guards, and my own wrath, no matter how you got here?"

"To offer you the services of myself and my men."

"A mercenary, eh? If you wish to join my army, see my recruiting sergeant—"

"Ah, but he's probably sound asleep at this time of night. As are all your soldiers, except for your stalwart sentry . . . and yourself. Besides . . ." His broad shoulders shrugged negligently. ". . . recruitment is for peasants. I prefer to speak to you directly, my lord. As noble to noble."

"A noble, you say? Who are you?" It was a challenge, intimating the young man's nobility was of such low degree, he wasn't worth a glance from the prince, that no one was of the same status as the *voivode,* and so could not speak to him as a peer.

"Marquis Damién La Croix, *Le Chevalier du Morte.*" With a flourish, the stranger bowed.

"The one they call *L'homme de nuit?*" Vlad managed to hide his surprise. His Transylvanian accent mangled the French pronunciation.

"You've heard of me?" He appeared slightly gratified.

"I've heard of you. And your *garde noir.* But I thought you a fable."

"Hardly, my lord." The young man smiled slightly, revealing slender, needle-sharp fangs.

"Sweet Jesu!" The prince reached for the crucifix, thrusting it toward his visitor who immediately turned his head and put out a hand to shield his face.

"Put away that holy relic, sire." His words were soft but anxious. "You're in no danger."

"Why should I believe the word of such a despicable creature?"

"Because I was once a noble such as yourself, and, in some ways, still am." As the prince placed the cross behind him on the desk, the stranger straightened and continued, "I've come to offer you my services, and that is all."

"So, you *did* fly through my window." The prince stared at him, barely hearing his words. "I always thought those tales were just that . . . stories to frighten children into obedience. Nevertheless, I prefer proof of my own eyes. Let me see your wings."

"If I must." With a slight sigh, the creature calling

himself *Le Chevalier* turned his back.

His riding coat was slashed from shoulder to waist on either side. As the prince watched, the broad shoulders flexed and twisted, there was a ripping sound and through the long, narrow slits, slender wings protruded. With the crackle of sails unfurling, they opened, swirling like a wide and fluid cloak.

"Is your curiosity now fed, my lord?" He whirled to face Vlad again, the wings disappearing in a whispered rustle. "Do we have an accord?"

"All mercenaries serving me are paid on their skill. What is your kind's price?"

"*My kind* . . ." Briefly, the words held a venomous edge. ". . . wish only one payment, sire. That which all men have in abundance." Briefly, the blue eyes seemed to hold a scarlet tinge. "We'll fight for you, my lord. For your glory . . . and all the blood we can drink."

The prince forced himself to stifle the shudder that statement caused. Instead, he nodded and held out his hand. With startling swiftness, *Le Chevalier* seized and pressed it to his forehead as he dropped to one knee. A second shudder threatened to escape and was quelled with difficulty as the back of the *voivode's* hand touched that chill flesh.

Blessed Christ, he's as cold as a corpse! And why not? This creature kneeling before him, who looked like a man . . . wasn't he, in reality, one of the *nosferatu*, the walking dead?

And he had just received them into the ranks of his army. *Dear God protect us all!*

"Rise, *Chevalier*." Nothing in his manner betrayed his inner thoughts. "Bring your men to the *castel*. They will be received without hostility, I promise. My men will be forewarned."

"Thank you, my prince." Standing, the Frenchman bowed slightly, then walked to the window. Opening the latch, he pushed it outward, so the night air came rushing in. As if in afterthought, he looked back. "There is one thing, Your Majesty."

"And that is . . . ?" The prince's answer was wary, as if expecting the creature to extract some deadly promise from him.

"You will protect my men and myself while we're in *Unsleep*. It may even be best if you change your battle tactics to night fighting. Ensure our safety while we're helpless, and I swear all your battles will be won, and you'll triumph over those you call your enemies."

"While you're in my service, you'll be safe, *Chevalier*." Vlad gave his word without hesitation. "I swear."

Nodding, the creature shrugged his shoulders, released his wings, and before the *voivode* could speak, leaped onto the ledge of the window. He threw himself into space.

Running to the window, Vlad looked down and then skyward. In the distance, a rapidly dwindling figure winged its way over the river.

And thus, Vlad Drakula opened his ranks to the *Undead*.

* * *

Landing a street away, Damién went up the stairs of one of the houses designated for the officers and thus left untouched, past the two guards stationed there and into the little bedroom off the landing. The girl wasn't heavy, her weight seemed even less than the armor he was wearing. Gently, he placed her upon the bed and sat upon its edge.

She didn't move. To his eyes, she looked as dead as he. Her skin had a bluish tinge, face bruised and bloody, the marks startling against the whiteness of her flesh.

Cautiously, he touched her cheek. It was chill, as if it had no blood to warm it. He turned her head, inspecting her throat. No marks. None of his men had been at her.

Had the mortal soldiers killed her? Was she going to die in spite of his bringing her to safety? Had the shock of being stripped naked and crushed into the frozen earth by the many bodies upon her own already taken its toll? He should have acted sooner, intervened, and simply demanded her from the *domnul* as his due.

He chafed the white hands, then dropped them, seizing a quilt. Pulling it free of the bed, he hurried to the fire where he held it out to the blaze. When it had absorbed some heat, he returned to the bed and placed it over her, rubbing her chest and belly with the padded cloth, massaging warmth into the cold body.

Soon, a faint touch of color appeared in the pallid flesh. In a few moments, she stirred, moaning softly. Tucking the quilt around her, Damién reached for the little pitcher and basin on a nearby commode, pouring water and dipping a towel into it. He swiped it over his own cheeks, smearing the blood so it gave his flesh a near-human pinkness.

Sitting down again, he began to clean her face.

She gasped, opening her eyes, hands striking out. He caught her wrists, and as she lay still, released them.

"'Tis all right. I took you from them."

Her clenched hands covered her face. Two blackened and tear-stained eyes peered at him through her fingers.

"You saved me?" At his nod, she stammered, "I . . . y-you . . . you were there, with the prince." Her breath came in a gasp, let out slowly. "Th-thank you."

"'Twas purely selfish." He wet the cloth again, wringing it before applying it to her throat where a series of red ovals that could've been love-bites if not so violently applied, were beginning to swell. "I want you for myself."

The girl didn't answer.

Gently, he pulled away the quilt, noting she made no effort to stop him. As the cleansing cloth moved lower, brushing across her breasts, removing the blood from a crescent of teeth-marks around one nipple, she trembled, biting her lip to keep from crying out.

It took all his will to concentrate on what he was doing. Her nakedness, that expanse of white flesh speckled with blood, the scent of her body, the smell of the soldiers' spill upon her, was almost strong enough to drive him into a rage of blood lust when his true intent was something quite different.

At that moment, the last thing Damién wanted was to feast on this helpless and frightened female.

Dropping the cloth into the basin, he stood and walked to the door, pausing with his hand on the handle to look back. "I must speak with the *domnul*. When I return, see that you're properly grateful."

Then, he went out.

* * *

In a nearby house, Drakula, freed of his armor, rested

his feet against the andirons in the fireplace and accepted the goblet of wine his lieutenant offered him.

It was a small dwelling but well-furnished and the wine a fairly acceptable Tokay. He assumed its owner had been a well-off individual, though his wealth hadn't done him much good against the Transylvanians' onslaught.

When Damién appeared, saluting him with his sword and asking, "What are your orders before dawn comes, my lord?" he countered with a question of his own, "Why aren't you out there, *Chevalier*? Taking your share of the Soldier's Reward?"

"I've taken my reward, *domnul*." The blue eyes followed his gaze, looking at the shadows the flames made on the wall, throwing dark figures into high relief before them. "You saw me."

"Ah, yes—the girl. She survives then?"

"She does, sire."

"For a little longer? For the night, at least?" the prince persisted. "What happens tomorrow night, when you awake? Will she lie cold and still in your bed? And when we ride out of here? Will you leave her behind to rise and feast on some other village's young men?"

"No, sire. I have no intention of *turning* the girl. I plan to keep her alive."

"To use as a human winepress, then?" Damién's answer surprised him. "To slake your unholy thirst?"

"Yes and no." There was a brief smile on the perfect mouth.

How can a man be so beautiful and still radiate such masculinity? the prince wondered. In his court, someone so comely would have been suspect of offering his backside to his fellows—and would soon have earned himself a place in the *Forest of the Impaled* for his perversion, a stout oak lance filling that place often pierced by a different type of weapon.

"How do you mean?" He remembered the hideous appearance of the *Chevalier* and his followers when they attacked. *How well they disguise themselves.*

Damién turned to the fire. Like his men, he wore full armor from the waist down, but only a breastplate covering from neck to belly. Tied at throat, shoulder, and waist, his back was naked, allowing his wings freedom. As he saw the movement of the muscles in those bare shoulders, the prince was again reminded of the night he had met the vampire.

"I intend no disrespect, *domnul*, but I doubt you or any mortal man can understand the loneliness my kind feels." He stared into the flames, one hand resting against the mantel. "I think . . . briefly at least, this woman may help assuage that loneliness . . . and when we ride out of here . . ."

"When we ride out?" the prince repeated.

"She'll come with me. When we fight again, she'll stay behind with the other camp followers, awaiting my return."

"Is there a chance she might damn herself and die by her own hand rather than submit to your desire?" Vlad allowed himself a moment's concern for one of his subjects. Since the night the handsome Frenchman appeared at his court with his soldiers of the night, he'd wondered about these unholy creatures, never actually calling them what every man knew they were. He also worried that accepting them into his army and paying them with blood made him as vile and accursed as they.

"There is always that chance, sire. After all, mortals are blessed with free will."

Free will . . .

The prince thought that over. In that case, since he had hired these Undead mercenaries without being forced, he could as easily dismiss them the same way. Or, if they protested, have Ragoczy and Jacza enter their tents during daylight and dispatch them.

Travel by night, my lord, attack when the sun goes down, protect my men and myself during the day . . . and we will fight for you, and you will triumph.

He had given his word. Vlad had determined early in his reign he would always be a ruler who kept his promises, both good and bad.

"The news of what rides with me goes before us," he went on, casually. "Do you know the peasants are saying I am also *nosferatu?* That I, too, am one of the *Undead,* and have summoned the children of the night to help me rid my country of these insolent foreigners aiding my kinsman in his fight against me?"

"Then you must allow yourself to be seen in daylight, sire, and refute those beliefs. Prove to one and all you are a mortal. I won't say a *mere* mortal," Damién spoke softly, careful to keep his voice neutral so he wouldn't appear to be toadying. "For you are a totally uncommon and exceptional individual. I daresay we will never see your like again."

And if I were able, he thought. *I would pray to the Unspeakable Power that we never do.*

Damién had never delved into the reasons why the prince chose to attack the townspeople he had taken a vow to protect, deciding *he,* least of any other, had a right to question or condemn anyone. There were unnatural monsters like himself and his men, and natural ones, like the man sitting before him, and he wasn't certain which was worse.

"What you have done for your country will be remembered in the coming centuries."

"Will you share a glass with me, *Chevalier?*" The prince raised his goblet, taking a long and satisfying swallow. "Or did you have enough . . . what do you call it? *Dark wine?* To satisfy yourself tonight?"

"Thank you, sire, but for now, I and my men are sated. At present, we require no sustenance, so, by your leave . . . ?"

Setting the goblet on a nearby table, the *domnul* waved a jeweled hand negligently. "Of course, go. Enjoy the rest of the night. Dawn comes soon enough."

* * *

In the bedroom, warmed by the fire and the blankets wrapped around her, the girl assessed her situation. After the soldier left, she cried, but now all her tears were gone. He told her he wanted her, had rescued her from death by rape so he might do the same to her, but not kill her. If that was the expected end to his mercy, he could've joined the others in their sport.

No, this soldier wanted something more.

She hoped.

He was a foreigner, she was certain. She had caught an odd intonation in his speech hinting of a birth somewhere other than Tara Romanesca. Briefly, she wondered where her sisters were and what had happened to them. Perhaps he'd saved them also? Could she dare hope for that much compassion from a mercenary? Would he possess more pity than her own countrymen?

When he returned, she would ask him to speak his desires plainly and if he said what she expected, she already knew how she would respond.

She had barely time to settle herself against the pillows, pulling the blankets up to her chin before she heard the clank of armored heels on the stairs.

The door opened and he stood there, tall and frightening in armor dulled with splashes of the townfolks' blood, his cheeks oddly pink against his pallor. At the same time, she saw something flickering in his eyes.

A promise of some kind, and . . . shockingly . . . a responding quiver in her own heart. *Oh, Sweet Savior, but he's handsome.*

He didn't move, studying her, as if to assure himself she wasn't about to fight him.

What good would that do? she asked herself. *With me naked and he armed with a sword?*

He walked over to a small chest, reaching for a decanter of wine sitting upon it. Pouring some into a goblet, he handed it to her.

"Well?"

She raised herself on one elbow, took the goblet, and sipped slowly, trying to properly form the answer to his question. The other hand held the quilt firmly against her breasts.

A foolish gesture, Damién thought. *Both I and half the men in the* domnul's *army have seen you naked tonight and probably a third have known your body as intimately as possible. Yet you would hide it from* me?

As she lowered the goblet, he walked away from the bed to stand before the fireplace. Holding out his hands to the flame, he wondered what she was thinking. The girl had been violated repeatedly, would she feel gratitude or hatred toward a rescuer who wanted to do the same, no matter what he called it? He wondered if she might attempt something brave but foolish, like trying to slay him.

Quickly, he looked around the room. No weapons handy, other than his own, securely attached to his cuirass by their chains and belts. Unless she knew what he was, and had something wooden handy, neither of those offered him any harm.

The girl lowered the goblet and sat up, letting the quilt fall into her lap. She took a deep breath making the battered but still-beautiful breasts lift, causing Damién's lust to surge a little faster through his veins.

She's going to be reasonable.

"I can be grateful for my life, my lord, if not for my dishonor," she said softly.

In it, he heard resignation for what was to come, as well as hope that he would be less cruel than the others.

"My name is Konstancza."

He didn't answer, merely continued watching her as she drank from the goblet again.

"My Lord, my sisters . . ."

"What of them?" He made his voice harsh so she would appreciate her own salvation. "I've no need for three women."

Without answering, she set the goblet on the chest and began to sob, very softly.

"Make certain your tears are spent before I return." Damién opened the door, and went out, calling to the guard on the landing to help him remove his armor.

When he reappeared, he was dressed as if to be presented at Court. Wanting to impress upon the girl her choice to live was the correct one as well as the fact that she was about to be tumbled by a noble, he had foregone the usual plain and serviceable clothes worn by a soldier when out of armor, for something more spectacular. A white linen shirt with a tight-fitting black doublet of watered silk under a knee-length open jerkin of emerald velvet. Below the doublet, his dark hose were visible to his waist, their buckled codpiece of a contrasting color.

The sudden intake of Konstancza's breath told him he had chosen wisely.

Throwing back the covers, she climbed from the bed and walked to him, eyes holding his, her bare feet making no sound though her step was firm and unhesitating. He noticed she kept her arms still tightly crossed over her breasts.

When she stood before him, she said quietly, "You saved my life and for that I'm thankful, my lord. How may I show my gratitude?"

He had no chance to answer.

Konstancza fell to her knees, arms encircling his legs, pressing her bare breasts against them. She raised her head to look up at him, and the movement brought her face on an exact level with his codpiece. Damién forced himself to be silent. What he wanted in that moment was to pull open the buckles and free his member from the restraining fabric, ordering the girl to arouse him with that sweet, beautiful mouth.

Instead, he took a step backward, catching her hands and pulling her to her feet.

"For the present, I would have you speak with me. I think we have much to discuss." He led her to a chair near the hearth and when she was seated, looking up at him expectantly, arms once more shielding her breasts, he took one of the blankets from the bed, wrapping it around her.

"Do you know who I am, Konstancza?"

"No, my lord." Her answer was prompt, with a childlike truthfulness. "I believe you are from France because of your accent and the way you pronounce some of our words through your nose as I've heard Frenchmen do."

Damién managed to stifle a laugh at that little insult. "My name is Damién. I'm called *Le Chevalier du Morte*."

She recognized his title, he could see that immediately, hands leaving her breasts to go to her mouth. "The one they call the Nightman?" Without giving him a chance to reply, she went on, "Oh, Sweet Jesus, have mercy. Then, you mean to kill me?"

She made the sign of the Cross, startled as Damién retreated several paces, holding up one hand, fingers spread to shield his face.

Taking a deep breath, she squared her shoulders, unintentionally making her breasts bounce enticingly, as she said with quiet resignation, "If I must die, so be it. I've been a good Christian woman and expect to find myself in heaven after you drain my poor body dry." In the next moment, however, she gasped in horror as the meaning of her own words sank in. "Oh, Lord. I-I won't go to heaven, will I? If you make me as you are, I-I'll become a vile creature—"

"You have nothing to fear from me, Konstancza," Damién assured her. "'Tis been long since I've had a mortal woman, but I swear I'll not force acceptance of my condition upon you." He gave a slight laugh. "I tried that once, and disaster followed. If you agree to stay with me, I swear to you you'll die in your own time, and a priest will give you *Last Rites*."

She didn't answer, too shocked by his reply to even shake her head, instead sat biting her lip and staring at him until he said, a little sharply, "Well? What do you say?"

"What if I refuse?"

"I'll leave this room, and when the prince's army abandons this place, I'll make certain you're taken over the border where you'll be safe. You—"

He didn't have a chance to finish what he'd been about to say. She was on her feet, standing so close her breasts brushed his chest.

"Do with me what you will, my lord, for I owe you my life."

Standing on tiptoe, she kissed him, gently, softly, didn't pull away or struggle as his hands closed about her. He returned her kiss with one rougher and more demanding. Pushing away the blanket, he peeled away the tattered remains of the night rail hanging around her hips.

Konstancza didn't move as the last strip of cloth fell to the floor, nor did she react when Damién kissed her again, lips roving across her breast, cautiously teasing a nipple, being careful not to cause her pain as his tongue stroked between the teeth marks. There was blood on her legs, still fresh from her assault, and also on the insides of her thighs.

Kneeling before her, he bent to lick away the sign of her defilement, tongue gently lapping the virgin blood. Her first faint moan brought him to his feet. Sweeping her into his arms, he moved to the bed, depositing her upon it.

He only showed his haste as he undressed, shrugging out of the jerkin, fairly ripping off the doublet. Pulling loose the strings tying his hose to his shirt, he let them drop as he slid the garment from his shoulders and tossed it aside, then pushed down his stocks and let them and his slippers fall atop the other garments . . .

. . . and all the while, Konstancza lay without moving, watching him with wide eyes . . . until the last piece of clothing was gone.

Briefly, he wanted to preen, display his body and allow her to accustom herself to the sight but his desire was rapidly taking hold.

She sat up, reaching out to cradle his half-rampant organ in her hands, placing a soft kiss upon the already moist tip.

Damién's lunge carried them both onto the bed and into a tangle of arms and legs. Somehow, he found himself cradled between her thighs, as he pressed his mouth against hers. Her hands roved over his body as if not knowing where to rest, exploring, stroking, their touch nearly driving him past the point of control.

She was open and ready, his cock straining to enter but he pulled away, raising himself on his arms to look into her eyes.

"Some of your blood. I must have it. One drop."

"Take whatever you wish, my lord." Her answer came as a harsh moan as she wrapped her hands in his hair, pulling him against her.

He kissed her throat. Turning his head, he dropped his fangs and raked one across the tender flesh, barely deep enough to break the skin, causing blood to well but not to drip. Licking across the little scratch, he savored that single crimson drop upon his tongue.

The wound healed immediately.

Of its own accord, his body reacted to the sweet taste, thrusting into her so quickly she cried out—not in pain but with satisfaction—and he pushed himself into her body again and again, while she clung to him. All the things he had planned to do, to be tender and caring, were forgotten as desire seized him. He rose to his knees, hands under her hips, lifting her off the bed, and with a bellow of fulfillment, poured himself into her before collapsing against Konstancza's breast.

Sated as he was, he forced himself to whisper, *"Sweet Unspeakable Name* . . . I vow, girl, 'tis a long time since I've tasted something so pure and unsullied. It fair overcame me."

She didn't answer, but stroked his shoulder, waiting until his breathing quieted and he rolled away.

"You said it has been a long time since you had a mortal woman? Exactly how long, my lord?"

He laughed slightly, a sheepish sound. "I vow I forget exactly. Several centuries at least."

He hugged her as she gave a little laugh of her own. Pulling her close, he kissed her forehead, brushing back the tumbled flaxen curls.

"What happens now, my lord?"

"Now? We sleep, Konstancza," Gathering her into his arms, he closed his eyes and lay still. Before she was lulled to sleep by the silence in the room, and not letting the fact register she heard no breathing except her own, he roused to say, "Don't think to escape or try to slay me while I'm helpless. There's a reason I left the door open."

"Why did you?" Until that moment, she hadn't realized the door to the hallway was ajar.

"The guard outside will hear if anyone leaves this bed during daylight and will investigate and prevent my being harmed." he informed her, coldly.

"The guard. He *heard?*" She didn't hear the threat, only that one fact. "He heard everything we did?"

"Aye." There was a quiet, self-satisfied laugh. "And has probably spilled in his stocks or is pressed into the shadows practicing self-abuse about now."

"Then let us sleep, My Lord." She wouldn't tell him she had no thoughts of trying to escape. Settling herself against him, she snuggled into his arms. As Damién's laughter died away and he became still once more, Konstancza also slept, too quickly for her to think she lay in the arms of a corpse.

***

The soldiers didn't try to hide their astonishment when Konstancza rode into camp with the *Chevalier*.

"So, the wench got herself a protector," someone spoke from the ranks. "She'll think twice once his fangs are in her throat, I vow."

The speaker fell silent as Damién turned, looking over the helmeted heads as if searching for someone. Pulling his horse to a halt, he dismounted and came around the animal to help Konstancza from her mount.

"Stay here. I must speak with the *domnul*."

She nodded, tightening her grip on the animal's reins and looking around a little anxiously. Damién understood why. The men who attacked her were somewhere in the soldiers standing around them and she was frightened they might seize her again.

"You won't be harmed," he assured her, then walked away.

He had gone less than ten feet when someone spoke behind her. "Well, pretty one. How do you like sleeping with the dead?"

Konstancza whirled. Behind her stood a young man in the garb of a mercenary. For some reason, that reassured her. Vague as her memories of that awful night were, she remembered the men raping her wore uniforms. She glanced over at Damién who stood in front of the prince's tent, in deep conversation with His Majesty.

"Afraid to answer? Afraid he'll see?" The boy leaned a little closer, breathing a waft of garlic and *gulas* in her direction.

Konstancza shrank away. He touched her arm, stroking roughly.

"You're a pretty wench and deserve to be under a hot-blooded man. When you tire of dead, cold flesh, let me know. We can meet in the daylight, where he can't come."

When Damién bowed to the prince and started back to where she stood, the soldier scurried back to his fellows gathered around a nearby fire.

Immediately, he saw the look on her face. "What is it?"

"Nothing—'tis nothing," she assured him, certain what his reaction would be if she told him.

"You've been frightened. Who?" Damién fell silent, staring at her. One hand closed into a fist. Though she continued shaking her head, he demanded, looking around, "Which one is he?"

"My lord, please. 'Twas was nothing. Don't harm him. I beg you." She touched his arm and his hand relaxed.

Smiling, he brushed his fingers against her cheek, then pulled away, striding toward the group around the fire. One man squatted with his back to them. Seizing him by the shoulder, Damién jerked him to his feet, spinning him around.

"Hold!" The soldier's shout held genuine fright. "What is this?"

"You know full well what it is," Damién grated, one hand going to the mercenary's throat and lifting him off the ground.

The soldier began to choke, gagging and kicking.

"You spoke to my woman, tried to entice her away from me with your warm body . . . and your warm blood . . . which could soon be very, very cold."

The last words were delivered in a low growl as he released the boy, dropping him on his back in the snow.

As the soldier looked up at him, cringing, Damién went on, "You're fortunate she has asked me to postpone the hour of your death."

Whirling, he stalked back to where Konstancza stood. Taking her by the arm, he caught the reins of their horses in the other hand, and led her to his tent. Behind him, he heard the young soldier vomiting into the snow as his fear-stricken stomach rebelled.

Damién smiled quietly.

* * *

Thus, began three months of contentment. A long time for a mortal but only a few moments in a vampire's continuity. Ever afterward, Damién would consider the brief time he spent with Konstancza one of the happiest periods of his existence.

Whenever he returned from a battle, she was waiting with hugs and kisses and a tub of hot water to wash away the blood. Bathing him herself, she aroused him with the caress of the washcloth against his battle-weary body. She never asked whose blood he wore or how many had died to stain his armor so. She was warm, loving, and attentive, and as eager to be taught about lovemaking as he was to teach her.

It would've surprised many to see him sitting beside her as she played a song upon the lute he had retrieved from the charred ruins of her home, or reading to him from a book of poems the prince sent one of his men to purchase for her. When she dined, he sat with her, nursing a goblet of wine he didn't drink but simply held to nurture the illusion of normalcy.

This is how it would have been between 'Toinette and me, if the Plague hadn't spoiled our lives, he thought. *If I hadn't been so cowardly and chosen immortality over taking my chances of escaping the Scourge.*

Though he would never express it, he was extremely grateful for being allowed to experience that brief taste of domesticity.

* * *

At present, the battles were over, so they returned to Tirgoviște, the prince's palace. Damién and his men took up residence in one of the unoccupied upper stories, drawing heavy velvet drapes against the sun, assured by the *domnul* they could sleep safely.

Servants brought Konstancza her meals and anything she requested and for a little while, she appeared happy, but soon, Damién noticed a change in her behavior. At first, he thought it imagined, deciding she was merely having one of those mysterious Woman's Times he'd barely learned about and had no occasion to explore before he lost his life. He'd already decided he would send her to other quarters during that time, not wanting any scent of blood inflaming him and making him lose control and harm her.

After she continued thus for several weeks, and he found nothing foreign in that wonderful human fragrance, he realized this wasn't the case and decided to confront her.

It was late in the night. He and his men had foraged well and now his woman was with him in their chamber, where she sat beside him, staring into the fire.

"My lord . . ." Her voice sounded timorous as if she feared speaking to him.

"What is it, sweet one?" He was sated and sleepy, wanted nothing more than to crawl into bed with her and hold her until morning came.

"Would you answer some questions for me?"

"What kind of questions?" What could she possibly want to know? She'd been very circumspect in not asking about his unnatural state.

"I-I . . ." She hesitated, then said, in a rush, "W-we were always told men who became the walking dead a-are unable to take women. 'Tis why they drink their blood, substituting that for having carnal knowledge of them. But you and your men . . . How can you be so different?"

Damién laughed. He'd been expecting something truly weighty, and the question was so harmless.

"'Tis never been true, Stanczi, except for the old ones, those who've forgotten the sweetness of a woman's body. They become obsessed with blood because that's the only pleasure they can still take, while myself and the others . . . We're still young. We've forgotten nothing and even when we take blood, even when we kill, we give a momentary pleasure."

That answer seemed to satisfy her for she nodded and went on, "Can any of the younger ones get a woman with child?"

"An immortal doesn't require descendants." His reply was a little sad, though he tried to hide it. *If we had lived, 'Toinette and I would've had a family, many sons and daughters to carry on the La Croix name. Now, 'tis as dead as I.* "Only mortals procreate so their line will live on . . . so they won't be forgotten."

She fell silent and didn't speak again.

The quietness in the room was unbroken except for the crackle of the fire until Damién said, "You seem out of sorts tonight. Is anything the matter?"

"Why would you ask that?" The sound of his voice seemed to startle her. She looked away.

A bad sign. Damién was well acquainted with the avoidance of a person's gaze as a prelude to lying.

"Tell me what it is, Stanczi." He made his voice quiet when what he wanted to do was order her to answer, and added softly, "You know I'll find out."

At that gentle threat, she went a little pale though she shook her head. "'Tis nothing, really. I-I'm just fatigued lately, and . . . I don't sleep well."

He knew she told the truth. Even deep in *Unsleep,* he sensed her restlessness. He studied her profile. She was too pale. That and the other things were all symptoms of a night visitation by one of his kind.

"Has one of my men been at you?" he demanded. Seizing her hands, he searched for bite marks, caught her chin and turned her head, but the blue veins in her wrists were untouched. Her throat was also unblemished.

"No, my Lord . . . I'm . . ." Abruptly, she burst into tears.

"Come, sweetling." Damién reacted as any man, living or dead, might. With dismay. "What's this?"

She sobbed that much harder. When his arms went around her, she mumbled against his chest, "Damién, my Lord, you know I've been faithful . . . I love you . . . I'd never betray you."

She continued crying until he pushed her away, saying with slight irritation, "Stanczi, I've no doubt of your fidelity. Just tell me what the hell's the matter."

Pulling from his embrace, Konstancza wiped her eyes, took a deep watery breath and spoke the words Damién never expected to hear.

"I'm with child."

* * *

For an instant, he simply stared at her. He didn't demand how it could have happened, only said quietly, "One of the soldiers who attacked you."

Sniffling, she nodded.

"What do you plan to do?"

"Do? My lord, what can I do?" She looked at him as

if he were a fool.

"Why, you can rid yourself of it." His expression mirrored her own.

Damién had no idea how such things were done, but he knew it was possible. There had been an old woman in the village under the protection of his father's *château* who was regularly visited by the serving maids he and Armand forced into their beds. The old witch had prevented her patron's son and the *Vicomte's* heir from populating La Croix with their bastards.

"Destroy an innocent child?" Konstancza shook her head. "I can't do that. 'Twould be murder."

"You'd rather have a bastard then stop an unborn life?" He couldn't believe it. "Don't be noble *and* a fool. Being born a bastard is bad enough, Stanczi. To be a bastard conceived in rape is even more terrible."

"'Tis written *Thou shalt not kill*—"

"Don't quote that holy drivel to me." He was beginning to become angry, listening to her being so stupid. "A mortal body can't tell when love is or isn't felt. It simply reacts to the seed planted inside it. You were forced to conceive this child. No priest would condemn you for ridding yourself of it."

He could see she wasn't listening, the way she kept shaking her head, repeating softly, "'Twould be a sin."

"Very well, then." With a sigh, he accepted her decision. Forcing himself to smile, he put his arms around her and pulled her close. "It appears I'm going to have an heir, after all."

She looked up at him. "What do you mean?"

"You don't think I'm going to turn you out, do you?" He laughed softly and kissed the tip of her nose, wiping away the tears with his thumb. "I'll leave the prince's service and take you back to France, to my home. Your child will be born there."

As he hugged her, feeling her lean against him with a sigh, he muttered more to himself than to Konstancza, "I wonder what my men will say?"

***

What Armand de Chevigny said when Damién spoke to him was surprising.

The next evening, after all returned from seeking their sustenance, he summoned his second-in-command, who listened in stunned silence.

"I release you and the others from your oath to me. You may stay here and continue to fight for the prince, if you wish."

"We'll return with you," Armand answered. "I and the others have had enough of these Romanians. They eat too much garlic. We'll be glad to return to France."

Though they could have merely flown away by night—for who would dare stop them?—Damién begged a formal release from the prince, and he and his men were duly discharged with Vlad Tepes' gratitude . . . and unspoken relief.

The following night, a little caravan of wagons and horses left Tirgoviște for the province of Limousin in central France, where Damién had been born and died. On horseback were the *Chevalier,* Armand, and five of his men, armed and in battledress, the other six driving the wagons. In those wagons was a cask containing mercenaries' pay for thirteen men for nine months' service, six women choosing to accompany their undead lovers to a foreign land, their clothing, jewels, and baggage . . . and Konstancza, the most precious item of all.

Six months later, they arrived, pulling up their wagons in the courtyard of *Château La Croix,* overlooking the little village of the same name, where Damién and his forebears had ruled for over five centuries before the Great Plague struck.

The courtyard was silent, the stones as dead as they themselves. The *château* was in terrible shape, silent witness to the devastation the villagers had wreaked upon it, partially burned, the stones weather-worn and falling.

A fitting place to dwell, Damién thought.

"Damién." Armand rode his horse alongside his friend. "The doors have been sealed. How will we get inside?"

Abruptly, he remembered: how the priest had nailed crosses to the doors of the *château* after routing him and his followers from its halls. Unable to seek shelter inside, they ravaged the village in revenge, frothing with wrath and anger, before dispersing.

"Have one of the women remove them," he ordered. "The crosses won't harm them."

Ha! Didn't think of that, did you, holy man? That we might have humans with us if we returned? Briefly, he wondered where the priest's bones lay now. He'd like to find them, dig them up, and scatter them to the winds.

The crosses taken down and tossed outside the walls, the *château* was once more ready to be entered.

"There are many suites inside," Damién told his men. "Take whichever you chose. Armand, do you remember which are mine?"

That brought a grin. "How many nights did I climb that old oak outside your window and toss pebbles against the panes to lure you to go a-whoring with me? I think I know where it is."

"Then take Konstancza's things there, will you?" Damién dismounted, handing his horse to one of the others, and turned to lift Stanczi from the wagon seat.

He carried her inside and into the great salon where his father always received visitors and supplicants from the village, where he and LeMaitre had covered the floor with corpses. It was empty and filled with dust, a few broken pieces of pottery and furniture littering the floor. His footsteps were a hollow echo as he stopped before the hearth with its giant fireplace so huge five men could have stood inside without touching each other.

Above the mantle was a portrait, or what was left of one. It had been slashed and torn, strips hanging out of the frame, only half of the face and one arm still intact.

"A souvenir of my faithful peasants," he said softly. "They wouldn't even leave my image undamaged."

Konstancza didn't answer, merely tightened her grip around his neck.

"A dead *château*, empty rooms, a destroyed portrait . . . not much of a homecoming is it, Stancza?" He allowed his bitterness to show. "Too bad all those who did this have long since died."

Turning, he left the salon and carried her to the rooms Armand had made ready for them.

* * *

Yvette DuPont was preparing supper for her family—

ratatouille, her husband Jean-Paul's favorite.

They were all seated around the large table in the kitchen, Jean-Paul, their eldest son, Louis, his brothers, François, Jean-Baptiste, and Claud, their daughter, Philippa, and baby Vincent in his highchair near his mother's place at the table.

"Hurry, Yvette," Jean-Paul called. "I'm starving for that wonderful stew you've made."

Humming, she wrapped pieces of quilted cloth around the handles of the soup tureen and lifted it, glancing casually out the window as she turned.

The tureen fell to the floor, shattering and splashing the scalding liquid onto Jean-Paul's boots. Yvette screamed.

"Yvette, *chérie*, what is it?" Immediately, her husband was on his feet, skirting the steaming mass of eggplant and vegetables staining the kitchen floor. When she didn't answer but continued screaming, he caught her by the shoulders, giving her a shake. Louis had gotten up also, starting toward his mother, then hesitating as if uncertain what to do. Behind him, the other children looked at each other in concern and the baby, seeing his mother in distress, began shrieking at the top of his lungs.

Pressing her face against the bosom of Jean-Paul's shirt, she continued sobbing while he helplessly patted her shoulder, until at last, she managed to get enough breath to gasp out, "The *château*. There's someone in the *château*. I saw a light."

"Nonsense!" Jean-Paul's expression changed from concern to condescension. "Your eyes play tricks. You merely saw moonlight reflecting off the stones."

"No." Yvette shook her head, protesting weakly, and

raised one hand, pointing with a trembling finger out the kitchen window. "L-look for yourself."

Slowly, her husband turned and stood stock still, staring at the dark silhouette of the château several miles away from the village . . . and the one bright point of light in a high, tower window.

"*Mon Dieu* . . ." His voice was a bare whisper as he crossed himself.

Guiding Yvette around the mess on the floor, he moved her away from the window.

She extracted the still-shrieking child from his chair and began comforting him, trying to distract herself with this mundane little task.

"Louis." Jean-Paul gestured to his son still standing by the table. As the boy came to stand beside him, he said, "Go to Étienne Carvel. Tell him the demon is back."

The boy didn't move, directing a frightened stare to the window.

"Go! Now!" Jean-Paul pushed him, and Louis turned and ran to the door. Throwing it open, he bolted out into the night, not even taking a lantern with him to light his way.

* * *

"'Tis true," Étienne Carvel announced. "He has returned."

"You're certain 'tis *Le Chev*—" someone began.

"Don't speak that name," Étienne shouted.

"Perhaps 'tis merely some travelers stopping to rest," Jean-Paul suggested. "Or gypsies."

"If only it were. No, I sent two men to investigate. 'Tis

L'homme de Nuit, all right."

"Why did he come back? How did he get inside?" Jean-Paul asked. "How could they remove the sacred seals?"

"They have humans with them."

That was explanation enough.

"What shall we do?" someone asked.

"*Oui*," another spoke up. "Do we simply sit around and wait to be butchered?"

"Of course not." Étienne appeared contemptuous of their fear. "We do what our ancestors did. Chase them out and seal the castle again."

"And then be slaughtered like he did our ancestors?" Jean-Paul asked.

"Some of them survived." For the first time, Étienne sounded uncertain.

"Oh, *oui—some* of them. Not *your* ancestor, or mine, Étienne. They both left young wives and half-orphaned children. Do you want that for your Emil and *petit* Robert? Or perhaps you'll survive, and he'll take your *bébés* instead?"

"What would you suggest?" Angrily, Étienne turned on his friend. "Do you have a better answer?"

Jean-Paul looked thoughtful. "Perhaps I do."

"Then—*au nom de Dieu*—tell us, DuPont. *Rapidement.*"

* * *

They had scavenged enough furniture from the unoccupied rooms to give all the women beds. In the dining hall, the table still stood; at present, Damién was seated, writing rapidly on a piece of parchment ripped from one of the ruined volumes in what was left of his father's library.

There were no inkwells or writing utensils available, so he untied his sleeve, took his dagger and slashed his arm above his wrist, ignoring the women's gasp as the blood spurted and dripped onto the table. Concentrating on his forefinger, he flicked a one-inch nail like the sling-blade on the knife of a *coupeur des bourses* and calmly dipped it in the pooling blood. Then, he smoothed out the wrinkled parchment and began to write.

There was no sound in the room but the scratch of Damién's blood-soaked nail upon the treated sheepskin.

Presently, Konstancza, seated at the other end of the table, got up enough courage to ask, "My lord, what do you write that is so important you use your own blood as ink?"

"A deed, my dear Stanczi." Damién looked at her with a smile.

"A deed? But who—"

"For you, dear one. I'm deeding the *château* and all its lands, including the village of La Croix to you and your baby." A quick smile crossed his lips. "Your child may be *un bâtard* but with all the revenues this land will bring him, he'll be a *bâtard riche* and people will respect him for that, if nothing else."

Before Konstancza could protest, he signed the parchment with a flourish and looked over at his second-in-command.

"Armand, you'll be my witness."

Armand didn't move. "Will that be legal, Damién? A dead man witnessing the signature of another dead man? Surely no court would honor such a document."

Frowning because he hadn't thought of that, Damién

looked around at the women gathered near the fire.

"Then one of you will witness. You're all alive. You—Anike." He gestured at a pretty brunette who stood up and walked over to the table. "You'll witness my signature."

"But Lord Damién . . . there's no pen."

"Use your nail, as I did. They're long enough." Seizing her hand, he looked at her fingers, then stretched out his arm so she might dip her forefinger into the cut.

Shuddering, the woman scratched her bloody signature under his as witness and hurried back to her seat as Damién called to another woman to sign as second witness. When this was accomplished, he waved the deed in the air for a moment, before offering it to Konstancza with a flourish. Silently, she took it, looking at the bright red script rapidly drying to a dark brown. Before she could speak, one of Damién's men appeared in the doorway.

"My lord, there's someone here asking for an audience."

"Ah, our first visitors." Damién caught Konstancza's hand and kissed it before he looked up. "One of the villagers, no doubt, come to pay his respects to the returning lord."

His words were ironic and angry. Raising his arm, he drew his tongue across the wound, licking away the blood, and healing the slash. He held out his hand and Konstancza carefully tied the ribbon at his wrist, closing his sleeve.

"Very well, Henri. Show our visitor in."

The people who came through the door were a surprising group, a man, a woman carrying an infant, four young boys, and a little girl, her thumb stuck in her mouth. The woman and the children stopped just inside the door.

The woman looked around in fright, then kept her eyes fixed upon her husband. She clutched the baby tightly and didn't move except to pat its back now and then as it grew restless. The man continued walking until he was within a few feet of the table.

Once he stopped, Damién fixed him with a rude stare, demanding, "Who are you and why have you asked to see me?"

* * *

"Master—" Now that he was here, Jean-Paul was having second thoughts about his plan and instantly regretted bringing his wife and children into this den of the unholy.

He looked around at the men and women standing near the fire. The women were human, he was certain, but the others? They appeared human enough, except they were all so handsome and tall, and strong looking. As if they could fight all day and not tire, and afterward, carry off a half dozen women and pleasure them all into exhaustion and demand more. No mortal male should look as these creatures did.

Though Jean-Paul at first questioned why a woman would allow herself to be damned by bedding one, now that he had seen them, he felt he knew.

All his life, he'd heard the tales of how his ancestor and the other men of the village stormed the *château* and drove out the vampire *chevalier* and his followers, but he'd always half-believed, thinking it a made-up story explaining the deserted but beautiful *château* overlooking his village like a dark and brooding bird of prey.

Now, however, he knew the stories had been true.

That he was now standing in the presence of the creature who had ruled his ancestor's village two centuries before, *Le Chevalier* La Croix, the Nightman.

"Well?" Damién was impatient. "Speak up."

Taking a deep breath, Jean-Paul gathered all his courage. "Why have you come back, my lord?"

"Why?" That seemed to surprise *Le Chevalier*. "Do I have to have a reason to return to my home, the place where I was born . . . and died?" His smile was unpleasant, firelight flickering off his fangs. "To whom do I speak, by the way? 'Tis only polite to give me your name."

"J-Jean-Paul DuPont."

"Ah, Jean-Paul DuPont . . . there was a DuPont in that nasty little group who ousted me from my home over two centuries ago."

"*Oui*," Jean-Paul allowed. "My ancestor."

"Have you come to emulate that ancestor who, if memory serves me correctly, died when I ripped out his throat?"

Jean-Paul took a deep breath. "Will you make us your nourishment, lord? Do you intend it to be as it was before? Will you kill us all?"

"Is that why you're here? To find out my intentions and report back to your *copains*?" Without waiting for an answer, Damién went on, "I could prevent your leaving here, you know. You could be dead in an instant, and in a matter of hours, your fellow villagers hanging over vats to catch their precious fluid."

Jean-Paul felt his heart sink. He was going to die and also his family. He had brought them to their killer. They had trusted him and now they would die at the fangs of this terrible, merciless, beautiful, damned soul.

"Or did you come for some other reason?" The cruel voice changed, becoming speculative. "Perhaps you'd better tell me. *Now*."

Taking a deep breath, Jean-Paul looked directly at *Le Chevalier*, his gaze meeting Damién's with a bravery he didn't feel. "I've come to offer you an alternative, my lord. An alternative to killing everyone."

Damién looked surprised. "Go on."

"I've come to give myself and my family for your use, sire."

"You're offering yourselves in exchange for your friends' safety?" There was incredulity in *Le Chevalier's* voice. He glanced at the others. They also looked surprised, and perhaps a little shocked.

"I'm still fairly young and strong," Jean-Paul went on. "If you and your men are careful, I can last many years and supply you with much of . . ." He stopped and swallowed loudly. ". . . what you need."

"True." Damién looked thoughtful, resting his elbow upon the table.

One sleeve came away spotted with the undried blood on its surface. Jean-Paul paled a little as he saw the red stains on the white fabric.

"However, you won't last forever. What are we to do when we've at last drained your fine body dry?"

"My wife—" Jean-Paul gestured at Yvette who raised her head, swallowed loudly and took a step forward, clasping the baby who had fallen asleep, to her bosom. She dipped a graceful and totally incongruous curtsey to Damién but didn't speak.

"A lovely little lady." Damién made his tone lascivious, his gaze hot, and Yvette flushed as she felt the heat of those blue eyes upon her. At his side, Konstancza shifted her weight, and he stretched out a hand and seized hers, squeezing it tightly. "A tasty morsel, I'll wager."

He drew his tongue across his lower lip as if licking away her blood. Yvette shivered slightly. Damién pulled Konstancza's hand to his mouth and kissed it.

"Not as tasty as you, though, my love."

She gave Yvette a smirk making the little woman blanch.

"She can have many children, sire," Jean-Paul was fairly babbling now, to distract Damién from Yvette and what he was thinking. "I can sire more b-before I . . . and after I'm gone, my sons will marry and provide others. There will always be DuPonts for your pleasure, master."

He stopped, averting his gaze, wondering how he could have been so mad as to believe his plan would work. How he could have dared look *Le Chevalier*, his lord and master whether Undead or alive, in the eye.

"Just don't harm my friends, I beg of you." It came out in a whisper.

For a long moment there was silence, only the crackling of the fire making any sound. Behind Jean-Paul, Louis moved slightly, as if impatient. The other children were seemingly petrified.

When Damién spoke, his words sent Jean-Paul's mind into total confusion.

"*By the Unspeakable*, you're either brave or a fool. I choose to believe 'tis the former. You've nothing to fear from me, Jean-Paul DuPont, nor my men. We wish merely to live here in peace. Go back to your friends. Tell them they won't be harmed. My men and I will go elsewhere for our nourishment."

For a moment, Jean-Paul was lightheaded with elation. *We won't be harmed.* In the next, he thought of the full impact of *Le Chevalier's* words. *Some other village will suffer but we are saved.*

"Does that ease your mind?" It was a silky-soft hiss. Damién was on his feet so quickly Jean-Paul jumped backward. He waved a hand at the door. "Go back to your village, DuPont, and tell them what I've said. I wish to be *Le Chevalier de La Croix* and nothing more. If they leave us alone, we will do the same. Now, go."

* * *

"It took you long enough to get here," Emil Carvel snapped, as Louis DuPont came out of the shadows of the oak grove into the sunlight.

"I had to wait until my chores for the morning were done," the boy replied. "Then I told Papa I was going to church. To thank God for delivering us from the Unholy Ones."

"Do you really believe what that *Undead* bastard said?" Emil looked at his friend with disdain. He was older than Louis, bigger and stronger, and known in the village as something of a bully.

Emil had been present with his father at the meeting three days previous in the town hall and had silently laughed at Jean-Paul DuPont's assertion that he could prevent slaughter on either side.

When Louis' father returned with the news that the Nightman stated he would offer no harm to the people of La Croix, it sent him into a spasm of ridicule to see the men of the village, his father included, acting like such fools. *Believe that monster?* If Étienne Carvel hadn't been one of them, he'd have wished *Le Chevalier* would swoop down and slaughter every one of the *imbéciles*.

It was up to him, Emil decided, to save his elders from themselves. When he sent a message to the young men of La Croix to meet him at noon on the road leading to the little church, none thought to disobey.

"He gave his word, Emil . . ." Louis began.

"Word? You *debile* . . . you believe him? What's the word of *le Damne* worth these days?" Emil spat into the dust and gestured at the little glob of mucous angrily. "That's about it right there!"

"But he—" someone else started to protest.

"Oh, *certainment*, he may not touch any of us for a few days. Just long enough to lull us into a sense of false security, but then—" He swung around to include all of them in his gaze. "Pretty soon, you'll wake with fangs in your throats, and the dying shrieks of your brothers in your ears."

"*Nom de Dieu.* What must we do, Emil?" It was evidence of their fear and of his control over them, the others didn't question what he said at all. Only Louis looked rebellious, but Emil was certain he could handle the younger boy. "Our fathers believe *Le Chevalier*. How can we protect them?"

Emil smiled. "We do as our ancestors did. Go to the *château*. Stake them where they lay in their unholy sleep. Leave their ashes for the wind to scatter."

"But there are human women with them," Louis protested, appalled by the scene his friend described. "What about them?"

"What about them?" Emil shrugged. "Aren't we more

than a match for a group of females? Especially ones who've been weakened by their *sans mort* lovers?"

There was a vague and uneasy mutter of agreement, as if all the young men were hesitant about attacking and overpowering a group of women, no matter their choice of paramours. Sensing this might cause some of them to back away from his scheme, Emil decided to force them to act.

"Come. We'll do it *now*."

"Now?" someone shrieked.

He fixed the speaker with a glare.

"I-I mean . . . *now?* In broad daylight?"

"Would you wait for *nuit?* When they wake and are strengthened and can fight back?" He raised one hand into the air, shaking his fist. "*Non,* we must go now, while the sun still shines. And slay them in their coffins."

He started down the road leading from the village to the *château* but had gone only a few feet when he realized he was alone. Turning, he glared at them.

"*Laches!* You're afraid to fight for your families? Very well, when *Le Chevalier* flies over your house, Jean-Philippe, and drags your baby sister from her bed, shut your ears to her screams. When he ravages your *maman* before he tears out her throat, hide under your bed, Jacques. Bah! I'll go alone before I ask such as you to help me."

With a sneer, Emil stalked away, wondering how far they'd let him get before—

"Emil! Wait!"

He stopped, didn't turn around. Running footsteps brought them crowding around him.

"None of us are cowards." Jacques stated. "Of course, we'll go with you."

"What must we do?" asked Jean-Philippe.

"We need stakes . . . holy water . . . and a crucifix." Immediately, Emil delegated tasks. "Jean-Philip, take your father's axe and chop down a couple of those saplings planted near the church. We'll sharpen those into stakes. And—"

"I'll take some flasks and get holy water from the church," Jacques volunteered.

"And I'll bring my father's crucifix," Emil added.

"B-but that was your great-grandfather's," Louis protested. "It was blessed by the Bishop himself. It—"

"—will be that much stronger in helping us fight them," Emil finished for him. He caught the younger boy by the arm. "Are you coming with us or not?"

They stared at each other. Louis was the first to look away. Silently, he nodded, so overcome by an emotion he couldn't identify he was unable to speak.

"*Bon.*" Emil gave him a shake and pushed him down the road in front of him, shouting to the others. "We'll meet back here in three hours. We'll have plenty of time before the sun goes down."

* * *

"Damién, wake up. Oh, God, wake up!"

For a moment, he didn't understand as he floated out of the dark haze of *Unsleep* into consciousness. He didn't want to awaken, felt drugged and sluggish.

Someone shook him.

"Damién, *please*!" It was Stanczi, her voice strident with desperation.

He forced his eyes open, looking up at her standing

above him. She had thrown a robe over her nakedness. It hung open, exposing the fullness of her belly, heavy now with the child. She shook him again. "Damién!"

He caught her wrists.

"I'm awake, sweet. What is it?" He glanced at the windows, shuttered and nailed shut. Sunlight seeped through the cracks in the wood, making little sparkles of dust motes on the floor. "*Merde*, 'tis daylight. Why have you awakened me while the sun shines?"

"Th-the villagers . . . they broke in." She took a deep breath, seemed for a moment about to burst into tears, then steadied herself and went on, "Th-they're going from room to room . . . Three of your men have already been destroyed."

"Armand?" He sat up, throwing himself from the bed as she clumsily backed away, picking up the robe at its foot and handing it to him. Damién shrugged into it, cinching the belt at his waist.

"He's warning the others. They—"

A shriek of mortal pain made her whirl, staring at the door. She caught his arm, fingers biting into his sleeve. Damién pulled away, heading for the door at a run.

"Stay here."

He didn't wait to see if she obeyed but flung the door open and ran straight into the arms of two young men standing on the other side. They were as startled as he. Before he could recover, they had seized his arms, throwing a rope of garlic around his neck and rendering him as helpless as a babe. He couldn't even struggle as one of them dropped a chain over his head.

Damién bit his lip to keep from screaming as the brush of the silver cross against his bare chest sent the flesh burning. They dragged him down the stairs and into the Great Hall.

He could hear footsteps stamping through the halls, the crashing of doors being broken inward, shouts and women screaming, once or twice a shriek of pain followed by sudden silence. At the foot of the stairs, a vaguely man-shaped outline of dust scattered under their boots as they carried him into the Hall.

There were other men in the Hall, all young, all obviously peasants and he guessed they were all from La Croix. He recognized none of them except one, little more than a boy, the peasant Jean-Paul's son.

They slung him at the feet of a taller boy who was obviously the leader. Damién lay unmoving, cursing the fact he wasn't able to get up but had to lie before this peasant like an exhausted hound.

Loud cursing sounded as two more men appeared, Armand, magnificently naked and struggling furiously, captured between them. He was also imprisoned by garlic ropes, a crucifix dangling from his neck. There were burns on his chest where the sacred object touched, the flesh still smoking.

Armand snarled and turned his head, snapping at one of his captors. The boy leaped away, reaching into his pocket and extracting a little bottle. Flipping the top off with his thumb, he flung it at the vampire, so the contents splashed his face and neck.

With a shriek, Armand struggled to escape, shaking his head in a frenzy of pain as the holy water soaked into his skin. One of his captors was knocked to the floor by a flailing arm. Someone else ran to take his place, pressing a sharpened stake against the vampire's ribs.

Shrinking from the stake's point, Armand stopped fighting. He wavered on his feet, breathing in long shuddering gasps, the left side of his face a seared ruin.

Damién raised his head, attempting to get to his feet. He was seized and jerked upright, two stakes digging into his throat and chest.

Another of his men was dragged inside, naked and helpless. His woman ran behind, striking the men on the back and shoulders, and cursing them violently. One of the men released his hold on the vampire and turned on her so viciously she cringed. He raised one hand, hesitated, then turned his back, tightening his hold on her lover.

The young man at whose feet Damién had been thrown looked at them, then over at another who stood behind him, holding a crossbow. He nodded.

The man raised the crossbow and pulled the trigger. The bolt sailed through the air and buried itself in the vampire's breast. There was a shriek as he stiffened, then collapsed. They released him, letting his body fall to the floor.

"Michel! No, no!" Behind them, his woman wailed his name, and flung herself onto his body. She hugged him tightly, pressing a kiss on the pale forehead already disintegrating under her touch.

"You bastards!" She turned a look of total fury on his killer. 'You think your God will reward you for this? 'Tis murder. He'll curse you, and if he doesn't, I will."

She began muttering in her native Romanian, pointing one hand in the archer's direction.

He put a hand over his face and clutched his cross. She began to sob, hugging the rapidly dissolving remains of her lover to her breast.

"Kill her," the leader rasped out.

They all stared at him.

"But . . ." Louis protested. "She's done nothing . . ."

"She's lain with one of these *sans mort*. She's as vile as he. She may have put a curse on us. She's probably a witch. For that, she deserves to die." He nodded at one of the men who stood behind the woman. "Do it."

The man took a step forward, drawing his sword. The woman was bowed over what was left of the body, eyes closed, rocking back and forth in grief. He raised the sword and swung it.

Her head flew across the room, striking the floor and rolling to the hearth. For a second more, her body stayed upright, then fell onto the ashes of her lover, blood gushing from the severed neck. It twitched, then lay still.

There was total silence in the room. Someone suddenly bent double, vomiting onto the floor. Another began to pray, clutching his cross while a third sobbed softly. Young Louis looked horror-struck. Only Emil appeared unaffected.

"Take what's left of the creature's body and put it in the fireplace. The woman's too," he ordered and when it was done, told them to feed the fire so both were consumed. As the smell of singed hair and burning flesh crept into the room, he looked at Armand, stoically suffering the pain of his burns in silence.

"You're brave, when it comes to killing helpless females and those drugged by daylight," Damién said. He spoke softly, controlling the fury he felt at his men's destruction and the murder of the woman, but it was as if he were shouting into the room's silence. "How brave would you be if we weren't shackled by these holy objects?"

Emil smirked. "You're never going to find out, vampire."

Two more men appeared in the doorway. "The other rooms are empty. They must have escaped."

Briefly, Damién's heart lifted. Some of his men had survived.

"Into the noonday sun?" Emil's voice was scornful. "They're hiding somewhere within the *château*. Search all the rooms, the upper stories, the wine cellar . . . they're here somewhere."

Damién felt a sinking within his chest. As long as it was daylight, though they could move about inside the *château*, his men were trapped. Eventually, they would be found and dispatched.

Raising his head, he looked at Armand, through *Life* and *Undeath*, his oldest friend. He met a gaze as bright and as his own, and now, as resigned.

It appears we've finally lost, mon compagnon, Armand's look said.

Damién managed to shrug without seeming to do so. *I'll not beg for mercy*, mon ami, *'tis been a good two centuries . . . if I must go to Hell, let me do so cursing them!*

From the hallway, came the sound of bare footfalls. Konstancza burst through the open doorway, looking around wildly. She saw Armand's mutilated face, shuddered, and looked over at Damién, visibly relaxing as she saw he was as yet unharmed. Then, she turned on Emil.

"Get out of here. Leave this place, *intrus*." She spat the words at him.

Emil merely gave her a mocking glance. "Who are you, demon's whore, to order me to do anything?"

"I'm the owner of this *château*." She raised one hand

and they saw that she held a rolled scroll of parchment, shaking it at him as she spoke. "This is my deed of ownership, and you've committed trespass and vandalism by breaking in here. Go. Now."

She was shaking with fury, stopped, panting loudly, her free hand clutching at the heavy weight of her belly visible through the gaping robe.

Emil laughed. "I don't think I need fear the *magistre* when I've done the province such a service. Who'll listen to the words of a foreign harlot who sleeps with demons over those of a pious Frenchman?" He gestured at Damién. "Get him up. I want the honor of slaying this one myself."

They pulled Damién to his feet, holding him immobile between them. Emil raised the stake he held in his hand. He ran toward Damién, gaining momentum for the thrust of the pointed piece of wood.

Damién didn't move, continuing to stare at Emil, and braced himself. The peasant stopped in front of him. The stake came down, aiming for his heart.

Konstancza threw herself between them. The point of the stake struck her in the breast, sinking in with a dull tearing sound. Dropping the scroll, she gave a pain-filled gasp and clutched at the stake. Emil stepped back with a horrified shout, then stood there, seemingly paralyzed with shock as she sank to her knees, then fell to the floor.

Stunned as they were by what had happened, his captors' hands went lax. Damién pulled away. He should've turned on them and slain both then and there, but he was concerned only for Konstancza, his Stanczi, *his darling,* lying in a pool of blood at his feet.

Kneeling, he lifted her into his arms. Miraculously, she

was still alive, opening her eyes to look into his.

"Oh, Damién, 'tis so cold . . . but . . . I've no pain. Dami, it doesn't hurt."

He didn't tell her that meant she was dying, that the shock of the stake entering her heart had numbed all her senses. Instead, he kissed her forehead, brushing back her hair. He could feel the blood dripping over her ribs, filling the hand under her back. He looked up at Emil.

"I promised her she wouldn't die unshriven. Fetch a priest." He meant it as an order; it came out as a plea.

"Why should I care if the bitch gets *Last Rites*—" Emil began, only to stop as Damién shot him a murderous glare.

"I'll go," Louis said. "I'll get *Père* Alphonse."

He was across the hall and out the door before anyone could speak, running footsteps disappearing as he dashed outside.

No one moved. The men holding Armand continued to do so. Damién clutched Konstancza to his chest, stroking her hair and murmuring a string of words and phrases with no real meaning, and she lay in his arms, eyes closed, breathing becoming slower and shallower.

Emil could have killed him in that moment, but not even that coward moved.

"Damién . . ." She whispered his name so softly he almost didn't hear. "I'm so sorry my baby won't be born, but perhaps 'tis best this way . . ."

He couldn't answer.

It was a remarkably short time when they again heard Louis' footsteps in the hall and the boy burst into the room, the priest in tow. *Père* Alphonse looked around, saw the bloody splashes on the floor. He gagged slightly at the hovering smell of burning flesh and hair, and then saw Damién kneeling with Konstancza in his arms.

He crossed to him, pausing as Damién looked up.

"I promised her she would go to heaven," he said quietly. "I promised her *Absolution*."

"You had no right," the priest replied. "Only God can do that."

He was startled when the vampire abruptly looked chastened and hung his head. Setting down the little box he carried, he opened it and knelt beside Konstancza's body.

Her eyelids fluttered. She looked from the priest to Damién. "Th-thank you, my love."

The priest leaned forward, "Daughter, do you wish to make your confession in the hope of receiving Absolution for your sins, and entering into the kingdom of heaven with Christ your Lord?"

Damién forced himself not to wince at those words, holding her hand tighter. There was an answering pressure from Konstancza's fingers.

"I . . . do . . . Father."

The priest looked at Damién again. "Give her your *adieu*, creature, for once she's been blessed, you are forbidden to see her again."

Silently, Damién kissed Konstancza's forehead. Her arms went around him, and she pressed her mouth to his. Releasing her into the priest's arms, he stood up. Immediately, his captors came to life, seizing him and dragging him from the room.

"Leave," the priest ordered. "All of you."

One by one, they trooped out into the hall, slamming the door.

It seemed only a few minutes before the priest re-opened the door of the Great Hall.

"'Tis over," he said quietly, grasping the box he carried as if he expected someone to snatch it from him. His hands and the front of his robe were bloody. "She has gone to be with the Father."

He fixed Damién with a speculative stare.

"She loved you, though I can't fathom why. And, I think you must have loved her, too."

"I did, priest, but I doubt you or any mortal could understand."

Shaking his head, the priest walked out of the *château*.

Emil found his voice. "Well, the bitch is dead. Now, let's rid the world of some other festers on God's skin."

With a scream of rage, Damién straightened his arms, flinging his captors against each other. As they crashed to the floor, he caught at the garlic and the chain and heaved them over his head, ignoring the slashes of fire searing through his fingertips.

"You fool!" Damién's voice was a hiss of rage. He leaned over Emil, mouth open, fangs sparkling in the rays of the now-dying sun. "Did you think the sun would stay in the sky forever? 'Tis setting, you *idiot*! You took too much time in your revenge. Your chance to slay us is gone."

Behind him, as if this were a signal, he knew Armand and the others were also fighting back.

Once they were free of the bonds of garlic and crosses, they made short work of the mortals. Most of them died where they stood. A few managed to escape, running frantically to the supposed safety of the village.

Emil lay on the floor, pinned down by Damién's

weight upon him while Louis was held motionless in Armand's grasp.

He leaned closer, breath hot upon the peasant boy's cringing skin. Damién's tongue flicked out, running a wet streak across Emil's cheek. A tear of fright trickled from the boy's eye, making a second trail through it.

"Please . . . no . . . don't . . ."

"You'll beg me? Now? After what you've done?" He gave a short, cold laugh. "I might have let you go if you had only killed my men, but Stanczi—she was no threat to you and she was carrying a child."

Damién raised his head as Emil began to weep, gabbling wordlessly, the sound mixed with tears.

"Her child was innocent of any sins, and you murdered it. And for that alone, you're going to join the damned."

Emil's scream was cut off in mid-shriek as Damién sank his fangs into his throat, bit down, then jerked backward, ripping out the jugular. Blood sprayed the air, Damién's face, and spattered against the wall. For several minutes, he knelt, a portion of Emil's torn veins dangling from his mouth as the blood gushed and ran and slowly stopped and the jerking, kicking body lay still.

Staggering to his feet, he spat out the piece of tissue and turned to the totally petrified Louis, held in Armand's steel grip.

"As for you . . ."

Louis closed his eyes, lips moving rapidly but silently. He didn't struggle, merely stood praying quietly while tears seeped from under his closed lids and slid down his cheeks.

"Open your eyes."

Falling silent, Louis obeyed.

"I made a bargain with your father that you, you *enfant stupide*, have broken, but you did go for the priest. You brought him to ensure my promise to my Stanczi was kept. For that, I give you mercy, Louis DuPont." He looked at Armand. "Let him go."

Armand didn't argue. He released the boy.

"*Merci, Seigneur . . . merci . . .*" Louis babbled.

"Silence!" Damién roared and Louis cringed against Armand and was quiet. "Get yourself far away from here, Louis DuPont, and never show your face in La Croix again. Once more I intend to punish the village for this crime against me, but I will spare your life for what you did for my woman." He raised a hand, finger pointing to the open door and the darkness outside. "Now, go!"

Without another word, Louis bolted for the door.

Damién turned back to Armand. "Come, *mon ami*, let's go hunting."

***

Once more, the village of La Croix was ravaged, but this time, *Le Chevalier's* revenge was more complete and more terrible than before. Every household, every man, woman, and child, every animal in the stables or the farmyards, was killed. None were used for sustenance, their blood staining the floors of their cottages, and flowing out the battered-in doors to soak into the darkened soil. Afterward, they set fire to the buildings.

. . . and the priest stood in the doorway of the church, praying, as he watched the flames consume the souls of his parishioners.

Only one family was spared.

As they reached Jean-Paul DuPont's house, and Armand prepared to crash through the kitchen window, he was stopped by Damién's hand upon his shoulder.

"Leave them. Jean-Paul acted in good faith. His son was foolish but helped save my Stanczi's soul. Let them survive."

* * *

"Well, Damién, what shall we do now? The *château's* been sealed again. This time with crumbs of the *Host* and holy water sprinkled over the thresholds. Someone must have doubled back while we were busy. Else that priest did it." Armand looked furious. "We should have killed him, too."

"It wouldn't have been easy," Damién replied, "once he took refuge inside that church of his."

"What do we do now, master?" one of the surviving *garde du nuit* echoed Armand's question. He landed beside Armand and began to preen his wings, scraping his hands across the broad black expanse and licking the blood off his fingers.

"Now?" Damién looked a little thoughtful and a trifle tired. "Now, d'Este, I think 'tis time we parted company."

The others looked surprised. Some started to protest, then all fell silent as Damién went on.

"Together, we're too big a target. Separately, we may survive longer." He waved a hand at the *château's* bleak silhouette. "You've been faithful soldiers. I thank you all for your loyalty, but now—'tis best we go our own ways."

No one spoke. Slowly, one by one, they unfurled their wings and flew away into the darkness.

When at last they were alone, the only sound the far-off crackle of the flames still burning in the village, Armand asked, "And you and I? What of us?"

"You plan to stay with me then, *mon ami?*"

"*Oui.* Unless you order me to go. You're *mon frere,* Damién."

"Then *you* chose."

Armand looked thoughtful. "To Calais, then."

"Calias? The seaport?"

"*Oui.* I understand England is beautiful this time of year."

"To cross open water, we'll need mortals to help us. Servants to protest us while we're helpless."

"On the docks there are many homeless children. Pretty little boys who'll gladly exchange some of their youth and blood for clothing and regular meals. They'll be loyal servants if promised those regular meals keep coming."

"*Pretty little boys?*" Damién looked surprised. "You say those words with a certain relish, *mon ami.* After all the females we've pursued and bedded, is there something you haven't told me?"

"No more than I didn't tell my father, Damién. Because I thought you wouldn't understand any more than he." Armand's confession was a calm one. "I love *les femelles, oui*—but I like *les garcons* even better."

"Oh well . . ." Damién shrugged as if his friend's answer was of no import. "In that case, I'll leave the selection of our new servants to you, *mon compagnon,* so the choices will be *tres compatible.*"

Armand's laughter was louder than the crackle of the dying flames as they turned their gazes toward Calais and flew away into the still-darkened night.

Again, I had lost my home but that was really no concern. I had lost my fortune, but money was always easy to obtain. I had lost my Stanczi and that would forever be a bleeding wound in my heart. Having once again tasted the sweetness of love, now knowing I could be found acceptable in a mortal woman's eyes, I longed to continue knowing that joy. I vowed I would search for another Konstancza, one who would love me in spite of myself, a woman to once more fill me with the happiness that, for a short, short time, had been mine.

It was inevitable that someday Armand and I would part company, he to seek his own fortune in the world of Humanity, I to continue my search. We would meet from time-to-time, our paths crossing as the world got smaller, but we would never be the companions we were back then. I would form other liaisons, other friendships but none would be as close as that with my almost-brother, until that oh-so-brief meeting with a certain Espagnole . . .

CHAPTER 3

Domingo
Paris, France
April, 1789

The darkened room echoed with low moans and deep liquid sounds, as well as an energetic creaking of the ancient bedstead.

It was a not-so-elegant little bed chamber in a not-so-elegant little *hôtel* in the eighth *arrondissement* of the *Ile de Paris*, facing the *Place de Concorde* near the Seine, shabbily furnished, but with a certain decadent *ambiance*.

Heavy drapes were drawn tightly over the mullioned windows and the only illumination in the room, other than a single oil lamp glowing feebly through its dusty chimney, came from the great brick hearth in which a fire rapidly consumed the logs fed into it earlier in the evening. Sending its light into the darkness, it touched the figures in the massive four-poster bed, lighting pale, naked flesh with an unnatural, rosy glow.

There were four bodies in the bed, two *poules* picked up outside a little tavern near the *Champs Élysée* and the two young men riding them most enthusiastically.

Turning his attention from the buxom redhead beneath him, Damién looked upward, giving his attention to the large, gilt-framed mirror miraculously suspended above the bed. In it, he could see the reflections of the two women—legs splayed, arms clutching empty air, as they writhed in the sway of desire.

No one else was visible. The *poules* had been glamoured, of course, to ignore the lack of reflections in the overhead mirror. It was only by turning his head and looking at the body beside his could he see his companion's bare backside bobbing violently.

That made him smile slightly. Merde, *the Spaniard is really giving his little filly a trouncing.*

He'd seen the young foreigner outside the little coffee shop, drunkenly bargaining with the two *trollops*, and—being fascinated by the way the redhead's *trayons* strained to escape the bonds of her bodice—decided to barge in and take her for himself, figuring the *étranger* was so in the embrace of *la vin* he wouldn't know he'd lost her. It was only as the other turned toward him and he saw the malachite oval on the silken cord hanging around his neck that he realized the man was one of the *Brethren* and backed away with apologies.

"No, *mi hermano.*" Dark eyes recognized his own gemstone, the Brethren's mystical aid for warding off enemies, regenerative power, and maintain a supernatural link with each other. "There's enough for two. Come, we'll share."

Quick to accept, Damién reciprocated by offering the use of his *hotel*, and led the way . . . and here they were, bouncing away, and enjoying every naked, delicious, sweat-soaked moment.

The Spaniard still wore most of his clothing. He'd

been so eager, he'd simply tossed aside his great coat and tricorne, and with the impatience typical of an *Espagnole*, pulled down his trousers, pushed the woman onto the bed and leaped into her. Damién had been a little more dignified. At least he'd folded his cape and managed to shuck his own *pantalon* and *chemise* before attacking.

Turning his attention back to the redhead without missing a single thrust, he bent to press a kiss against one heavy breast before seizing the nipple between his teeth and nibbling on it gently. He wanted to sink his teeth into the blue-veined globe, feel her blood flowing smooth as milk into his mouth but so far managed to restrain himself. His desire, however, was growing. He could feel it as he wrapped his arms around her heated body, gathering her against his chest.

It wouldn't be long before he'd allow his lust to overcome him.

Faster . . . faster . . . he thrust inward once, a second time, then gave a cry, throwing his head back as he pushed a final time, continuing to spasm as he heard an echoing sound from the other side of the bed. As if he'd done nothing more strenuous than take a deep breath, while hoping the *poule* didn't notice he hadn't breathed in quite some time, he said conversationally, "*C'est fini* with this one. Want to swap, *mon ami*? I have a fondness for *les blondes*."

"*Seguramente*."

Releasing the woman, he crawled on hands and knees to the Spaniard, who moved toward him in the same fashion. As they passed, however, the Spaniard reached out, placed his hand behind Damién's neck and pulled him forward, kissing him on the mouth. Damién raised one hand, cupping his fellow vampire's chin with his fingers. For just a moment, the blood on their lips mingled, each tasting the sweetness on the other's mouth, tongues flicking at lower lips to steal the lingering drops.

Then, they exchanged places and the Spaniard settled between the redhead's heavy thighs, spreading them wide and falling forward against her round soft belly. Damién threw a leg over the little blonde and began to mount her with as much enthusiasm as he had his own woman. As he started to lean against her breasts, however, something hanging around her neck caught the firelight, a silver glint—a cross, a small silver cross, on a delicate chain, nestled between the round, white teats.

He caught himself before he landed on it, managed to keep from cringing away, but couldn't stop from throwing up his hands protectively.

"Why are you wearing that thing?" *Remerciez le diable*, he had to force the tremor out of his voice.

"Don't you like it? 'Tis very expensive." Sliding a finger under the little crucifix, she lifted it from the deep valley of its resting place.

Damién bent backward to escape the Holy Power radiating from it. Merde, *how can something so small be so strong?*

Plainly, she was puzzled by his reaction. "Most of my gentleman like me to wear *la croix*. They say it give them holy vigor." She smiled as the thought struck her. "Why, 'tis the same as your own name, *Monsieur.*"

Damién didn't like being reminded his surname was that of the sacred object that could confine him. Keeping his eyes averted, he growled, "Take it off."

"But—"

"*Mi compadre* is allergic to silver." The Spaniard spoke

up, resting his cheek on the redhead's balloon-like breasts. He brushed his lips gently across one nipple, tongue licking lazily as he gave a soft, satisfied moan. "Do as he says, *dulce.*"

The redhead wound her hands into his hair, pulling him back to face her. She thrust her pelvis upward, then wrapped her arms around his neck, kissing him deeply.

The Spaniard gave a groan of satisfaction and as she released him, his slim hips continued to buck against hers.

Pouting a little, the blonde unclasped the cross, dropping it on the bedside table.

"There," she said, as she lay back down again. "Is that bet—"

Damién's mouth came down on hers, forcing the rest of the sentence down her throat, along with part of his tongue. When he raised his head, she was gasping for breath and laughing at the same time.

"*Dieu*, I should have removed it sooner."

He managed not to wince as she said the *Name that Must Not be Spoken* and kissed her again to prevent any more holy words from escaping. By the time he moved his lips to her throat, she was moaning softly, no thought of speaking coherently entering her mind.

Gently, he brushed his mouth against her neck, trailing tiny kisses along its length. She had a slender, pale throat. He could see the distended veins pulsing rapidly, engorging with the blood of her arousal. He'd noticed those delicate blue veins while they were in the street, couldn't wait to sink his fangs into the soft flesh surrounding them, but had forced himself to allow his comrade the right to the first taste.

That the Spaniard agreed to swap before doing so

made him feel even more affably inclined toward him.

He licked gently along the tender skin of her throat, tongue leaving a moist, gleaming trail. She moaned again, clutching at his shoulders, nearly rising off the bed to meet his movements, attempting to take him deeper within her. Her legs locked themselves around his waist.

Damién turned his head, dropped his fangs, and brushed them against her neck, a bare caress, not enough to break the skin. Nevertheless, she reacted.

"Ouch! Did you bite me, *M'sieu*?" Somehow, even in the darkness, she managed to give him a coy look.

"Did it hurt?" Not that he cared, at this stage.

"Well . . . no . . . but bites are expensive. Sometimes they *do* hurt and that will cost you." She slid her arms to his neck, looked into his eyes, and was lost.

"*Chérie*," he whispered softly, holding her with his gaze, feeling her will slip away.

Though her eyes were still open, and she continued moving against him, he knew she was already *fascinez*. Beside him, he could hear the Spaniard whispering something in his own language, and he was certain he was beguiling the redhead the same way.

"If it hurts you, I'll give you an extra *franc*."

As usual, greed overruled physical safety. With a sigh, she released him, turning her head, and even being so helpful as to pull the long blonde curls out of the way. Damién pressed his mouth against her pale skin, eyeteeth grazing across the beating vein. Without actually biting, he pushed against the rapid pulse, letting the mere pressure of the rushing blood against his teeth puncture the skin. The sudden spurt of liquid into his mouth made him nearly cry out with the pleasure of it. Stifling his outburst by sucking heavily on the rapid flow, he let his mouth fill before swallowing, closing his eyes in ecstasy.

Ahhh, 'tis so good.

It had been several days since he'd fed, and because of that, this feeding was that much better, the blood sweeter, the pleasure almost . . . *exquis*.

On his third swallow, he was aware of a tingling bitterness on his tongue, accompanied by a rapid spinning of his brain, dizziness worsening as he sucked harder.

Damn, there's opium as well as whiskey in her blood.

A little bonus. He might actually have to give the *poule* that extra *franc* after all. He swallowed again, drawing out more of that delicious, drug-and-alcohol-filled serum, shoulders heaving with the taking, embrace tightening around her. Beneath him, the blonde gave a soft sigh and went limp, her arms falling gracefully onto the bed.

A heavy hand came down on his shoulder.

"*Amigo, cuidado.* You're taking too much."

Damién raised his head, his satiated eyes meeting the Spaniard's brown ones, red-tinged now from the surfeit of blood within them. Taking a deep breath, he nodded, and forced himself to pull away, sliding an arm under the woman's shoulders and raising her.

"Merciful goodness," the redhead exclaimed. "Did she faint?" She gave the Spaniard an arch look, nodding at Damién. "Your friend must be some *homme* to make Odette swoon like that." She fixed him with what she obviously thought was a limpid gaze. "I'd like to be made to feel thus."

Dulce, he was tempted to say. *You already have. You just don't know it.*

Instead, he pushed her back onto the bed, kissing her

aggressively. When he released her, she was gasping for breath and actually feeling a little lightheaded.

"*Jesu, Espagnol.*" She didn't notice Damién's slight grimace and the curious stare he gave his companion who didn't even flinch at sound of the sacred *Name* but simply raised himself on one elbow to smile at her a little smugly.

Odette was conscious now, looking a trifle embarrassed as Damién whispered in her ear, explaining how she'd apparently succumbed to the drugs and drinks she'd had earlier, cautioning not to let it happen with other customers who might not be as understanding as he. While he talked, he was getting her off the bed and into her clothes, even kneeling to slide on her stockings and shoes, ironically thinking what a sight he must appear. Totally naked, blood smeared on his chin, and kneeling at a whore's feet assisting her to dress. Looking over at *Le Espangol* who was calmly shrugging his trousers and stockings into place, he indicated with a jerk of his head that the Spaniard should do the same.

With a flourish and a bow, his gesture was obeyed, the Spaniard leaving his trousers hanging around his hips to minister to the redhead, and abruptly, the two *poules* found themselves hustled out the door, the coldness of francs in their palms.

"—and one extra for you, *chérie*, as I promised," Damién said as he dropped the coins into Odette's hand.

"*Merci,*" the redhead simpered, seizing the Spaniard and slathering a moist kiss upon him before dropping her pay between the deep division of her breasts. She twiddled her fingers in a farewell gesture. "*Bon Soir, messieurs.* Don't forget us if you need . . . entertaining . . . again. Manon and Odette."

The two tottered down the hall as the Spaniard pushed the door shut and set to tucking in the voluminous tail of his shirt. "Well, *compadre?*"

"Ah!" Damién leaned against the wall, kissing his fingers and flinging them into the air. "*Deliciéux. Totalement deliciéux.* Especially the little blonde."

"You were a trifle greedy, *amigo*. I had hoped to sample her, too. You barely took a sip from *la dulce* Manon."

Damién shrugged. At the moment, he was so engorged, he didn't want to think of drinking another drop. He stifled a belch. "I'm saving her for another day."

"Fair enough. Then so shall I." He was struck on the chest by the back of the other's hand. "And now—I need to rid myself of some less pleasant liquid. Where's your chamber?"

With a flourish, Damién gestured to a narrow door set in the far wall, trailing along as the Spaniard hurried toward it. He got there just as his guest hiked up his shirt, seized his member and aimed it at the porcelain chamber pot on a small stand near a walnut commode on which an ironstone basin and pitcher sat.

As the amber stream struck the bowl, Damién leaned against the wall. Glancing down, he frowned suddenly.

"You're staring," the Spaniard stated quietly. "At a most private spot. *Por favor*, after all that enjoyable fucking we were doing, don't tell me you like *los niños* better than *las mujeres?* That would disappointment most terribly, *compadre.*"

"What'll happen if I do?" Damién asked, smiling slightly at the melodramatic tone in the other's voice.

The Spaniard's mouth quirked. "I'll tell you I don't kiss on the first assignation."

"No? What about that little *baiser* you gave me earlier? With tongue, too."

"I was carried away in the heat of the moment. It was a kiss for a brother. It meant nothing."

"*Non?*" Damién pretended to pout.

"You fondled my cheek," the Spaniard reminded, with an uplifted brow.

"I was trying to keep my balance," he rationalized.

"If that little caress was any indication," came the reply. "Your balance has already been tilted."

Damién laughed out loud. "I leave that kind of behavior to others. Women, whether under me or on their feet, are enough trouble, without asking for more by seeking out the stronger sex, too." He shrugged. "I'm French. That kiss was simply a sign of my regard for you."

"I didn't have any doubt," the Spaniard replied. "But you *are* staring. Envy, perhaps?"

"Not in the least." Damién's answer was a little too quick. "I think our cocks are about equal, if it comes to that. However—" He hesitated slightly. "*Pardon, mon ami,* but, if you'll excuse my saying so, your tool seems to be missing something."

"Of course." The Spaniard didn't appear bothered by this statement. Giving his organ a shake, he released it, letting it fall to nestle against his thighs, and dropped his shirt, hiding it from sight. "I'm a Jew."

Damién nodded as if he'd known this all along, though he'd never expected a Spaniard to be anything other than *le Catholique*. He also never realized other religions might also be plagued by vampires. He had thought his kind only existed within the Christian framework.

"That explains why you weren't bothered by the cross,

or Manon's little exclamation." He looked thoughtful. "A vampire who isn't affected by crosses. *That* could be useful."

"If it had been the Seal of Solomon," the other replied, buttoning his *plackette* under the shelter of his shirt. "It would be a different story." He chuckled softly. "You should have seen the faces of the *peones* on *el estado de mi padre*. They would continue to wave their crosses at me and call for their *Jesus* as I tore out their throats."

He shrugged, waving both hands expressively.

"Of course, none of it did any good."

"How did it happen?" Damién was curious.

"Wrong place, wrong time. By the way, *mi nombre* is Domingo de Leyenda, *Conde* de la Torre."

Making a leg, Damién bowed low. "*Enchanté, votre Seigneurie*. I'm Damién La Croix, *Chevalier* du Morte."

"Your name is really La Croix?" As he straightened, the Spaniard chuckled disbelievingly. "That must take a lot of explaining." He walked back into the bedroom, stopping so quickly Damién nearly ran into him. "*Damnacion!* Is that sunlight I see through that crack in the curtains?"

Peering over his shoulder, Damién confirmed it was.

"What am I to do now?" There was genuine concern on the pale face. "My rooms are far from here. I'll never make it before the sunrise is complete."

Placing a calming hand on his shoulder, Damién said, "Never let it be said the *Chevalier* du Morte let a fellow *sans mort* go out into daylight. You can stay here. As my guest." He gestured to the bed, then looked back as he thought of something. "You do carry native soil with you, don't you?"

"*Por supuesto.*" Reaching into a trouser pocket, Domingo produced a small leather bag with a drawstring around the top. "I never go anywhere without it."

"Good." Damién flipped back the coverlet. "Sprinkle a little here, and let's get to bed." He glanced at the window. "That sun seems to be rising quite rapidly."

"You're planning on sleeping here, too?" He was fixed with a suspicious dark stare.

Damién ignored the implication.

"But of course." He turned back the other side of the coverlet, revealing a coarse layer of soil sprinkled on the sheet beneath. "My coffin is in my suite with my servant and—like you—I'd never make it. Already the sun pulls at my bones."

"Well, then—" Untying the bag, Domingo thrust thumb and forefinger inside, lifting out some of the contents and dropping it onto the bed, spreading it evenly with one hand. He pulled the *duvet* from the Frenchman's grasp, dropped it into place, smoothed out the wrinkles, and checked to make certain his trousers were fully closed.

"Not that I don't trust you."

By now, Damién was also getting dressed, tucking his shirt into his waistband. "Trust is essential in any relationship—even amongst *étrangers*."

They settled themselves side by side, nodded to each other and lay still, snared as neatly by the call of *Unsleep* as two fish caught in a *pecheur*'s net.

* * *

Domingo de Leyenda was a Spanish Jew. As a man he would have been fifty years the Frenchman's junior, as a vampire, he was nearly two and a half centuries younger.

In spite of being Castilian Jews in Ferdinand and Isabella's Catholic-ruled Spain, the Leyendas managed to survive by pretending conversion. Under the protection of their pseudo-religion, they flourished undetected, practicing their true worship in secret. After the youngest son of the then-present *conde* was *turned* by an *Undead* passing through on his way to France, their true Faith held them in good stead when young Domingo began his nocturnal depredations.

While Dom fed, the *peones* bled, wielding their crosses with fervor, wondering why their holy relics had no effect against the foul fiend, never once thinking of the obvious. As ravenous as only the young can be, he nearly decimated his immediate family before his vampire sire managed to bring his appetites under control, and thus found himself heir to the estates and *castillo* which he would never have possessed if he'd lived.

Damién La Croix had been a noble in his own domain, a soldier in many lands, and now, in a time when having blue blood in one's veins, even someone else's blood, was a potential danger, masqueraded as a commoner to protect himself. Domingo, being a foreigner and new to Paris, had no knowledge of what was fomenting in the city.

It was in Paris, in the year 1792 that the two *sans morts* met.

* * *

Domingo opened his eyes, staring into a face only inches from his own. With a snarl, he flung himself from the bed, mouth open, fangs sprung to attack, striking the man's shoulders and bearing him to the floor.

"*Imbécile*!" Damién was off the bed, struggling to pull

him off the man who was offering no defense whatsoever. "Hold. That's my servant, Georges. Don't kill him."

"You call me *imbécile?*" Dom gave him an angry look, retracting his fangs. "It wasn't I who couldn't detect *la blonde* wore a cross. How could you not sense it?"

He got to his feet, dusting his knees and stepping back to allow Georges to stand.

"I did sense it," Damién lied, defensively. "I merely allowed my lust to take over and ignored it."

"And could have gotten yourself permanently marked," Dom pointed out. "That would be *una verguenza* . . . and an embarrassment. To have that sign you hate seared into your chest,"

"Yes, well—" Looking around for some way to distract the Spaniard from this subject, he nodded at Georges who still lay on the floor. "Aren't you going to help him up?"

"Why?" He was given a look of pure Spanish distain. "Is he disabled from being knocked on his ass?"

Shaking his head, Damién offered Georges his hand, pulling the servant to his feet.

"So," Domingo looked dramatically surprised. "*Es verdad*, what I've heard. France is truly becoming a place where *liberté, égalité*, and *fraternité* are taking their insidious hold over even the nobility."

"What would you know of *égalité?*" Damién demanded. "And how do you know I'm noble?"

"Oh, one does hear rumors of such things." A lace handkerchief was pulled from a sleeve, followed by a wave of one pale hand. "Peasant unrest, and other drivel, even in *España*. Though one hopes 'tis only that—rumors."

The handkerchief brushed against the fine Spanish

nose as if to wipe away an unpleasant smell, and he *tsked* loudly.

"I never thought I'd see one of the *Brethren* being overcome by it, however. As for your being noble? 'Tis obvious. You have a manservant and a suite elsewhere. You were definitely a *caballero* before your demise."

Damién ignored that, thinking of what else the Spaniard had said. He had also heard the rumors and seen the truths, indeed everyone in Paris had. Treatises nailed on building walls, booklets distributed at booksellers, articles in newspapers, discussions in the coffee shops.

There was trouble just below the surface of the beautiful spectacle Paris offered to the traveler, and those who heeded it were already adjusting their lives accordingly so as not to be swept away when the bubbling pot of anger overflowed. It was best during uncertain times to do nothing to draw attention to one's-self; Madame Guillotine could chop off a *sans mort* head as easily as a human one.

Being always dependent upon humans for their welfare during daylight, most vampires, even the noble ones, already had a more equal relationship with their servants than their living counterparts. Damién had always felt he treated Georges most fairly, and also the other *wharf boys*—the homeless youngsters he and his friend Armand had recruited so long ago, giving them shelter and clothing in exchange for their blood and loyalty. Besides, once it was well-known that a human servant, if faithful enough, might be *enthralled* and given near-immortal life . . . *that* definitely caused fidelity.

He was about to give a heated answer to the Spaniard's insulting remark, when Domingo burst into laughter.

"No, *amigo*, don't be angry. I meant nothing. *Carram-*

ba. Are all *los Frances* as thin-skinned as you?" The handkerchief was tucked once more into his sleeve. "I'm very aware of how much I owe my own servant, Emilio, and treat him accordingly."

"My apologies, *mon ami*, but 'tisn't wise to criticize those sentiments so loudly—even in jest. The wrong ears might hear." Damién gestured to the richly brocaded coat Domingo wore, and at his own unadorned, dark broadcloth. "It might also be a good idea for you to tone down your apparel somewhat. An elaborate showing of wealth isn't a good idea these days."

"Now *that* will make my sister very unhappy."

Georges picked up his tricorne, dusted it with his sleeve and presented it to the Spaniard with a bow.

"Your sister? Is she one of the *Brethren,* also?" Briefly, Damién wondered if Spanish vampires were different from others. Did entire families join each other in becoming *Undead*? Would Domingo's sister be available for a little trifling, perhaps? He was perfectly willing to help cement Franco-Spanish relations.

"No, but when I died and plainly showed no interest in staying that way, she reminded me I'd need human help during certain hours." With a bow making the servant smile, Dom took the tricorne from Georges and settled it upon his head, carefully smoothing the long black hair, clubbed with a slender satin riband so it hung down his back. "I agreed and set about seeking a trustworthy servant but she'd have no part of that. *She* would be my human helper . . . and she kept after me until I gave in and made her so."

"*Merde.*" For a moment, Damién looked shaken. "You took your *sister*?"

"It was mainly to shut her up." There was a truly Spanish shrug. "It wasn't as if I *turned* her or anything. I swear I never touched her while I was alive. That would have been a sin, in any faith. No," he shook his head. "I simply gave in to her nagging and *enthralled* her. Ysabela Lysetta is ten years older than I and has always tried to run my life."

He turned to the fire, holding his hands out to the blaze.

"It was easier to give in than to argue. Afterward, I found Emilio, to act as my *criado* and actually do for me while letting Lysetta think she's running things." He winked. "It keeps her out of the way."

"*Les femmes* . . . ah." Damién nodded in sympathy. Though he'd had no older sisters in his life, his mother had been much the same, always worrying about her only child and trying to coddle him into helplessness.

"As to wearing the poorer clothing . . . I suppose that would mean eschewing jewels and other adornments, also? Ostrich plumes, pearl earrings, glass-heeled slippers?"

"'Tis best. The plainer, the more acceptable."

"Ah . . . she definitely won't like that." Domingo turned to the window, then looked back, bowing to both Damién and Georges. "Now, I'll take my leave, *señores*." His eyes met Damién's once more. "*Gracias* for a most enjoyable evening, *Señor le Chevalier*, and I hope we'll meet again."

He disappeared, leaving the curtains swaying slightly in the silence following his departure. Damién went to the window, pulling back the heavy drapes.

In the street below, Domingo looked up, doffed his tricorne and swept them a salute and a bow, then started briskly up the darkened street.

Dropping the curtain, Damién shook his head.

"I imagine I'll definitely see more of that one," he said, a little ruefully. "We'd best keep an eye out for him, Georges."

There were soon other things to distract me from one straying Espagnole. A few months later, the Bastille was stormed, and the Revolution with its subsequent Reign of Terror burst into all its hideous glory. Georges and I fled to England where we were welcomed (reluctantly, I might add) into the ranks of Les Elus, the vampire fraternity of Great Britain. I wasn't enchanté about becoming part of une organizacion Anglais, but it seemed best at the time, especially since it offered protection for a foreigner while I became acclimated to this new home.

As with a newcomer to any place, I found those I liked and those I merely tolerated among my confrères.

Chief among the latter was Lucien St. Albans, a dark, saturnine Roman who condescendingly gave me a reticent courtesy. Lucien was Chief Councilor of Les Elus—the Council of Vampires—his controlled demeanor hiding a coldly passionate nature. His admirers laughingly called him the Dark Prince. I won't repeat the soubriquets his enemies gave him. It was Lucien's duty to make certain all sans mort followed the rules in whatever endeavor we found ourselves, especially when dealing with that group of hapless and benighted humans calling themselves the Black Swans.

Black Swans were so addicted to the thrill of sating vampiric thirst, they willingly did so. In my part of the world, that was unheard of, at least in the way the Swans did it. Oh, in Europe, we had our followers, of course, but mostly they were fascinez, chained to us by the blood-thrall . . . our servants, doing for us that we couldn't do for ourselves because they could still move about in daylight. They supplied us with blood when we weren't able to forage on our own, but those Black Swans . . . Sweet Unspeakable Name! They *flocked to pre-arranged* soirées—*replete with wine, food, and music (for them), where they offered themselves to whichever* sans mort *wished to sample, in exchange for the intoxicating exhilaration only a bloodletting could give.*

For some, it became quite addictive.

I was invited often to these fêtes, *and I went, first out of curiosity, then out of need. It was definitely easier and safer than searching out a victim on London's streets. It was there I met the two other* L'Anglais sans mort *whom I would come to call my friends.*

One was Morgan D'Arcy, Earl St. Averil. Blond, tall, dashing, Morgan had been a cavalier, fighting for the return of the Stuarts to the throne but later succumbing to his own particular type of vampirism far away in my own France. He still held a grudge against the Scots for deserting the monarch he claimed as a friend, and even after all this time would expound on it if given the proper cue. Pour him a couple of goblets of blood and he was ready to vent an embittered spouting: "Promise him kingship then desert him in battle. We watched the cowardly buggers slipping away every night."

I didn't care one way or the other. At the time of Morgan's adventures with his Royal copain, *I was in Europe, so I missed the entire affair. Once I'd heard the story twice, I always made certain His Lordship didn't get in his cups when I was with him. Nevertheless, Morgan was an amiable companion, and I was often invited to join him on his jaunts into the realm of carnal pleasure.*

I found these vampyres *(as they preferred to spell it) different from their European brethren in many ways, the primary one being the method of their conversion. They weren't so much* turned *as* transformed . . . *infected as it were, by something transmitted during the blood exchange from sire to fledgling. It would be centuries before they could put a name to it, viruses not being in the general medical vocabulary at that time. This breed of vampire was differ-*

ent from myself in other ways also. They weren't affected by holy water or garlic. They didn't possess our wonderful wings but had the advantage of being able to see themselves in mirrors, a trait coming in terribly handy when associating with humans who were forever posturing and primping before the damned things.

Still, for all our differences, we shared one major benefice and one fatal flaw ... we were all immortal and none of us could tolerate the rays of the sun.

Morgan used to joke that in this case, it wasn't only the European Undead who occasionally made ashes of themselves.

As talented as he was handsome, I could always find Morgan wherever a pianoforte was in evidence, and Lucien generally somewhere within viewing distance. The Dark Prince had a passion for Lord D'Arcy which wasn't returned, though Morgan was aware of it. As a result, my friend teased and taunted and insulted, letting Lucien know he was knowledgeable of his feelings but was never going to have them fulfilled as he flaunted his many conquests before the Grand Councilor's burning black gaze.

I personally felt Morgan was playing with a very deep-smoldering and truly dangerous fire, but that was his problem, so I stayed out of it.

The other friend was Tristan McLachlan. The name was Scottish, but Tristan had come from Ireland during a time before Scots and Irishmen divided themselves into two countries. His name meant 'sad stranger' in Celtic and Tristan proved himself just that, for no matter how many times we met or whored or satisfied our thirsts together, he always kept something of himself hidden, even from me.

It was because of Morgan I left England ...

Chapter 4

Morgan D'Arcy, et al
England
June 10, 1790

They were lounging at Royal Oak, Lord St. Averil's country home in County Devon, a place Damién had visited so many times he now had his own suite there. It had been a long night, filled with much wine and laughter, a swirling miasma of warm, perfumed flesh and brightly-colored gowns, plumed heads and flirtatious laughter behind unfurled fans. Now they were both easing themselves into the stillness before dawn arrived.

"Damién, my friend, I'm leaving England." Morgan spoke out of the blue, with no warning whatsoever. He raised his goblet, finishing the dark red liquid serving as the vampire's wine.

Now that they were alone, he'd dropped the glamour he always threw out to hide his blatant differences from mortals, and his ever-present fangs and cat-like pupils were in evidence.

"I won't say I'm surprised," Damién murmured. "Because, frankly, nothing you do surprises me. Not now. May

I ask, why? It isn't Lucien, is it?"

That brought a harsh laugh. "My dear Damién, the day I leave a country I love because of Lucien St. Albans, is the day I bare my chest to some vampire hunter's stake."

"Just wondering." Damién made a vague gesture with his own glass. "I know he makes it difficult for you—thwarting every suggestion you make, refusing to listen to any plan you propose. And doing it for no other purpose than because he knows it angers you... just as you do the same to him."

"*Oui, nous nous faison pas?*" Morgan agreed, laughing. His mother had been French, and he often spoke to Damién in his own language. To make him less homesick, he said. "We do seem to continually rub each other the wrong way, don't we?"

He looked very satisfied as he said it. Probably thinking of the last time he'd left the Grand Councilor totally chagrined and fuming under that saturnine exterior.

"So... your very obvious inclination to never—to put it delicately—see eye-to-eye, set aside, why are you leaving?"

"Very simple. I'm bored. I feel the need to see new places, new people... taste new blood..." As if to emphasize this, his tongue flicked out, drawing lightly across his lower lip.

"Where are you going? France isn't the safest place for foreigners just now, and I wouldn't recommend Russia... too cold. They tell me Spain's good this time of year. The *señoritas* have blood of the right temperature to warm even an Englishman no matter the season."

"None of those. I'm going to the New World. Our former colonies. A place called Charles Towne, in fact—

or Charleston, as it's now been rechristened. Personally, I like the former name better."

"Named after your beloved King." Damién instantly regretted saying that and was relieved when the expected diatribe didn't begin.

He'd heard of Charleston, been curious about it, in fact. Once he also thought of journeying to America but just as quickly talked himself out of it.

It was too far away. A whole ocean away, in fact . . . over a sea very wide and filled with moving, salty water, something a *sans mort* could never cross under his own power. Traversing the Channel had been hellish enough. Damién had no idea what sailing across such an expanse of salt water might involve.

"*C'est correct*. And I've just had a fantastic idea." Morgan gave him that wicked look indicating some novel form of mischief had sprung to life inside his handsome head. "Why don't you come with me?"

"To America?" Damién's former thoughts came flooding back.

Why not?

He had nothing to keep him in England. Not really. None of the women here were very interesting after the first ten minutes, and those who were had long passed the half-century mark, making their brains more attractive than their bodies. He'd heard the land across the ocean was filled with more wonders than merely its people, and he did have a curiosity as to how the blood of those *indigènes* might taste.

"Won't that be difficult? Going by ship, I mean?"

"Not really." Morgan shrugged any problems aside. "I have my manservant, you have Georges. They can do whatever needs to be done while we lie in our berths during the day—claiming severe *mal-de-mer, of course*—"

"Oh, *naturellement*," Damién murmured.

Mal-de-mer. Hm. Even the name didn't sound pleasant. How would that condition affect a *sans mort*?

"—and roam the decks at night. I imagine we can find a couple of stowaways to sustain us, or perhaps a transportee or two."

"Still . . ."

"Don't worry." One of those finely shaped pianist's hands that would later make him famous on stages from London to Moscow and ports in between, rested on Damién's arm, tightening in persuasion. "There'll be no problem. You'll see. What say?"

Damién thought about it. For exactly two seconds more.

"You've convinced me. When do we leave?"

Thus, I abandoned the United Kingdom for America, where I would remain. The former colonies became my new home, a land where all were supposedly equal but some were more equal than others, and vampires didn't figure into that *particular equation. Not just yet, at least. There, I would find great beauty and great squalor, and—hopefully, the woman I was still seeking, but so far hadn't found. Perhaps, I consoled myself, that was the reason . . .*

. . . she awaited me in the New World.

CHAPTER 5

Kate
Charleston, South Carolina
April 28, 1792

The water in the harbor was dark but not still. Ships anchored at the landing rocked and swayed as the Atlantic current rushed onward to become the Kiawah River seeking inland. Fog rose from the whitecaps, creeping thick and white onto the docks.

Behind the tower of hogsheads filling the front of the warehouse a few yards from the wharf, Katherine Blackwell shivered and drew her shawl tighter around her shoulders. The knitted length was still damp from last evening's downpour, though she considered herself fortunate to have had enough presence of mind to snatch the triangle from the privet hedge as she ran from the backyard. Once dry, it would be some protection, though scant, against the chill night air.

She supposed she should consider herself lucky it was early spring and not mid-winter; else her frozen corpse would be lying on this spot. Instead, she crouched, shivering slightly, watching the door of the tavern situated on the dirt street facing the warehouse.

Her aunt, owner of the tavern, had an agreement with the warehouse owner to store the wine cellar's overflow in the warehouse until the huge casks were needed. At that time, several bunged before shipping would be carted across the road and around to the back of the tavern where they were rolled down the ramp into the cellar and lifted onto racks. Then, spigots replaced the bungs, and the wine was ready to be poured.

My aunt . . . Kate's pale lips curled slightly as she thought about her mother's sister, charged with protecting her orphaned niece. *Someday you'll pay for believing that lying libertine of a husband over your own flesh and blood* . . .

But not yet. Just now, Kate's only concern was finding some place to keep out of the expected continuation of the previous night's storm, and perhaps a little food. Having no skills other than domestic ones, and now bereft of her virginity, she knew of only one way to get what she needed. By becoming exactly what her aunt had already accused her of being.

The night before, she'd faced that fact while huddled behind the barrels, and reluctantly accepted it as the only solution. She had no other relatives to turn to and doubted going to the authorities would serve any good purpose. Her aunt had been commended for taking in an orphaned child and she was certain if questioned about her niece's absence, would quickly paint herself as the wronged woman and again be applauded for driving away such a viper in her bosom instead of gaoling her for lewd behavior and adultery. Especially since that would be admitting her beloved husband had been Kate's partner in that lewdness. As it was, being labeled *wanton*, even with no further proof, would keep Kate from obtaining honest employment anywhere in Charleston.

There was a whisper of sound behind her. Kate stiffened, looking around.

"Wh-who's there?"

No answer.

Only night noises, she told herself, shrugging and tightening her hold on the shawl. It was a little dryer now, felt a bit warmer, she convinced herself.

When the sound came again, she ignored it. She'd heard rustlings and scampering all night, or imagined she had, as she curled into a corner formed by several casks. She'd slept very little, envisioning all sorts of vermin and creatures scurrying about in the dark.

The source of the sound moved slightly, this time making no noise. He'd been watching her for some time, first out of curiosity, then concern, as he wondered, *Why is a human hiding in the darkness, especially one so young?*

In spite of the scent of fear surrounding her, she smelled delicious, her blood as fresh as a field of flowers. Nostrils quivering as that unsullied sweet fragrance filled them, he melded into the shadows under one corner of the eaves, settling in to watch.

Occasionally, he moved slightly, deliberately brushing against one of the barrels or flicking off a few splinters of wood, making them fall to the dirt—something to cause her to turn and peer into the darkness. He wanted to see if he could frighten her into leaving her hiding place but no . . . whatever she intended, she meant to see it through.

Therefore, he stayed also.

The tavern door opened, spilling light and a spate of

laughter into the dark. Two men came out, both weaving dangerously. One staggered toward a horse tied at the hitching rail to one side of the door, the other followed, laughing at his friend's attempts to mount the animal. It took several tries, though the horse was patient and never moved or shied as his rider got half-way onto his back, then tumbled off again. Doubtless he was accustomed to that if the way he waited was any indication.

At last, with his companion's laughing assistance, the sot achieved his seat, gathered the reins, and kicking the animal in the ribs, started off at a slow amble. The other waved a farewell, then stood a moment watching his friend's wobbling retreat, as if half-expecting to have to run after him and assist him out of the roadway.

Once the sound of hoofbeats died away, he turned, wavered slightly, and started at an unsteady pace toward the docks.

Kate drew in a deep breath. She hoped he wouldn't get too near the water and fall in, drunkenly drowning himself before he got to where she stood.

Earlier in the evening, there had been a woman wandering the riverside. Kate had been tempted to speak to her, ask her for help, but the sudden realization of her occupation stopped her.

Unfashionably dressed in an out-of-date gown, the tart's full bosom bulged above the deep cut of her ruffled neckline. The gown itself wasn't open as was the style to show the highly decorated petticoat beneath, though its tight bodice advertised she wore no stays. Her skirts drooped limply—no bum-roll or bustle—and barely skimmed ankles trim in their black stockings. Perhaps the most notable thing about her was her footwear. Red satin with buckles cut in false stone shapes adorned her shoes, a lady's ballroom slippers gracing a harlot's feet, and probably costing her several nights' drubbing for the pride of wearing them.

Even with her ill-dressed hair, the woman might have been considered comely but for the layers of white lead powder and Spanish wool-roughened cheeks. Kate could see several places where the rough wires had actually caused bleeding when dragged over her skin, but the powder didn't hide all the smallpox scars pitting her forehead and jaw.

She'd stood before the warehouse for quite some time, one expensively clad foot tapping impatiently on the cobbles before an early-night patron decided to leave the tavern. He wavered a moment as if trying to decide which way to go, then stumbled toward the street leading past the docks. The harlot waited until he was perhaps twelve feet away.

With a sigh, she shrugged back her shoulders, plastered a bold smile on her carmine-layered lips and stepped directly into his path.

Briefly, they spoke in low murmurs. He dug into his waistcoat pocket, placed something in her hand. Together, they continued in an uneven trail up the street, his arm around her waist, holding her tightly against his body.

Kate hadn't been able to hear what was said but she'd already made her decision. When the next man came out of the tavern, she was going to do as the tart had done. Accost him, say something to entice him, and . . . If she was lucky, perhaps he'd let her spend the night and give her a meal before he sent her on her way.

If I'm lucky. If not . . . With a couple of coins in her

hand, it wouldn't matter.

The drunkard had gotten past. While she was lost in thought, he'd wandered on up the roadway.

There was a scrabble and a skitter behind her. Kate ignored it as the tavern door opened again.

Another staggerer, this one worse off than the other two. He took a step, tripped and nearly fell, righted himself and began a determined, if somewhat, wavering march along the same path the first had taken.

Kate took a deep breath, wishing she had been able to hear what the whore had said. *Good evening, sir, are you taking a walk?* She was certain it had been nothing that polite. *If only I knew what to say. And the way to say it.* At the moment, having been gently brought up was a curse.

He was getting closer. She stood up, preparing to step from behind the barrels.

"You don't really want to do that, do you?" Someone spoke behind her.

Gasping, she whirled, staring at the man not five feet away. "Wh-where did you come from?"

"I live here." He chose to misunderstand her question, coming out of the shadow of the warehouse's eave.

He was tall, his face shadowed by the short brim of his hat, and further hidden by the upturned collar of his greatcoat. It was unbuttoned, revealing the curve of his cutaway. Between his coat's turnover collar and the top button of his richly embroidered waistcoat peeked a sheer frill of a ruffle. Other ruffles fell out of his sleeves and over his gloves.

It was so dark she couldn't tell what color his clothing was. Everything seemed to blend into the shadows, from the top of his hat to the toes of his riding boots.

The approaching footsteps were coming closer. She turned away.

"Don't." A hand caught her arm, pulling her backward. Her shoulders struck a solid chest, and she was held tightly against his body.

Fear knifed through her.

What does he want? Is it my fate to be killed by this stranger?

He didn't seem intent on harming her . . . not yet, at least . . . merely preventing her from stopping the approaching man.

A desperate idea flashed through Kate's mind. *I'll cry out. The man'll stop and I'll pretend he rescued me, convince him to take me home with him and . . .*

Even as she sucked in air to scream, a hand clapped over her mouth.

"Shh."

She forced her body to go limp. As he relaxed his hold, she lunged forward, from behind the barrels directly into the drunkard's path. He skidded to a halt, waving his arms like a tight-rope walker keeping his balance.

"What's this? Hullo, there." He aimed an owlish leer at her. "Where did you come from?"

"I-I've been waiting for you." She glanced over her shoulder, didn't see her assailant anywhere. Had he run away?

"Re-al-ly . . ." The words were drawled in a stream of whiskey-laden breath making Kate want to fan the air.

She forced herself to smile, knowing it must look a ghastly caricature. He didn't notice, leaning forward so steeply, she feared he might tumble bum over head.

"Got somethin' for me, do ya?"

"Uh . . . yes . . ."

A crooked finger beckoned. "So come closer, gel . . . let me see."

Kate did as he asked.

"And they're beauties, too. One hand seized her shoulder, the other plunging into her bosom. His hand cupped her breast, thumb rubbing against the nipple.

Kate was startled to feel it perk and harden while her mind felt nothing but revulsion.

"Take your hands off the lady."

She didn't have to turn around to know it was the stranger. He hadn't run away after all but was still intent on playing the hero.

"Lady? What lady?" The drunk peered around with exaggerated care, eyes wide. "No one here but this *hooer*."

The hand tightened. Kate winced.

"Nevertheless, you'll remove your grubby fingers from her bosom, else you'll find my glove in your face." The stranger pulled off his right glove as he spoke.

"'Od's blood!" The hand recoiled as if burnt. "If you want the tart that much, take her. I've enough troubles without fighting a duel over some li'l roundheels."

Without waiting for the stranger's reply, he wobbled past at an unsteady gallop, heading up the darkened street.

Kate turned on the stranger. "Why did you do that?" she demanded.

"You've very welcome, my dear." His reply was ironic. He had an odd intonation, telling her he was a foreigner. "I think you know."

Sliding the glove back on, the stranger turned to look at her.

"Because you want me for yourself." She made it a

statement and was surprised when he smiled and shook his head.

"If I spend my money on a woman, 'twon't be one I have to teach what to do. Did you think to get a bed for the night and a warm breakfast in the morning and a coin when he sent you on your way with a pat on the head? Stupid child."

His anger hurt, more so because it was true.

"You'd have gotten a drubbing and possibly the pox and been kicked into the street as soon as he took his pleasure. *Get the money first* . . . that's the whore's cardinal rule. You don't even know enough to do that."

"I supposed you do?" An odd hope stirred within her. "Are you one of those . . ." What were they called? "P-procurers? Can you teach me what I need to know?"

"*Sweet Unspeakable Name.* Don't insult me, girl." His laugh was rueful. "I'm much, much worse, if the truth be known, but in your case . . . I truly mean you no harm."

She shook her head, clearly not believing. No *gentleman* lurked in the shadows, grabbed a woman and muffled her so she couldn't cry out, not without meaning some kind of mischief.

"There's a clean bed and a warm fire waiting for you in my home, if you wish it," he went on. "Come with me and you won't have to spend another night hiding among these barrels waiting for sots."

"How'd you know I'd been here all night?"

"I've been watching you. I think you knew I was here."

She remembered the rustlings and other little sounds. "That was you? Why didn't you show yourself?"

"I wanted to see what you would do. Just how desperate you were."

"So now, you know." She was ashamed, and still confused as to what he really wanted.

He studied her intently a moment. She could almost feel his gaze burning her cheeks.

"You're very young."

"I'm almost eighteen."

"That's young from where I stand."

She thought that an odd thing to say, since he looked to be only four-and-twenty or so. Perhaps he meant in experience.

He touched her cheek, finger caressing the line of her jaw. The tanned calfskin was soft against her skin. Unconsciously, she leaned against his hand.

"And so very, very innocent."

"Innocent? Not anymore." Kate gave a choked half-laugh and began to sob. Before she realized it, he'd drawn her to him, cradling her face against his chest.

"Go ahead and cry, child. Let it out."

Somehow, her arms went around his waist, and she was crushed against the sleek satin of his waistcoat, smelling the gentleman's scent of sandalwood in the fabric. His own arms closed around her. A gloved hand stroked her hair, and he didn't speak as she sobbed out her unhappiness and desperation against him.

When at last her tears ended with a soft gulp and a cough, he pushed her away to look into her face. A hand brushed an errant strand of hair from her forehead, one gloved finger wiping away the tear-tracks on her cheek. They left a dark stain on the leather.

"My offer's there for the taking, child. A warm meal, a bed for the night, and . . ."

". . . what do you want in return?" she asked, as

harshly as she could.

". . . if you wish, you can leave in the morning." He ignored her question and held out his hand. "Will you accompany me? Please?"

Perhaps it was that one word. As if he were politely begging. Nevertheless, something kept her from nodding.

He hesitated one moment longer, then shrugged and dropped his hand and turned away. Before he'd taken four steps, Kate found herself running after him. She caught his fingers, tightening her own around them.

He didn't slow his pace, nearly dragging her behind him. She had to run to keep up with his long strides, as he went on, "I apologize for not having transportation. If I'd known I was going to find you, I'd have brought my coach. As it is, we'll have to walk."

He slowed to look down at her, giving her a smile that gleamed under the streetlamps and sent an arrow of warmth into her heart.

"You don't mind, do you? Walking, I mean."

In that moment, Kate would've followed him anywhere.

They seemed to walk forever, the length of Meeting Street.

Charleston was built on high ground, ten feet above sea level, but the stranger's home was even higher than that, on a hill overlooking the town. By the time they reached it, Kate was certain she would have to be carried the last steps of the way.

The great walled gates loomed before them and the curving driveway, until at last, they stood before a beautiful brick mansion with a cream-colored door encased in a finely decorated transom and frame.

Kate looked up, mouth dropping open in awe.

The house was beautiful. Set at angles to the drive, it was built in what would later be called *Charleston single house style*, windows enclosed by carved frames and cornices contrasting whitely with the rich red of the fired brick. Two stories loomed above, with white porch railings and curtain-wreathed doors opening onto the balconies. Though rooms on the main story were lighted, no illumination shone from those above them.

Releasing her hand, the stranger lifted the horseshoe-shaped brass knocker and brought it down, striking the door.

The door opened. Light poured out. A man dressed in the livery of a well-to-do house servant was silhouetted in the golden glow.

"Georges." The stranger stalked past him.

"Master, you're back. But so early?" He looked past the gentleman, seeing Kate who timidly trailed him inside. "And bringing a guest?"

"As you say, Georges." He took off hat, coat, and gloves, thrusting them at the servant who accepted with the ease of long practice. "The young lady will be staying the night. Open one of the guest bedrooms."

"She appears very young, sir." As he turned from placing the garments in a nearby closet, George glanced at Kate, then fixed his master with what appeared to be a disapproving frown.

"That's why she's sleeping in a guest room." The stranger caught Kate's hand, tugging gently but insistently. "She'll need a meal, also. Is there anything left from your supper? Have Cook stir up something filling."

With that, he pulled Kate down the hall and into a

door open on the right.

It was a parlor, small and cozy. Obviously not a place to receive visitors, but where the family gathered at the end of the day. Comfortable chairs huddled around the hearth, a loveseat and a larger settee behind them with small tables strategically placed here and there holding figurines or sculptures. On the walls, paintings hung between massive *armoires* and bookcases.

A fire blazed cheerily in the hearth. When the stranger released her hand, Kate rushed to it.

"Georges, a blanket. She's wet and chilled."

Holding out her hands to its warmth, she let the flames' heat creep over her. The fire burned behind a copper-latticed screen protecting the crimson Persian carpet from escaping sparks and cinders.

She looked up at the elaborately scrolled mantling.

Above it hung a portrait of a dark-haired man in ancient garments. The painting had been damaged; someone had slashed it with a knife, and there was a large section of the canvas missing where the left arm should have been. Part of the face had been disfigured and had obviously been repainted because the colors looked brighter and smoother. There was something in the way he held his head and the almost-direct gaze of his eyes reminding her of the man standing behind her.

An ancestor?

He hadn't spoken, just walked to the sideboard and took a thick crystal decanter from among those sitting there. Pouring a scant amount of wine into a goblet, he offered it to her.

Kate took it, sipping cautiously.

It was strong but sweet tasting, held the flavor of cherries blended with the alcohol. There was barely enough for two swallows, so he obviously wasn't attempting to overcome her with strong spirits.

As Georges returned with a soft blanket that he draped over her shoulders, the stranger stepped to one side, leaning against the mantel, one arm resting on the beautifully carved rosettes along its border. Gathering the blanket about herself, Kate seated herself in one of the chairs. She kept her head down, studying the goblet and the few drops of wine left in it, more to avoid that straightforward gaze than for any other reason.

"Your wife won't care that you bring home strays at all hours?" She thought herself clever to determine his marital status in such a way.

"I doubt it since I have none." The question seemed to sadden, then amuse him. "Before you indelicately go further... I've no mistress, either. No female in this house warms my bed."

Before she could answer, Georges re-appeared, bearing a tray upon which rested a covered dish. At his master's gesture, he placed it on the table next to Kate's chair, whisked off the cover and disappeared again, carrying the cover away with him.

The most delicious aroma floated to her. Kate's stomach, empty for a day and a half now, reacted accordingly... with a loud, appreciative growl.

Embarrassed, she clutched that organ convulsively, beginning an apology, "I-I'm sorry..."

"Don't be."

She could detect more of that accent, now. Not Carolinian, not even American, she thought, but she hadn't enough experience with foreigners to tell which country.

"Please, go ahead and eat. I know you must be famished."

Reaching over to the tray, she lifted the plate, setting it on her knees, took the knife and fork and tucked into the best meal she'd ever eaten. Small new potatoes cooked in butter and sprinkled with chives and parsley, a thick slice of beef, braised in its own juices that were also soaking into the two slices of buttered brown bread lying next to it, and green beans boiled with bacon. There was a goblet of something dark on the tray also, and after gobbling down two of the potatoes—and startling herself by her lack of manners—she reached for the glass, tasting tentatively.

Grape squash.

She rolled the tart-sweet liquid on her tongue before swallowing. Yes, the stranger definitely didn't want her unconscious but alert and responsive. That thought sent a shiver through her, startling her even more as she realized it wasn't completely a fearful one.

He spoke only once as he seated himself across from her, smiling slightly as if watching a child.

"Please, eat slowly. No one's going to take it from you, and I don't want you having a bellyache from swallowing your food without chewing it."

Reprimanded, she reddened, but did as he asked, chewing slower and savoring each mouthful until it was completely consumed. As she laid fork and knife upon the plate and leaned back with a sigh, he stood and came toward her. She stiffened; he merely took the plate from her lap and returned it to the tray, then tugged on the bellpull by the hearth.

While Georges returned to take away the tray, he silently watched her. As the door shut again, he cleared his throat slightly. Kate turned back to look at him.

Oh, dear Lord, he's so handsome.

Young, as she'd thought, long dark hair, almost black, tied back loosely. Dark brows and blue eyes, definitely foreign, and full of some kind of . . . *a myriad of expressions* . . . mischief, longing, desire? Could he be a rake, a foreign *roué*? She'd heard of those but had no true idea how one looked.

Kate blinked and felt herself relax. *'Tis time to make him state his intentions.* She decided to be bold, and sk.

"Well, sir. You've fed me and warmed me and now I think 'tis time we spoke plainly with each other. Who are you and what do you want?"

"You're correct, and I agree we should now be introduced. Who am I? Damién, *Marquis* La Croix, *a votre service*." He made a leg, bowing with one hand touching his heart, then held gracefully open-palmed toward her.

He straightened, waiting, one perfect brow arched inquisitively.

"I— Uh . . . Katherine . . . Katherine Blackwell, sir." Pushing back the blanket, Kate stumbled to her feet, bobbing him a dip of a curtsey. She rested one hand on the arm of the chair. Truly that dark blue gaze made her feel too weak to stand.

"Katherine. Are you called *Kate*, perhaps?"

"Y-yes sir."

"But not just any Kate, I'm thinking." He considered her a moment, forefinger to his lips and what he said next startled her. "Nay, *'tis Sweet Kate. Plain Kate and bonnie Kate, the prettiest Kate in all Christendom, Kate of my consolation—*"

"*Taming of the Shrew*," she acknowledged. "My father

quoted that particular passage to me often." She was startled to feel her eyes sting as she said that.

"Yet it makes you sad to think of him." He was too observant. "Why?" he persisted, frowning slightly.

The way his dark brows dipped into a vee as his expression changed intrigued her. She had the most absurd notion to reach out and stroke away the lines appearing on his forehead.

Truly, you're too young to have worry-wrinkles, sir. Her hands clenched together as if to prevent them from following through.

"Did he cause your current circumstance? What parent would place his child in such straits as that?"

Kate didn't answer. She tried to, but the tears began immediately as she thought again of what had happened and how wickedly she'd been treated and now the *marquis* dared, even mistakenly, to blame her father?

"Here now, none of that." A handkerchief appeared, plucked from a sleeve, the fine cambric pressed into her hand.

As she blotted away the tears and stifled more, he took her hand and led her to the settee. Flipping up the tails of his coat, he seated himself, pulling her down to sit beside him.

"Now, tell me. Why were you hiding on the docks and what happened to make you willing to sell yourself to a stranger for a night's lodging?"

Twisting the handkerchief between her fingers, Kate obeyed.

"I'm an orphan," she began. "My father was a schoolmaster in the Shenandoah Valley where my parents and my younger brothers and I lived until a fever swept through and I was the only one to survive. My only other relative is my Aunt Margaret, so I was sent to her as soon as my family was buried..."

* * *

Margaret Blackwell had always been jealous of her younger sister. First to be married, though to a gentleman come down in the world since he had to teach others' offspring, Alice Blackwell had been of such a sweet disposition she'd never suspected her older sibling's hate. She had been eighteen when she was courted and subsequently married to James Blackwell. Margaret, three years older, and remarkably plain as well as big boned and ungainly, would be thirty-two before she married, and then to a much younger man more attracted to her dowry... that, and the fact that as eldest daughter, she would inherit her father's tavern when the old man died.

Josiah Daniels was twenty-five and seven years' his wife's junior and that should've been enough warning but Margaret was desperate. She was willing to ignore rumors of his womanizing as well as the warnings of friends that he was more interested in her money than her body. After their marriage, he was steadfastly unfaithful but remarkably discreet, so Margaret turned a blind eye to his dalliances as long as he serviced her regularly.

If they'd had children, perhaps she might not have continued to be so bitter when letters from Alice told of the births of Katherine and later her brothers, but Margaret never quickened, continuing childless and becoming more embittered as the years and her sister's family increased.

When she received news that everyone except her niece had perished in the fever sweeping through the Shenandoah, she experienced a moment's flash of vindication and a desire to toss the letter into the fire while laughing in glee. Now the pretty daughter . . . the one her father and everyone else had cosseted and pampered so . . . was no more, a mere mound of tamped earth in whatever churchyard existed far away in Virginia, and she, the late-married, childless one, had triumphed.

Publicly, she welcomed the orphaned child, letting her generosity be known throughout the town, while privately putting Kate to work in her home as little more than a servant. Granted, she slept in the house and not in the little cabins in the back where the slaves lived but other than that, the girl was treated no better than the West Indian man and the two women Josiah had bought at the Slave Emporium.

Kate helped Mariah cook; she served her aunt and uncle at table, eating in the kitchen with Mariah, Jessamine, and Caleb as they had their own meals at the rickety old table. She washed the dishes, swept and mopped the floors, helped Jessamine with the laundry, and every night staggered upstairs to her dormer room in the attic to fall into an exhausted sleep.

In spite of this minor abuse, Kate was grateful for a home and expected to stay there for a long time, or at least until her aunt decided to marry her to someone who could be taught to handle the tavern. As it was, she caught the eye of the wrong man.

It began shortly after her seventeenth birthday when her uncle began complimenting her. It was as if he'd abruptly realized she was one of the family and not merely someone sent to be a servant for them.

Kate thanked him politely, but she got the feeling something in his flattery *wasn't quite right*. Then, odd little incidents began, as Josiah's attentions became more overt . . . his fingers lingering on her own as she served him from the platters at the sideboard, body brushing against hers when they passed each other in the narrow hallways. Once, while she was bending over the wash pot, stirring the clothes in the soapy water as it bubbled and boiled over the fire, he stood watching her for several minutes.

The water was hot, steam rising from it as the fire blazed on that spring day, and Kate had rolled up her sleeves and unbuttoned the top two buttons on her dress, allowing some cool air to touch her damp skin. She'd felt definitely uncomfortable under his hard stare but continued with her work until he turned and walked into the house again.

For the next three days, Josiah neither said nor did anything to worry Kate. On the fourth day, however, he made his intentions unmistakable. Leaving Margaret at the tavern handling the customers, he came home, followed Kate to the second-best bedroom where she was changing the linens, locked the door behind him, and proceeded to rape her.

Afterward, she had no true memory of what happened, other than Josiah's weight pressing her into the bed, sudden pain and his harsh grunts as he plunged again and again into her body, and his broken cry of satisfaction. Climbing from the bed as she sobbed in shock, he stuffed his now-limp tool back into his breeks and re-buttoned the take-down front.

"Don't think to tell Margaret of this. She'll not believe

you. Nor will anyone else." Unlocking the door, he walked out, leaving Kate in a puddle of his spill spotted with her own blood.

She believed what he said, and her silence made Josiah bolder. He began coming home several times a week, dragging Kate into the nearest bedroom. At night he often stole from Margaret's side while she slept, coming to the little dormer room where he would abuse the girl again and again while holding one hand over her mouth to stifle her cries.

His ill-treatment might have continued, except one day, Margaret did something he never expected.

She followed him home.

It had been raining all day and the hostel part of the tavern was full of weary, water-soaked travelers wishing nothing but a dry bed. The public room itself emptied early because no one would venture through the downpour. Leaving Caleb in charge of the tap, she hurried home, expecting some intimate time with her husband. Instead, she found Josiah sprawled naked upon the second-best bed, with Kate kneeling between his thighs, sucking on his yard while she chafed his cods between her palms as he'd ordered.

What followed was chaos . . . Margaret beating the girl while shrieking invectives, Kate trying to explain as she dodged the blows, and Josiah scrambling into his clothing and protesting his innocence above the din: *Th' demmed li'l trollop seduced me, Meggie. Enticed me . . . I couldn't help m'self!*

Dragging the girl down the stairs, Margaret slung her out the door and into the downpour, locking it before Kate could recover. "Out, you little wanton! Into the street where you belong."

"Aunt, please. Listen. It isn't true. He lies." Beating on the door with her fists, Kate begged and pleaded as one by one the lights in the house were extinguished, except for that in the bedroom where Josiah was now expiating his sins by giving his wife the groaning of her life. When that lamp also darkened and everything was quiet, Kate knew she wasn't going to be allowed back in.

The rain has lessened now. Pulling a shawl from the hedge where it had been spread to dry, she held the sodden garment over her head and began to run. With Josiah's accusations still ringing in her head, she didn't know where she was going, simply wishing to get as far from the house as possible. When she found herself at the docks, her first thought was to fling herself into the water and escape her humiliation in the most final way. Self-preservation prevented that, and instead, she hid among the barrels in the warehouse where she cradled her bruised fists against her face and at last burst into the tears she hadn't shed in all the months of her abuse.

* * *

". . . and that's where I was when you ruined my chances with that gentleman," she finished.

"Ruined? Perhaps," Damién answered. He gave her a half-smile. "Or mayhap I've simply given you better ones."

It was as she thought. He wanted her for himself, but she wanted to hear him say it.

"I've told you all, sir. Now answer my question. What do you want?"

"Nothing."

He spoke so flatly, she frowned.

"Nothing?"

"Well . . ." There was that flicker of a smile again.

Kate found herself answering it before she could stop. She forced the frown back into place.

"Perhaps, *something*."

"What? Exactly."

"Not what you're thinking, I assure you." He sounded so earnest. "I've answered both your questions, Kate, but I'll tell you more. Who am I? I'm a lonely man."

He stood, returning to the sideboard to select an odd antique decanter and pour its contents into a goblet.

"I'm a foreigner, as you can tell. I wish to make your country . . . your city . . . my new home." He took a small swallow of the dark liquid, savoring it as if to give himself a moment to collect his thoughts. "I'm also a rich man, and my money has opened many doors to me. It enables me to have any woman I want, for as long as I want, but none of them interest me."

Once more he returned to the settee but didn't sit. Instead, he stood looking down at her, twisting the stem of the goblet around and around in those long, aristocratic fingers.

"I'm lonely, child. Most desperately. While there are women in this town who can give me pleasure, none can give me what I really seek."

"What is that, sir?" *He has money, a beautiful home, and a handsome face. He's welcome in the houses of the well-to-do and obviously pursued by women. What more can he desire?*

"I wish someone who will accept me for who I am . . ." His voice sank to a whisper, as he added, "In spite of what I am . . ."

He's lonely? This handsome, titled man is lonely?

Before she could voice her disbelief, he went on, "That's all I ask of you. I give you free run of my home, your own bed where you may sleep alone, good food, and in return—"

"All I have to do is give you the pleasure of *my company*?" She dared give the words an ironic lilt. "Read to you, perhaps play the pianoforte, talk to you and listen to your cares and woes?"

"If you can read, *oui*. If you play the piano, even better. And—I wouldn't go so far as to say I have cares and woes, but— That's more or less the gist of it." He lifted one of her hands, kissing her fingers gently.

Kate shivered as his lips touched her skin. They were so cold. He looked down at her, those wonderful eyes meeting hers.

"Bring some small pleasure into my life. Would you do that for me?"

She didn't believe a word he said. *He wants something more, but I do owe him. For tonight at least.*

"This is a serious thing you ask of me, sir, and something not so hastily decided," she hedged. "May I think on it tonight and give you an answer? Tomorrow?"

"That's fair enough." She was bathed in a smile more brilliant than all the others he'd bestowed upon her so far. "For now, though . . ."

In one motion, he pulled her from the settee and swung her into the chair by the fire, whipping the blanket out of the way and tucking it across her lap.

"Sit here. Get warm. Your hands are still icy."

When she obediently settled herself and had accepted a small glass of wine, with a murmured, "Thank you, sir," he went on, "*Non, ma petite.* You must call me Damién."

"Damién . . ." she repeated his name slowly, tasting it as she had the wine.

There was a knock at the door, and he looked toward it.

"I must leave for a few moments. Stay here and keep warm." He went to the door, opened it and went out.

A murmur drifted through the wood, Georges' voice, his own answering.

Kate finished her wine and placed the glass on the nearby table. In a few moments, the meal she'd consumed, and the warmth of the fire mingled with the softness of the blanket to conspire against her. She started to blink, then to nod, and was soon asleep in the chair.

She didn't wake when Damién returned. Lifting her small body, he cradled her against his shoulder for a moment. Then, he carried her upstairs to the guest room.

"Send one of the serving women to undress her," he ordered Georges as he placed Kate upon the bed. Damién waited until the *valet* disappeared before he touched the pale, tangled hair, brushing it back from the girl's face.

So young, so tender . . . perhaps she's the one I've been looking for. Someone not wise in the ways of the world, someone not yet set in society's unyielding molds . . . Kate, will you be the one I seek?

"Mastuh?" Zephorah, one of the *enthralled* slaves, appeared in the doorway, brushing sleep from her eyes.

"Prepare the little one for bed," he ordered. Bending, he brushed a kiss across Kate's forehead, and left her in the slave woman's care. "*Rêves doux, ma petite.* Sweet dreams."

* * *

Damién's happiness had returned. It was so much as

it had been when Konstancza was with him, he was astonished.

Kate filled his existence with a joy he hadn't felt since the night he'd been accepted by that ravaged Romanian girl three hundred years before. He had only to close his eyes as he sat with her by the fire to imagine he was once more at *Château La Croix*.

For the first time in centuries, his heart was calmed. He was content.

He found the girl witty, as well as well-read, no doubt the result of being a schoolmaster's child. His laughter, never before heard in the mansion, now rang through its corridors with startling clarity. The first time the servants heard it, they stared at each other in consternation. Now, a month later, they barely acknowledged the sound, it was so commonplace.

"I vow I've never laughed so much before. You're good for me, child."

"Do you really think so?" She held an embroidery frame in her lap, plunging the needle in-and-out of the tightly stretched cloth, creating delicate stitches forming an elaborate "C" onto a square of linen destined to be a dinner napkin.

"Indeed, I wouldn't have said it otherwise."

"In that case, will you answer me two questions?"

"Anything." Transferring his goblet to his other hand, he waved it in a grandiose gesture.

"Stop calling me *child*."

"That's granted easily enough. I'm sorry if I insulted you with that label, Kate."

Child? Oui, she is that, but so much older than her years in some ways. I think the abuse she's suffered has aged her.

"What's your other request?"

"Tell me who you really are, and what takes you away from me every day. Where do you go when you leave our home?"

"Ah, that's three questions." It thrilled him that she said *our home,* but he wouldn't tell her that. Not yet anyway. He was always hedging away from the truth, skirting it with partial falsehoods. "Which shall I answer?"

"All my questions, Damién." She gave him her most winning smile, just short of cozening. "Please?"

Damién might be centuries old, but in that moment, he was like any older man with a pretty little chit flattering him. He liked it . . . and gave in, too easily . . . or appeared to.

"Very well . . ." With a loud sigh as if the telling exhausted him. "As to your first question: I've told you. I'm the *Marquis* La Croix, tenth to hold that title. A stranger to your shores but now a new inhabitant."

"And the second?"

"I have business in town to attend, and that's what takes me from your most pleasant company every day."

"You're a noble, not a businessman," she protested. "To which buildings do you go? Why does it take all day, allowing you to return only as the sun goes down?"

"I'm a noble, *oui,*" he agreed. "But I must carefully handle my money else it may soon be gone, and I'll be a penniless man with simply a title. For that reason, I invest my money, Kate, and also to show my faith in my new country. It's an all-day affair, checking on each and every place to which my funds have gone."

Kate let him think she accepted that explanation, but secretly, she felt there was more to her savior than he would say.

Though he might be absent during the day, he always made certain he appeared when night fell, escorting the girl into the dining room for their supper together. It was a supper he pretended to eat, moving morsels about the plate with his fork, while in reality, the only thing he consumed was the rich, dark wine in the goblet Georges gave him, refilling it as the meal progressed.

Afterward, they would sit in the parlor for a while, where Kate played the pianoforte or they had a game of chess or simply talked, and then Damién would lead her up the stairs, kiss her fingers, and leave her at the door of her bedchamber while he walked to his own. Once he was certain the girl was asleep, he left the house, in search of his own nourishment.

It might have continued so if Kate hadn't decided to satisfy her curiosity about her benefactor. By now, the girl accepted the fact that Damién meant her no harm, that he did truly wish only her companionship, though she thought that odd in someone as young as he appeared to be.

With that knowledge, however, and her apparent safety, came something else . . . the desire for revenge. She wished to make her aunt and uncle pay for what they'd done. A man as rich as the *marquis* could get that for her, she was certain. That would come later, however. For now, the mystery of Damién's whereabouts during the day intrigued her and she determined to solve it before broaching that other subject with him.

Perhaps, she thought, *he goes somewhere he doesn't wish others to know. Perhaps my knowing it can be used as a lever to gain his aid in avenging myself if he refuses.* Since he was a foreigner, it might be that he wouldn't wish to involve himself in a family scandal.

Kate had learned much of the deviousness of her fellow men in a very short time, and decided if she had to, she would force Damién to help her.

Though he thought her a clever girl, Damién had underestimated just how much. Kate noticed the strict routine of his schedule . . . his absences during the day, appearances only after sundown. She found it odd that, though he'd professed to have a bevy of female admirers, he always retired at the same time as she, and never went out at night. Neither had she heard a sound from his room telling her he'd smuggled some female into the house, and she's questioned why he needed to secretly bring someone into his own home anyway. Surely not for her sensibilities? Not as aware of men's base natures as she now was. She felt a little ashamed as she thought that, for she found herself unable to ascribe Josiah's same carnality to her protector.

She was determined to learn where he went and why. And she would begin the next day.

* * *

Kate slept fitfully that night, awakening every few hours until the moment the sun came up. There was no sound through the house at all; it was too early yet for even the cook to be awake. Dragging a chair to the door, she sat and opened it wide enough to see the entrance to Damién's own chamber across the hall. Now she would be able to watch him leave and somehow contrive to follow him.

Damién didn't appear. The door never opened, and soon, she heard stirrings as the servants went about their tasks. Georges arose to supervise them. Though she sat for a good three hours, staring at the *marquis'* doorway, it remained closed. At last, as the grandfather clock in the front foyer chimed nine o'clock, and she heard the footsteps of the girl Damién had chosen to be her abigail coming up the stairs, she hurriedly replaced the chair by the hearth and threw herself back into bed, feigning sleep as the girl knocked on the door.

Later, upon seeing Georges, she asked, "When will His Lordship be coming down to breakfast?"

"The master left the house hours ago, mistress," was the valet's smooth reply. "He breakfasted before his departure."

Liar, she thought. *If he left hours ago, 'twas in the middle of the night.*

She stationed herself near the foyer, finding one excuse or another to keep the front door in sight most of the day while at the same time, preventing the servants and Georges from being suspicious. By the time the sun went down, she was not only exhausted and bored but also running out of excuses and welcomed Georges' announcement, "Mistress Kate, supper is ready."

"Master Damién is late," she stated the obvious. "However, I think we'll start without him." She went to the dining room.

In a few moments, Damién was there also, showering her with apologies and excuses for belatedly arriving for the meal.

"No matter. You're here now." She waved his excuses aside, wondering, *Did he really just arrive, or has he been secluded in his room all day?* "I trust you have a good appetite?"

She said it with a teasing smile hiding the desire to confront him.

"You didn't while away the hours at my aunt's tavern, eating pickled eggs and drinking ale?"

"An awful-sounding combination, *ma petit*." He grimaced as he allowed Georges to seat him at the table. "I swear, *non*. I'd let nothing prevent me from enjoying my meals with you."

"I had thought to see you before you left," she said, shaking out her napkin and spreading it across her lap. "It seems I didn't get up early enough."

"*Oui*, I was up and gone before you stirred." Was it her imagination or did the goblet he held out for Georges to fill tremble slightly? "Some of my meetings are quite lengthy and I must be there in the truly early hours."

He took what seemed to Kate to be a rather large swallow of wine. He was always served from the same decanter, the one she'd seen him drink from that first night, an ancient, fired-pottery bottle. Ugly, Kate thought, compared to the others on the sideboard. It looked to be very old and Damién told her it had been in his family for generations. She'd been intrigued by the wine it contained, so dark it was almost black in his glass.

"Is the wine to your liking?"

He set down his goblet, looking at it as if surprised by her question. "*Oui*. Very. A good vintage." This was said to Georges, who nodded and returned the bottle to the sideboard.

"May I have some?"

"Of course. Georges, some of that *carmenere* for Mistress Katherine."

"No," she said quickly. "I wish to drink what you're

having, Damién. Georges, pour me some of the same."

Her heart beat a little faster as she ordered the servant, something she'd never done before.

Instead of returning to the sideboard, Georges paused, looking back at his master.

Damién shook his head. "Some of the *carmenere*, Georges."

"Why can't I have the other?" She knew she sounded like a spoiled child, but she was certain there was something about the wine he was hiding from her. "That you're drinking?"

"'Tis a special blending, only for the La Croix family," he responded in the same way, as if he were placating a child. "We never allow anyone not a family member to drink it."

"That's very selfish." She affected a pout. Before, that had always won him over.

"'Tis a strong wine. You wouldn't like it." On this, it appeared he couldn't be moved. "The *carmenere*, Georges."

She accepted the wine, admitted it was a good choice and fell silent, continuing her meal without further prying.

After their usual sojourn in the parlor, Kate asked to be excused. She didn't have to feign being tired; because of her sleeplessness of the night before, and her sentry-duty in the foyer, she truly was. Damién admitted his early day had tired him also and escorted her to her door.

Going inside, she waited for Zephorah to arrive and help her prepare for bed, impatiently suffering the girl's ministrations while listening for Damién's door to open again. She didn't hear it. Once the slave was gone, she again positioned herself before her door, looking out into the corridor.

She dozed lightly; the sound of footsteps in the hall awakening her. Peeping through the crack, she saw Damién hurrying toward the stairs. In a few moments, she heard him speaking to Georges and the outer door shutting. The odd thing was, she heard no sound of coach wheels or rattling of harness.

Does he walk to town each night?

Determined to see him when he returned, she remained at her post, leaning with cheek resting against the wall and falling into a deep sleep. Only when the clock struck three did she awaken, footsteps on the stairs seeming to echo the heavy *ding-dong* of the timepiece.

When Damién appeared within her vision, she thought he looked odd, and it took her several moments to realize how his appearance had changed. He looked much healthier than he had at supper that night. His face was fairly glowing, those high-sculptured cheeks rosy with a blush any maiden might envy. His full lips touched with enough pink to draw attention to their fine shape. Thinking back, she remembered other nights when he had appeared so, while over the length of a few evenings, his color seemed to fade. He would gradually become paler and paler, his cheeks sallow, his lips colorless, skin dull... Then, abruptly, he would look... *normal*... again.

What does it mean?

The click of the lock brought her out of her reverie. Replacing the chair, Kate hurried to her own bed, surprising herself by falling quickly into sleep, though one thought remained with her even when she awoke... *I must get into Damién's room.*

* * *

The next morning, Kate had her own breakfast, didn't bother asking where the master was, and pottered around the house until noon. After a light dinner, she tried to appear casual as she headed up the stairs, announcing she was going to rest. At Damién's door, she paused, hand hovering over the handle. Sudden doubts seem to batter her.

What if I'm wrong? What if he leaves the house by some way I'm unaware of? Perhaps there's a secret entrance or something. If so, why does he go out again at night? Surely, he isn't carousing somewhere, for he didn't look drunk when he came in, and the changes in his complexion...

Taking a deep breath, she seized the handle and pushed it down. Nothing happened. The door was locked. After all her thoughts, that disappointment made her tremble with frustration.

Why does he lock his door?

Foolish question. In his home, he could lock any door he pleased without a reason.

Still...

Whirling, she hurried down the stairs, going to the kitchen where she knew a set of keys hung on a peg by the servants' entrance. There was one key very different from the others. That had to be the one opening the bedchamber door. It wasn't difficult to slide that key off the ring.

It amazed her how no one paid the least attention as she returned the ring to the peg, and, with the key clenched tightly in her hand, hurried back upstairs. The key worked; it clicked in the lock and at her push, the door slid silently open. It took her a few moments to replace the key, then she was back up the stairs, hand on the handle, opening the door and going in.

Whatever she'd expected to find, she was disappointed. She found herself in a sitting room much like the parlor downstairs, though smaller, a comfortable chair by the fireplace in which a small blaze crackled. A desk, bookcases and tapestries adorned the walls. These looked very old, however, some of them actually threadbare in spots as if moths had gotten to them. She wondered why Damién would have such obviously old things about, then decided they must have sentimental value for him.

On the mantel was another antique wine bottle. Kate decided to satisfy her curiosity once and for all about the special wine vinted *just for the La Croix*. Seizing the decanter, she worked out the cork. A pungent and unpleasant odor wafted from the bottle. Raising it to her lips, she took a sip, recoiling as the cold, thick liquid struck her tongue.

"Ugh!" She spat into the fire. It flared and spluttered. Hastily, Kate closed the bottle and returned it to the mantel. *What vile stuff. How can Damién drink that?* It certainly had none of the delicious flavor of the *carmenere*.

She wiped a hand across her mouth as if to remove the aftertaste from her lips. That scent . . . and the taste . . . it was familiar somehow . . . thick and sticky, bitter with a vague meaty tang. Like . . .

. . . *blood* . . .

Backing away from the hearth, Kate ran through the adjoining door . . . into Damién's bedchamber.

That room was deadly dark except for the glow of a single oil lamp by the bed. Heavy draperies crossed over each other at the two windows, folded in such a way not a speck of sunlight could penetrate. The furniture was heavy and masculine. A clothespress and chiffonier, a chair near the hearth, a chest at the foot of the bed. The bed itself was swathed in draperies also, heavy velvet like those on the windows overhanging sheerer ones to keep out insects during the summer. Through the sheers, she could see the flickering rays of the lamp lighting *something* in the bed.

Kate brushed back the draperies. In the next moment, she backed away from the bed in horror, hands to her mouth to prevent screaming.

Damién lay there, hair loose about his shoulders... naked and still... covers pulled up and folded to his waist. His arms lay by his sides, atop the sheets.

Like a corpse's.

"Damién?" Kate seized his hand. It was cold, as if there was no blood in it. She forced herself to clutch it tightly as she shook his shoulder. "Damién, wake up."

He didn't respond. It was then she saw... His chest wasn't rising with the gentle breath of the sleeping.

He wasn't breathing at all.

Kate released his hand. It fell to the bed. A dead, white thing.

When she'd shared her meals with her aunt's slaves, Mariah and the others had told her of the evil spirits of the West Indies, the creatures of the night their own ancestors brought with them from their homelands when they were carried away into slavery. They spoke to the impressionable child of the *nzambie*... a resurrected creature with no will of its own... the *dhuppy* with its thousands of razor-sharp teeth... and the *vampyr*, the corpse appearing as a man, immortal as long as it drank the blood of the living.

How can you stop them, Mariah? she'd asked, eyes wide with fear. *What can one do to protect herself?*

The slave's answer had been short and brutal. *You takes uh big knife an' chops off 'is head. An' once you does dat, da vampyr, he ain't gonna bother nobody evuh agin.*

Now Kate had all her answers and regretted learning them. Why did she pry so? *Oh Damién.*

A dagger lay on the mantel, a sword next to it, a long blade in a shagreen scabbard, the rough, untanned leather so shabby and worn Kate wondered why Damién would possess such a thing. He never wore a sword and the weapon looked nothing like those she'd seen some gentlemen wear so she assumed it must be inherited. Another family relic, like the antique wine bottles, and the tapestries.

She had a brief wonder if the others knew what their master was . . . Georges hadn't already used a knife to end his existence. Was it fear? Could it possibly be loyalty?

Was it left to her to be the one?

'Tis his *sword, one he used in some other life, and now* . . . She hurried to the mantel. *Now, it will be used to end this one.*

Was there was irony in that?

The blade was so heavy it nearly fell from her hand as she pulled it from the scabbard, clanging to the floor. Fearfully, Kate glanced back at the bed. No movement, no reaction.

She dragged the sword over to the bed, the point of the blade digging into the carpet. It took all her strength to raise it above her head, muscles in her arms tensing to bring it down.

Am I strong enough? Can I sever his spine with one cut?

For several minutes, she stood with the blade of the sword poised. Doubt staying her hand.

Damién has never threatened me. He may be a creature of the night, an undead corpse preying upon the living, but he's offered me only kindness and friendship. He saved me. But . . . How many people has he killed?

The sword fell to her side. She dragged it back to the hearth, returning it to its scabbard. Then, she rearranged the draperies so no one would know they had been disturbed, and left the room, setting the lock. As it snapped shut behind her, she ran to her own room, throwing herself on the bed where she sobbed out her confusion.

She stayed there the rest of the day, answering Zephorah's knock, "Miss Kate, you be all right?" with the excuse that she was tired and would be down when Master Damién came home. When she heard his door open and his footsteps descending the stairs, she waited a few moments, then got up and went to the ironstone pitcher and basin on a nearby commode, washing the tears from her face and joining him downstairs.

Told by Georges of her taking to her bed during the day, Damién inquired after her health. He appeared no different than he had ever been, though her perception of him was now changed. Pleading the excuse of having not slept well for several nights, she returned to her room soon after dinner.

She waited until he had gone, waited until the house was silent before she returned to the kitchen and once more got the key. Locking the door behind her, she took the chair to the other side of the bed where anyone entering wouldn't be able to see her, and sat, waiting for Damién to return.

The sound of the door opening awakened her. Kate straightened in the chair, watching as Damién came into the bed chamber. He didn't see her, removing his coat and placing it on the chest at the foot of the bed. As he began to unfasten his stock, unwinding it from around his neck, she saw there was a dark stain on his shirt-front, red spattering the neckpiece, and a corresponding smear at the corner of those full lips.

Taking a deep breath, she got to her feet and that made him notice her.

"Kate?" His hands stilled in unwrapping the stock. "What are you doing here?"

"Waiting for you." She walked to where he stood, stopping a few feet away, out of reach.

"My chambers aren't the best place for that." He spoke in a chiding tone, still sounded so much like the man she had come to trust it tore at her heart.

"I wanted to be certain I saw you when you returned. Why did you go out?"

"Must we go over this again?" His tone held sight irritation at having to repeat himself. "My businesses . . ."

"At so late an hour?" she interrupted.

He looked surprised that she still questioned him. "There was an emergency."

"Don't lie to me more, Damién."

Nothing to do but tell him, Get it over with. No matter what happens.

"I know the truth. I saw you. Lying in that bed like a dead man." She waved a hand at the draperies. "I know what you are."

"What am I, Kate?" He released the stock, hands falling to his sides. "What is the truth?"

"You're a monster." She had to keep from crying as she said it. "A demon preying on the people of this town. How many of Charleston's citizens have you killed?"

He exhaled a deep sigh. That startled her because it

sounded like relief . . . and resignation.

"I kill no one. I . . . take . . . what I need and tell them to forget."

His confessing so easily shook her. His voice was quiet, though his look was wary, like that of a wild animal sighting an enemy.

"So. Now I've confessed to you. What will you do with the knowledge? Will you betray me to the authorities?"

Though common sense told her not to, she met his gaze, seeing nothing but sadness in their depths.

"You've been kind to me, Damién. You've never threatened or harmed me. How could I ever betray you?" Kate stepped closer, so close he could seize her if he wished . . . and kill her. "You said you wanted a woman who'd accept you in spite of what you are."

She touched his cheek, startled by the heat pulsing through it, wondering briefly whose blood caused that warmth. Her fingers trailed to his lips, wiping away the red smear.

"I'm that woman, and I'll keep your secret because I love you.

When she kissed him, she was startled by the strength with which his arms went around her, crushing her body against his. His mouth pressed hers, lips forcing her own open, tongue intruding to claim her own. She could taste that cold, bitter tang upon it . . . abruptly becoming sharp and hot and sweet.

She pulled away to whisper, "Make me yours. Tonight."

Damién eagerly obeyed.

Carrying Kate to the bed, he taught her a man could love with passion while still being gentle.

Damién's loving brought with it an ecstasy Kate had

never realized could exist. Nothing Josiah had done to her had prepared her for it.

She's expected pain and brutality, briefly shrank from sight of the stiff, spear of flesh aiming at her. Realizing her fear, even after her declaration, he'd restrained himself, calming her with kisses and caresses until the moment she touched him without hesitation. When she responded and her body lay suppliant and liquid under his . . . when he rested between her slender thighs, sliding inside that narrow wetness, Kate felt her fear melt into astonishment and pleasure.

There were tears, but of relief, stifled against his shoulder before the passion engulfed them again and again. Twice more he loved her that night and when at last they slept, it was in each other's arms, with an exhausted contentment Damién was certain few men and women had ever given each other.

"You're mine, now, Kate. Be assured I'll protect you forever." No mention was made of his turning her. As with Konstancza, he'd made that clear. "I'll never take your blood or attempt to make you as myself. If that happens, 'twill be because you ask me of your own free will."

She started to speak, but warm fingers pressed against her lips.

"*Non*, don't say anything now. That's something you must give much thought, not decide while passion overwhelms you."

Obediently, Kate kept quiet. Though certain of Damién's devotion, and in the fire of her delight in discovering the pleasure his body could give, she felt ready to set about achieving what she desired most.

* * *

Damién's happiness lasted another month before Kate brought up the subject. From the moment she'd declared her love for him, he'd been so changed, she sometimes had trouble believing he was the vile creature Mariah had described to her.

Changing his feeding habits, he now went out only when the need became necessary, when the blood receded from his bones and his face became as pale as someone ill. Indeed, it was only after one or two of his mortal acquaintances remarked on his pallor that he again began to venture forth more often, all the while apologizing to Kate for doing so.

Though he had no sense of her being there, she spent a good portion of her day cuddled beside him in his bed. In spite of the plan in which she hoped to involve him, Kate truly did love Damién and wished to be with him whether he knew it or not. At night, of course, he escorted her to his chamber where he made love to her with an abandon he hadn't experienced since his first nights with the unfaithful Antoinette.

After their third night together, he'd even dared assemble Georges and the slaves in the foyer and announce to them that from that time onward, they were to consider *Missus Kate* his wife and mistress of his home, something that astonished Kate and apparently pleased the others no end if the smiles they bestowed upon the two were any indication.

It came to Kate during that time that she'd now been absent from Charleston society—or at least her aunt's portion of it—for nearly three months and hadn't really missed it one bit. Nevertheless, the desire to see Margaret and Josiah pay for her ill-treatment hadn't lessened during that time. Neither had Damién's freely given love changed her intent.

She broached the subject that night, as they sat by the fire so domestically. He with his dark wine, she with her embroidery.

"Damién, I truly love you."

"And I you, *amour.*" He smiled, looking over the rim of the goblet at her. "Is there any special reason for that declaration now?"

"No, I ... yes ... She studied the initial on the napkin on the hoop, needle tracing the delicate scarlet thread in the stitches. "I was just thinking you've taught me how physical intimacy can be a pleasure for both a man and a woman ... how ..."

"That isn't something to be discussed where others might hear, love," he chided, glancing toward the open parlor door.

She was startled to see him flush slightly. *Why shouldn't he?* she asked herself. *He fed last night.* She had come to fear his leaving her to hunt. Not for his own safety, she told herself, but because of what it would mean for her if he were apprehended and destroyed.

"I understand that, but I wished to let you know, while I had the courage to dare speak of it." She was clutching the hoop tightly, forced her hands to release it into her lap. "Josiah was so cruel to me. I-I wonder if he'd ever mistreated Mariah or Jessamine that way. If so, being slaves, they have even less recourse to justice than I."

"True," he agreed, returning to his wine. His frown told her he'd never considered the lot of slaves one way or the other, something only a person like she, who'd been nearly one of them, might. "Though I've personally never taken one of my slaves to my bed, I know 'tis a common practice."

"I'm certain there are others who are not slaves he's also violated," she persisted. Picking up the hoop, she began methodically stabbing the needle through the cloth. Again and again, not making a stitch, just puncturing the fabric. All the pain and humiliation came back to her and she wish it was the flesh of Josiah's yard she stabbed with the needle's-point.

"What are you getting at, Kate? Say it plainly."

"I wish to accuse him, Damién. Go before the magistrate and denounce him and get justice for myself and all the other women he's defiled."

"That might not be such a good idea, *chérie.*"

It surprised her when he didn't immediately agree to her plan. *Man,* she thought uncharitably. *Superior creature.*

When she scowled, he went on, "It happened over three months ago. I've made one or two trips to the tavern and found your aunt has spread the story you stole from her and ran away with a traveling whiskey drummer. If you suddenly reappear and make this accusation, I've a feeling no one will believe you."

"You think I should keep quiet?" she demanded, jabbing the needle into the cloth again. She struck her finger. A bright spot of red appeared next to the top curve of the *C.* "That even as your wife, with the backing of *le Marquis* La Croix, I would be disbelieved?"

"Even so." To his credit, he did look sad as he quashed her plans. "Our marriage is in no way legal. Though I've been more or less accepted, they would see you only as a foreigner's mistress, and a tavern owner's runaway niece who stole from the woman taking her in when her parents died."

Kate fell silent. Inwardly, she seethed, anger at Damién for what he was saying because she knew it was true, fury at Josiah and Margaret for once again being seen as the injured parties, rage at being helpless to get her revenge. She struck the needle against the embroidery frame. It snapped.

"Oh," she said matter-of-factly. "I've broken my needle." She sat there, staring at the metal hoop in her hand and at the bloody spot of her finger. "And I've stuck my finger."

"My poor darling." Immediately he was out of his chair and kneeling beside her, taking the injured hand in his. He kissed the tiny wound, tongue caressing her finger, licking away the blood.

Kate shivered as a flash of desire swept through her. She fought to subdue it.

I mustn't let him distract me. Not now.

Looking up at her, he smiled. "I know you wish retribution, but 'twill be best to let the whole thing go. Forget it. You have me and I swear no one will ever hurt you again. Let it die."

"Of course," she managed to murmur, while silently swearing, *Something will die all right, but it won't be my desire for revenge.*

* * *

It wasn't Damién's night to hunt so he made love to Kate instead. It was glorious and as passionate as always, and as she lay panting, near-faint beneath him, she was almost persuaded to give up her plan.

Almost.

Once her heartbeat slowed and breathing quieted, and Damién lay beside her in that condition he called *Unsleep,* the thoughts came thundering back.

Around five o'clock, she got up, dressing quickly. Taking from the mantel the dagger lying beside the sword, she tucked it into her sleeve as she hurried from the house before Georges or the others stirred. Though it was still dark, the nearing of the sun to the horizon in preparation to rise would keep Damién captivated in sleep. Kate knew what she had to do, and she decided to go ahead and do it. Before she weakened and allowed Damién's love to make her change her plans.

Reaching town, she hastened along the street leading to her aunt's home. As at Damién's residence, no one was stirring yet. In fact, very few people were on the streets at that very early hour. Hurrying to the back of the house, Kate stood on tiptoe, feeling around the top of the door frame. Margaret had secreted a key there; Josiah was always forgetting his own, especially on the days when he took over the late nights at the tavern. Now, his forgetfulness would be his downfall.

She found the key, opened the door and went inside, tossing it upon the table.

The house was quiet; only a few squeaks and pops of settling timbers broke the silence. Kate started up the backstairs, pausing once as she stepped on a board that creaked loudly. After a few moments, she continued climbing.

On the second floor, she hurried to the room her aunt

shared with Josiah. Even if she hadn't known the way, the loud snores issuing through the closed door would've guided her.

Outside, she paused a moment, then pulled the dagger from her sleeve. Her heart was beating so fast, she could barely breathe. Briefly, she thought of Damién and the love he offered and what he'd said. What she would lose if she went through that door. She brushed it aside.

They don't deserve to live.

Pushing open the door, she went in.

She did it so quickly it was a disappointment. Neither Josiah nor Margaret awakened as she hovered over them, slashing the blade across their throats in one swift motion. They were lying so close together, she made one cut do for both. There were only a couple of liquid gurgles as they tried to breathe and began to strangle in their own blood, then a spasmodic twitching of limbs and both bodies lay still.

The amount of blood surprised her, it seemed to splash everywhere . . . upon the walls, the headboard, all over the bedclothes and herself.

Is this how it is when Damién hunts? Except for that one time, she'd never seen any blood about his person at all. She was also startled to feel a violent disappointment. *Why don't I feel better? I did what I wanted. Made them both pay. Why don't I feel vindicated?*

All she really felt was stunned, a dull, hard ache in her chest as if she'd been struck a heavy blow or run into something knocking the wind from her.

Turning, she walked out of the room and down the backstairs. In the kitchen, she found Mariah stacking kindling in the fireplace to make a fire. Margaret always unlocked the kitchen door allowing the slave inside before she went to the tavern.

"You needn't do that, Mariah," she said calmly, stopping at the foot of the stairs.

The slave jumped, dropping the log she held as she spun around. "Lawd, Miss Kate. Where'd yo' come frum? An' why doan I need ta mak' uh fiah?" She took a step closer, staring at the stains on Kate's dress. "Miss Kate, what's them marks? They looks lak blood!"

"It is." Kate caught the slave's hand and placed the knife in it. "I've killed the Master and the Mistress. To pay them back for the wicked way they treated me."

The next few hours were confused in her mind. Mariah screaming for Caleb and he forcing himself to go upstairs, then coming down gray-faced and trembling. Jessamine sent running for the magistrate who appeared, also hurried upstairs and returned as shaken as were the others crowding into the little kitchen . . . the doctor, the minister. All of them stared at Kate where she sat at the table, smiling and nodding pleasantly to each who entered.

After a lengthy discussion, they took her along to the gaol, placing her in a cell though still hesitant of housing a female there, but there were no other prisoners, so they deemed it proper considering her crime. Somewhere in all the confusion, she asked for Damién and surprisingly, they believed her story of being his wife, and notified him.

Georges told them he was out of town and would return that night. When the sun was down, he appeared at the prison door, shaken and white-faced, this time not through lack of nourishment. He didn't berate Kate as she expected, just seized her hands and kissed them and assured her he understood and would retain a lawyer to represent her.

He got the best in Charleston, and that good man filed a plea of commission of murder while of an insane turn of mind, but it did no good. Kate's confession, her emotionless attitude yet rational acknowledgement of fact did nothing in her favor. Just as Damién had warned—and Josiah before him—no one believed her story.

"Why didn't you speak up when this happened?" demanded the magister.

Her stumbling explanation that she was unable to gather her senses at that time, that only after marrying Damién had she begun to think rationally again, was received with doubt. The story Margaret had spread was accepted as the true one, and the fact that the *marquis* was absent during the two days of the trial did nothing to help her case. The jury accepted her guilt as so obvious even her husband didn't wish to be associated with her.

Kate knew she might have fed Damién to them, given him as a sacrifice to the townspeople while he lay helpless in *Unsleep*, and after the discovery of what he really was, might even accuse him of *enthralling* and making her kill for him but she refused to do that.

The jury had no choice; they found Kate guilty and sentenced her to hang.

* * *

The night before she was to die, Kate asked to see Damién. Previously, she'd sent word to him not to attempt to see her—the true reason for his absence—not wanting any more attention drawn to him than was necessary.

When he appeared, pale and wan, she immediately

asked, "You haven't been feeding? Why not?"

"In the Name of the *Unspeakable,* Kate!" he burst out. "My wife, the woman I love above all else, is going to die in the morning for double murder and you ask me why I haven't fed?"

Briefly, he looked away, running one hand through his hair. It was hanging loose about his face, just as he'd looked the night she'd first seen him as an *Undead*. She never thought she'd seen him look so distracted. His neckpiece was askew, the folds wrapped loosely, his shirt barely tucked into his britches. The handsome, self-controlled *marquis* had disappeared, only a frantic husband in his place.

"Why did you do this, Kate?"

The same question he'd asked her after his one visit that first night.

"I think you know why." She gave him a serene smile, taking his hand. "I love you, Damién. You must believe that." He kissed her fingers, kneeling beside the cot where she sat. When he looked into her eyes, she kissed him gently on the lips.

"I can't let them kill you. I won't."

It hurt her to see the love in his eyes and the deep, wild hope spring to life there.

"I once told you I'd never force you to be as I am, but . . . let me turn you, Kate. Let me save you."

She stared at him for so long, he caught her by the shoulders, shaking her slightly.

"Kate! Do you hear me?"

"It won't work." She sounded so tired, almost sluggish, shock still hanging about her like a shawl. "Mariah said a vampyr has to be killed by chopping off its head.

If I'm hanged, it'll break my neck. That's the same thing, isn't it?"

The sad look she gave him made him want to scream. "*Non.*" His hope still flared. "I-If I do it now, they'll think you died of heart failure. I can make the punctures small. They won't be noticed."

She glanced away, seeming fascinated by a cobweb hanging in a corner of the cell.

He burst out, ignoring the pain, "Kate, *for God's sake*, listen to me. Let me do it. 'Tis the only way."

Briefly, he leaned against her, face pressed into the hollow of her throat, savoring its soft warmth, listening to the slow, steady flow of her blood. It was so calm, as if she didn't have a care in the world. She touched his cheek.

"Kate. *Please*." That one word he'd spoken before, the one drawing her to him. That seemed to reach her.

He felt her nod, raised his head to stare into her eyes. Her lips barely moved as she whispered, "Yes, Damién."

"You must think of living, Kate, and nothing else." He spoke quickly, not knowing when the night-gaoler would return to send him away. "The will to live will bring you across and back to me."

Getting to his feet, he pulled her off the cot, pressing his mouth to hers.

One last kiss . . . to last a lifetime for me . . . forever for you, she thought as his lips slid from her mouth to her throat. She felt them caress the vein, licking it gently.

He often did that while they made love, running his fangs up and down in time to the pulsations. She'd never feared he would do more. Now, she didn't care. She didn't wince or even react when they sank in, and his mouth clamped over the wounds to prevent any telltale drops from spilling onto her collar.

There was nothing but that gentle, almost loving, sucking, as he drew her blood into his body, as the whispers started in her brain, getting louder and louder as she became weaker and weaker.

Kate refused to listen.

She didn't want to hear the whispers, didn't intend to pass from one life to another, more immortal one. *I do not wish to live,* she concentrated on that one phrase instead of the will to survive. Though she loved Damién, she didn't wish to become as he, had no desire to even continue living now that she'd had her revenge.

We never took wedding vows, my darling Damién. They contain the words 'Till death do us part . . . and now death shall part us . . . Forever . . . I'm sorry, I can't go with you . . .

"Goodbye, my love," she whispered so quietly he barely heard as her body went limp in his arms.

Damién held her for a moment, then lowered her gently to the cot. Sitting beside her, he held her hand and waited . . . and waited . . . until he felt the tug of the sun just below the horizon and the equal pull of *Unsleep*.

When Kate hadn't roused by that time, he knew she wasn't coming back, that it wasn't simply a delay as it had been with Antoinette and Armand. She'd never planned to *Cross Over*, but had let him think it to escape the shame of being executed for something she felt was a just action.

She used me. But she loved me, I know she did. She gave herself to me freely, though I promised her only my protection . . . and . . . she did say, Goodbye, my love.

Sighing, he released Kate's cold hand and called for the night-gaoler, and when the man arrived, blinking and rubbing his eyes, he took a deep breath and said in a trembling voice that was in no way feigned, "M-my wife . . . I think she's dead. I don't know what happened . . . w-we were talking and she . . . collapsed . . ."

He stood aside as the man unlocked the cell and rushed in, didn't hear what was said as he bent over Kate's body. All he could hear were those last words she had spoken.

Goodbye, my love . . .

I lost again, and this time, through no fault of my own. Or was it? If I'd agreed to help Kate, we might have been forced to leave Charleston but at least she would have lived to go with me.

As it was, her death was declared heart failure. She was buried in a small plot I purchased in the common cemetery, far away from her perfidious aunt and uncle's graves. I put the house up for sale and the Marquis La Croix left town the night after the funeral, seeking to bury his grief in travel. All I took with me was a single unfinished dinner napkin monogrammed with a crimson initial C, embroidered by Kate's own sweet hand.

In his elegy to his friend, Lord Tennyson says, "Tis better to have loved and lost than never to have loved at all. I might disagree with him there. Being one who has loved many times and always lost, I can only envy those who've never felt the sweet sting of passion and the equal stab of grief. For years afterward, I questioned whether Kate truly loved me or if she simply saw in me a haven until she could convince me to kill for her and when I refused, decided to proceed alone.

I prefer to cling to the final words she spoke to me, to believe that though she never intended to follow me into the darkness, she still had enough love for me to tell me goodbye with her dying breath.

After all other thoughts of her have been buried in the past, this is the one I choose to take with me into the future.

After losing Kate, I mostly ignored the rest of the Eighteenth Century, wandering disconsolately through it, waiting for a New Age to dawn. My meanderings brought me to New Orleans, where I was pleased to find the Creole lifestyle pleasant and more to my liking than the rest of the country at that moment. At least we spoke the same language—with some variations—and their customs made me feel somewhat at home. Even its many superstitions, the gris-gris, the celebrations of Baron Samedi, the Guedes or Spirits of Death, Le Grand Zombi, its many loa, and the practices of Marie Laveau did nothing to discomfort me during my stay . . . though sometimes those very customs were employed against me.

After all, Louisiana was a large state; there was enough room for me and all the practitioners of voodoo and obeah to survive more or less amicably.

I only grew dissatisfied with the arrival of that intense civil discord calling itself The War Between the States, or as the Southerners termed it, "The War of Northern Aggression." In later centuries, it would be termed the "Civil War of the States," but I always wonder, when has a war ever been civil? Whatever the meaning of the word, nevertheless, it was in itself a surfeit of bloody delight for the sans mort.

How profitable for the Undead Mankind's little aggressions have been!

We roamed the battlefields, draining the dead, releasing those still living from their torment, and in some cases, our ranks grew, as those who fought to survive rose to join us in our prowls.

Afterward, when New Orleans was occupied by conquering Union troops and those curfews and other atrocities were performed *upon that fair city, I deemed it time to depart for safer ground. So, one freezing night in December, I packed my coffin and stole away into the night . . . Heading West, as did many others also disenchanted and disenfranchised from life as they had known it.*

California, there I went! *Full of as much hope for a new life as they.*

The next century brought with it the promise of many things new and different . . . suffragettes . . . flappers . . . hippies . . . bath tub gin, pot, and love beads . . . Women's Lib—and wasn't that a delight, to actually be the prey for a change?—and wars enough to fill the entire world with blood. World Wars One and Two and all that followed were masterpieces of destruction to sate the most ravenous sans mort. Then there was the atomic bomb and threat of nuclear annihilation to all. Except my kind, of course. I walked through it untouched by that emotion I still sought.

I welcomed the New Millennium with hope. That with the beginning of a second thousand years, my search would soon be over.

CHAPTER 6

*Beth
Los Angeles, California
March 17, 2011*

Making a kiss at her image, Bess applied lipstick with a flourish.

Now for a little blush to remove the pallor from those wan cheeks. The brush flicked over high-sculpted bones. *Perfect!* Her face glowed vibrantly with Life—enough life for several people, in fact.

Critically, she studied her face in the mirror.

Is it wavering slightly? Were the edges becoming just a bit unfocused—or was it simply her imagination? She peered closely at the image. No, it was just as Damién had promised, as it had been yesterday when she looked at it . . . and the day before that . . . and the day before . . . and . . .

Not like poor Damién who had to concentrate to hold his likeness in the glass. Of course, he was *terribly* ancient, and she supposed as he got older, some powers were bound to slip just a *little*. It must give him a totally *helpless* feeling knowing he'd conquered the centuries, but once in a while forgetting exactly *how many* centuries it had been.

Vaguely, Bess wondered what would happen when she, at last, became like Damién. Would they have to find someone to care for both of them as she cared for him now? A paranormal caregiver of sorts?

Well, tonight, she wasn't going to worry about any future aging, or lack of it. Tonight, she was going out and having some *fun*! She was young, she was beautiful, she was wearing a new, red sequined mini-sheath, and Mark was waiting for her at a rave; she'd meet him there and they'd dance and kiss and . . .

Bess laughed out loud, then quickly stifled the sound before Damién could hear.

Tonight is my night to howl! Even if not very loudly. *Mark and I.*

Damién didn't know about Mark. So far, she'd managed to keep him secret.

How lucky can one girl get? An immortal lover and *a human one. And I don't know which is more scrumptious.* She thought of Damién's handsome face and Mark's won't-quit body. And their accompanying accessories. *Yum!*

Leaving her room, she tiptoed down the hall, stiletto heels in hand, pausing before the thick oak door with the brass fittings indicating the many locks and latches installed on the other side. Evidence of Damién's current paranoia. Taking a deep breath, she called softly, "Damién? Are you awake? I'm leaving now."

Do I actually expect him to answer?

The sun hadn't set though it was nearly eight o'clock, so he probably wasn't even conscious. *Damn that Daylight Savings Time!* Sometimes she felt as if it had been put into effect just to bedevil them.

"Dami?" She tried again, raising her voice slightly,

calling him by that nickname, knowing how he hated it.

My name is Damién, he had told her once, haughtily. *No one calls me Dami, and you won't, either.* But she did. Just to annoy him.

Like now.

She hated leaving him alone, wished he'd come with her though she knew the reason he wouldn't. Bess was well aware why he never left the house.

That damned accident.

Before then, she and Damién went out often. They had laughed together in the night and walked among the people in the city, relishing the noise and the crowds while he savored the lusty excitement for *Life* humans possessed, as well as those humans themselves, but now . . . ?

He was afraid to leave the protection the house offered. *Agoraphobia,* that's what he had, a morbid fear of crowds and open places, if that was possible. If it hadn't been so tragic, it would have been disgusting.

The accident did more than instill fear in Damién. The pain of his healing also drove Bess from his bed. Though she later returned when he was once more whole, renewing their love with its old passion, their *Closeness* had ended. Always afterward she would leave him to go back to the little bedroom at the end of the hall, to sleep.

As he did.

In silent isolation.

"Dami—"

She could envision him lying in the king-size bed. He had also developed a fear of enclosed spaces. Removing all furniture from the room. Pulling the draperies from the four-poster. Demanding to lie on satin sheets under which a thin layer of that odd paprika-red soil from the riverbed near his long-forgotten home had been spread. She could almost see him, imprisoned in the *Sleep-that-isn't-Sleep*, one hand curled on the pillow near his cheek (*none of that arms-folded-over-the-chest crap for Damién La Croix!*) with the gleaming black satin covering his cold, beautiful body.

Bess glanced at her watch, fidgeting impatiently. *Five after eight.* Mark was waiting.

She bent to slip on her shoes.

"Damién, I'm going. If you get hungry, there's something in the fridge—"

Still no answer.

She was almost to the stairs when the voice came—inside her head—startling her so she stumbled and clutched at the banister to keep from falling.

Beth . . . *Beth?* . . . *BETH!*

She recovered, snapping, "I wish you wouldn't do that!"

It didn't hurt but it always shocked her a little, a violent wiggle in the center of her brain, accompanied by the most delicious little chill, like someone running two fingers up her spine before lightly slapping the back of her head.

Sorry . . .

But he wasn't. Otherwise, he wouldn't keep doing it. His voice, like a whisper within her mind, went on, *You know I don't like leftovers. I'll wait and dine when you get back. Bring me something.*

"Damién, no!" She let a whine creep into her voice. "Not tonight. Just this once, can't I come back by myself?"

As usual, her wishes were ignored. *Pick up a burger or something for yourself. You know I hate to eat alone.*

Abruptly, he was gone, leaving in her mind that brief emptiness his departure always created.

"Okay," Bess muttered in defeat, wishing rebelliously Damién was *normal*. Wishing he would somehow find the courage to leave the house again. Wondering how she was going to explain to Mark when she had to leave him early to shop for Damién's *meal*.

Quickly, as if expecting to feel his voice calling her back, she ran down the stairs.

As she opened the door and stepped out into the coolness of the early evening twilight, Bess asked herself once again why she'd ever gotten involved with a vampire.

* * *

Lying in the cocoon of mind-darkness, Damién sensed her absence, body crying out at the loss. He needed Beth, loved her. She, of all of the women he had known since Konstancza now made his journey through Time bearable.

Because she'd stayed with him.

He was still thankful he'd decided to *walk* that night and had cut through the alley behind the little club, coming upon the two figures struggling in the dark.

A man and a woman . . . her purse lying on the concrete, a pair of twisted, hand-rolled joints and a cigarette lighter beside them . . .

It was obvious what had happened; they'd stepped outside to light up. The girl was either already stoned or drunk and her companion wanted something more than a little smoke. She hadn't been high enough not to refuse, but too wasted to fend him off. He easily overcame her through sheer strength, had her on the pavement, straddling her body as she kicked and flailed beneath him.

Damién, waiting for the outcome with a *voyeur's* interest, was rewarded with a luscious view of slim legs in black fishnet stockings, white flesh peeping over their tops as she struggled and bucked beneath the heavy weight pinning her down. As a backhanded swipe knocked her momentarily unconscious, he decided it was time to step in.

Leaping the ten feet separating them, he seized her attacker, hurling him against the row of trash cans at the opposite building's back door. As he'd expected, the man was a coward when confronted with someone more or less his own size.

He picked himself up, stared at Damién a moment, taking in the tall figure as well as the thickness of the chest and arms in the dark jacket. With a deep breath, he disappeared down the alley at a hobbling run, thus saving his life, and Damién turned back to the girl, the one he was *really* interested in.

She lay half-sprawled on the pavement, skirt hiked up to reveal a truly delectable length of thigh, looking up at him with a highly unfocused stare. When he held out his hand, she smiled drunkenly, taking in the shoulder length dark hair and his elegant but somber clothing.

"Thanks, my hero."

Wavering briefly, she successfully placed her own hand, carefully manicured with black-lacquered nails, in his after the third try. He pulled her to her feet.

Eyes so black-rimmed they looked bruised stared at him. He'd always marveled at the Goth's penchant for black-on-white make-up while he layered on tanning solution to give his own pallid complexion color. *If only they knew*...

"I'm Nightshade," she whispered in what she considered a seductive manner, he supposed. To his ears, she merely sounded out of breath.

Damién laughed. "No one's called Nightshade. What's your real name?"

She didn't argue, simply answered, "Elizabeth... Elizabeth Ann..."

"Well, Elizabeth Ann... Ah, yes... *Elizabeth, Eliza, Betsy, and Bess... all went together to seek a bird's nest... they found a bird's nest with five eggs in it... they each took one and left four in it*..."

She was looking at him now as if he'd lost his mind. Probably thought him stoned out of it, another patron who fortuitously stumbled outside in time to be a dark knight.

"Now, which one are you? None of the above, I think. Beth, perhaps?"

She nodded.

"Then... Beth, let's get out of here."

"What about the rave?" She made a little grimace, nodding toward the still-open back door to the club.

"Come with me and you'll get more than a rave." He nudged the trampled joints with the toe of his boot, kicking them toward the trash cans. "And a better high than these can ever give."

"Is that a promise?" She hesitated. Not from fear, he thought, but weighing her options.

"More than a promise, I assure you." He made his leer comical enough not to seem threatening. "Come with me, babe, and I'll give you something you've never had before."

"Promises, promises." She affected boredom.

"Not a promise, my dear. Whatever I say, I deliver."

That did it. She gave him a much wider smile, linking her arm through his as she wobbled against him to keep her balance, and gazed up at him with eyes owlishly dilated.

"Cool."

She had come home with him, to the house behind the wrought-iron fence past the avenue of dark trees. When she learned what he was, she accepted it with only the slightest of protests. "But I thought you were just a *Goth*—not a *real*—you know."

It was almost a year before she could say the word *vampire* aloud. Now, three years had passed, and he had been more than happy in Beth's presence ever since.

And then, he had his accident . . .

How could he ever explain how he felt that day, when the sun had risen, striking the trees—and then himself, as he lay helpless in the grasp of the drug-saturated blood he had taken from that intoxicated body in the alley?

Eyes dazzled by visions of screaming stars and shattering bursts of light, while his fingers frantically groped along the walls of buildings seeming to bend and melt under his touch. Clawing through the dark alleyways like a blind man, he hadn't dared try to *transform* and fly, the ability seemed taken from him. He couldn't remember *how*. But somehow, he made it as far as the long driveway curving off the highway past the stand of pines before collapsing completely.

Tiny rivulets of fire were feeding on his bones as the first ray of sunshine struck. His clothes began to smolder, centuries-old flesh igniting like brittle paper touched by a match.

Beth saved him, dragging him up the drive and into the safety of the house but the damage was done. Having been caught in daylight, once seared by the purifying touch of the sun and, knowing it might happen again, Damién refused to leave the house. It became his refuge, his haven.

He no longer went to his victims; now, they came to him.

Now, he sent Beth out at night, and she never came back alone . . .

* * *

"*Shhh.*" Beth put a finger to her lips as she opened the front door. "We've got to be *very* quiet."

"Why?" Mark asked. "Do you have a roommate?"

She hadn't wanted to bring him here but he insisted. After all, they had enjoyed innumerable hours at *his* place. Now, it was *her* turn to play hostess. She'd definitely wanted Mark to make love to her in her own bed since that first night but—why, *why?*—did he want to do it *tonight*, with Damién, craving and empty, lurking upstairs?

In fear of what would happen, she'd refused him for months, but tonight, still angry at Damién's demand, something reckless and rebellious stirred within her, and she'd agreed.

Dami will never know, she told herself. His feeding schedule was off-kilter. He refused nourishment for weeks at a time, lately had developed a tendency to keep sleeping to ward off hunger pangs. And when Damién slept, it was a true *Sleep of the Dead.* If they were quiet, he'd never sense they were there.

I can handle Damién, Beth kept repeating. By the time

they got to the house, she'd convinced herself she could get away with her scheme.

He'll just have to go hungry, she decided defiantly. Tonight was *her* night, and hers, alone. After Mark had gone, she'd awaken Dami and tell him some lie as to why she hadn't brought anyone home with her. He'd believe her. He had no reason not to. And tomorrow night... She'd make it up to him.

Looking up at Mark, she said, "No, not a roommate, exactly."

"Who, then?" He leaned toward her, starting to kiss her again, not really interested in the answer she gave whenever he raised his head.

"My..."

Kiss.

"...employer..."

Kiss, mmm.

"...he's an..."

Kiss, lick, kiss.

"...old guy..."

Kiss, tongue, tongue.

"...really ancient..."

Kiss, kiss, kiss.

"...an invalid..."

"And you're his nurse?" He was only mildly curious, went back to dragging his tongue across her earlobe again.

"In a way." She pulled out of his embrace and tiptoed toward the stairs, tugging on his hand gently. Silently, Mark followed her.

As they passed Damién's door, she pointed at it and put her finger to her lips again. Mark nodded and copied the gesture, and they went by quietly, not making another sound until they were inside her own room with the door safely shut. After that, there wasn't much need for talk. Mark quickly got her out of the red sequins and lost his own clothes somewhere. He was more than ready, cock stiff and straining as he scooped her into his arms. Then, they were together on the bed in a pleasant tangle of bare flesh and satin sheets.

He rolled against her, body warm and eager, planting a row of kisses across her shoulder and up her neck. As his mouth lingered on her throat, Beth momentarily felt a desire for Damién's cold-as-ice kisses. For an instant, she missed that delicious tingle surging through her as she felt those chill fang-tips gently grazing her flesh.

In a few moments, the warmth of Mark's touch drove away the longing. She closed her eyes, allowing herself to become lost in his humanness, wanting his mortal lovemaking now as she would also want Damién when he touched her. When he loved her with that cold mouth and pressed his icy flesh against hers and his climax filled her like the flood of a snow-filled river.

Mark gave her pleasure and more than once she had to stifle the cries she could have given. Each thrust and retreat burned like a fiery spear of flesh as it penetrated the tunnel of her body, then slid free to invade again. Oh yes, her Mark was a shagmaster *par excellence*.

You're so good, handsome mortal boy. So delicious and you fuck so fine. She wanted to scream it at him, bit her lip instead. Yet when she felt the rush of his heated release, heard his final groan muffled against her breast, the thought still came, *How dare I compare any living man to Dami?*

Afterwards, with Mark half-dozing, she sat studying

his naked body, letting her gaze rove possessively over it. Reaching out, she cupped his resting cock in her hand as if weighing its power. She bowed her head to press a kiss against the soft smoothness of its crown, letting her tongue brush languidly. Then, she satisfied herself again, teeth pressed to his unresisting flesh to suck his blood to the surface and directly through the skin, making a deliciously brutal *hickey*. She was becoming quite adept; it was a power she'd just discovered in herself, one helping her understand Damién better. She told herself it bonded her closer to him, a surprising bonus of their association, though he was yet unaware of it.

Later, she kissed Mark consolingly on the thigh, lips grazing the sensitive flesh gently before raising her head to study his face, relaxed and depleted now of its passion. He and Damién would seem the same age, she realized, until one learned otherwise. Mark had blue eyes and dark hair, also . . .

. . . just like Dami.

Why hadn't she noticed before that they looked so much alike? Had she deliberately chosen Mark because of that resemblance, wanting to be loved by a *living* Damién as well as an *Undead* one?

This revelation made her stiffen slightly. As if sensing the movement, Mark came wide awake, reaching out to pull her back to lie beside him. "Come here, you."

Before she could say anything, the bedroom door slowly swung open, and they looked up to see Damién framed in the doorway.

He was wearing a pink turtleneck sweater and jeans. In spite of the long black hair lying unbound about his shoulders, he looked as un-vampirelike as anyone could.

THE NIGHTMAN'S ODYSSEY

In fact, he appeared a little curious, frowning slightly as he peered in. A young man wandering in to see what a roomie was up to.

In that moment, none of them moved. When he took a step into the room, breaking the spell, Mark seized the sheet, pulling it up to hide Beth's nakedness and his own.

"Who the Hell are you?"

Damién ignored him, one hand going to the malachite pendant around his neck, stroking it gently as he always did when he was upset. "Beth, I thought you were going to let me know when you got back."

For a moment, his accent was very pronounced.

"I-I . . ." For the first time in her life, she couldn't look at him.

Mark was still stuttering angrily and that focused Damién's attention on him.

"You weren't very quiet, you know. You woke me as soon as you opened the front door."

"Beth?" Mark looked at her, eyes narrowing. "*He's* your employer? The sick old guy?"

"Is that what you told him?" Damién laughed, displaying gleaming canines. "*Bethie.*" He shook his head as if chiding a naughty child.

"What in God's name is going on here?"

Damién flinched, taking a step backward, rasping out, *"Don't say that!"*

Before Mark could move, he had recovered and was sitting on the edge of the bed, looking into the blue eyes, immediately noting their likeness to each other.

"Tell me, Elizabeth." Those pale eyes turned toward her, then flicked back at Mark again. "Is this an accident or do you want me to feast upon myself?"

"Please, Dami, don't." Beth found her voice. "I *love* him."

In one of the few moments of cruelty she'd ever seen from him, Damién pursed his lips slightly, looked falsely injured, and said, "And all this time I thought you loved *me*." Shrugging, he turned to Mark. "*Women*. Who can understand them?"

By now, Mark had recovered. "Now, wait a minute! I don't know what's going on between you two—"

"That's obvious," Damién agreed, his voice dangerously quiet.

"—but whatever it is, it looks a little kinky, and if you think I'm going to join your little party—"

"My dear Mark, you already have." His reply was too soft.

That stopped whatever Mark had been going to say. "How do you know my name?"

"I know everything. *Everything!*" He hissed the last word at Beth, and she felt fear stab through her as she realized how foolish she'd been to think she could keep Mark's existence from him.

One hand went to her mouth as she looked away, knowing what was coming. Knowing she couldn't prevent it. She'd brought Mark here. Brought him here and placed him in Damién's hands. *A lamb thrust into the jaws of a wolf.*

"This wasn't supposed to happen," she whispered. "Dami, please . . . please, don't."

"Don't worry, Beth." An icy hand went under her chin, lifting it, forcing her to look at him. "I'm not jealous. Believe me, I understand."

"Well, *I* don't!" Mark put in petulantly.

"I'll treat him just like all the others." Damién ignored

his interjection. "I promise."

"*Others?*" Mark echoed. He was making frantic movements to get out of bed. Damién's weight on one side of the sheet and Beth' grasp of its other corner prevented him. "What others?"

"Just be still . . ." Damién said, conversationally. His hands went to the bare shoulders. ". . . and it won't hurt a bit."

"*Don't touch him!*" Beth' voice was shrill. "He's not for you, Dami."

"Now, just a min—" Mark began.

Beth's hand struck his chest, knocking him out of the way. Momentarily breathless, he lay there, watching Damién and his girl snarling at each other over his prone body.

Like dogs over a bone.

It was the last coherent thought he would have for quite some time.

"If he's not for me, who *is* he for?" Damién demanded.

"*Me*, that's who," Beth shouted recklessly. "He's *mine*."

"Well, hell, can't you *share?*"

"Not this time."

"And what am *I* to do? Damn it, Beth. I'm hungry. I need *sustenance*."

"It's not my fault you keep going on these starvation diets," she flung at him. "You know it's not healthy to continuously skip meals."

"You know I've been gaining weight—" Damién began.

Folding her arms over her breasts, Beth shook her head stubbornly.

At that point, Damién's hunger got the best of his control. Eyes alight with a feral brilliance, he seized Mark by the shoulders, lunging with open mouth, three weeks' craving driving him against the unprotected body. Before the hapless young man could move, his fang-tips sought the vein and struck.

Mark fought to escape, sheer terror engulfing his mind. One fist pounding Damién's chest, the other hand grasped at a sleeve of the pink sweater, trying to escape from the drawing, insistent mouth.

Don't fight, a voice whispered. It seemed to be coming at him from all sides. *Relax . . . accept . . .* A haze of shadows filled his brain . . . His ears were ringing . . .

"Dami. *No.*" With a scream, Beth came to life. She fell on him, beating his shoulders with ineffectual fists as she saw Damién's body heave with the pleasure the *Taking* was giving him.

Mark's body stiffened, jerking slightly. With a single ecstatic sigh, his eyes rolled upward, and he went limp in his captor's embrace, lax fingers slipping from the pink cashmere.

Giving a deep shuddering breath, Damién released Mark, laying him upon the pillow. The neck-wound was ugly, the edges ragged and bloody, not his usual neat little pin-prick bite. He'd been *too* hungry . . .

As he straightened to face Beth, there was blood running down his chin. It dripped onto the front of the sweater, a red drool making a contrasting crimson spatter against the soft pink. Pulling a handkerchief from his pocket, he wiped his mouth.

"I'm sorry. I didn't mean to—" came from behind the white cloth rapidly becoming red-stained. "Damn, it's s-so *pure*. He doesn't smoke, drink *or* use drugs, does he? Where did you find this kid, anyway? A Sunday School ice cream social?"

Beth didn't answer. She was looking at Mark's unmoving body, and the gaping tear in his throat where the blood was starting to dry.

"You've killed him," she whispered, the words a flat monotone. Her throat felt scorched, filled with centuries of dust.

"No, I haven't." Damién returned the handkerchief to his pocket and smiled at her. A missed drop of blood ran down one incisor, glistened on its tip, and fell onto his lower lip. He licked it away. "I didn't take any more from him than any of the others, in spite of the rather ungentle way I did it. In a few hours, he'll be wide awake and ready for some of your tender loving care. Which I give you my permission to ladle out as enthusiastically as necessary."

Damned generous of you, she thought. Aloud, she said, "He's dead, Dami. He's not breathing."

"Nonsense." He bent over the pale body, staring at the still chest. His nostrils quivered slightly as if scenting something. Then he straightened to look at her in total surprise. "He— Did he have a weak heart?"

"Mark was as healthy as a horse."

"How could he die?" He looked bewildered. "I didn't take enough to kill him."

"It would if someone else had fed, before you . . ." Beth began.

"*Who?*" Damién turned on her so quickly she jumped. She didn't answer, simply looked guilty. "You?" He didn't believe her. "*How?*"

He touched the boy's chin. Mark's head lolled, baring

the damaged neck. "There aren't any other wounds."

She flipped back the sheet, exposing the naked body. The answer was obvious. Damién stared at the blue vein in the groin-bend of the waxen thigh, at the little red scabs dotting it like needle-tracks. The look he turned on her was murderous.

He seemed to be choking.

"You never said it had to be taken from the *throat*," she said defiantly.

"And he *let* you?"

"He never knew. I did it *afterward*. After we loved. Quite often, as a matter of fact. While he slept, then ordered him to ignore it. I did it again tonight . . ." Her voice trailed before rising defensively, "I just wanted to know if I could."

"How? I haven't turned you, Beth. How could you—"

A negligent shrug. She had no answer for that, really. "It was an experiment. I just want to be like you, Dami. You know that."

"*Sweet Unspeakable Name!*" Beth was still mortal. He'd never expected she might develop a desire for the dark wine, or an extension of his own powers. "A fine time for you to decide to become Madame Curie. This is just great."

"I didn't like it," she replied, as if that made it all right.

"Liar," Damién snapped. "Why do you keep doing it, then?"

She didn't answer, looking away.

Damién stood up, raking one hand through his hair.

"Do you realize you've made me a murderer? Seven hundred and sixty-two years I've been careful. And now?" He gestured toward the window. "It's an hour before sunrise and I've a corpse on my hands!"

"It'll be okay, won't it?" she asked. He gave her a blank look. "I mean, in a little while, won't he *arise*? H-he'll be like you? *Undead*?"

He took a deep breath, trying to control his anger and at the same time wanting to laugh at her stupidity. "I hate to disappoint you, darling, but it doesn't work that way. *Un-Life* has to be *bestowed*. It's been over two hundred years since I've done it." With his Kate; seven hundred since Antoinette and Armand. Two failures, one success. "I doubt if I remember how."

"Is that why you've never *turned* me?" Briefly, she looked disappointed. *In him or in his admission?*

He ignored that. "Your young man is dead, Beth. Totally and irretrievably."

"Oh no."

"Save your grief," he snapped. "We need to worry about ourselves right now." Quickly, he looked around the room. "Where are his clothes?"

"Mark's dead? Really *dead*?" Beth's voice was soft. And lost.

"As the proverbial doornail, my dear," came Damién's cold reply. "Here." He picked up the garments lying on the chest at the foot of the bed, tossing her the shirt.

Beth caught it, clutching it to her breast. *Mark's shirt*. Mark, whom she'd helped to kill by taking his blood and weakening him. There was a tiny pink spot on the front, where she'd splashed her pomegranate margarita while trying to drink and dance at the same time. She crushed the garment against her face, inhaling the scent still clinging to the fabric . . . the still warm fabric, the still living young male scent, his after shave, a tinge of sweat.

How could I have been such a fool? Mark had paid for her stupidity.

"Help me get him dressed."

"What are you going to do?"

"Not *me*. *We*. He has a car, doesn't he?"

"A Jag. It's in the drive."

He glanced at the pale face again. "We're going to put him into the car. You're going to drive us." Damién had never learned to operate an automobile. He still didn't trust machines that moved under their own power. "To his home. I'm sure you know the way."

Beth winced at his sarcasm.

"We'll put him in his bed and let the police try to figure out what happened." Dropping the clothes on the coverlet, he slid one arm under Mark's shoulders. "Now, when I lift him, put the shirt—"

Mark turned his head and sighed, a faint wheezing exhalation.

Beth screamed and Damién nearly dropped him.

"*He's alive!* Oh, Dami, he's *alive!*"

"He can't be," Damién snapped, stubbornly.

"Then, he's *Undead.*"

"If I could, I'd thank that *Name* I can't speak." Damién stepped back from the bed, staring at the supposed corpse, whose eyes were now open. "Though I don't understand why."

He'd *turned* the boy, there was no doubt, but the fact that he hadn't intended to . . . No time to worry over that just now.

While Beth hugged him and murmured silly little endearments, Mark struggled to sit up; he saw Damién and pushed her away.

"You son of a bitch. I don't know what you did to knock me out but— Damn, my throat hurts." One hand went to the already half-healed wound, coming away blood-stained. "*What did you do to me?*"

"Mark," Damién spoke gently, his tone a contrast to the boy's furious ones. "I know this is going to be a shock but you . . . Well, to put it bluntly, *you died,* and . . ."

Mark was staring at him. Surprisingly enough, there was no fear on his face. Only anger.

"*You,*" he stated flatly, "are crazy." Throwing back the sheet, he scrambled out of bed, wavered a moment, then recovered and reached for his clothes. As he pulled on his slacks, he said, "Beth, I'm getting out of here and you're coming with me."

She didn't answer. She was too busy sliding into the red-sequined mini, thinking it might be best to be fully clothed for whatever was coming.

"You can't leave." Damién argued, mentally cursing the younger generation and their inability to listen to anyone not a peer. "It's going to be daylight in a little while."

"So?" He was dressed now, reaching out to seize Beth's hand. "Come on."

"Mark, you're *Undead.* If the sunshine touches you, you'll burn like dried leaves."

He didn't listen.

* * *

Mark aimed himself at the door. Damién attempted to stop him but the boy already had the *Undead's* swiftness, if somewhat uncoordinated. He and Beth were down the stairs before Damién had time to move. By the time he got to the top of the staircase, the front door slammed shut.

He reached it, throwing it open. Mark was starting the engine of the Jag.

"Come back inside," Damién pleaded, looking toward the trees. The sun was beginning to glimmer through the branches. He could feel his own fear quivering in his gut. "You won't have a chance. *Please.*"

In answer, the Jag's engine roared to life. Mark sent the car squealing down the driveway as the first rays of sunlight peeped over the treetops.

Damién darted back to the safety of the foyer, slamming the door. Hovering beside the bay window, he watched from the shelter of the velvet curtains as the beams of light shot over the trees and through the tinted windshield into Mark's eyes, closing his own in sympathy as he heard the boy scream. He knew how it felt, red-hot pokers of light, piercing the pupils, sizzling into the brain . . .

Mark let go of the wheel, putting his hands over his face to shut out the brightness. The Jag veered off the driveway, striking the curbing and bouncing into the air. The car sped onward and smashed into one side of the open iron gates, as his body crashed through the windshield, landing a few feet away. A spray of gravel and crushed flower petals flew into air before the Jag rolled onto its side.

Before he realized it, Damién was out of the house, racing down the drive. He felt the sun's heat on his face, was aware of a sense of space and distance and total vulnerability. Shutting his mind to the fear and the memory of pain, he concentrated on the figure in the grass, now sitting up, one hand to his head.

As he got nearer, Mark stood up.

"I'm still alive," he said, wonderingly. "I went through the windshield, and I didn't get killed." He touched his forehead. The impact wound splitting the skin was nearly half-healed.

"You're already dead," Damién told him curtly.

The sun was hot on his back. He could feel it penetrating the sweater, his skin starting to sting. *Got to get this young fool out of here and back inside.*

"Then, it's true." Mark looked at his hands. Little wisps of smoke were beginning to curl from his fingertips.

"Let's get back inside."

"Beth . . ." Mark ignored him. "Where's Beth?"

Together, they ran to the car.

She was pinned in the wreckage, the passenger's side of the dashboard shoved against her chest. Somehow, they managed to pull her free, Mark lifting her out to Damién who clutched her small body to his as he sped back to the house, the boy behind him.

The sun had nearly cleared the trees.

"Damn, my skin's on fire," Mark cursed. It was. Literally.

Damién didn't answer. He could feel the heat encircling his own body, ready at any moment to explode into destruction. Fear as well as concern for Beth made him run faster. The holy light above him sapped his strength, preventing him from moving as quickly as he wanted.

Mark slammed the door shut a second before his sleeves ignited. Damién left him standing in the foyer, slapping the little flames into oblivion.

Upstairs, he placed Beth on the bed, knowing as soon

as he saw the bloody bubbling at her mouth nothing could be done. When Mark arrived a few minutes later, shirt still smoldering with an accompanying smell of burnt fabric, he told him so.

"No, you can do something," the boy said stubbornly, and Damién knew that between the car and the bedroom, he had accepted what he had been told. "I-I believe you." He shrugged and smiled, sheepishly. "What else can I do?"

"If you'd done that before," Damién couldn't resist pointing out, just a little waspishly, "none of this would have happened."

Like a child being chastised, Mark avoided his gaze.

"Save her. Make her like us." he whispered. "Please."

"I can't." Damién tried to explain. "I didn't intend to kill you and I certainly didn't intend to *turn* you. What happened was an accident, a-a fluke. You wanted so much to live you *overcame* an accidental death. Beth's unconscious. She doesn't even know she's dying."

Mark looked at him angrily, eyes burning in the bloodless face. "*You* can save her. You're our *master*."

By now, Damién was frantic. In a few minutes, the sun would be fully risen, sending its deadly rays pouring into the bedroom. He had to get the curtains closed, get himself and Mark—his *fledgling*, his responsibility—to safety. He didn't have time to argue. *I don't need this.*

"If I could do it, will you accept the consequences?" He didn't have time to go over all the fine points of being *turned*. "You may love Beth, Mark, but so do I. If I *turn* her, she'll be bound to me, just as you are. Do you really want a *ménage à trois* for eternity?"

"I'll take my chances," came the reply. "Just don't let us lose her."

Damién glanced toward the window. The sun was halfway above the trees. *Hurry . . . hurry . . .* "All right. I'll try."

Gently, he cradled Beth in his arms.

"She always wanted to share my existence," he said softly, "Let's hope that desire still exists within her."

He pressed his mouth against the feebly throbbing throat. Briefly, he forgot everything as he tasted the bright flow. He'd taken Beth's blood before. Their lovemaking usually ended with his cock up her tight little tunnel and his fangs in her throat, but this time, it tasted different. He was now savoring the sweetness of Mark's blood pulsing through Beth' veins.

I love you, Beth, always have . . . I didn't intend for my fear to drive you to this boy . . . Come back to me. To us . . .

There was a pounding in his ears, his own heart convulsing with a tremor as the blood of two mortals surged and blended in his veins. And then . . . the thud died away and all he heard was Beth's wounded heart . . . *beat, falter . . . beat . . . beat . . . stumble,* and . . . *stop . . .* as nothing passed through it.

This wasn't the way I wanted to give you Immortality, Beth. He raised his head and gazed into her pale, still face. *I wanted to make it a Celebration. A beginning of the journey we'd take together. And now . . .*

Mark broke the silence. "When will we know?"

The sun was making shadows of the window frame on the bedroom floor.

Gently, Damién let Beth slide from his arms.

"It's daylight now. If I succeeded, Beth will awaken tonight." He could already feel the pull of *Sleep-that-isn't-Sleep* upon him. "I have to rest."

"And me?" The boy looked at him, the *fledgling* seeking guidance from his creator. All the belligerence was gone. All he seemed now was a frightened child, waiting for reassurance from an adult. "Where will I—"

"Here. It's only fitting you sleep in the bed where you died." Damién drew the curtains closed, making certain his body was shielded by the thick cloth. "Go ahead and get into bed," he went on and his voice shook with an emotion he didn't even want to name. "I'll tuck you in."

Obediently, Mark undressed and lay down beside Beth, putting his arms around her. By the time Damién pulled up the sheet, he was already half into *Unsleep*. Gently, he brushed back the tousled hair from Beth' face and kissed her on the forehead.

As he straightened, Mark roused slightly, clutching at his hand.

"Don't leave us," he whispered. "Sleep here. We're both your *fledglings* now. Protect us, master. *Please*."

His fingers entwined through Damién's like a child seeking comfort. Damién didn't argue. It was getting late and he was tired, *Unsleep* tugging at his mind like a hook piercing a fish. *Why not sleep here?* The air of the house was saturated with the dust of his Native Soil; he could sleep anywhere within its walls.

He dimmed the lights and returned to the bed but he didn't sleep.

Couldn't.

* * *

Instead, he waited . . . crouched beside Beth's body, look at Mark's sleeping form. Chin resting upon his up-drawn knees, he watched and waited, while outside the day swelled and burned and died. Waited for the sign that his Gift had been received, that somehow Beth had sensed what he was trying to do, until at last, touching her cold, unmoving flesh, he knew it was no use.

Beth is dead. She would never walk beside him in the darkness. He'd never again hear her footsteps on the stairs. Never hold her body close or make love to her again.

He had failed.

Beth is dead. Food for the worms, and while her lovely bones rotted in the earth, Mark would awake, as immortal as he, usurping her promised niche in Damién's existence. Childishly, the cry curled within him. *If I can't have Beth, I want no one!*

Certainly not this clinging, defenseless *male* fledgling...

With a defeated sigh, Damién knew what he had to do. He'd done it before, so there shouldn't have been any hesitation. But this time... If Beth had been with them, he would accepted Mark, wouldn't have protested his presence at all. He would've gladly shared her with the boy. It wasn't as it had been with LeMaitre and Antoinette, for Beth still loved him. *But Beth is gone...*

"I'm sorry," he whispered as he slid his arms under Mark's body and lifted him from the bed.

Effortlessly, he carried the boy to the window, kneeling to place him gently upon the floor.

"I want Beth, you see, and only her. No one else," he went on softly, leaning over the still figure.

His words fell on unhearing ears; nevertheless, he was compelled to explain.

"It would be different if Beth were with us." Slowly,

he got to his feet, turning toward the window, reaching out to grasp the curtain cord, pressing himself against the wall, out of harm's way. "I can't... I *won't* let you take her place."

Damién pulled the cord. With a jerk, the curtains parted. Sunlight filled the opening, pouring in to bathe Mark's body in golden light. For a moment, his pallid flesh glowed in a glittering aura.

Damién turned his head, one hand shielding his eyes. He heard the first faint crackle as the boy's body burst into flames, the sound growing louder as it was consumed.

Finish it.

Skirting the circle of light, he ran to the bed, the roar of the flames loud in his ears. Hastily, he pulled Beth's body from the sheets, not as gentle as he had been with Mark because now, he had to hurry.

"You win after all, boy."

Standing as close as possible, he let her body slide from his arms onto Mark's flaming corpse. For a moment, they clung together, her head resting on his chest, as they would be always. For Eternity.

The flames rose, obscuring everything.

Damién looked away. This time, he didn't want to see the destruction of those two helpless bodies. This time, there was no revenge in his heart, only a deep, searing sadness. He might not shed tears but his soul was screaming as he heard the flames crackle.

When it was over, when only a blackened pile of ashes remained, faint wisps of smoke floating above it, he drew the curtains closed again.

Without looking back, Damién left the room, returned to his own, and settled himself in the huge satin bed.

As before, he felt no shame in what he had done, not in his betrayal of Mark's trust nor the destruction of Beth' body. It was fitting they be together, while he . . . .

Since the day he witnessed Antoinette's betrayal, he had sought a companion to accompany him on his journey. There had been many women, some mortal, some not, and many were willing to go with him, but always, inescapably, he lost them . . .

I thought it would be different with Beth.

Now, he was truly alone, by his own actions, committed freely . . . damned again as much by this as by his *Undead* state.

It had been inevitable, he supposed. Perhaps this was intended all along, no matter how much he fought it. That he should always be cursed to walk the corridors of Eternity in solitary damnation. Possibly that was his punishment for thinking he could escape the death Heaven had assigned him.

"So be it," he whispered.

Damién closed his eyes. *Unsleep* surrounded him like a sheltering cocoon, sweeping into his brain. He needed to assume tranquility before it overcame him. In the midst of his desolation, a sudden thought, seized from the random turmoil of Mark's dying brain exploded into being inside his own.

A movie is being shot . . . the boy was to have been an extra and had wanted Beth to go with him but he'd never gotten the chance to ask her . . . *a horror movie. How appropriate.* Damién's mouth curled into a smile. Could there be a better place to make his re-entry into the world of the Living?

Yes, he would leave this house, once more brave the

Outside. Among actors in make-up, he would be unnoticed, the selection of his prey thought part of the plot...

... and who knows? Perhaps he would find another Beth...

With sudden anticipation, Damién gave himself up to the darkness.

Once again, I had loved and lost, but ever the eternal optimist—or perhaps the eternal fool—I still believed I would someday find the one I sought, though the centuries and the women came and went and I was left as empty-hearted as ever. I had found solace and charm in America and thought to make it my home forever, believing if I were to find what I searched for, it would be in this beautiful land of free life, free thought, free love . . .

. . . and so, into the Future . . .

2140 was a banner year for the Undead, *thanks to a discovery by one Christopher Landless, vampire and former Restoration footpad, for it was through his endeavors we followed Mankind in conquering the stars. A good man, Kit . . . I found him an amiable drinking companion and a good friend in the short time I had his acquaintance. His findings enabled us to travel the galaxy as free as our human counterparts, boldly going where no* Undead *had gone before, and opening new hunting grounds for slaking our thirsts. However . . .*

UNDEAD EXIST; SCIENTIST CALLS FOR EQUAL RIGHTS FOR VAMPIRES.

That was the headline on the New York Times/Planet, *New York City, NY, on August 18, 2390, the day Undead and Human existences changed forever.*

Up until that time, we were considered just myths or something the socially disenfranchised toyed with in their aberrations. The day social scientist Karoly Gregoriu Gregorevica marched into the General Assembly of Planets in the Terran World Capitol at Charleston, South Carolina, and dropped his seventy-five disc bombshell on the podium, normalcy flew out the window.

He'd been watching us for twenty-five years, and the astounding part was: we never even noticed. Too busy reveling in shedding our Earthbound chains, I suppose.

Soon, there was legislature to protect us, laws to provide us with the nourishment we needed. Now we were no longer hiding in the shadows but actually mixing with those we formerly considered both our enemies and our prey. We were no longer monsters but merely "hemoglobin addicts." Even with that ridiculous onus, it was a relief to be so free.

It didn't last, of course. One little slip and everything came tumbling down, though that mistake took over eighty-five years to happen. In the end, it was Mother Nature herself who betrayed us, as if she could no longer bear seeing her true children consorting with the misbegotten creatures of the night.

For the crime of a few, we were all condemned, hunted down and captured. Those who fought were destroyed, the rest overcome by holy relics and transported to internment camps on whichever world they were found. In those prisons, we would continue our unnatural lives surrounded by moats of running water, guarded by men wearing crosses and other religious symbols for protection. It should have been brutally laughable.

It held no humor at all, not in the least, for now, the entire **Undead** population was at the mercy of Humanity. Oh, they cared for us, made certain our prison was comfortable and we got the nourishment we required. Truly we were the most well-tended animals in any zoo, but it's the nature of Mankind to destroy that it fears, and we all wondered how long it would be before we joined all those other species they had assisted into extinction.

CHAPTER 7

*Michel
New Orleans, Louisiana
November 15, 2575*

"Who's that?" Michel Boudreau stepped to the railing of the guard tower, looking down. It was his first night at Bayou Compound, and he'd been staring at shadows for hours.

"Where?" David, the other guard, peered over the railing.

Below them, a man stood in the mist, a vague figure at the edge of the cliff, looking out over the water flowing past the island. He thought he saw broad shoulders rise and lower in a sigh.

Abruptly, there was a girl beside him. One minute she wasn't there, the next she was. Mist coiled around her, blending with the white gown she wore. She looked up.

"Please—" Hands raised, pleading, eyes red and strained as if she'd been crying. So distressed, so beseeching. "Please, help me!"

"What the hell?" Shouldering his rifle, Michel started toward the ladder. *Got to get down there. Fast.*

"Wait." David's hand caught his shoulder as his other

clutched the ornaments around his own throat. "Don't."

Michel tensed to pull away. Fingers tightened and he felt his skin tingling. He relaxed, feeling the sense of urgency evaporate.

The man spoke to the girl. For a moment, it seemed they argued, her hands waving expressively. She looked upward once more and back at him, shoulders slumping. He put an arm around her, drawing her close and pressing her face against his chest. They disappeared into the mist.

"Where'd they go?" Michel blinked. The air below them swirled thickly, its center a high dense column.

"That questions marks you as a newbie if nothing else does," David snorted, releasing him and sliding his rifle off his shoulder. He leaned out, aiming the weapon downward, the beam of its site-lamp raking back and forth through the mist. "Didn't you read your manual?"

"Of course, but—" He thought a moment. "They're in the mist?"

"They *are* the mist. Better check *Chapter Two* again."

"Shit." Now, he could see. Two faint body-sized columns moving against the vapor, away from the tower and toward the camp, getting smaller and smaller.

"*All employees will immediately assist in restraining a fellow guard if he shows signs of enticement-toxicity,*" David quoted. "It's part of the job description."

"Still . . ."

"They can sense us, you know," he went on, walking back along the parapet as they both should've been doing for the past few minutes.

No guard was supposed to stay in one spot for very long. The entire 360-radius had to be viewed every fifteen minutes, even in the dense mist.

...ice floated back to Michel, ghostly disembod-
...cially fresh meat, though not so much the meat
...blood. Scent someone new as soon as he steps
...sland. Didn't you feel it when you got here?"

...experienced something, Michel knew that. A
...ness, sudden, brief whirling as if his brain had
...d, or he'd had two stiff shots of *arrière-grand-
...shine. *Was that what David meant?*

...led. "Yeah." He thought about the girl. "She
...pitiful. I was just going to see what was the

...y're pitiful all right." There was no sympathy in
...er guard's voice. "Not one of them has had a fresh
...dy since coming here and that's been eighty years."

"I wasn't really *enticed,* or whatever you want to call it."

"Right."

"I don't even like women." He'd make that plain right now.

"Sure."

"I mean, that makes me immune. Right?"

"Look, *bon-bon* . . ." Somehow, the way David said it kept that little epithet from sounding like the insult it usually was. Even in the current permissiveness, gays were still given *le battez froid.* "It doesn't matter which sex you like. Once they call, you're susceptible to that glamour vampires put out."

"If that's so, why weren't you affected?"

"Who says I wasn't? I just latched onto my amulets." He gestured at the heavy silver necklaces, each one with the symbol of a major Terran religion and several minor pagan ones. "And let their holy power flow through me."

"Is that what I felt when you touched my shoulder?"

He remembered again that tingle, like a minor e...
son.

"And that's what stopped you. Not me."

Michel thought about that a moment.

"Better get your manual out and reread it. If yo... looked it over the first time."

The mist was quiet now, like layers of ragged m... floating above the ground. Even the river was invisibl...

"David?"

"Hm?" He'd reached the end of this side of the tower, the guardhouse in the center blocking him from Michel's sight. "Get to patrolling. The Fed doesn't pay us to have a gabfest."

"Wh-what would've happened to me?" Michael began his own tour of his side of the parapet. "If I'd gone down there?"

"If you'd survived, you mean?" There was a chuckle. "Wouldn't call it *surviving*... dying and coming back. You'd be put in here with the rest of them. Because if you *did* come back, then you'd be just like *them*." David appeared on the other side of the guardhouse. "Don't ever turn your back, Michel, or underestimate them. You've heard of people raising wild animals as pets and then one day the critters suddenly attack their masters?"

Stirred by a sudden night breeze, the mist swept upward. Michel nodded, realized David probably couldn't see, and said, "Yes."

"That's how these... things... are. They may look like people but they're not. They're wild animals. Beasts. And you'd better never let down your guard because sure as you do, they'll attack. Now—" As far as David was concerned, the conversation was over. "Let's get back to what we're being paid to do."

Michel studied the wisps of mist surrounding him. It was like tiny wet fingers pressing through his uniform, caressing his face. He shivered. "You never answered my question. The man. Who is he?"

"That's Damién. Their leader. Don't worry. You'll meet him. When he's ready."

Damién . . .

He liked the name. It made the shivers go away.

* * *

"Excuse me, sir, is this seat taken?"

"Don't be cute." Lucien St. Albans didn't look at the figure standing by the booth. "Sit down and quit pretending this is a social function."

He raised his drink and took a bare sip, not bothering to hide his grimace of disgust. Morgan D'Arcy slid onto the seat opposite, setting down his own drink, something bright red in a martini glass.

"The drink is not to my Lord's liking?"

"Keep it up and I'll show you what *is* to my liking." It came out between gritted teeth before he could stop it. Lucien set down the glass, studying it intently, angry that once again he'd let his emotions show and Lord St. Averil was the one bringing them out. "Why must you persist in doing that?"

"But, Lucien, what else can I do to entertain myself these days?" The question was sarcastically innocent and vicious at the same time, sounding even more so when spoken in that languid, Restoration drawl. "It's not like I can fly away to New Orleans or somewhere to party all night."

"You—"

"Well, Morgan . . . engaged in your favorite pastime, I see." Damién appeared beside them, drink in hand. "Doesn't Lucien-baiting ever go out of style? Move over."

Without asking, he sat down next to the Englishman and looked around. "A booth. *Très confortable*."

"I'm afraid even teasing Lucien doesn't satisfy my need for variety tonight," Morgan complained. "The booth? Lucien was here first. I imagine he wanted some privacy. To sulk."

"Morgan, once again, you go too far. But it's not sulking," the other vampire corrected. "It's more . . . introspection."

"In other words, you're feeling sorry for yourself." Morgan raised the glass, taking a delicate sip. "Ah, at least tonight, they got the proportions right."

"*Oui*," Damién tasted his own drink. "It's damned difficult to make a proper *Purple Martin* martini, isn't it?"

Nodding his agreement, Morgan set down his glass, studying it in exact imitation of Lucien's own posture, though this time there was no irony in the movement.

They were in the *Blood Bank*, as they'd christened the little building. It was furnished like a small private club with booths and tables, the only structure in Bayou Compound not a below-ground bunker. A fairly attractive place with low lights giving an aura of intimacy, a music system whose wall-length speakers sent out something low and soothing to mingle with the hum of voices. It also had a bar stocked with the watered-down plasma of three cold-blooded species, and twelve warm-blooded ones, none of them human.

The others were standing around in little groups,

some dancing, some talking, murmurs floating to where the four sat. They could've eavesdropped, but at the moment, none appeared to care what their fellow inmates were saying.

From this vantage point, several couples were visible in the booths, engaging in suggestive conversation and flirtations. In public, that wouldn't lead to anything more than a few desperate and passionate kisses, perhaps one or two amorous little nips upon the throat, a gentle sipping of blood.

Anything more serious was forbidden; no Undead ever took blood in quantity from his own kind unless he intended to bond or destroy. Since they were all prisoners, no one wanted to bond with someone he'd be stuck with forever, and since they didn't know how many of their kind were left, no one wanted to destroy another.

A few were more bold; in a far corner, just enough into the shadows so their movements were unseen unless one was specifically looking, two of the more exhibitionistic were locked in an embrace of frantically caressing hands and rapidly thrusting hips.

That would give the Humans a shock, Damién thought, watching briefly out of the corner of his eye. Even in this day and age, with all the knowledge the *Undead* had foolishly exposed during that so-called *Time of Acceptance*, many humans still believed vampires impotent. Of course, the older *sans mort* supported that myth, clinging to it like a badge of honor. The sad fact was, they also professed to believe it . . . in spite of performances like the one going on not twelve feet away. They'd even been known to publicly and loudly refuse a *femme sans mort's* advances. They wanted to believe it, he supposed, because it kept them in their dream of the *Good Old Days* when everyone was free and it was *Open Season on Humans* and the *Undead* were a mysterious entity to be feared.

There was a combined gasp of orgasm. Damién looked away in disgust, sorry he'd weakened even for a moment and become the *voyeur*. It certainly had done nothing for him, except make him angry. The lack of pride his kind often displayed still managed to infuriate him.

"Sorry I'm late." Puffing slightly, Domingo appeared, holding a pilsner of an almost colorless liquid. "Got unavoidably detained."

"Looks like you got avoidably *blown*," Damién gave the Spaniard's disheveled clothing a slightly envious glance.

"Hear, hear." Morgan raised his glass again. The level had gone down considerably in a remarkably short time. "You didn't get that high color simply by flying from your bunker, old chap. Who is she?"

"Greta." Dom didn't deny it. He sighed and settled himself by Lucien who merely slid over a little more but didn't speak.

"Greta." The way Damién said the name made them all look at him. "So that's where she went. She tried to lure that new guard tonight. I talked her out of it. That's the fourth time this year."

"She's young still. What's she now, three hundred?" Morgan was prone to making allowances for newer converts. More tolerant. "Give her time to adjust."

"I do. And continue to do so." Damién flicked Dom a bare wink. "Might have known she'd go to the Spanish Stallion to work off her desire."

"I don't mind being used." If anything, Dom looked proud. "Not in the least. I enjoyed it as much as she did.

More maybe."

That was answered by a laugh from Damién, a sarcastic snort from Morgan, and silence from Lucien, who continued to steadily consume his drink.

"Is that an *Albatros D'eau-de-vie fine?*" Dom studied the fluted goblet currently raised to the Roman's lips. *Brandy Albatros* . . . an elaborate euphemism for albatross blood mixed with a dash of fine brandy. "That's pretty potent stuff, Lucien. You'd better take it easy."

"And if I don't wish to?" was snapped at him.

That surprised them all. Lucien was usually the last to show distress. His ineffable calm and ability of control were the traits earning him the position of Grand Counselor of *Les Elus,* a position he would still be holding if it presently existed. Confined as they were, with no knowledge of the outside world other than the few facts the guards let slip if they dared break the rules and speak to them, they had no idea if any vampires were still at large or whether the network so carefully set up over the centuries had collapsed altogether.

"Just saying," Domingo answered and let it go at that.

Of all the non-human fluids of sustenance, that of the albatross was one of the most potent; merely drinking the plasma led to rapid inebriation. It had to be ingested slowly, and since the blood of ocean birds was very salty, the drinker usually needed two or three more glassfuls of something less saline to slake the thirst it caused. No matter the second liquid, it always combined with the first to make a powerful solution. Vampires generally had to be carried out of the *Blood Bank* after consuming one *Brandy Albatros.* The empty glass pushed to one side told them this was Lucien's second.

The former Grand Counselor was known to hold his liquid refreshment. *And this proves it,* Damién thought, admiringly.

"Don't disparage Lucien's choice of poison," Morgan spoke up, finishing his martini. He raised a hand, snapping his fingers and a pretty girl in a waitress' shift materialized, swept the glass away and reappeared to place a second before him. He nodded at Dom's pilsner. "I don't know how you can palate that stuff. Hell, it isn't even blood!"

"Spoken like a true viral mutation, *amigo.*" Domingo lifted the pilsner, drank, and lowered it to wipe the foam off his upper lip. "But it makes a very delightful variety of taste. Ahhh . . ." He offered the glass to Morgan. "Try it, you'll like it."

Taking it from him, Morgan took a careful sip, handed the glass back, then sat there, rolling the scant bit of liquid around on his tongue. He choked slightly and turned his head as if looking for somewhere to spit.

"Allow me." Damién whipped a handkerchief from his breast pocket.

"*Merci.*" Morgan passed it across his mouth, folded it very precisely once, then twice, and placed it at the back corner of the table. "My gratitude, Dami. In another moment, I swear I might have embarrassed all of us." He rounded on the Spaniard, glaring at him. "Damnation, Domingo, that has to be the most vile taste in existence. How can you stand to allow it into your mouth without upchucking? What is it anyway?"

"Essence of asparagus and broccoli, blue-green algae, and kelp juice. Very filling."

"For a grasshopper, perhaps," came the answer with a truly British sniff. "And not a drop of blood in it? Why would they even put something like that in the stock here, anyway?"

"They think we're gigantic aphids, perhaps?" Dom appeared amused by Morgan's reaction.

"All I can say is, we've come to a sorry pass when one of us is reduced to drinking vegetable juice to get some variety in his diet. Remember when we used to search for someone with a rare blood type? Just for the hell of it?" Morgan was on his way to finishing his second drink, already waving his hand to summon the waitress again.

"Better slow down a little, *ami*," Damién warned.

Lucien set down his glass, clearing his throat ostentatiously. They all looked at him.

"I wish to leave." He aimed the words at Dom. "Would you please get up so I may do so?"

So very formal. And quiet. All three tensed.

Uh-oh. Lucien in a polite mood was a warning it might be the lull before a very bad storm. It'd been a long time since anyone had vented violently. And if it was the *Dark Prince* . . .

Damién found himself suddenly wishing it would happen. Looking at the other two, he knew they were thinking the same thing.

Without speaking, Dom slid out of the booth. Lucien followed with as much grace as possible when performing such an act, then bowed to all three with the formality of someone leaving a drawing-room, and walked away.

There wasn't a wobble in his step nor the hint of a stagger, his back ramrod straight beneath the dark jacket. Even if he were sloshed out of his mind—and none of them had evet seen Lucien St. Albans in such a condition—he'd never show it to the public.

"He's still bitter about your being chosen over him as leader here, I think." Morgan made the statement matter-of-fact. The waitress had brought his third martini but he was showing no urgency in drinking this one, thankfully. He studied the long fall of black hair between Lucien's shoulder blades, how it never even swayed as the dark vampire walked toward the exit.

"Hell, I didn't want that dubious honor and still don't. I'm willing to cede to him any time he wishes," Damién replied. "I've told him that and he refuses to accept."

"That's because he won't be second choice. Lucien's proud, we all know that." Morgan was silent a moment, before saying, "He's bored, that's all. Got a lot of time to think and that's always bad. For anyone."

"Who's that?" Damién's attention was caught by movement near the bar.

Someone he didn't know. A male, silver-white hair short and spiky, almost luminous in the dim light. He was dressed conservatively enough, in a form-fitting black robe resembling a cassock, its knee-high side-slits revealing black boots. At the moment, he was speaking to a *femme sans mort* and she was laughing, obviously flirting.

"Him?" Morgan looked in that direction. "That's Euclair Trianon. Just transferred from San Francisco Compound. He was giving them too much trouble so they shipped him back home. Guess they think we're tougher and can calm him down." He spoke with a raising of one eyebrow and a soft sneer.

"I hadn't heard of a transferee." Damién frowned. "I'm supposed to be notified before one arrives."

"Better watch it then. That's the way it always starts when they lose respect for you . . . first slipping up on notifications, then other protocols go, then . . . you're in total ignorance." Dom shrugged. "Probably just some bureaucratic slip-up. The note's sitting on some secretary's desk somewhere, I imagine, waiting to be sent here."

"What's his major maladjustment?" Damién brushed aside this seeming snub.

"He—" Morgan turned from his scrutiny of the white-haired vampire, leaning forward and lowering his voice. "It seems he liked teenagers, particularly young males nearing post-adolescence. Savaged them rather badly."

"That's all we need. A Predator."

"Don't be prejudiced, Dami. To the Breathers, we're *all* predators." Morgan's smile was ironic. "But then there are predators and there are *predators* . . ."

"*Gracias* for making that fine distinction," Dom murmured.

"We'll have to keep an eye on him," Damién said. "I understand one or two of the guards are barely in their twenties. Here's hoping they've got more sense than to fraternize. I suppose there are enough young ones within our own ranks to distract him, if necessary."

"Should we start seeking volunteers?" Morgan raised an eyebrow.

Damién didn't answer. Domingo finished his drink, asking, "Anyone want another?"

"*Morrr-gaannn* . . ." The soft purr caught them all by surprise. They hadn't even heard the woman materialize by the table.

"Lady Justine." The Englishman smiled. She was small and blonde and definitely something to make a man of any physical entity feel better just by looking at her. A Restoration beauty, and still one. And a friend of Morgan's since his return to London after that first New World visit. He struggled to his feet, not an easy thing to do when sitting in a booth, as Dom and Damién did the same. "How good to see you again."

As if they hadn't seen each other last night and the night before and the night before that and . . . back to the beginning of their so-far eighty-year imprisonment.

"You promised to play for me." She smiled.

"That I did." Morgan was suddenly eager to get away. To be in a beautiful woman's company, to begin a seduction starting with his rippling the piano keys and concluding with his playing Justine's body as skillfully as he did a Beethoven *Sonata*.

He tossed his head, slinging back that fall of blond hair. It was hanging loose about his face tonight, unhampered by any kind of tie and looked like an angel's hair, something His Lordship definitely wasn't. His knee nudged Damién's under the table, the signal for him to *get up and let me out*.

Damién hastened to obey.

"What would you like to hear tonight?" Morgan offered Justine his arm. As if they were about to take a stroll on the verandah of her now-lost manor house in Surrey. "Some Lizst? A little Schubert, perhaps?"

"I've the need for something lively," came her lilting reply. "How about a selection of Joplin?"

"Master Scott, it is then." They were at the piano now and in a moment, the bouncy notes of *Maple Leaf Rag* pranced into the air. With a few more bars, others gathered around the piano, asking for requests and Morgan and Lady Justine, sitting beside him on the bench, were lost to Dom and Damién's view.

"Morgan's lucky," Dom sighed. "He's got his music to keep him from being bored. I've got Greta, until we tire of each other. What or who do you have, Dami?"

"At the present, this fairly acceptable *Equine Collins.*" For once, he didn't even acknowledge that little nickname. "And a little later? Some delicious *femme sans mort,* or, if not, perhaps a good holobook."

"I'm not that desperate. To read a book," Dom declared.

"I don't call it *desperate*," Damién corrected. "I call it *having a restful evening.* Truly, there are some nights when I just wish to be alone, Dom."

"Don't make that a habit," his friend warned. "Otherwise, you'll end up like Lucien. Brooding. And that's never good."

* * *

It had been eighty years since the incident the newspapers called the *Bethel Bloodbath,* the occurrence bringing about the revoking of the *Vampire Treatment and Census Bill* and the instatement of a Federation *Agency on Undead Security and Apprehension.*

In 2495, a flock of vampires traveling through Earth's Blue Ridge Mountains had gotten caught by a sudden flashflood. Kept from reaching the local blood bank, their leader, Damién's friend Christopher Landless, forced them to suffer their isolation for three weeks, before giving orders to attack the little town located on the same side of the river.

Of the population of nearly five hundred, only a five-year-old child survived.

The AUSA was efficient and deadly. Vampire hunters were deputized, with authority to capture the fugitives any way they could, destroying only those not surrendering peaceably. The *Undead* were subsequently interned away from the cities, within ghettos on the main world of each sector, in areas surrounded by running water blessed to make it holy, accessible only by boat or a drawbridge lowered from the Human side. Guards carried rifles armed not with bullets but with cartridges of holy water, fashioned to explode on impact and douse its contents upon the unfortunate target.

Thanks to Dr. Gregorevica's observations, they even made allowances for the differences within the vampire population. Those transformed by virus-laden blood exchange were kept from simply diving into the moat and swimming to the farther shore by a guard-rail of Kelvin beams surrounding the entire island. Rifles had an ejection-switch internally exchanging their ammunition from holy water to liquid nitrogen if necessary.

Damién, Morgan, Lucien, and Domingo had been fortunate—or unfortunate, depending on how one wanted to look at it—to be together in New Orleans when they were apprehended. Damién hadn't been able to stay away from the Big Easy—or NOLA as the *sans morts* had all begun to affectionately call it—and the others, with him at the time, agreed to accompany him for a visit. They'd all been intelligent enough to surrender without a fight.

Processed, tattooed with the universal symbol of the vampire—a bat in flight—that indelible mark of identification painted into the flesh by a painstaking application of holy water for the *Nosferatu* Undead or seared with the modern equivalent of a branding iron for the Vampyre, they were brought immediately to Bayou Compound, an island in the swamps north of the Big Easy, the water around it blessed by the present Bishop to make it further impassible.

That was the only time Damién had ever seen Lucien lose control. He'd fought his captors as the doctor assigned to apply the tattoo bent over him, had to be physically restrained as he was stripped and marked. They'd all been forced to witness his humiliation though he never made a sound as the glowing bat-shaped laser wand was pressed against his flesh—and it *had* been painful, Damién would testify to that. Whether light or liquid, like a thousand tiny coals being thrust through the skin. He thought it was more the idea of being forced to cede his will to another's even for that short time—to *not* be in command—that had made the Roman react so.

In an attempt to soothe him, the three of them, even Morgan, screamed and made as much outcry as possible, contrasting their supposed fear to his silence as his skin had been marked. They never knew if Lucien appreciated their act; he didn't speak of it, and if any of the others alluded to the incident in any way, quickly changed the subject. He also never let any of them see that badge of shame, either.

A proud man, whether sans mort *or Breather,* Damién concluded. *So are we all, but Lucien St. Albans even more so.* He wondered if that pride, imprisoned as it now was, would eventually lead to the former *Grand Counselor's* downfall.

Then his "date" for the evening was there, looking sexy and delicious and he had no further time to worry about Lucien or any of the others. Taking his hand, she led him out of the *Blood Bank* to her own bunker. He would stay there until the following night, drinking some delicious *Equine Liquor de Andalusia* she'd wheedled from the bartender, and making furious and passionate love until the sun came up when they would cuddle together and slip into *Unsleep*.

* * *

"His name's Damién La Croix," David said.

They were taking their third-hour break, sitting in the guard house atop the tower. Michel wondered why they had to even go outside. From inside the little round room, they had a 360-degree view of the compound via security Spies, lights coming on automatically at dusk illuminating every inch of space except where the mist lay.

And neither it nor the cameras can detect which is real mist and which non-corporeal vampire. That's the reason we have to walk around outside, constantly checking, he answered his own question.

"According to his Bio in the files," David nodded at the computer screen embedded in the nearby desk. "He was a *Marquis* in *Vieille France*—" He gave the words a truly Cajun pronunciation. "— in the thirteen century, 1249 as a matter of fact. That was when that plague went through and killed most of the people in Old Europe. He chose to become a vampire rather than die." He shrugged as he dug into his pocket and pulled out a small metal case, flipping it open and offering it to Michel. "And he's been around ever since."

"Damn. 1249?" Michel selected a cigarette and held it to his lips as David ignited a lightstick and touched it to the end of the little briarwood tube stuffed with tobacco. "That's over thirteen hundred years." He blew a smoke ring into the air. "This is good shit. Where'd you get it?"

"And he doesn't look as old as I am and I'm twenty-eight. I got it from my *gran'mere*." David answered his question without batting an eye. "She grows it in a hothouse in the bayou to supplement her Federation pension. Keep that to yourself, by the way."

Michel nodded. He had no desire to be arrested for using a proscribed substance and tobacco had been Number One on the Surgeon General's List for centuries now. It was also still as plentiful as it was before, though now available only on the DarkSell market or through private growers like his partner's grandmother.

"Before our relief gets here, we'll make sure all the smoke's gone," David went on. "Don't want any tell-tale smell giving our little indulgence away. Those daytime guys are real *piqures*. Too bad we can't stand outside but one of the vamps might see and peach us or try to blackmail for a smoke."

"They use the stuff, too?"

"You better believe it. They're more into illegal vices than any human."

"Don't happen to have any coffee on you, do you?" Michel wondered. "Smoking always makes me thirsty."

"Sorry, *bon-bon*. If you want to trip on that vice, you're on your own. Tobacco's as far as I go. Where would I brew it, anyway?"

"No prob. I've got some instant stashed away at my digs. I can wait until I get home." He decided to get back to the subject. "You were saying about this Damién . . . ?"

Damn, I like saying his name. Damién . . . Da-mi-ennn . . .

He smiled at how foolish that was. Intrigued by a man's name. It sounded as if it ought to be moaned in the dark ... *Daamiieennn*...

"Not much more to tell. He's the leader here, the one we go to if there are any problems and the one who comes to us if they have a grievance. He's suave, cooperative, sophisticated, and..."

"Is he handsome? I couldn't tell the other night." Michel hated the eagerness creeping into his voice as he asked the question. Shit, that sounded so *gai*. David hadn't laughed at him or done anything to indicate he looked down on him but he didn't want to push it. "I've heard all *Undead* are to-die-for."

"And many people have probably done just that." David laughed and walked to the door, tapping his ash-filled cigarette-tube on the railing so the residue fell out and was swept away by the wind. "You finished? I'll take back my tube, then."

As Michel handed it to him and he shook it clean also, he went on, "Yes, he's handsome. They all are and they'll fool you with their apparent friendliness. You just remember what I said about wild animals." He shook a warning finger and returned the two tubes to the case, picking up his rifle, and fanning the air with his free hand. "Now, let's get back to work."

* * *

"Why do you keep coming here?" Morgan asked. Tonight, he'd walked with Damién to the cliff's-edge. "Do you enjoy torturing yourself? Indulging a little masochistic streak?"

"Not particularly," came the quiet reply. "I just don't want to forget."

"Neither do any of us but we don't continue rubbing salt into the wounds by longing for what we no longer can have."

"They shouldn't have put us in here, Morgan. I'm certain if we collar one of the lawyers with us and asked, they could find some loophole—"

"Don't you think we've already tried that? Dami, you know we've been looking for that very thing since we were apprehended, and so far—eighty years later—we've found nothing. Nada. Zilch. Zero."

"It's got to be unconstitutional, to imprison an entire species for the crimes of a few."

"We're not a precedent. It's happened before. We were there on a couple of occasions. Remember Manzanar in the Forties and that Black Mountain camp during the Terro-Albegensi War? Besides, where planetary security is involved, Individual Rights go out the window."

"Sometimes, the imprisoned were liberated," Damién persisted.

"And other times they were decimated." Morgan expected his statement to end the argument. "Is that the only reason? I seem to sense something else, though I can't tell exactly what it is."

"I don't know, either. All I can tell is there's something wrong, and I think it concerns that new guard. I felt it the first night he came on duty. When Greta acted up. That's why I keep coming back, and looking at the city's lights, and waiting for whatever it is to reveal itself." He gave Morgan a quiet smile. "Kind of killing two birds with one stone."

"Killing with boredom, you mean. You're never going

to get one and you may never find out the other. Guards aren't supposed to associate with us, you know. Though some of them get a weird titillation from doing just that. Did we ever do anything like that when we were human? Flirt with danger, I mean? I suppose we did. It's so long ago now, I sometimes have trouble remembering."

"Or just don't want to?"

Morgan ignored that. "Well, must go. I've a sudden desire to lose myself in some Rubenstein for a while." He touched Damién's shoulder lightly. "Give it up, and come with me."

The only answer was a shake of the dark head. Shrugging in return, Morgan disappeared.

Damién didn't watch him go. Something was about to happen, he was certain. He had experienced a *frisson* as soon as he arrived at the cliff-edge, a brief stirring as if a stiff breeze of emotion swirled around him. Just like the other night. Sensations so tangled they were unintelligible. And tonight, something new. A heavy dose of . . . *curiosity?*

It has to be the new guard. I know the other one. David. Cautious, friendly enough but careful, follows the rules at least where we concerned, because I'm sure that smoke I've smelled is tobacco and it comes from up there. No, it has to be the rookie, whatever his name is.

There was movement above him. A soft *whirr*. Someone coming down in the lift. Boots crunching on the soft river sand.

Damién didn't turn around, just waited until whoever it was stood about eight feet from him. Then, he said quietly, "Please don't come any closer. You'll burn me with your amulets if you do."

"Sorry." It was the newbie. Very young, by the sound

of his voice. "I didn't realize—"

"In that case, you should read your *Manual*." He unknowingly repeated what David had said on Michel's first night. "Why are you here? You should be up on the tower. Watching from a safe vantage-point."

"I-I wanted to introduce myself. And to ask you something."

"So? Which shall we do first?" He turned to look at the boy now, and as he did so, realized *boy* was a true description. The kid couldn't have been more than twenty, so callow it made Damién's nerves sing just to look at him. Not overly-tall, the dark green uniform complementing his slender body and *café au lait* coloring.

A wafting in Damién's memory. Of the many Octoroon Balls he'd attended in New Orleans, where young women of mixed blood were paraded before potential lovers. Remembrance of the ones he'd sampled and how delicious such tender blood tasted. Young men like this one had been present, also—sloe-eyed and cream-skinned, acting as waiters and footmen to their more-pampered sisters. The boy would've fit right in. Briefly, Morgan's description of Eauclair echoed in his head.

He summed up the boy in three seconds. Fresh-faced innocence. *Probably working this night job to put himself through school. And doesn't realize how very dangerous it is.*

Most sentries were young recruits who didn't understand the danger; they simply saw the high pay rate, *Hazard Pay* because like any prison, there was always a chance a prisoner might attempt to escape. Because of the nature of those confined in Bayou Compound, a guard could be brutally savaged if it happened. Like all young, they thought it wouldn't be any of them. They were immortal.

Oh, mes enfants, *if only you knew about* real *immortality.*

Once the boat was gone, a sentry was as much a prisoner as they, only his communicator available to summon aid. If he could get to it.

Damién's nostrils quivered slightly as the scent of Michel's nicotine-laden blood wafted to him. *And using the hard stuff, too. Hm. Perhaps he isn't so innocent.*

"I'm Michel. Michel Boudreau." Unthinking, he held out his hand. When Damién didn't reach for it but simply stood there, he let it drop. "Sorry. I forgot. Not to suppose to touch."

"Damién La Croix." There was a slight inclination of that dark head. "*Vueillez vous rencontrer.*"

"Merci." It wasn't Cajun French but he understood.

"We are now introduced. What's your question?"

"You come here every night. And look out over the water at the city. Why?"

It was Morgan's question over again. Damién sighed.

"Isn't it obvious?" His answer was a little sharp. "Why would any prisoner stare at some place he isn't? Because I miss it. Even after all this time. Because I resent the fact I'm here and the people there are free and laughing and not put away somewhere because of something a few of their kind did." He turned back to look at the winking lights on the opposite shore. "Punishing all for the crimes of some isn't justice."

"They don't know who did it," Michel tried to defend the Justice Department's decision. "This was the safest way to make sure—"

"—the perpetrators were punished? And an entire species with them?" Damién made a sharp impatient gesture, and gave a slight grunt of pain. "Let's not talk on it further. All it does is make the loneliness worse."

When he looked at the boy this time, he seemed to move stiffly.

"What the matter? Are you hurt?" Michel put out a hand, then jerked it back quickly.

"Just my wings."

"W-wings?"

"I haven't used them in eighty years now and they've been bothering me for some time . . . folded away as they are. They're becoming cramped. They need to be exercised to prevent atrophy." He looked up at the sky. "Damn, I'd love to fly above this place."

"Why don't you? Oh . . . right . . . the barriers."

At points around the cliffs, lasers had been set up, rising from their Kelvin beam bases. Over their heads, red beams criss-crossed the island. Anything flying through the field from either above or below—and several unfortunate birds had already been victims—would be incinerated immediately.

"The beams are thirty feet up," Michel went on. "You could fly below that height."

"That's not *flying*. I need to *soar*. To rise above the clouds, then swoop, and feel the air currents on my face, float on them . . ." Damién's voice died away. He seemed to have trouble speaking. "You can't possibly understand."

"Can't you . . . uh . . . let them out? Like standing and stretching your legs, so to speak?"

"Doesn't work. I'd want to use them. It would only make the longing worse." He nearly staggered as the waves of sympathy struck him and briefly, couldn't bear it. *Pity? From this human?* He stiffened. "I must go."

Michel was left standing alone in the mist. He didn't

even have time to blink.

***

"You're a fool," David greeted him as he stepped out of the lift. He resumed his pacing on the parapet. "And you're going to get yourself killed. I should report you for *blatant disregard of the rules.*"

"Why don't you?" Michel picked up the rifle he'd deliberately left behind. Another blatant disregard.

"Because you'd get fired and I'd have to break in a new partner and . . . damn it, kid. I like you." David looked away a moment as if embarrassed. "As a working buddy, I mean."

Michel didn't answer, merely took up his post. David walked to the other end of the platform before speaking again.

"OK. You're curious about Damién La Croix. Just be careful. Bayou Compound has never lost a guard to an inmate and I don't want the first one to be on my watch. Take your rifle with you next time."

"What makes you think there's going to be a next time?"

"He's a vampire. And you've got the beginnings of a crush." The guard's shoulders dipped in defeat. "Of course, there'll be a next time."

***

"We're anachronisms," Damién declared. It was another night at the *Blood Bank* and he was sitting with a fluted goblet of Royal Black Swan plasma before him, sipping it very cautiously.

"In what way?" Domingo asked. He plunged the swizzle stick he held into his own drink, stirred vigorously, and watched the platelets on the bottom rise in a single scarlet trail to mingle with the amber serum.

"We're something that shouldn't have existed past the Nineteenth Century, when people stopped believing in us."

"They believe in us now, old chap," Morgan pointed out. "That's one reason we're in this damnable place."

"You're right," Damién set down his glass. "Still, think of all we've seen and done. The people we've known. We've been eyewitnesses to human history. And where do we end up? In a concentration camp for a crime we didn't commit."

"Morbid reminiscences, Dami." He could tell Morgan was making an attempt to head off this particular diatribe before it started. The same way Damién used to try to sidetrack his own anger over Charles Stuart's betrayal. "If you've got to talk about it, write your memoirs. It'd be a best-seller."

"Who'd believe it?" Thankfully, Damién joined in the sudden whimsy.

"Well, no one could refute it, could they?"

"*Sí*," Domingo joined in. "And with the royalties, we could hire a Philadelphia lawyer and get our handsome selves out of here."

"If the *Committee for the Humane Treatment of the Undead* doesn't spring us first." Morgan raised his drink and took a hasty gulp.

"What's that lunatic fringe group up to now?" For

once, Lucien looked interested. He wasn't drinking tonight, refusing to partake of any of the Federation-supplied *serum-with-a-few-red-corpuscles-in-it* passing for blood. Probably a reaction to his near-over-imbibing of a few days before.

Recently, Damién had learned a surprisingly number of humans believed vampires have been imprisoned unfairly, their Civil Rights violated. Of the same opinion as he in that only those participating in the Bethel Incident should have been arrested and tried, they had been petitioning since the first incarcerations for the *Undead's* release. A recent outbreak of violence on Albidon-7 Compound with a guard arrested and convicted for killing some inmates, then later found innocent when the real culprits were captured, had made the group renew its efforts. Damién hoped they were successful for more reasons than one. One of those destroyed in the unpleasantness on Albidon had been his friend Kit Landless, and though he'd like the Englishman, since it had been his order starting the whole thing, he now felt the scales of Justice were balanced.

"I'm beginning to understand the meaning of the term *stir-crazy*," he muttered. "Perhaps that's the real punishment. The humans intend to *bore* us into oblivion."

"You're getting too melodramatic." Morgan leaned forward. "Are you drunk?"

Damién shook his head. "Not yet, but I'm getting there."

Lucien gave him a sardonic, completely *Dark Prince* look but didn't say anything.

"Good." The Englishman picked up his mug. "I was afraid you were serious."

"Damn it, D'Arcy, I *am* serious." Damién pushed the

drink to one side, as if confronting his friend. "Human life is all so petty. I mean—all I wanted that day I met LeMaitre was to live . . . to escape the plague and continue my existence . . . and I did it, at the cost of my family, the woman I loved, my happiness . . . my soul . . ."

He picked up his glass and studied its contents glumly, started to drink, then set it down again. The others fell silent, studying their own drinks, except Lucien who merely looked bored.

"And now . . . where am I? *Trapped* . . . Somehow, it all seems such a waste. So futile . . ." His voice faded away.

All sat in commiserating silence.

At last, Domingo held up his glass. "Ah, to hell with it, *compadre*. To better days, and soon."

"Hear, hear." Morgan touched his own goblet to the Spaniard's.

"I'll drink to that," Lucien surprised them all by declaring. Pulling Morgan's glass from his fingers, he drained the last drops from the mug. Replacing it in his hand, he smiled coldly. "From your lips to God's ears, my friend."

Surprisingly, no one cringed.

* * *

"He's not here yet." Michel glanced at the holoclock above the guardhouse door as it silently counted up the minutes. "I hope nothing's happened."

"Will you listen to yourself? Jesus, kid, you sound like some girl on her first date." David let his concern show in anger. "For God's sake, Michel. This is a vampire, not a boyfriend."

"He could be," Michel retorted before he realized it,

David's unreasoning anger catching him off-guard.

"Don't even go there. You're shouldn't be doing this, Michel."

"Doing what? I'm merely taking one of my two legal rest breaks."

"Right, and the fact of that *break* always coinciding with Damién La Croix's appearance is just that? A coincidence?"

"As you say . . ." Michel had the nerve to smirk slightly. "Besides, we haven't done anything wrong. You know that. You're always watching, I've seen you. He's never touched me."

"And he'd damn well better not. If he so much as lays a finger on you, I'll cover him with so much holy water, he'll dissolve on the spot."

"Please. You wouldn't do that, would you?" Michel actually looked frightened.

"I might." David decided to let the threat stand. He'd probably just go down there and break it up personally. Firing his rifle would involve filling out a slew of reports and having a hearing, and so far, he had nothing negative on his employment records. "Just remember that."

He turned away slightly and Michel looked downward past his shoulder as the mist coalesced into a vague man-shape.

"He's here." He headed toward the lift. Briefly, David blocked him. Michel scowled.

If he doesn't move . . .

"Rifle." The other guard held out the weapon. Michel took it and stepped into the lift.

As it started downward, David told himself he was a fool and should be brought up on charges of *aiding and abetting.*

* * *

"Bon soir." The words came out breathlessly as if he'd been running. On the way down, Michel's pulse suddenly shifted into overdrive; by the time he reached the bottom of the tower, he felt as if he was galloping down the home stretch.

"Michel." Damién turned to bestow a quiet smile of welcome. "We must stop meeting like this."

That made the boy smile, also. *He actually made a joke. Damn.*

Damién appeared to be listening to something. The smile was replaced by a scowl of concern. "Your heart's racing. Are you ill?"

"How could you . . . You can hear my heartbeat?" Michel looked awed. "No, nothing's wrong. I'm just excited to see you again." He gave Damién that shy smile winning over more boyfriends than he could remember.

"And I'm glad to see you, too." Apparently, vampires were no exception. Damién visibly relaxed. "Though I can't imagine why you look forward to standing here in the mist talking to someone such as I."

"How can you say that?" Michel gave him a disbelieving stare. "It's fascinating to listen to you. You've been so many places, done so many things, Damién. Don't you realize what it means, to hear about all that? Especially to someone who's never been away from New Orleans?"

"I see." He shouldn't have been surprised to hear his own words parroted back to him from this mortal. "The old Othello-Desdemona complex."

"Who? Are they vampires, too?"

"Hardly, *mon petit*." The endearment slipped without his noticing it but Michel did and his heartbeat quickened even more. "That's something you'd have learned about if you'd continued your education."

"I'm going to," the boy answered, confirming what Damién had originally thought. "As soon as I have enough money. That's why I took this job." He hesitated, then rushed on, "I'm glad I did. If I hadn't, I wouldn't have met you."

"And that's something I wish to speak to you about."

"Really? Why?"

"This isn't right, Michel. Our meeting like this." After leaving the *Blood Bank* the night before, he'd had time to think about the boy. Of the way this naïve youngster treated him, that he was obviously developing an infatuation, and the fact of their speaking to each other was breaking the first rule a guard was taught. "In fact, it's very wrong."

"What's wrong with it?" The boy looked puzzled. "We're just talking. You said you were lonely. I-I thought you'd like company. Someone to talk to."

"I am. And I appreciate your concern, but . . . You aren't supposed to speak to me, Michel, much less be in my company like this." He gestured, glancing upward.

Michel followed his gaze, seeing David leaning against the rail, his rifle aimed downward.

"Your partner's got your back. See?"

"You wouldn't hurt me."

"No. *I* wouldn't but others . . . I won't go into the whole vampire sensory dynamics but you're a temptation, child, and you've placed yourself severely in harm's way as well as jeopardizing your job by doing this."

"I'm not a child. I'm twenty-two." The words came out stubbornly.

If Michel had thrust out his lips in a pout, Damién wouldn't have been surprised. *Damn it, didn't he hear anything I said except that one word?*

"From where I stand, that's an infant." Damién hurried on to get it said. To brush aside the one friend he'd made in the last eighty years and rid himself of the only relief from the tedium of a prisoner's life. For the boy's own good. "We're breaking the rules, Michel, and that's why I won't be coming here again. Tonight is the last time you'll see me."

"What? No!" Michel went pale, then flushed, his blood slowing, then rushing so fast, Damién was almost overwhelmed by the frantic change in its tempo. It took great control not to stagger as the frantic *thrum* of racing liquid swept through him. "You can't."

"I can and will, boy." He made his voice harsh, an elder speaking to a disobedient youngster. "This is—"

"Damién, don't leave me, please. I love you." Michel looked ready to burst into tears. He glanced upward.

David was gone from the railing. Pulled back by duty to patrolling the parapet.

I've got to do it now. This'll be my only chance . . .

Before the vampire could move, Michel closed the space between them, throwing himself against Damién.

His arms closed around Damién's waist. There was a momentary attempt to pull away. Because of the silver, no doubt. Michel was glad he'd had the foresight to close his shirt, hiding the amulets and putting a layer of fabric over them. A brief calming when there was no pain, then hands went to his shoulders, pushing slightly.

He caught Damién's face in his hands, pulling his head down, pressing his mouth against the vampire's. *He's so cold. I never realized . . .* There was another start, a stiffening of the body in his embrace. *What's he going to do? He's so much stronger than I am.*

The momentary *frisson* of fear disappeared as he felt the answering pressure of the mouth on his, arms tightening around his body, a frantic flick of tongue . . .

"No." Damién pushed him away so quickly he staggered.

"Don't do this, Damién." Michel regained his balance, realizing the vampire could've tossed him against the tower's wall if he wanted to. *Even with his strength, he was careful. He didn't want to hurt me.* "I'm begging you."

Damn it, in a minute I'll be crying. He could feel his eyes sting.

"Michel." There was a deep sigh, as if Damién were regaining control. "I apologize for that. I don't usually . . ."

How to say it? *I don't respond to the embraces of young men? I did it only because that's the first contact I've had with a human in eighty years and the longing for a warm body was too much?*

"Don't apologize. I wanted it. I want more. You can have me, whenever you want." The words tumbled out, frantic, heart-felt. He had to get them said before Damién became mist and left him.

"You don't know what you're saying. But I do. I don't traffic with children . . . and that's exactly what you are, Michel. I also don't deal with vulnerable young men." He backed away, putting even more distance between them. *"Goodbye."*

He whirled, sending up a wave of mist, melded into it, and was gone.

"Damién. Don't. Come back." Michel was calling into empty darkness and knew it. For a few more moments, he stared at the curling white clouds. His chest was beginning to hurt, a heavy pain deep within his heart, spreading through his body.

He's gone. I chased him away. I've lost him.

Hurriedly, not caring if David was again watching, he ran to the base of the tower. Stepping just under the eaves where the latrine door loomed, he leaned against the polyconcrete, pressing his forehead against its cold, rough surface and gave in to the pain, shoulders heaving.

"*Petit le pauvre.* You shouldn't cry so. He really isn't worth it."

Someone had seen? Witnessed his humiliation and rejection? Gasping, Michel whirled around, reaching for the rifle. He raised it. "W-who's there? Show yourself."

Movement within the shadows. A figure emerged, arms raised. A man, white-haired but young. Dressed in nondescript dark clothes. Some kind of robe.

"Don't shoot. I'm unarmed." He smiled as he said it, as if to softened the tension in the air.

"Give me your name and number," Michel snapped. Even with tears running down his cheeks, he managed to remember his training.

Should've remembered it before, you idiot.

"Certainly. Eauclair Trianon," he bowed slightly. "Number Seventy-five."

Seventy-five. Other knowledge clicked into place. Inmates were assigned numbers according to when they were captured. *He was caught early.*

"Y-you aren't supposed to be here. Get back to the c-compound." He tried to sound authoritative, knew his voice trembled. A latent tear followed the others. He sniffed, ruining the entire tough-guard effect.

"And you should get back to your post. You aren't supposed to be here, either," Eauclair reminded him. "I saw it all, you know." He didn't move. Appeared to be waiting.

"And? So?" Affecting a nonchalance he didn't feel, Michel decided he could wait, too.

"Do you have any idea why Damién rejected you? Really?"

"Because he's not into boys? Because he doesn't want to jeopardize his position with the AUSA? It doesn't matter." Michel shook his head. "He doesn't want *me*. He made it plain enough."

"Neither of those things. If Damién wanted you, he'd have you, and the *Agency on Undead Security and Apprehension* be damned." Eauclair paused to let that statement sink in.

"What, then?" Michel loosened his hold on the rifle long enough to swipe at his eyes with his sleeve, then quickly caught it again.

"Humans are prey, boy. Our sustenance. Some of us make them our lovers also, but not Damién." There was a slow smile, almost as if the vampire were enjoying some secret. "He never plays with his food. For sex, he turns to his own kind." He heaved a regretful sigh. "You'll never have him. Not as long as you're mortal."

"I guess I've really lost him," Michel muttered. "Because I can't change that."

"Can't you?" The slow smile grew larger. "There are ways."

"What ways?" It was a suspicious question as if he expected the vampire about to spring some joke on him.

"Think about it." Eauclair nodded and disappeared. A trail of mist floated from under the tower.

"Michel? Michel!" Before he had time to try to figure out what the vampire meant, he heard David's frantic call.

Stepping from under the eave, he got into the lift just as it started up, moving so quickly he had to hang onto the handrails to keep from losing his balance. At the top, he stepped out and nearly ran into David, standing there with rifle raised.

"Where the hell were you? I was about to come down and begin a search."

"I-I had to take a leak." He couldn't meet David's eyes, went over to the rail, looking across the river.

"Alone?"

"Stop it. Yes, alone. I . . . Damién won't be coming back any more." He didn't turn around, saying the words to the night air. "I hope that makes you happy."

"*Relieved* is more like it." As if sensing his despair, David said, "I won't ask questions. Just remember, it's for the best."

"Yeah. Right." Michel whirled, stalking down the parapet. "I've got to check the southern and east perimeter. I'm late in my rounds."

Behind him, he heard David move in the other direction but he ignored the sound of his partner's bootheels on the planking. Instead, all he could hear were Eauclair's last words: *You'll never have him. Not as long as you're mortal. There are ways . . .*

* * *

Damién himself was unhappy also, but for a different

reason. *I just gave up the only things giving me any pleasure . . . looking at New Orleans' coastline and someone new to talk to. To save an infatuated mortal's job. Damn it. I had no idea the kid was gay. Perhaps it's just as well. For both of us. I certainly couldn't respond the way he wanted. That kiss was reflex, nothing more. And Morgan's right. I shouldn't keep torturing myself by wanting to go back to Orleans when I know I never will . . . It was the right thing to do, but . . . Damn that stupid human. And damn me for letting myself be drawn in and flattered so.*

He didn't look up as chairs were drawn up to the table and the others dropped into them. "Don't say anything. I don't feel like talking."

"Aren't we in a mood tonight?" Morgan didn't listen, of course.

"What's wrong, Dami?" Domingo apparently wasn't going to be quiet either.

What's the use of asking for silence when no one obeys?

"I have a feeling someone's heart got broken tonight."

So even Lucien's going to break radio silence. Just great.

"You gave the kid the brush-off. Right?" Morgan guessed. Lifting his glass, he said it as casually as he might have mentioned the moon was full that night. "And there was a scene, I imagine. Hurt feelings? Tears, even?"

Damién didn't answer. Pushing back his chair, he stood and walked away, heading for the bar.

"Dami, wait."

"Let him go," Lucien said quietly. "He's hurting, too, in case you can't tell." He studied his own drink. Something very weak and tasteless tonight.

"Not as much as the kid, probably," Morgan dipped a forefinger into his drink, holding it up to let a single crimson droplet fall onto his tongue. "Mmm."

"You can't possibly imagine how it feels to be rejected by someone you care about." Lucien continued staring into the transparent liquid.

"No, I can't," came the soft, smirking drawl. "But I imagine you're going to enlighten us. Please, spare me the reminiscences."

"Shut up, D'Arcy. I mean it." For a single searing second, Lucien looked up, black eyes boring into Morgan's blue ones. Then, he also got up and walked over to where Damién stood.

* * *

Damién, how could you do this? I miss you so.

It was a week later. True to his word, Damién hadn't returned to the tower, though Michel was there whenever the time he should have appeared rolled around. His thoughts had been in turmoil since the moment the vampire disappeared, and Michel would've been the first to admit that what had started as curiosity then melted into infatuation was now a *fixation,* an *idée fixe d'amour,* one he harbored and fed and had no intention of letting go.

He'll come back. He has to. Even if he doesn't want me, he won't be able to resist the lure of New Orleans' lights, he told himself.

Truthfully, he didn't want to let go of the memories he had of being with Damién, the things the vampire had spoken of, the longing in his voice as he told of people long-dead. Michel was uncertain what he himself had said in reply. All he knew was that he hadn't properly conveyed the emotions Damién's words engendered in his own soul, and he'd convinced himself what Eauclair told him was true. *He only rejected me because I'm human. If I was a vampire as he is, we'd be lovers right now.*

Damién La Croix had now become his obsession, in his every waking thought and most of his dreaming ones. More than once, he'd awakened from images of passionate sex with the vampire, slipping from sleep into consciousness with an explosive orgasm. That was shocking and at the same time the most pleasurable experience he'd ever had, and he didn't want that to stop, either.

He fed his fixation by thinking of Damién while he was on duty. *Where is he now? What's he doing? Does he think of me, of how he broke my heart? Is he trying to forget with some young Undead male?*

That usually brought on a spate of jealousy he told himself was unreasonable, followed by the sudden stiffening of a hard-on so demanding he usually had to relieve it then and there. Or as soon as he could get to the latrine.

Once, David had horned-in as he'd headed for the lift.

"Where are you going?"

"To the latrine. Got to take a leak."

"You've been doing that a lot lately," Suspicion in every word. "Got a kidney problem?"

"For God's sake, David. You're not my mother. Quit with the questions."

"You don't need to go down there. It's a stupid place to put the *latrine*, anyway. Just hang it over the railing and let fly." That was what David always did, opening his fly, pulling out an impressive organ—which Michel might once have responded to if his partner had given any encouragement—and spraying a golden stream downward. After making certain which way the wind blew, of course. "I won't peek."

"Sorry." Michel's response to that attempt at good-natured humor was anger. *Damn, if I don't get out of here, I'm going to cream in my shorts.* "I was always taught not to pull out my pecker in public. And to piss into a toilet."

He stepped into the lift, slapping the controls and keeping his back to David so he wouldn't see the tent in his trousers.

The lift seemed to take forever to reach the base. Once there, he propped the rifle against the latrine door and pulled his pants open, thankful once again they were made of silscloth which could be ripped apart, then closed simply by being pressed together again.

His erection sprang out as if spring-loaded and he wrapped his fist around it and started pumping, keeping a mental image of Damién before him.

"Still at it, I see."

"Go away, Eauclair." *Damn it, not who I want to see right now.* His hand didn't stop moving as he spoke. *Soon, getting close.* He didn't want the vampire there when he came.

He was certain he'd been lurking every other time. The mists had been unbelievably heavy, but this was the first time he'd actually been visible and Michel didn't like that at all. A vampire *voyeur? Hell, why not?*

"But no, *petit.*" The vampire was in front of him before he realized it, a cold hand pressing down on his moving one. The chill seemed to spread over his cock, slowing his hand, making his erection wilt. *No, damn it!*

Eauclair's whisper was in his ear . . . soothing . . . monotonous . . . "I've watched you abuse yourself long enough. Let me help. You shouldn't have to put yourself through this torture. I can make it better, *mon doux.*"

The sound was so hypnotic. Michel blinked. *Damn, I*

feel so tired. Maybe that's what jerking off every ... single ... night ... does to a man, but ...

Suddenly, he was too exhausted to fight, didn't push the vampire away as hands gripped his shoulders. His own hand slid from his rapidly softening cock, fell to his side. In the next instant, he was staring at Eauclair's face, at that smooth, white skin and black eyes, as hands slid from his shoulders to his hips, fingers digging through the cloth into his skin.

The vampire smiled, then the smile became a widening grimace as his tongue flicked out. It was long and sinuous and forked.

Like a snake's.

Michel felt a single moment of revulsion as Eauclair's head dipped and that slender tongue wrapped itself around his tool, drawing it into the waiting mouth.

Are they all that way? Would it disgust me if it was Damién's tongue, split and slender, winding around my cock?

There was a soft, milking sensation, a sensuous tightening and release, *tightening and release...*

When he came, it was so satisfying, he nearly collapsed. The only thing keeping him on his feet were the vampire's hands. He hung in that grip for what seemed minutes, until his breathing slowed and his heartbeat returned to normal, finally raising sated, sleepy eyes to meet that dark, bottomless gaze. *Strange, his hair's so white but his eyes are black...*

The tongue unwrapped itself from his flaccid cock. Red welts encircled it, fiery crimson lines appearing as circulation rushed in. Eauclair waited until he'd stuffed it back into his trousers and the silscloth was once again rejoined before he spoke.

"Did you like that, *petit?*" He didn't wait for Michel's dumb nod. "It could always be like that if you were one of us. Think of that."

"I have," Michel mumbled, not wanting to admit it but finding he couldn't keep from saying the words.

"And?"

He didn't answer.

"Give yourself to me, Michel. Let me bring you *Across.*"

"And be enslaved to you? No thanks." In his misery, Michel had finally read the *Manual* from cover to cover, and he was now aware of the relationship between sire and fledgling. "It's Damién I want, not you." Some ridiculous sense of politeness made him add, "No offense intended."

"How can I take offense if you speak the truth?" Eauclair laughed. "My supremacy over you doesn't last. It's only to teach you what a newcomer should know. Once that's done, you'd be free to go to him, Michel. To have him love you. As you want. As *he* wants."

"H-he wants that, too? But . . ."

"He told me. He's miserable, too, Michel, but he won't act. He can't, because he's our leader. He doesn't dare." Black eyes met his, knowing the boy was too inexperienced to realize it was all a lie, that he would be bound to his sire forever, or until Eauclair tired of him and tossed him aside. *If Damién wants my leftovers, he's welcome, after I've had my fill.*

The boy was weakening. He was going to give in, he could feel it. He—

Instead, Michel pulled away, reaching for his rifle. Once it was in his hands, Eauclair had no choice but to step back. When the boy disappeared around the corner of the latrine and he heard the lift start upward, he limned into the mist, taking his flaring of success with him.

It won't be long now.

* * *

Michel was feverish and frantic. It had been three weeks since Damién's rejection and though he wasn't certain, for several nights, he thought he'd seen a frosty shimmering in the mist at the point where the vampire had always stood.

Coming to look at the lights of the Big Easy beckoning across the river or to look for me? The latter he hoped, and wished he'd been on the ground at the time. Would he make his presence known or simply stay in that ethereal form, insubstantial as the water droplets shrouding the air?

He didn't know and he didn't care, all Michel wanted in that moment was to do whatever to took to have Damién speak to him and be with him, again.

When the appointed time came and went, he headed for the lift but tonight David placed himself in front of the open doorway, body completely blocking his entrance.

"You're not going. Michel, this has got to stop."

"Says what army?" he snarled.

My God, he's completely out of control. David had watched his partner sink with sickening speed, deeper and deeper into his delusion. He'd tried talking to him, encouraging the kid to go to the AUSA staff shrink—though that would be admitting he had a problem and perhaps get him fired—and did everything short of going to their superiors, but now . . . He'd had enough.

"No army. Just the head of the *Agency on Undead Security and Apprehension*. I reported you, Michel." He felt like a traitor as he said it, though it was the right thing to do, and something he should've done after that first night.

"Reported . . . ? No."

"I told them the whole thing. Took me an hour to fill out all the forms," Even in this tense moment, that still griped. "Told them how you'd disobeyed orders and fraternized with an inmate, how he'd refused to let it go on . . ." That absolved Damién and didn't jeopardize his standing with the authorities. He was too good at handling human-vampire affairs to have that happen, David realized. ". . . but how you've been furthering your fantasy of being with him to the point of dereliction of duty."

"Y-you . . ." The kid couldn't get the words out. He appeared to be choking, mouth open, eyes wide.

"Tomorrow you're going to be called to headquarters and your position here terminated."

"Y-you've gotten me fired? You son of a bitch."

"It's for your own good," David defended himself, tightening his hold on his rifle. "You don't belong here, Michel, and the sooner you get away, the sooner you can fit back into the real, normal world."

"I don't want a normal world, you traitor." David didn't have time to dodge as Michel brought up his own rifle, catching him under the chin. His head snapped back as he fell inside the lift, weapon flying out of his hands to land on the parapet. Michel's boot caught him on the jaw. "I want Damién."

Too stunned to move, he could only lay there as he was dragged from the lift and dropped on the floor of the parapet. From far away, he heard the quiet buzz as the lift started down.

* * *

"Eauclair?" Michel didn't wait for the lift to reach the base, leaping out as soon as it was within four feet of the ground. He fell to his knees, righted himself and looked around. "Are you here?"

Mist whirled and gathered. Before the vampire could form inside it, Michel had unfastened the silver chains with their crosses, crescents and other symbols, from around his neck. He tossed them behind him as Eauclair appeared.

"Do it!" He didn't give the vampire time to say anything, just ripped open the neck of his uniform shirt, closing his eyes. "Now."

Hands touched his shoulders. Cold breath on his cheek. A kiss trailed to the edge of his jaw, that wicked, forked tongue licking down his throat . . . A sharp sting, followed by a rush of desire and . . .

. . . *pain* . . .

. . . like he'd never felt before as the fangs sank in, nearly meeting in his flesh, and the blood spurted and he fought to get away . . . and his heart began to beat frantically . . .

"Think of surviving, boy . . . only of that . . ." The whisper was inside his brain, coiling through the dark recesses.

Survive . . . got to do that . . . for Damién . . . Damién . . . That was Michel's last thought as the whispers got so loud they drowned out the furious pounding of his heart and it faltered . . . slowed . . . fluttered furiously . . . and stopped

...

***

"Michel? Where are you?"

Eauclair heard the lift go up and almost immediately start back down again. Raising his head, he pressed a kiss against the pale, bloodless lips and let the boy's body fall to the ground. He faded into the mist as he wiped Michel's blood from his mouth, and by the time David stepped out of the lift, only a few swirling drops of vapor showed where he'd been.

"Michel!" The guard ran to the crumpled body, rolled it over, gathering it into his arms. He saw immediately there was no use in trying resuscitation. Michel's face was bloodless, lips gray, skin already cold. His eyes were rolled back, no iris visible, mouth slack. Even his tongue had no color. "Oh, Michel. *Vous jeune imbécile stupide!*"

For a moment, he knelt there, cradling the boy against his chest, as his own shoulders shook in surprising grief. Raising his head, he called out one word. "Damién!"

***

"What is it?" The answer came so quickly David jumped. Seeing the body in his arms, Damién didn't give him time to answer. "What happened? Who did this?"

"I thought you might tell me. You didn't?" David's look held no fear, his amulets giving him the courage he needed to face the vampire.

"Don't be stupid. I'd never do such a thing." Damién knelt beside David. Gently, he touched Michel's cheek, shaking his head. "Poor child. Why?"

"That doesn't matter. I think you know the answer anyway. What we need to worry about now is what this is going to do to you and the other inmates."

"Why do you care?"

"I don't, really, except I don't think it fair for everyone to be punished for the actions of one. That's exactly why you're all in here in the first place, remember? You've said it enough yourself. I heard you telling Michel."

"And now this poor child has done the same thing to us." Damién brushed his hand over Michel's eyes, closing them. In the next moment, he flinched slightly as the boy sighed and turned his head, eyes fluttering open again.

"Damién?" He sat up. "You're here?"

"Oh no." It was breathed behind him. David shifted his weight, releasing his hold on Michael's arms. "You let one of them *turn* you. Michel, you idiot."

"Say whatever you want." Michel turned his back on his friend, his attention on Damién whose expression mirrored David's horror-struck one.

"Do you realize what you've done?"

"Of course." Michel made it an obvious statement. "I've guaranteed we can be together. I'm like you now."

"What does that matter?" Damién's answer was harsh. "I don't want you no matter what you are."

"But . . . he said . . ."

"Who? Who did this?"

Michel ignored the question. "He said, you wouldn't touch me because I wasn't *Undead*. That you . . ."

"*Enfant stupide!* I won't touch you no matter if you're alive or not. I may prey on males but I don't have sex with them. You've died for nothing, boy."

"Y-you mean, you don't want me? I died for you and you still don't want me?"

It made a pain in Damién's own heart to see the realization of his useless sacrifice appear on Michel's face. It stayed there only a second before a bleak determination took its place.

"Well, I won't be put in here. I won't spend eternity wanting you if you don't want me."

"You don't have any say-so in the matter—" David began,

Spinning, Michel struck out, knocking David aside as the guard reached for him. Before either could stop him, he ran to the cliff's-edge, fumbling into his pocket for the key-card killing the power surging through the posts. One swipe of the card into the slot and the beams wavered and disappeared, allowing him to pass through and slide down the bank to the river's edge.

Immediately, a high-pitched squall ripped through the air; a warning signal floating over the island, also sending an impulse to AUSA Headquarters, notifying them the guard-rail had suffered an unauthorized breach.

With the *Undead's* swiftness, Damién got there before David, who scrambled down the incline, reaching the vampire's side just as Michel flung himself from the bank.

He struck the water with a loud splash and immediately sank, only to bob to the surface as the holy water rejected him. The current bubbled and boiled, its blessedness reacting to the damned vampiric flesh floating in it. Michel floundered, arms above his head as he sank again. He was directly in front of them, only two feet or so from shore but the bank was a sheer drop-off underwater, a dozen feet deep at that point.

Catching David's arm, Damién leaned out over the water, reaching for the boy's hand. Feeling the holy vibrations of the water below him, he wavered slightly, then caught one wrist, tugging the struggling body toward shore. David released him and grasped the other and together, they began to pull Michel out of the water.

He was lifted, head and shoulders above the roiling waves, continuing to struggle against them. His grasp slipped. Michel was dunked again before David once more caught his hand. Still fighting their grasps, the boy slid under. The water spouted upward, splashing against them. Damién cried out as drops of water splashed his cheek, his skin sizzling. He ignored the pain, tightening his hold on Michel's wrist. Red foam swirled in a sudden whirlpool, flowing outward.

The boy stopped struggling.

Damién gave a sharp jerk, falling onto the bank as Michel's arm separated from his dissolving body.

David stared a moment, then looked at what he held in his own hands. Dropping Michel's armless hand on the bank, he staggered to his feet, whirled and vomited into the sand.

Damién got to his feet but otherwise didn't move, just stood there, holding the arm and listening to David empty his belly. It was several minutes before the guard turned, coughing and wiping at his mouth.

"Oh God." He ignored the vampire's wince. "He . . . dissolved . . . like sugar in water . . ."

"That's why we don't go near it," Damién said quietly. He dropped the arm. With a dull *thunk,* it landed near the hand. "Are you all right?"

"You mean, am I recovered from seeing someone I

thought a friend liquify before my eyes?" There was a soft, mirthless laugh. "Yeah, I guess I am." David gestured at Damién's seared cheek. "How about you?"

"It'll heal. I'll have a scar." Damién brushed fingers against the red weal. "*Il n'importe pas.*" He shrugged. "So . . . what do you do now? Make a report of some kind, I suppose. *Bien.* I'll wait at the base of the tower while you call your superior. I imagine they'll wish to speak to me."

Above them, the siren's wail still rent the air. David ran back to the wall, using his own card to silence the alarm. Then, he walked back to where Damién stood.

It was several seconds before he spoke. He looked at the two body pieces at their feet, over to the tower, and back to Damién. "No. I'm not going to do call anyone but I *am* going to do something else."

"You have a plan? I'm listening."

"If I report this, there'll be more news coverage and investigations and hearings than either of us want."

"I'm aware of that, and though I have no idea what will happen, I'm certain none of it will do us any good, so I repeat: *You have a plan?*"

"We put those—" He nodded at the arm and hand. "—into the river. His body's already gone. They'll dissolve also. No body, no crime."

"Won't he be missed?"

"I'll just tell anyone who asks he didn't show up for work. They'll check his apartment, find him gone. I'd already reported him. Maybe he decided not to wait to be fired but took the easy way out, and left for parts unknown."

"You're being very dispassionate about this. I thought Michel was your friend."

"He is . . . was. But he wouldn't listen to any of my warnings. I suppose this could be considered my fault since I didn't stop him but it's like I told him. No guard here has ever been killed and I don't want the first one happening while I'm on duty. Self-preservation, man."

"Yes," Damién agreed, sadly. "In the end, that's what it always comes down to, doesn't it?"

He waited while David gingerly picked up the arm and hand and dropped them into the water. Together, they started back up the bank, walking side by side, something Damién decided David hadn't yet realized. He waited as David again used his card so they could get through the barrier, this time punching in a code so the alarm didn't activate.

At the same time, they both saw the silver chains laying near the lift.

"What about those?"

Without answer, David scooped up the chains. Cupping them against his chest, he ran back to the water, slinging them into the current. They made a very small splash as they sank.

"They'll think he sold the silver and used the money to leave town," he said as he returned to where Damién stood. "You'd better go. I need to get back to my post."

He was startled when a cold hand caught his arm. Stiffening, David reached for his rifle as Damién said, "You need to say something . . . some words . . . or a prayer."

"Yeah, guess so." David's answer was sluggish with latent shock. Damién was certain he was feeling Michel's death more than he was allowing to show.

Damién released him, looking out over the rapidly

tumbling water. *Look at it, flowing so swiftly. Not caring it now holds bits of a dead man's bones in the dirt of its bed, or the blood of a foolish boy who loved so unwisely reddening its currents.*

David walked back to the water's edge. Damién looked away as the guard crossed himself and clasped his hands together. He fumbled into the mass of chains around his neck and extracted a crucifix, holding it up.

"Lord, Michel was misguided. He didn't understand what he was doing. Guess you could say he was temporarily insane. Whatever his reason, please don't hold it against him. He was a good kid, anyway. Let him into Heaven or, at least, don't send him to Hell." He kissed the crucifix, dropping it back into the others. "*Au Nom du Père, du Fils, et du Saint-Espirit, amen.*"

This time, as he passed through the fence posts, he reactivated the beams. David made a mental note to notify Headquarters and tell them the warning they'd been sent was a malfunction. A bird had flown through the beams, causing a disruption and sending out a signal.

When he reached Damién's side again, the vampire raised his head. "You liked him. You really cared about Michel." The dark eyes seemed to probe into his brain. "More than you let on, I think."

"I'd have made him a better lover than you." David's answer was short. "I let him think I was straight."

"Sins of omission are sometimes worse than sins of commission."

"And I'll carry that sin with me for the rest of my life." David sighed. "I doubt if it would've mattered if he'd known."

"You'll never know, will you?"

"No, and that's the saddest part." David looked up at

the tower, slinging his rifle over his shoulder. "Time to get back to work. Going to be lonely up there the rest of this night." He gave Damién a tiny, tentative smile. "Wouldn't want to keep me company, would you? Kind of hold a wake for Michel?"

The brief shake of that dark head gave him the answer he expected.

"Guess I'll do my mourning alone then."

Slowly, he trudged toward the lift. Damién waited until it was heading upwards. As he faded into the mist, he saw David wipe his fingers across his eyes.

There was an investigation but it went as David predicted. The conclusion was that Michel decided being a camp guard wasn't the life for him, and since he was about to be fired anyway, he'd sold the amulets, and used the money to leave town. David got another partner, one who followed the rules. Though Morgan and I made our own inquiries, we never discovered who had turned Michel, and thus were unable to carry out our own punishment for that breech of AUSA's rules. I would always carry some guilt with me for not handling the whole business with more diplomacy. My excuses are my own loneliness that I allowed Michel to feed, and the surprising fact that, in all my thirteen hundred years, I'd never been approached by anyone of the gay persuasion. Difficult to believe but true. If I'd taken a little more time to be gentle in my rejection, Michel might have lived to allow David to comfort him. As it was, my anger thrust him away and sent him into that spiral of destruction.

I thought of that often as I looked at New Orleans' lights, until the guilt drove me away from them completely. I was as responsible for Michel's death as the unknown vampire who turned the boy, and that was another sin to lie heavily upon my conscience as another century dawned. I had no idea I would face that century in freedom.

Within another six months, that Committee for the Humane Treatment of the Undead *triumphed. In a hearing lasting six weeks, the* Agency on Undead Security and Apprehension *declared that, with Christopher Landless' destruction at Albidon Compound, they considered the one responsible for the Bethel Bloodbath now punished and all other vampires absolved of the crime. Within another two weeks, liberation pro-*

ceedings began, and we were free again.
   Or were we?

It may take several millennia for the truth to sink in, but at last, it does . . . even through this thick sans mort *skull. Eventually, I realized I would never find the woman I was searching for. I had lost her when I chose to become* sans mort, *as I lost my family and all the others I had loved. I purposely made myself this way, placed myself outside the pale of human existence and human love, and for eternity I would pay that price.*

At last, I bowed my head to the inevitable, and continued my existence alone. As I was meant to do all along . . .

Chapter 8

Alysse
New York City, New York
April, 3304

"Damién, is it you?"

He'd been strolling down Park Avenue, heading back to his hotel after doing a little hunting when that question came from behind him. Turning, he saw Domingo standing there.

Nothing like the last time he'd seen him, dressed in sweats and trainers, having just come in from a night run along the perimeter of the moat surrounding their internment camp upriver from New Orleans. Now, he was in business suit and wingtips, and sporting a moustache—of all things—in a time when facial hair was strictly unfashionable.

"Domingo, how surprising but good to see you." As if they'd been apart only a few days instead of a few centuries.

He caught the hand Dom held out to him, performing what he had come to call the *hetero-human bump*. Grasp the right hand, seize the shoulder with the free one and pull the person toward you so chests collided. Then, a quick slap on the back and separate—the accepted greeting between males these days.

"How long's it been? You look great, *compadre*. Are you headed anywhere in particular?" As usual, the Spaniard shot a volley of questions at him without giving him time to answer. "Have you fed?"

"Just finished." Damién hoped any passersby hearing that would think he meant dinner. He'd waylaid a homeless person stopping him to beg a credit or two, drank his fill, then left him with an antique coin worth several hundred. He hoped no one would kill the poor fool and steal it.

"So have I. But look—here's a Starbuck's." Dom glanced up at the holosign floating before the little shop. "Why don't we go in and have an *après diner cafe*?" Without waiting for an answer, he seized Damién's arm and walked toward the door, dragging him along.

Luckily, the automatic doors could also be opened manually; that was one problem with being *sans mort* . . . electronic equipment couldn't detect their existence so wouldn't work for them. Damién had been often stranded outside buildings while people tried to figure out why their equipment *malfunctioned*. Being a business open to all, vampires didn't have to be invited in, so Dom pushed open the door and went inside, releasing Damién as he did so.

The shop was a Starbucks Century Thirty-four, boasting that recently-revived ancient practice of forcing patrons to queue themselves before a cashier to get their beverages. Damién had always referred to that with the unkindly description of *guiding hogs to a trough*. The college student took their order for "two *expresso grandes*—is that acceptable, *amigo*?" shoved the two plasticon cups across the counter and looked past them to the next in line.

"So . . . how have you been?" Dom ignored the cooling coffee which would end up being poured out after he left the shop. "Recovered from our concentration camp ordeal, have you?"

"Don't even mention that." Damién gave a theatrical shudder. "I don't want to think about that part of my life again, and I wouldn't think you would, either. I'm just thankful they didn't figure out some way to keep track of us after we were all released."

"That's what they said, anyway," Dom agreed, darkly.

"What do you mean?"

"They've such advanced technology these days, *amigo*. Had some then, too. Who's to know if they put some *nanobots* or something in the plasma they so kindly supplied us every week and are even now monitoring our whereabouts . . . or tracking devices in the water of our tattoos?"

"*Unspeakable Name*. Dom, you're not becoming a conspiracy freak in your old age?" Dami laughed to cover up the fact he'd often had the same thought but ascribed it to the persecution complex he'd developed and kept for several decades after being released. He changed the subject to something safer. "What have you been up to?"

"Oh, nothing much. Keeping a low profile, as they say. I stay in touch with my stepdaughter's descendants whenever I can . . . pop up in California every decade or so and stay a few days, pretending to be a distant relative from *Nuevo España*. She kept my name, you know."

He shook his head, picking up the rigid little cup and tilting it slightly so the coffee inside—not the real stuff, but a cereal substitute—swirled around. Coffee had been second only to tobacco on the *Proscribed Substances List* for centuries now and illegal to possess or consume. Probably because of that fact, many *sans morts* delighted indulging in both.

"I really loved that kid. She cried when we staged my death, even though she knew the truth. It hurt me more than I can say when she died."

Damién didn't answer. That was the most difficult part of being immortal, leaving behind those one had developed a true affection for. They were both silent for a moment before Dom spoke again.

"How about you?"

"Oh, I go wherever the mood strikes me, footloose and fancy-free, as they say . . . got a condo in Miami, a townhouse on the West Coast and a penthouse in the Big Apple. I have an art gallery here. Supposedly, that's the source of my income." He smiled slightly, thinking about a restored short film he'd seen in a cinema museum in Miami once. *Dracula Bites the Big Apple.* He wondered how many nibbles the *sans mort* had taken out of the city in the past two millennia.

"Have you kept in touch with anyone from the camp?"

After being freed, they'd dispersed quickly, as if fearing even gathering in pairs might bring them to the wrong attention and they'd be hauled back again. They'd all agreed not to advertise what they were, assuming mortal personas. Hiding under false identities, pretending once more to be human. Human attitude helped; many were actually ashamed of that portion of their social history. They neither asked where the *sans mort* went nor wanted to know, just accepted their disappearance with some relief and pretended they no longer existed. Today, no *sans mort* in his right mind would dare admit his immortality. Pretty soon, humans might even question that such a thing had ever happened.

In this instance, *Critical Erase Theory* dive-bombed a new low. With that perversity History shows now and then, the vogue of believing in mythical vampires was once more on the rise.

Back to *Square One*.

"We see each other from time to time . . . my old friends and acquaintances . . . Lucien, Morgan, Armand . . ."

"It's a wonder that camp managed to stay in one piece with so many alphas in it." Domingo shook his head, remembering. "Lucien was determined to run everything, Morgan didn't care one way or the other as long as he had that blasted piano, I sided with Morgan, and you— Our reluctant leader . . ."

"That certainly shot Lucien down in flames, didn't it? Everyone unanimously picking me. Well, we all managed to survive and come out of it. Morgan's even re-established his career, I see. Under a slightly assumed name. Morgan Averil . . . kind of appropriate."

"That was a good idea, translating his title like that." Dom agreed. "I've done the same occasionally. Once even called myself *Dominick Sunday*. No use tempting Fate by keeping the same name through the centuries. Sooner or later someone's bound to notice."

"Law of Averages," Damién agreed.

"So. Are you going to the concert tonight? I understand the New Millennium-Carnegie is sold out."

"How could I miss it? I bought a ticket as soon as it was announced." He'd always enjoyed Morgan's music. It had been one of the few things making their imprisonment bearable. To once again hear the melodies he could extract from a piano . . .

"I'll be there, too, and at the after-performance party. Got a special invitation. You?"

"I'm not sure . . ." He'd gotten an invite in the mail. Engraved, on creamy, heavy bond but Damién wasn't certain he really wanted to see the blond pianist face-to-face again. It would stir up memories he preferred stay buried . . . of that hapless young human Michel, how he had tried to save him . . . "Will Lucien be there do you suppose?"

"He's in London at the moment. Some problem with establishing a Black Swan club here in New York. He really wasn't happy to leave right now, you'd better believe it." Dom glanced at his watch, getting to his feet. The timepiece was just for show. It didn't work; *sans mort* negative energy did something to the electronics. "Well, guess I'd better get going. I'll see you tonight then."

And he was gone, before Damién could agree or manage an excuse not to be there.

***

Morgan got a standing ovation the moment he appeared, a tall, slim figure encircled by a single spotlight on an otherwise darkened stage. The evening clothes he'd chosen for this performance were similar to the ones he'd been wearing the first time Damién saw him shortly after he arrived in London at the end of the Eighteenth Century. Flamboyant in their own way . . . a tailed evening coat pre-dating the Regency style, stovepipe-legged pants, gleaming white silk shirt with a white waistcoat embroidered with silver thread, and a cravat looped gracefully around his throat. His blond hair was tied back by a wide black ribbon.

It was currently the style for men's hair to be very short, almost shaved, long hair favored only by those in some field of public entertainment, so that was how Morgan got away with that shoulder-length mane. Hairlessness of head and body was the rage, though Domingo had sworn he'd never shave anything other than his face, and woe be to the valet or *coiffeur* daring to come within fifteen feet of his Family Jewels with a razor. He might keep his own hair closely-trimmed but he'd never understood why a man would voluntarily shave his cock, and though he had a few women actually flinch when they'd seen the dark thatch covering his body, once under vampire enchantment, they hadn't complained, didn't give a damn, then. He imagined he could've been as hairy as a bear and there wouldn't have been a whimper.

On Morgan the long hair looked good. It fit perfectly the romantic image he projected and the music he played. *Prince Charming at the pianoforte.*

As the applause died away, Damién settled himself, listening as his friend walked to the piano he'd managed to miraculously find again after his release. Though battered and chipped, its tone was still impeccable and its outer shell had been restored to perfection.

He closed his eyes as Morgan flipped up his tails, seated himself on the bench and raised his hands to strike the first notes . . .

* * *

The backstage pass was there for him, just as the invitation promised. The guard checked his name off the list in his HCU—a combination cell phone/miniature computer unit, attached a holographic name tag to his lapel—it floated like a spiraling star—and gave him directions to the reception suite, waving him inside.

He went through a dark hallway, around a corner and found himself in a large open area brilliantly lit, filled with people, and alive with voices, laughter, and music . . . with Morgan in the middle of it. No sooner had he stepped out of the dimness of the corridor than he was spotted.

"Damién! *Mon copain.*" Saying something to those around him—mostly women, Damién noted, and all dazzled by that vampiric aura—Morgan rushed forward to perform the obligatory greeting, then stepped back. Those blue eyes gazed at him as if he truly were happy to see his old friend.

They exchanged pleasantries.

Damién asked about Morgan's wife. Isabeau was a Southern belle and a well-known scientist and their love was a tempestuous, on-again/off-again *affaire,* at the moment more off than on, though Morgan had confidence they would be reconciled soon . . . *again.* In the meantime, he was playing the field until that reconciliation occurred, when he'd become a completely faithful husband. *Also, again.*

Damién got invited to dinner in a couple of weeks, then Morgan was swept away by his agent who had found some bigwig wanting to sponsor a concert on the West Coast, and he was alone again. He accepted a drink from a passing waiter, raising it to inhale the alcoholic scent, recognizing it as *Dom Perignon Avant Millenium Deux.* Leave it to Morgan to ask for the best, even if he couldn't drink it. And to get it, because he was worth every penny. Then, he simply stood there.

Not for long.

"Dami!" It was Domingo, resplendent in evening suit with a scarlet vest and cummerbund, hurrying toward him. He held the hand of a young woman. "I've someone I want you to meet."

They stopped before him. The girl was young, much too young to be at such an event, he thought, recognizing her as one of those who'd been standing near Morgan. She should be at home with her nanny. Dressed in a white sheath of some sheer stuff seeming to simply be wrapped around and around her slender body. He wondered how it managed to withstand the pull of gravity since he saw no straps or ribbons. Then he looked at her face and forgot about the dress.

She was familiar. Somehow. Blonde, blue-eyed. So small and innocent-looking, but older than he'd first thought. Still, so very, very young, possibly not more than twenty-one. There was an odd glowing aura about her, twinkling like little stars with spaces of darkness. He knew he'd never seen her before but there was something about her reminding him of someone he'd known.

"Damién La Croix, may I present Alysse Constance La Croix. Alysse is from *La France Nouveau*." Dom looked satisfied at the little start Damién gave upon hearing his surname repeated, saying as if just realizing that fact, "Hey, same last name. Perhaps you two are distantly related?" He smirked slightly and bowed to the girl. "Now, my dear, I've done as you asked, and must get back to my date."

He nodded toward a dark woman in red, standing near a table of *h'ors doeurves,* winked at Damién, and walked away. Damién accepted the girl's offered hand, bowed and released it.

She asked to be introduced to me? Why?

"Well, Mr. La Croix, do you suppose we *are* distant relatives?" The girl's voice was soft and quiet but it wasn't simply low-pitched. It was weak, and Damién thought he detected a brief breathiness. He had to lean forward slightly to hear.

He inhaled deeply, trying to pick up her scent. There were too many mortals around, too much perfume and aftershave and alcohol and food smells. He could barely detect the subtle, young female fragrance, and something else . . . A brief unpleasant whiff. *Is she ill?*

"I rather doubt that, Mistress La Croix—may I call you Alysse? Having to repeat my own name each time I speak to you will become tedious after a few moments." He pretended to drink his champagne, looking out over the milling bodies. To his right, Morgan was feigning reluctance as he strolled to the piano, allowing himself to be "persuaded" to play something.

"Please, I'd prefer it anyway."

"To answer your question . . . *non*, I doubt we have any connection. My family left France a long time ago."

Morgan touched the keys, *Traumerei* floated over the voices . . . soft, sentimental, sad . . .

"You can be so certain without any knowledge of which part of the country I'm from?"

That stopped him momentarily. *Damn, should've asked that first, then denied it.*

He had a sudden sense that in spite of being so young,

she was also very sharp.

A spout of laughter made her turn slightly, looking over her shoulder at a young man standing near the door.

"My brother, the *marquis*." She waited a fraction of a moment as if studying his reaction to that. Her accent was barely noticeable, even less than Damién's own. "We're from *Village La Croix*. In Limousin. You're familiar with it?"

Marquis *La Croix? How can that be? I was the last one. And I personally burned the village to the ground, along with the* château.

He'd made it Konstancza's tomb, as well as her funeral pyre. He struggled not to let his confusion show, knew he failed as she smiled.

Who are they? Really? Imposters working some kind of scam, pretending to be Neo-European royalty?

"I was unaware that particular title still existed. I'd always thought that branch of the La Croix family died out during that plague they had back in the thirteenth century or whenever it was." He forced himself to sound suitably vague. Would someone in this millennia know of such ancient history?

"And yet—here we are." She spread her arms as if presenting herself to him once more and stepped closer. Damién surprised himself by moving a pace backward. It made him appear afraid, and that angered him. *Of a girl barely out of her teens who isn't as tall as my shoulder?* He fought to hide it.

What she said next only added to his confusion.

"I'm glad you came tonight. I was afraid you'd ignore the invitation. When I suggested it to Morgan, he was doubtful, too."

She asked Morgan to invite me? What's going on?

"And miss seeing my old friend?" No need to let her know he'd almost done exactly that. "Believe me, hearing his rendition of Liszt's *Festival at Pesth* was a delight. I doubt anyone else could make that music sound so carefree and charming."

Morgan had left the piano now, again acting the host.

She made an impatient sound. "Please, Damién, no more games. I know what you are."

"Other than an independently-wealthy Frenchman and a friend of Morgan Averil, famous concert pianist?" He decided to play it for laughs. Things were getting more confusing.

"I know about Morgan, too." She glanced to where his friend stood, watching as he left one group and approached her brother—the *faux marquis*—speaking to the young man and laughing at his answer. "In fact, it was he who helped me find you. Unknowingly."

"I didn't realize I was lost." *What the hell does she want? What does she know?* He wasn't certain just how much to say. They might merely be talking at cross-purposes. This could just be some odd form of flirting, but the girl's words had such an ominous undertone, he didn't think so.

"You hid your tracks well, but I've a vast amount of money at my disposal, and my brother has enough influence to get me any information I wish." She looked satisfied. "You didn't stay hidden very long. Or your secret either."

"And what secret is that, *chérie*?" He felt cold slither down his spine. Knew what she was going to say even as those beautiful pink lips opened to speak the words.

"That you're a *sans mort*, of course." At least she whispered them. No one around paid the least attention. "Other than I, only Alain knows, and I'm certain you don't want anyone else to be aware."

"What do you want?" Coldness engulfed him. She wasn't bluffing. "I—"

"Alysse?" Her brother's call interrupted.

Damién realized he had no idea what he'd been about to say, only that her words made the oddest sick feeling in his stomach. Something he hadn't felt in a very long time. Not since the day the bounty hunters carried him, bound and gagged, from the boat into the internment camp.

Fear.

"It looks like Alain's ready to go. We're renting a house while we're here. Out on Long Island. Why don't you stop by tomorrow evening? For drinks?" Her mouth quirked a little as she said that. She fumbled in her small evening purse, bringing out a tiny hand unit. "We can talk more. Do you have your Hand Computer Unit with you?"

He answered by retrieving his own from a breast pocket, holding it up. She tapped hers against it. There was a sharp little *beep*.

"Our address and how to get there. See you around eight?" She raised one hand in a fluttery wave, then hurried toward her brother who was waiting impatiently. He was young also, only a few years older, Damién noted, and as blond as she. When she was a few feet away, she looked back as if remembering something.

"To answer your question, Damién . . . I want you to help me die."

* * *

The next night, Damién landed at the La Croix estate. His valet, also subbing as chauffeur, had no problem following the directions Alysse had sent to his HCU. Jean-Louis piloted the *Rolls Aero-Argent* skillfully, and they arrived within a few minutes of eight o'clock, landing on the little strip before the house. He was greeted at the door by the butler who ushered him into the drawing-room and hurried away to let "Mistress Alysse know you're here, Master La Croix."

He had time to roam the room briefly, glancing at some laser-prints grouped on one wall. Landscape scene . . . some ancient buildings . . . one looked disturbing familiar. He leaned closer to get a better look . . .

"Damién, I'm so glad you came." She was there, filling the room with that faint glow. As Damién turned to look at her, it seemed to flicker and grow dim.

"How could I resist after those cryptic remarks you made?" He took her hand, bowing over it as before, inhaling quickly, trying to separate the scents he now detected.

Away from the swirl of odors at the reception, it was much easier, but no less confusion. There was the essence of young mortal female . . . a subtle blending of oils and waters making up her perfume, some kind of emollient lotion, and something else. As before . . . faint but bitter. He still didn't recognize it but knew he should.

"Especially that last one."

"I'll get to that in a moment." She brushed aside his reference to her wishing to die. "I imagine first and foremost, you'd like to know why we've appropriated your surname, and exactly what I know of those thirteenth-century La Croix you spoke of last night."

"If it leads to an explanation of why you think I'm a

sans mort, I most certainly do." He was going to continue denying it until she proved her knowledge to him in no uncertain terms.

"If you still insist on pretending . . ." She shrugged and sat down on a nearby Victorian settee—the genuine article, he was certain—motioning for Damién to sit also. He carefully chose a chair opposite, facing her. That made her smile slightly. "Let's see. Where to start?"

"How about with who you really are." It was said a little sharper than he intended. If her brother was renting this place, he had to have money, so why would he need more? He'd done a little Info-Surfing on the Web last night, found a great deal on the *le Marquis* La Croix and sister, and all of it appeared legitimate. If they weren't into some elaborate confidence game—and their very youth would indicate they couldn't be very practiced at it yet— what was it?

And why me as their target?

"You first." She looked as if she were playing a guessing game of some kind, eyes sparkling. "Admit who you really are, and I'll do the same."

Stalemate. There was no way out of it. So, he'd do it. He had to know. Afterward, if she tried to spread a rumor, attempting any kind of blackmail, he'd simply say he was humoring the child because he thought she was into some fantasizing little pastime. Then, he'd caution her brother against letting her be so indiscreet again. Turn it back on her, embarrass her, if necessary.

"Very well." He sighed in surrender and it wasn't all an act. "I'm a *sans mort*. Damién La Croix, tenth *Marquis* La Croix. Born in 1225, died in 1249. There. Satisfied?" She didn't say anything, but her look was triumphant.

"Now, your turn."

"Very well." She took a deep breath. "My real name is Alysse Constance La Croix. And my brother is truly the *Marquis* La Croix."

"I thought you were going to tell me the truth." He let his annoyance show. "I've confessed something very dangerous about myself and you still give me that lie?"

"It isn't a lie." She made soothing motions with her hands though she didn't look fearful.

"*Non.*" Anger made him forget his former decision. "I remember very well burning *Village La Croix* to the ground and my home with it. After I was attacked."

"You killed everyone in the village and there was no one left alive in the *château.*" She made it a statement. "Did that twice, if I remember correctly."

"That's right." He thought again of returning to the *château*, walking into that room where Konstancza's body lay upon the floor in a pool of drying blood. He'd picked her up, carried her to the table and arranged her dear corpse upon it, carefully folding her encrimsoned skirt over her legs and silently cursing those who'd left her lying there so immodestly. A last kiss to her cold lips and he thrust his hands into the still-glowing fire, lifting out burning embers with his bare hands, listening to his flesh crackle and sear as he tossed the coals onto chairs and the floor. Watching with satisfaction when fabric and wood began to smolder and burn.

When he stalked out, the place had been in flames, consuming Konstancza and her unborn child along with his hopes.

"Are you certain?"

"What game are you playing, girl? *Merde!* Let's stop this

verbal dancing around each other. Speak plainly and tell me exactly what you mean." Damién got up, staring out the open doors into the garden. It was lit by solar-powered fairy lights, set into the border of liriope lining the paved walkway winding though the flowers.

She nodded, more a graceful inclination of that blond head, agreeing. He didn't see that, keeping his gaze intently on the open doorway.

"There was always a legend in our family. That we were descended from a foreign woman who'd been mistress to the last *true* La Croix." Her voice was softer now, that vague French accent more pronounced. Damién turned to look at her. "It was said she was killed when the villagers stormed the *château* attempting to drive him away because he was supposedly a *sans mort*."

"A *legend*, you say. Very well. I'll confirm it. It's true. She was killed, protecting me. She and her unborn child died, getting between me and a stake." He paused, swallowing loudly as a sudden fullness welled inside. "And no—the child wasn't mine. That didn't matter. I accepted it. But they both died."

"Did they?"

"Please." His sigh was heavy as he returned to the chair. Suddenly, he felt more than weary, as if feeling all those centuries on his shoulders. "No more riddles."

She must have sensed that internal change for she looked apologetic.

"I'm sorry. I didn't mean to upset you. I had pictured this as a dramatic but happy scene. My revealing ourselves to you . . . you admitting who you are . . . sort of a crazy family reunion."

He didn't answer, just gave her a quiet look, waiting.

"The truth, Damién... She—was her name Konstancza as we were told?"

He nodded. Her knowing that couldn't surprise him now.

"Konstancza died but her child lived..." Damién's head jerked up, his eyes staring into hers as she went on, "The story goes that the priest called gave her *Last Rites*..."

***

He listened to her confession, carried out Extreme Unction, *and was putting the small bottle of holy oil, his prayer book, and his stolla back into the little box he'd brought with him. Konstancza lay with her eyes closed. She didn't appear to be in pain; the wound in her chest had stopped flowing and he was certain she'd soon be gone. He studied her face.*

A beautiful woman. And obviously a pious one. How could she love such a godless creature? And the child she carries. So sad for it to die. Whose was it? Everyone knew sans mort *were unable to have carnal knowledge of females. How could—*

With a gasp, Konstancza opened her eyes. One hand seized Père Alphonse's wrist. "Father, my baby—"

There was a liquid gushing and a ripping sound. She bit her lip to stifle the scream. Blood trickled down her chin and he heard a faint, muffled mewing.

Pulling his hand from Konstancza's, Père *Alphonse touched the hem of her skirt, gently lifting it away from her bent knees. What he saw made him start in amazement.*

Between Konstancza's thighs lay an infant, still attached to its mother by the blue-mottled cord. It moved slightly, giving that weak cry again, little arms waving. Alphonse's startled gaze swept over the tiny body . . . blood-smeared, covered with birth-slime . . . a boy. Alive.

Konstancza moaned slightly, head moving from side to side. Her breathing was getting shorter, more stressed. He had to hurry. Had to let her see her child before she left them. An abandoned dagger lay nearby on the floor. He seized it and cut the cord, knotting the slippery, bleeding end with his fingers, and lifted the infant in his arms.

"My child, you have a son." He held the baby where she could see it without lifting her head. She touched it with one hand, fingers stroking along the little cheek. The baby gave a soft whimper, then quieted.

"Baptize him, Father. Quickly. Let me see that before— Name him Damién.*"*

He would've protested calling such an innocent miracle after that godless creature but it was a mother's dying wish. With one hand, he fumbled with the box, got out the oil and whispered, "Damién La Croix, I baptize thee in the name of the Father, the Son, and the Holy Spirit, as it is your mother's wish. Grow and flourish and become a holy, god-fearing man." He turned to look down at Konstancza. "There, my child, he's—"

Sightless eyes stared into his. As he reached down to close them, he hoped she'd lasted long enough to know the child was taken into God's fold. He also realized he had a problem.

The sans mort *mustn't know of the child. He had to get him away. The infant had fallen asleep, as if the holy oil on its tiny brow had soothed it. He was so small, like a cherub, the pale floss on the little head fine as angel's hair.*

It would fit in the box . . .

When Père Alphonse *left the château, he took Konstancza's child and the paper he'd found near her body—the deed to Damién's* château—*with him, safely tucked inside the box . . .*

***

As Alysse fell silent, Damién said, "If only I'd known . . . Thank you for telling me my darling Konstancza's child survived but I still don't understand why you've done this. Or how you can claim the lands in Limousin."

"I'm coming to that," Alysse answered. "You see, the priest took the baby back to the church—"

"They rebuilt it then?" She gave him a questioning look. He admitted with more than a little shame, "I-I burned it, also. Twice. Once, while I lived. In a rage."

"Oh. Well, I suppose they did. It's still there, and we've been told it dates from the early fourteenth century." She resumed her story.

***

Père Alphonse hurried back to the church. It was getting dark and he was certain with the falling of night, the sans morts *would free themselves from their captors and a bloodbath was in the making. Going to the little shed behind the church, he set the box in the straw and quickly milked the one cow the church was allowed to keep, taking both bucket and box back into the little kitchen. There, he freed the baby from the box, seeing with relief it still breathed. Dipping a piece of cloth into the milk, he stuck it into the little mouth. When it was sucked dry, he performed that act again and again until the child burped slightly and fell asleep.*

It was then he became aware of the flames reflecting on the clouds and heard the faraway screams and knew the villagers were being slaughtered. He stood at the door of the church, holding the sleeping child and watching Village La Croix's *death struggles and wondered if he would be next.*

Once, he heard the flapping of wings, and something striking the roof. Soon the timbers were burning and he hurried to his room in the cellar, crouching there on his cot with the child still in his arms as the church burned above them.

Much later, the survivors appeared at his door, making their way to what was left of the church—Jean-Paul DuPont and his family, and soon after, a terrified Louis. Learning who the baby was, he snatched it from the priest's embrace.

"He spared me," the boy shouted as Père *Alphonse tried to calm him. "I caused all this. His woman died because of me. He gave me back my life and the only way I can thank him is to raise this child for him."*

* * *

"And that's what happened," Alysse concluded. "The DuPonts moved into the surviving rooms of the *château*. They buried Konstancza's ashes in the church yard, and sent out messages to other villages, asking for settlers to come and bring their village back to life. Any traveler or vagrant passing through was encouraged to stay. Louis married and raised young Damién as his child. Using the deed, he took the La Croix name as his own, claimed the estate for the boy and continued to live there. From the ashes of the *château*, they managed to salvage several casks containing foreign coin, and from that small wealth, the La Croix family became again a rich and noble one."

"And you're named for her." That appeared to be all Damién had heard of the last part of her explanation.

She nodded. She seemed surprised he should appear so dazed.

Poor child, he thought. *How can she know of what I lost the day Konstancza died and what she's just given back to me?* Briefly, he wished he could fall to his knees and speak God's name in thanks without bursting into flame.

"I've pictures of the *château*. Would you like to see them? You could tell me how close to the original they were able to make it."

Silently, he stood and allowed her to lead him to the grouping on the wall. Now, he knew why the building was so familiar. He looked at it as he'd been doing when she entered. Closely. Yes, it was similar to his home but the shape was a little different. There was two less stories and undoubtedly less rooms.

"It's . . . similar enough," was all he could manage. His eyes were stinging. *Tears? Now? After all these years?* Blinking, he looked down at her. "Thank you for that explanation, *chérie*. Now, the rest of it? Your wish?"

He was certain that would be the most important of all the things he'd learned this night.

"Let's go outside. I'd like to show you the garden."

Obediently, he followed her through the open doors onto the paved walkway with its fairy lights.

* * *

"This is a lovely place," Alysse said. She took Damién's hand as they went down the path. It felt warm and trusting in his cold one and he didn't pull away.

He liked her touch. Her hand felt as if it belonged in his. He remembered how Konstancza had liked to hold his hand, warming it with her kisses.

"We have one like it back home and when I die, I'd like to be buried there, among the roses. Or . . ." She swung around to look up at him. ". . . perhaps not, if you're agreeable."

"That's morbid talk." He ignored the insinuation, hoping he'd imagined it. "Why do you believe you're going to die, Alysse? You're too young to have thoughts like that."

"Because it's true." She pulled her hand from his. "I've a rare circulatory disease, Damién."

Is that what I sensed? Incipient death running through her delicate veins?

"That doesn't necessarily make it terminal. With all the things they're doing in medicine these days—"

"—no one can help me. I have only a few months left. As far as the entire medical community is aware, I'm the only one with this particular condition, and no one has the faintest idea what to do." She gave an unhappy little laugh, eyes bleak. "Isn't that ironic? My brother has enough money for three men. We can colonize planets, go beyond our own system into other galaxies but no one and no amount of credits can save one specific human life."

"What—"

"I'm not going to bore you with explanations. All you need to know is: It's fatal and no one can do anything about it . . . except perhaps you."

"Non." He didn't hesitate, didn't even have to think about it.

"No? Just like that. Wouldn't you like to think it over?" She didn't appear surprised by his refusal.

"I can't, Alysse. Not even for you. Especially not for you." He was struck by the parallel between his own situation and hers. He'd wanted to escape the death staring him in the face, just as she was attempting. He'd chanced upon LeMaitre and seized the opportunity. It had been a questionably fortuitous accident, but Alysse had hunted him down, relentlessly, with one specific goal in mind.

"Don't speak so quickly, Damién. Also, don't think I'm doing this on a whim. I thought this over for a long time before I began searching for you. It wasn't easy . . . even though I've been the family historian since I was fifteen. But I had the time, the *expertise,* and the money, and my brother's connections, and I succeeded." There was a brief smile. "Though picking up your trail again after the Liberation was really a trial."

They stopped near a tea olive bush. She snapped off a twig, pressing the sweet-spelling little buds against her nose, inhaled loudly before turning to him again.

"Don't refuse me now, Damién. Think about it . . . how it'll enable me to continue my good works . . . and keep your Konstancza alive for you."

She held the sprig of flowers against his cheek, stroked the leaves down it. It tickled slightly.

Damién breathed in the scent. It awakened another memory . . . of the flowers filling the vases lining his parents' home in La Croix. The scent turned cloying, filled with death. He moved his head, turning away from the suddenly-sickening fragrance.

Alysse moved closer, her hand sliding to his shoulders, her voice dropping to a soft, insinuating whisper. "*Turn me, Damién, and I'll be your Konstancza. I'll take her place. I'll do anything and everything for you . . .*"

Standing on tiptoe, she pulled his head down, pressing her lips against his. It was awkward at first, he was so much taller. Then the kiss strengthened, became more forceful. It wasn't a shy, virginal brush of lips but a caress with determination and will-power behind it. Damién was suddenly very aware that Alysse might be one who could cross the Veil and awaken as a *sans mort*. He was also shocked to feel himself responding to the brush of that frail young body against his.

Unlike some, he'd never preyed on one he considered a child. Young adults, he'd accept, but anyone whose age he questioned ... He'd once or twice actually maneuvered a glimpse at identification holocards to assure himself he wasn't becoming that kind of predator, holding firm to his belief that youngsters were too guided by their emotions to be competent in such a serious decision as sharing their blood. But with Alysse ...

He had no doubt she knew exactly what she was doing. Also, that she didn't want him but would gladly trade her body for what his could give her. He also knew in that moment, he wanted it, also. One hand came up, encircling her back, pulling her closer while the other brushed across her young breasts, fingers caressing a nipple, feeling it peak and harden. He was hardening, too, lower down, his cock rising and stiff, driving of its own motion against her slender thighs, suffusing itself with blood, while his tongue wanted to taste hers.

He could hear her heartbeat increasing, pulse suddenly racing, that death-dealing blood thrumming through her veins. He felt his fangs drop ...

"Non!" Damién pushed her away so quickly, she staggered and nearly fell. He caught her arm as she regained her balance.

"Why not?" She stared up at him. He was certain she was going to burst into tears. Surprisingly, she regained control.

"I've only *turned* three people in my life, Alysse, and two were terrible mistakes. I swore I'd never do it again, and I won't. Not even for you. I'm sorry."

The sad part? He really was.

"You're sorry?" She jerked her arm from his grasp, throwing the sprig of tea olive to the ground. "That'll be little comfort when I'm dead and buried. Will you come to my funeral and give my brother your condolences? If you do, be sure to tell him how you could've saved me . . . to stay with him . . . to continue my life . . . and wouldn't."

"Alysse, be reasonable. I didn't come by my decision without much thought. Sometimes . . . if a person has hidden vices, perhaps isn't even aware of them, becoming *sans mort* brings them out. They change. And not for the better."

"I don't have any bad habits. I'll still be myself."

He wondered if that was true. This iron determination . . . that could easily become something else. He shook his head.

"Very well." If he thought she'd accepted his refusal, her next words killed that idea. Angry and petulant, like a child refused a much-wanted treat. "You're not the only *sans mort* around, you know. There were plenty at the reception the other night. My research got me a list of them. I'm certain I can find someone else who'll be a little more obliging. Your friend Domingo, or perhaps even Morgan himself." She smiled, and it was startling in its smugness. She touched her breast, sliding fingers down her ribs. It was a shocking, sensual gesture. "Morgan likes me."

"He'd never do that." He felt a twinge of doubt as he spoke. Domingo, would refuse, he was certain, but Morgan ... The Englishman might be persuaded by the girl's fatal condition.

"I think you'd better go now, Damién. Suddenly, I feel very tired." She sank onto the stone bench, turned away from him.

He stood there a moment more, then hurried up the path back to the house. Inside again, he asked the butler to send someone to have Jean-Louis bring the car around, then waited on the front stoop for it. As he stood there, he realized what that unknown scent in Alysse' blood had been. The pheromone of death ... as tempting as an aphrodisiac for some of his kind.

It would draw them to her as nectar attracting a bee.

***

His first act the next night was to get in touch with Domingo. The Spaniard's reaction was as he'd expected.

"Damién, I should be insulted you'd even ask me that, but I understand. Believe me when I say, your young lady is safe from me." Dom poured and offered blood brandy. "Unfortunately, there may be others not so disciplined. I think you should warn her brother so he can watch her."

"Don't you suppose he already knows? She says he's aware of what I am."

"But not necessarily of her plan. Tell him."

"I will," Damién promised. "After I speak to Morgan."

***

Speaking to Morgan wasn't all that easy. He was in the middle of that week-long engagement at New Millennium-Carnegie and—unlike the first night with its reception and partying and schmoozing—prone to disappear into his penthouse immediately after the performances. That particular night was a Saturday, so Damién was certain Morgan would be ready for a little night-howling, performances or not. He'd managed to send word backstage, getting through to the valet, Trevor, who promised to relay his message.

When he reappeared after the curtains closed and the crowd vacated the theater, he was admitted and given directions to the guest dressing room. Trevor was there to greet him, bustling about laying out clothes while Morgan sat on a bench before an elaborate dressing table with a well-lit mirror.

"Dami!" He smiled at Damién's barely noticeable wince as he turned to look behind him, catching his friend's sidle out of sight of the looking-glass.

For once, Damién felt a stab of envy. *Lucky devils, having an image. The Church had taught* sans mort *have none because they have no soul. Does this mean* Vampyres *still retain some vestige of humanity?* He's never thought of that before. It prickled a little.

"Sit down. This won't take long. Those blasted Klieg lights are devilish hot. Makes even a vampyre sweat."

Getting to his feet, Morgan hurried into the bathroom where Damién could hear water running and multiple splashes. When he reappeared, he was scrubbing his face with a towel.

"Trevor said you wanted to talk to me?" Morgan removed the shirt he'd worn onstage, draping it over the back of a chair. He dabbed at his chest and neck to blot the last stray drops of water.

"That's right, I—" Damién was distracted by sight of his friend's bared chest, the hair so pale it was almost invisible. "You aren't following that disgusting trend, are you?"

"What?" Morgan's eyes followed his gaze. "Good Lord, no." He shrugged as he reached for the shirt Trevor held, exchanging it for the towel. "It's all there, just not too visible. You and I have never had any reason to view each other naked, old chap, so you couldn't possibly know."

He spread his arms and did a turn in the center of the room.

"This, Damién, is my natural appearance, as God—unfortunately or not—made me. Though I really don't think about *that,* any more. Fact of the matter, it's mostly *glamour.* It helps when I'm stretched out naked on a bed with a woman. Usually, anyway. Though there was that one . . . She was practically ecstatic. University professor, I think. Gave me a lecture on my adherence to the *prevalent cultural non-hirsute tendency,* which wasn't exactly what I wanted at that precise moment. Kept going on and on, "My God, your skin is so bare . . . so smooth . . . so silky . . . Morgan, you're perfection . . . I have to touch you . . ." His voice went up in a sarcastic falsetto. "Trouble was, she never did. Not that I don't appreciate a compliment now and then, but she kept talking and talking . . . I *enthralled* her to shut her up. Damned distracting."

He slid off the stovepipe trousers, stepping into a more modern pair. Damién thought about what he'd just said and laughed, shaking his head.

"Leave it to you . . ." was all he could choke out.

"How about you, *mon cher Français?*" came the amused

question. "Still wooly as a bear? Probably keeps your tool warm in winter, I imagine."

"Never mind my... Morgan, I've something very important to discuss."

"So?" He closed the shirt, tucked it into the waistband of his trousers and looked at Damién. "Discuss."

"It's about Alysse La Croix..." That was as far as he got.

"Isn't she the most delightful little creature? Trevor, can you help me here?" Morgan turned his attention to his hair, getting the comb caught in a tangle. The valet took the comb, deftly did away with the little knot and tied it back. "Delicious, too, I might add."

"Morgan, I swear, if you've..." Before he realized it, Damién was at the dressing table, one fist raised.

"Hey! Relax, old boy, I was just joking." Morgan was on his feet, surprise on the aristocratic British features. "Is that jealousy I see? I'm not trespassing on your territory, am I?" He pretended to peer at Damién. "No. Something else. What is it, Dami?"

"Alysse is sick. She's dying." He decided to be as blunt as possible. "She's looking for someone to *bring her over*, and I turned her down."

"And you're wondering if she came to me." Morgan didn't ask any questions. Rather, he seemed to be considering what to say. "Yes, she did."

"And...?"

"And... I told her I'd think about it."

"Think about it? Morgan, you can't. She doesn't know what it involves."

"Damién, my old friend, I think the young lady knows exactly what becoming *Undead* involves. As a matter of fact, we talked it over in great detail when she put the idea to me. Went over all the pros and cons. I didn't sugar-coat it, explained how the Vampyre aren't the same as you *sans mort*. That with me as her sire, she'd be transformed into a new, separate species. She told me you'd refused her. Also, why she'd chosen you to start with, so I understand what she means to you. But . . . ."

"D'Arcy, I swear, if you do what she wants, I'll . . . ."

"What will you do? Challenge me to a duel? Kill me? Damién, I think you need to go home and calm down. You're letting your concern for this girl get out of control. Find yourself a woman and fuck her and yourself into exhaustion. You're getting a reputation as *celibaitaire*, did you know that? Forget about Alysse La Croix. She's beyond your help." He walked to the door, holding it open. "I'm meeting Alysse in half an hour and it'll take that long to fly there, even in my Jag. Come on, I'll walk you out."

"Don't do this, Morgan." That was all Damién said as he went through the door.

"Do what?" came the calm answer. "I'm merely taking an attractive young woman on a dinner date."

Damién was certain he knew who was going to be the dinner but he'd already said enough. Anything more and Morgan would probably react as he didn't want him to.

* * *

Domingo wasn't much comfort.

"I don't know what you expect me to do. Morgan isn't some adolescent we can pen up in his room until he comes to his senses. You may as well accept the fact the girl's determined to become a *sans mort* and if she can't get you, or Morgan or me to *turn* her, she'll find someone else—and before you ask, no, she hasn't come to me. Yet. There are plenty of us around, Dami. And many Vampyre, also." Dom unconsciously parroted Alysse' words back at him. "It won't be difficult for her to find someone less disciplined."

Damién's glare nearly froze him in his tracks. He actually stumbled as he sat down.

"Or perhaps not. You've no guarantee she'll find anyone to agree, you know. After all, we're not suffering such a deficit in the *sans mort* population we need to add a new member to the mix. Especially one so well-known." Damién relaxed slightly, only to tense again as Dom, not knowing when to shut up, went on, "Besides, if she has to be turned, wouldn't you want it to be someone who'll be gentle and compassionate and showing some care? Not a *sans mort* who'll just drain her and leave her to recover alone? There's been too much of that recently and Morgan would never do that, *ami,* not with the rituals the Vampyre utilize. He'll at least stay with her and help her adjust."

"If I have my way he won't get a chance. I'll kill him if he touches her, Dom. And I'm going to warn Alain, too. Tonight."

* * *

As Damién's limo landed in the drive, another was flying away. He had a scant glimpse of a red Jag *Conquerer* winging its way skyward, and a blond mane visible through the windscreen as he got out of the car and headed toward the door.

"What was Morgan Averil doing here?" he demanded as Alain came down the stairs to greet him.

"... and hello to you, too," Alain's greeting was slightly sarcastic. He and Damién had become friends during his visits to the estate to try and talk Alysse out of her mad scheme but this, his fifth visit in as many days, was beginning to grate on human nerves. "If it's any of your business, Morgan and Alysse had another date tonight and he's just brought her home."

"Is she all right?" he asked, a little too anxiously.

"Is she still alive, do you mean? Yes. No marks on her throat, no more anemia than usual. Really, Damién, you're beginning to sound like an anxious mother. That should be my department, don't you think?"

"In that case, why aren't you worried? I've told you what she wants to do yet you still allow her to go out— alone—with someone like Morgan Averil." Damién was aware he was painting his friend, perhaps unreasonably, with the blackest brush, but he couldn't help it.

"As far as I can tell, Morgan's been the perfect gentleman. Unlike you, who have been acting like a near-lunatic. Damién, this has to stop. Alysse was certain she's seen you lurking outside several restaurants she and Morgan have been to, and you have to admit it's damned suspicious for you to appear within a few minutes of her returning home every time they go out together. If I didn't know better— and I hope I do—I'd say you're merely jealous."

"Jealous? For God's sake—" He nearly bent double as pain seared through him. Gasping, Damién fell against a chair. He was barely aware of Alain's arms around him, helping him into it. "Sorry. Shouldn't have said that."

"I can see you're really upset." There was a reassuring

pat to his arm. A brandy thrust into his hand. "Here, drink that. Then go home, and relax."

"Perhaps I should try to talk to Alysse—"

"No. She's doesn't want to see you. I promise you, she's all right. And even if she isn't, remember it's her choice." Briefly, Alain looked a little wistful. "I hadn't planned to say this, but . . . I don't want to lose her. So I've . . . told her I'll accept whatever happens."

"Then, may that *One Whose Name* I can't speak have mercy on both you young fools." Tossing down the brandy, Damién held his breath against the alcoholic sear down his throat, handed the snifter back into Alain's hands and stormed out.

* * *

"Can this thing go any faster?" Damién demanded. "I could've flown there myself twice by now."

"Sorry, master." Georges's calm tones didn't work this time. He could see his master wasn't to be soothed. "I have to keep under the speed limit. It won't do for us to be stopped by an air traffic cop."

"No, of course not." Damién threw himself against the seat, leaning his elbows against his knees, face buried in his hands.

She's gone. That was the word greeting him when he'd arrived at Alain's tonight. He'd spent half the day thinking over what the boy had said, worrying over Alysse being turned by Morgan or someone less scrupulous, worried and fretted and—yes, admit it, even muttered something that could've been mistaken for a prayer on two occasions—until at last, as the sun was slowly sinking, he'd fallen into fitful *Unsleep*.

At nine o'clock, Georges had worriedly checked on him, and Damién awakened with his decision made. If Alysse was so determined to damn herself, he had to make one last effort to dissuade her and the only way to do that was to take her with him while he hunted, show her exactly what she'd become when the hunger struck. He'd skipped feeding for several days now because he'd been so concerned with her welfare and at the moment, he was bordering on ravenous. If seeing a *sans mort* at his worst didn't deter her, nothing would. And if she still insisted, he'd do as she asked.

He dressed, ordered the car brought round and went to the La Croix estate.

He knew something was wrong as soon as the butler opened the door. The man didn't smile, his guarded but friendly attitude gone. Instead, he simply stared at Damién as if he didn't recognize him before shaking his head slightly as if to clear it and saying in a quaver, "Master Damién . . . I . . . we aren't receiving visitors yet . . ."

"Gerald, what is it?" He was afraid he knew but it had to be said. Aloud.

"Oh, sir . . ." The man's dignity shattered. Tears ran down his cheeks, transforming his attempt at austerity into a crumpled mask of sorrow. Shaking his head, he waved Damién in. "I-I'll get Master Alain . . ."

Opening sobbing now, he disappeared through a door into a part of the house Damién had never been. There were loud murmurs, then Alain appeared, eyes reddened, manner subdued.

"Damién, this isn't a good time. Come back later when the arrangements have been finalized."

"What arrangements? Alain, I need to see Alysse. Now."

"The viewing will be tomorrow afternoon. You can see her then. I'll leave word to allow you entrance in the evening." Alain turned away.

"Viewing? What the hell are you talking about? What's happened?"

"She's gone, Damién."

"Where did she go?"

"Don't play stupid. I can't take it. She's dead. It . . . it happened shortly after she and Morgan got back last night. She . . ." he hesitated, swallowing a sob. "Please, just go before I say something I shouldn't."

Alain turned and ran back through the open doorway, leaving him standing there.

Damién returned to his car, ordering Georges to take him back to the city as quickly as possible.

Morgan . . . he did this, damned that beautiful child. After I begged him not to. Why didn't I stop him? I should've known he couldn't resist her. I should've done it myself. On and on, around and around, the accusations and now-useless thoughts kept whirling inside his brain. He remembered his last conversation with Morgan, and the only other thought in his mind: *I'll kill him for this.*

"Georges, take me to Morgan Averil's."

"Yes sir."

While Damién struggled to control himself, the car banked sharply, heading toward the house Morgan had rented in an upper class section of the city. Damién had never been there. He'd begged off the dinner invitation after the first time he and Morgan talked about Alysse.

* * *

A party was in progress. The house was well-lit, light streaming from every window illuminating the many limos and luxury cars lining the driveway. Some were sports models favored by the young, and Damién didn't doubt there would be many American recruits for the newly-founded US Black Swans that night.

Soon they'll have one less vampire to do the recruiting, was his only thought as he pushed open the door and went in without bothering to ring the bell. Brushing past the butler, not waiting to be announced, he rushed into the ballroom, standing there briefly getting his bearings.

The room was full of humans, *sans mort*, and Vampyre, the latter two all unmasked tonight. None were hiding behind glamour or any kind of sensory shield, all visible before the mortals there specifically to meet them.

Morgan was standing near the piano, the focal point of the room, holding court among a group of Young Things, all rich, all beautiful, all probably very bored and seeking the new sensation of being enslaved by the *High* becoming a Black Swan offered. He was saying something and they were laughing appropriately, the girls leaning closer, the young men looking envious. The fact that he could be here, in such good spirits and lining up another conquest while Alysse was barely cold from his deadly embrace sent Damién into a fury.

That bastard, partying when he should be with his fledgling. What did Domingo say about his being a caring sire?

No one had noticed him yet but they would in a moment. And after he killed Morgan, they'd probably descend on him, too, and give these bored rich kids a real show—vampires killing one of their own—but he didn't care. He'd—

"Damién. Welcome." That cool, quiet voice sank through his thoughts as sharply as a knife blade.

"Lucien. Hello." Stopping his single-minded charge toward Morgan who still hadn't noticed him, Damién greeted the *Les Elus* Grand Counselor. He didn't look at him as he spoke, but kept his gaze on Morgan, standing only a few feet away now. "When did you get here?"

Damn. This won't be as easy as I thought with Lucien keeping an eye on the proceedings.

"I arrived a short time ago. Just before Morgan's other guests."

Those dark eyes seemed to appraise him. Boring into his back as if they knew what he was planning. Lucien could sense his agitation though his demeanor didn't change. Just as unruffled and in control as ever—the *Dark Prince par excellence*—and he certainly looked the part tonight in a black suit and equally-ebon silk shirt, its pearl-gray ascot skewered by a ruby stickpin the only bit of color about his person.

A pseudo-gentle hand touched his arm. "You seem upset. Perhaps you'd better take a few moments to calm yourself, before—"

He didn't get a chance to finish. Jerking away, Damién launched himself at Morgan who had just sighted him. He'd actually dared to start toward them, one hand outstretched. Damién's onslaught carried them both to the floor amid screams from a couple of the girls and cries of surprise from mortals and vampires alike, his own shouts rising above it all.

"You son of a bitch! I told you I'd kill you if you

touched her!" His fangs were out now, glistening and stretched to their full-length. Too stunned by his attack, Morgan didn't try to defend himself. Briefly, he lay under Damién, staring up at the crimson wash in the blue eyes, sheer confusion on his handsome face.

A drop of spittle slid down a fang, splashing on the perfect chin and that jarred Morgan from his daze. "What the hell are you talking about?"

He didn't wait for an answer. Morgan bared his own fangs as he lunged. The next instant they were rolling over and over, each aiming for the other's throat . . . Morgan defensively, Damién intending to kill. Miraculously, hands seized and separated them before a single drop of blood could be spilled.

Damién was startled to find himself hauled upright by Armand. *Where the hell did he come from?* Morgan was being helped to his feet by Domingo, while a glaring Lucien placed himself between them.

Neither moved, exchanging murderously red stares. Morgan tensed, appearing ready to leap. Domingo's hands tightened on his arms, subduing him. Damién felt Armand's do the same to his own. They didn't dare commit the forbidden act of fighting around the man whose duty it was to ensure decorum was maintained at these affairs. There was no telling what Lucien would do if he was even touched.

"You two . . . take them into the drawing room." They were unceremoniously dragged away. Behind them, Lucien's unruffled explanation was already sending the others back into a party mood. "Nothing to sorry about. Just a demonstration of what happens when someone poaches on another's territory. We'll smooth it over. Everyone just go back to what you were doing."

Voices were already raised in chatter as he also left the room.

* * *

"There had better be a good excuse for your behavior, Damién. Otherwise, you're going to find yourself up on charges of attempted murder of a fellow vampire, and hauled before the Tribunal." That summed up Lucien's side of the business in one sentence.

"If I am, I'll plead justifiable homicide." Damién shot a vicious gaze at Morgan. "You bastard."

"Not at all. I'm proudly legitimate."

Domingo had released Morgan and the Englishman was completely composed again. His fangs well-covered, he raised a hand to brush his hair out of his eyes, smoothing the rest.

"I consider it a pity duels are no longer *en vogue*. Otherwise, I'd meet you on some secluded area with a sword. Attacking a friend for no reason borders on madness, *mon copain*."

"That's right. Make light of it. You . . . *l'ainglais porc* . . . *meurtrier des innocents* . . ." Briefly, every word of English Damién knew deserted him. "She's dead and you did it, even after I asked you not to touch her."

"What's he talking about, Morgan?" Lucien scowled from one to the other, the movement making the dead-black hair whisper against the shoulders of his jacket. "Is this about some mortal female?" He looked exasperated. "Will you never see them as anything more than a soothe to that carnal itch you get while you nourish yourself with their blood?"

"I haven't the faintest idea . . ." Morgan shook his head, then his expression changed with a sickening comprehension. "*She* . . . Dami, you don't mean Alysse?"

"Don't call me that. Only a friend should use that name and you're no longer my friend." Damién looked away.

"She's dead?"

Footsteps approached. A hand touched his arm.

Damién jerked away. "Don't pretend you don't know since you did it."

"When? What happened?"

"Why are you keeping up this charade?" He spun around to meet Morgan's eyes. Didn't like what he saw in them. Confusion . . . and a slowly-dawning misery reflecting his own. "She's dead. Shortly after you left her. It doesn't take a genius to figure out what happened. You agreed to what she wanted, and . . ."

He couldn't finish, just shook his head.

"Damién." That one word held more grief than he'd ever heard, except in his own voice. "I admit I was with Alysse tonight but she complained of being tired and asked me to take her home. I did so and left, coming back here. I'd offered to open my home to the Black Swans and decided I may as well join in since our date was cut short. I didn't touch her. I swear." He looked away again, shaking his head. "Please give me a little credit for honoring a friend's wishes."

Morgan's hand returned to his shoulder.

Damién forced himself to look back at his friend. Staring into Morgan's eyes, he made his gaze go further, seeking the thoughts telling him the Englishman was telling the truth. "If not you, then who?"

"Jacob." Lucien was in the doorway, calling to the butler who appeared as if materializing. "Please call the residence of the *Marquis* La Croix and ask about his sister's death. The number's on Quik-Dial I believe. And be tactful."

With a murmured answer, the butler disappeared. They all stood there, looking at nothing until he returned, speaking in a whisper to Lucien who nodded and dismissed him.

"It appears Mistress La Croix passed away early this evening from heart failure shortly after Morgan left. Her brother was with her at the time." His dark gaze impaled Damién. "You're very wrong in your accusations, Damién. Nevertheless, you've broken a rule at a gathering and we can't let it go unpunished."

The gaze swung to Morgan.

"As the wronged party in this situation, what do you wish to do?"

"Nothing." Morgan didn't look away from Damién. "Except to mourn the loss of someone we both cared for." His hand tightened on Damién's shoulder. "Damién, I'm so sorry."

It happened so quickly, Damién had no warning.

A sudden choking in his throat and then . . . He began to sob, great harsh wracking tears, sounding as if they were wrenched from the bottom of his heart. Not the tears of a mortal but those huge blood-red drops of the *sans mort* . . . wrung from the soul and so rare they were never seen except in moments of the direst grief.

Damién bowed his head and cried the tears he'd never been able to shed when he lost Antoinette, Konstancza, or any of the others. As he felt Morgan's hand on his neck, nestling his face against his shoulder with a pat to his back, the sobs grew louder in their intensity as two millennia of bereavement poured itself onto his friend's chest.

"Let's leave these two alone," was Lucien's quiet order, with no attempt to disguise his contempt at the emotional display. "No need for us to witness this."

No one spoke as the doors were opened. A brief wave of laughter and voices floated in, then was shut out again.

At last, Damién raised his head, meeting Morgan's eyes once more. "Forgive me, *mon ami*."

"Don't apologize."

"*Non*, I must . . . I should have trusted you more. Damn it, we're *amis de confiance*. Can you forgive me for doubting you . . . for . . . this whole unpleasant display?"

"Unpleasant? Really, old chap. I think it's something you've needed for quite some time. Good cry and all that. Just sorry you had to lose someone you cared for to get it." Morgan was becoming the stiff-upper-lipped Englishman, to cover the embarrassment he knew Damién now felt, and to a lesser extent, his own. "Been known to do that a time or two myself, but don't let that get around."

Damién nodded, allowing himself to be soothed by Morgan's act.

"I won't ask if you want to stay, so why don't I walk you to the car?" He opened the door, guiding Damién to the entrance as he spoke. "And tomorrow night . . ."

"What happens then?"

"You and I will pay our last respects to Mistress Alysse."

***

They weren't able to attend the memorial service, of course. If Alain had held it at night it would've raised too many questions. His requesting they be allowed an evening viewing was odd enough. The following day, he departed for Limousin, taking his sister home to be buried in the rose garden as she'd requested. He left word he'd be back. Later. After a suitable period of mourning.

***

A week after, a troubled Georges appeared at Domingo's penthouse.

"I'm sorry to disturb you, *Señor Leyenda*, but I didn't know who else to go to," he began.

"You're Damién's man, aren't you?" Dom thought he remembered seeing him in the pilot's seat of Damién's limousine one evening. As Georges nodded, he asked, "What's happened?" though he felt like saying, *What's Damién done now?*

"It's Master Damién, sir." The valet hesitated only a moment before bursting out, "H-he's been despondent ever since that little girl died. The French one? H-he's locked himself in the wine cellar, won't come out . . . it's been nearly a week now, and . . . this evening when I knocked on the door, he didn't answer."

"My God . . . I had no idea." All Domingo could think was how stupid Damién was being. He'd thought all this had blown over, that he had accepted what happened. Then he remembered his stepdaughter and asked himself if his reaction to her death was any different. He'd hidden in his own rooms for two weeks, in the dark, without feeding at all.

"H-he seems to think a great deal of you, sir, and I thought . . . if anyone could get through to him . . ."

"Of course. I'll come with you now." He pushed Georges toward the door, calling over his shoulder to his own servant, "Emilio, if Mistress Lysetta asks where I am, tell her an old friend is ill and I'm paying a convalescent call."

* * *

"There." It was an ordinary door, looking much like those in the rest of the apartment, though it had a wide, curved utilitarian handle rather than a doorknob.

"And you say he's been in there for nearly a week?"

"Five days, sir." The valet nodded.

"With no nourishment other than wine?"

"Wine . . . and his own specially-bottled blood."

"There's no other way out? No windows or any way to let light in?" Dom studied the door carefully.

"Sir, you don't think . . ." Georges stopped, swallowed and shook his head. "We call it a cellar, but it's just another room in the apartment, specially built to stay cool and dark. For the . . . liquid."

"That's good then." Domingo squared his shoulders and walked to the door. "*Gracias*, I'll take over from here."

"Thank you, sir." Georges stepped back, turning to the hallway. Just before walking out, he looked back. "Get him out of there, sir. Please."

Domingo waited until the valet was gone before striking the door with his fist.

"Dami, it's Dom."

No answer.

He waited a few moments, then knocked again. "You may as well open the door. I've nothing to do for the next month and I can stay right here until you open up."

There was silence. He heard a shuffling, the click of a lock and the door slowly swung open. There were no lights inside but he had no need of any. He could see as well as if the room were illuminated.

Domingo stepped into the darkness. It was cold inside, as well as being dark. The entire room was nothing more than a refrigeration unit, set at 53 degrees, the proper temperature for storing wine. In the back of his mind came the thought, *That's much too hot for blood storage. How does Dami get around that?*

Immediately, the door shut again.

Dom turned. Damién was standing near the door, a very changed Damién. His hair was unkempt and damp, hanging in his face, a face so pale the scar—gotten so long ago during their incarceration, and now so old—shone luminescent against his skin. It looked as if someone had poured something very wet and sticky over the dark locks. He was wearing a silk shirt that once had been white but was now wilted and bedraggled, tails hanging out of his trousers, the front splashed with stains of varying shades of red. Both wine and blood, Dom decided, if the stink of alcohol and metallic tang of hemoglobin floating to him were any indication.

"What do you want?" It was asked in a rusty croak as Damién took a single staggering step toward him and stopped. He held a bottle, raising it to his mouth as he spoke. Liquid splashed and spattered.

"I think you know." Dom dared snatch the bottle from him. "That's enough of that. Good God, Dami, what are you trying to do? Kill yourself?"

"Never heard of a *sans mort* dying of alcohol poisoning," came the slurred answer. Damién was so drunk he didn't even wince at the *Name*. "Or of too much blood."

"Do you want to be the first? Who knows what a combination of the two might do? Especially if taken in large quantities."

Dom looked around at the room, saw what looked like a walk-in freezer, its door flung wide among shelves built into the walls. *He has a separate freezer for blood.* Keeping it at 4-C, he imagined. Both shelves and freezing unit were nearly empty now.

"How much did you have stored here anyway?" He glanced down at the floor. "About six dozen bottles, if all these empties are any indication."

"Seven, but who's counting?"

"You should be. Do you really think it's going to help? This . . . liquid self-immolation?"

"She's dead, Dom."

"As we're all painfully aware." He couldn't keep the irritation out of his voice. *Give me strength to be understanding.* "Humans die all the time, Dami."

"I could've saved her."

"Dami—"

"I didn't really love her, but . . . she was Konstancza's descendant, Dom. I should've done it because of that. I could've gotten my Stanczi back. Kept her with me this time." He pulled the bottle from Dom's hand, slugging down the rest of its contents before it could be retrieved. It overflowed his mouth, dripping down his throat onto his collar. Wide crimson rosettes spread onto his shoulders. "But no. I had to be noble..."

The bottle crashed against the wall as Damién slung it. Shards of glass slid down the wall, trickling to the floor and mingling with the wine.

"I've been searching all my immortal life for a woman to love. I thought I'd accepted I'd never find her and then ... In Alysse, I thought I had, because she wanted so to live. Instead..."

Raising his head, Damién stared at the ceiling. His eyes glowed in the dark with a damp luminescence.

"I'm the world's biggest loser, Dom. Nothing but a damned supernatural soap opera..." He swung his arm wide, intoning in a sarcastic imitation of a holocast announcer. "Welcome, dear friends, to another episode of *Damién's Search for Happiness* ... asking the infinitely stupid question, *Will our hero ever find someone to accompany him through eternity?* And also the very obvious answer: *Not fucking likely!*"

A low chuckle floated to Domingo, so grief-filled it chilled his bones. It ended in a fit of coughing that died in a sob.

"Remember that old joke back in the Twenty-first century? *If you're the girlfriend, wife, or best friend of the hero, don't expect to last past the First Act? And definitely* don't *wear a red shirt.* Story of my life, *mon ami.* Over and over and over ... I'm a failure ... and it's taken Alysse's death to make me finally accept it. For real, this time."

"You did the right thing." Domingo said, stubbornly, though he thought his assurance sounded weak. "Refusing. It was the only thing you could do."

"Really?" Another laugh, this one a rude, drunken

snort. "Nice of you to say. I don't think so." Damién stopped, his tone changing, suddenly filled with surprise. "Oh, Dom... I feel so... odd... so... very..."

Domingo caught him as he fell.

***

"Where am I?" Damién opened his eyes, blinking blearily. He was staring at a ceiling that suddenly tilted, threatening to spill him off whatever he was lying on. Groaning, he closed his eyes again.

"In your room. In your bed, to be exact." The speaker sounded very far away.

He opened his eyes, stared, blinked again, saw someone sitting on the other side of the room and tried to bring the dark figure into focus.

"Alone?"

"*Sí.*"

"Damn. That's no fun. You could at least have tucked a female or two around me." He threw back the comforter, lurching upright. That proved too much of an effort and he fell backward onto the bed again, hands over his face. "Is it still the thirty-fourth century?"

"Yes. Unfortunately."

"Shit. I was hoping maybe I'd pulled a Rip van Winkle."

"I'm glad you can joke. That shows some improvement." Domingo stood and walked over to the bed, looking down at his friend. "How do you feel?"

"I don't have the exact word to describe my condition at this particular moment. Awful? Hellacious? Like Death-warmed over? Come to think of it... not even that comes close."

"Is that a surprise? You've just consumed eighty-four assorted bottles of wine and blood in five days. What did you expect?"

"I expected to die. Now?" A heavy, resigned sigh. "I guess I'm going to live."

"And I for one am glad to hear that. Now, then—" Sliding hands under Damién's arms, Domingo helped him sit up again. "Get up, have a shower. Please. You stink. *Eau de Vin et Sang* is not the fragrance for you."

***

When he left the penthouse, he left Damién in the care of a relieved Georges, bathed, dressed in fresh clothes, and reluctantly admitting he was ready to face at least another millennia or two.

***

"Dami, how are you?" It was six months later, and once again, Domingo and Damién met on Park Avenue.

"Fine. Good as new . . . or bad as ever . . . take your pick."

They moved out of the traffic of pedestrians, taking shelter under the canopy of a nearby shop window. Made small talk for a moment, neither alluding to Damién's little breakdown half a year before or the fact that he'd avoided everyone, including Domingo since then.

"I supposed you heard about Alain La Croix." Dom decided to risk bringing up that sensitive subject.

"*Non*. What?" The last news Damién had of the boy

was after his return to New York. He'd been in the process of setting up several trust funds in his sister's name, for impoverished but bright students. Not as visible as before, still in mourning, he'd explained to the media, but his philanthropic pursuits hadn't suffered.

"He . . ." Domingo's hesitation told him it was something he wasn't going to like hearing. "He was *turned*. Two weeks ago."

"What?" Damién's exclamation made several people stare at him. He lowered his voice. "After Alysse, he'd do something like that? Why?"

"Apparently, he decided the world needed him and his philanthropies more than he needed his soul, so he chose immortality over life."

"Who did it?" Once more, the murderous thoughts he had at Alysse's death came alive. *I'll find whoever it was and kill them . . . stake them out for the sunrise . . .*

"You aren't going off the deep end again, are you?" Immediately, Dom regretted saying anything.

"Just tell me what happened."

"No one knows. All that's certain is his appearance at a Black Swan to-do last night, where he selected a couple of partners and enjoyed them tremendously. There's been no report of his death in the human world, so he's going to continue with *Business as Usual* until such time as he has to change identities. He wants to see you, Dami. To justify it, I think. Do you wish to see him?"

"*Non*. I . . . I might say something I'd regret." Damién sighed. Mentally, he struggled to force the dismay from his mind. "Later. When I've finally accepted all this. I thought I had, but now . . . I've got to start all over again. Don't worry, *mon ami*." He slapped Dom's shoulder. "No histrionics this time, I promise. I just hope he has no hidden desires to ruin him."

"I think . . ." Briefly, Domingo struggled with his words. "I don't think Alain has any bad habits at all. In fact, after witnessing his performance at the Black Swan, I believe that was only to introduce himself to the rest of us. The boy's too much of a gentleman. I'm pretty certain he's going to see feeding as a necessity and nothing more. I don't think you have to worry about Alain La Croix."

Damién didn't answer. Once again, he thought it was a pity human life-spans were so limited.

He was startled to find his memories turning back to the thoughts he's had that day in the church in *Village La Croix* . . . of how ironic it was that a man's acceptance of Salvation didn't assure him immortality in this life but only in the next.

Once again, I had lost one I cared for. Though I might not have had the kind of love for Alysse that I had for the others, I had a connection with her making my grief much sharper and deeper. Eventually, I would see Alain again and his reasoning would make me accept his decision. He had been a good mortal and he was that unique creature, a good sans mort. *What he had been was carried over into his new existence, and that drove home to me that his sister probably would have been the same.*

Of course, now, we'd never know.

I doubted if I would ever stop regretting not doing as Alysse asked, but the question was moot at this point. She rested among her roses at Château La Croix, *her brother would bestow his financial bounties on the world for centuries to come, and I could go on as always.*

Alone.

I had told myself I accepted the inevitable; Alysse's death confirmed that belief. In spite of Domingo's interference, I became a recluse. It was easy, because of what I am. Most of our kind are generally accustomed to long periods, even centuries, of isolation from other beings, anyway. I confined myself within whatever apartment, condo, or estate I owned at the time, traveling with the change of the seasons, never venturing outside except to hustle from building to vehicle and back. I mourned that sweet child's death and her brother's crossing, and felt the last link to my home and the last tie to my mortal life disappear. It was about time, I suppose. Two millennia is long enough to cling to anything. I might have stayed that way forever, if one day Domingo—that proverbial bad centavo—*hadn't once more appeared . . .*

CHAPTER 9

*Gabrielle
Miami, Florida
May 1, 3500*

"You've got to stop this foolishness!"

"Is that what you call grieving for two lives lost too quickly? Foolishness?" Damién didn't look at his friend. "In that case, you've been *Undead* far too long."

"You know what I mean." Realizing in this frame of mind Damién might take almost anything he said the wrong way, Domingo quickly backtracked. "Of course, Alysse's dying was a tragedy, but none of us were the cause. You understood that as soon as you recovered from the shock. And Alain . . . Well, perhaps that was bad judgment on his part. But think of it this way: as long as he can keep his being *Undead* a secret, the La Croix name will continue to survive."

"Small comfort. I'd have preferred it survived the usual way, and if one day there were no more living La Croix, so be it."

Domingo didn't answer. He'd been in the city with his many-times great-stepgranddaughter—still posing as a distant cousin from *Nuevo España*, of course—celebrating her graduating from the University of Tampa-by-the-Atlantic. Knowing Damién owned a townhouse on one of the inlets, and on the off-chance he was at last receiving visitors, he'd made his way there that evening. To his surprise, his old friend agreed to see him.

It was a much-changed Damién, however. No longer debonair and well-groomed, the slovenly creature slouched before him in a faded exercise jersey, shaggy-faced and long-haired, was a shock to the system, even for Domingo, who'd long ago proclaimed himself unshockable.

Time to eat those words and get to work, he told himself as he surveyed his friend.

"Still..." Taking over the role of host, he helped himself to one of the decanters of Damién's blood brandy sitting on the bar. Splashing some into two small snifters, he offered one.

Damién accepted the glass, cradling it between his hands and staring into the rich crimson liquid. "I know this is no simple social call, Dom. Why don't you just say what you came here to say?"

"Since when can't I visit an old friend?"

"Since I purposely told you I didn't want to see anyone. Ever." He took a sip of the brandy. One hand touched the scar on his cheek, that souvenir of Michel Boudreau's demise. He stroked it absently. "You're lucky I broke my rule and buzzed you in."

"Dami—" Domingo saw him wince slightly as he used that nickname.

It was well-known he'd always hated it, but now... It conjured up some memory, he supposed. *Wasn't there some girl a couple of centuries ago who called him that? Something about a bit of infidelity with a human boyfriend and a fire . . .* He couldn't remember exactly.

"All right, I admit it. I'm worried about you."

That elicited a slight snort and a sigh.

"Therefore, I'm here to invite you to a small gathering I'm having tonight at my penthouse . . ."

Damién stiffened; he could see him preparing to refuse.

". . . and to bodily carry you there if you say *no*."

"In that case . . ." Damién gave up without a fight. He downed the brandy in one gulp, making Dom wince. Blood brandy was to be savored, one sip at a time. "I suppose I'd better save myself the embarrassment of being dragged out of here kicking and screaming and come quietly."

Dom's reaction was surprise, then relief.

"Good. Now then," he recovered, becoming business-like. "It's only a few friends . . . all *sinmuertos*, so you needn't wear a human persona tonight. Formal, by the way . . . have Georges dig out the dinner jacket . . ."

"Jean-Louis."

"What?"

"My valet's name is Jean-Louis. Poor Georges finally succumbed to old age quite some time ago."

"Oh." Dom had lost his own man, Emilio, the previous winter.

It had shaken him more than a little. Emilio had been with him since the beginning. *Thralls* lived much longer than humans, but eventually, their bodies did betray them and die, no matter how much their wills were devoted to their masters. He was now seriously considering *turning* his sister in order to prevent losing her, also.

"Sorry. I hadn't heard."

"I asked Alain to bury him on the estate since he was born there." Damién accepted his friend's late condolences with a nod. "That was the last time I spoke to him."

"Well, he's doing well. Dying didn't change him a bit. Still the philanthropist and all-around good boy." Domingo brushed aside any more talk of Alain La Croix. "Now, hurry. Shower. And shave, unless you intend to keep that brush on your face. And let's go. I'm the host so I have to be there when my guests arrive."

Damién hauled himself from the spot on the black leather couch where he seemed to have taken root and headed upstairs. Once showered, he and Jean-Louis considered his long-unshaven face as well as his now waist-length hair.

Already in tune with his master's vagaries and iconoclastic fashion sense, the valet opted for an imperial, an accepted form of beard nowadays, and his deft fingers fashioned it easily. Then, they shortened the dark hair to shoulder length, pinning it back with an onyx-studded clasp. Since he was unable to see his own image in a glass—of which there were none in the penthouse except a small one in the valet's own room—Damién took Jean-Louis's word that he now looked presentable.

Apparently, he was telling the truth, if Dom's reaction was any indication when he returned downstairs to rejoin his friend.

"*Maledicion*, Damil!" Gesturing at his own face, and the mustache adorning his upper lip. "Do you ape me, *amigo*? How will the females know which one of us to choose?"

Damién was actually laughing as he got into the waiting limo.

He'd swear he heard bells, a carillon of chimes, sweet voices singing a wordless melody. Looking around as if dazed, he wondered why the others didn't hear it also, and why everyone was staring at him.

She smiled. He was lost.

Fifteen minutes later, they left together, returning to his townhouse for an evening of passionate and fervent lovemaking.

Three hours after that, Damién came up for air, rolling over to breathe into the darkness, "I've been searching for you for three thousand years, did you know that?"

"That, *ma cher*, has to be the most original line I've ever heard." Her laugh was gentle as she raised herself to nip at his throat. "Unfortunately, I can only reply that I've been looking for you for only two thousand."

Putting his arm around her, he drew her close, startled to feel—or thought he did—warmth radiating from her body to his. Perhaps another sign of their mutual destiny? Together, they generated that heat only lovers could make?

"Am I too old for you?" He made it a facetious question, though he knew she heard the anxiety under it.

"I like older men." She didn't take time to think. Another kiss to the underside of his chin, a soft hand touching his chest and sliding downward under the sheet to rest against that thick, wiry hair nestling his Jewels. "I like men with experience and humor and gentility. You're everything I want, Damién La Croix.

"What shall we do about that?" He turned to look at her and the glow in her eyes, shining at him in the darkness filled him with a happiness he would swear he'd never experienced, not with any of the others. "You de-

***

As the host, Dom was the first one there; as his guest, Damién was the second. The others arrived on time. It was *de rigeur* to be prompt to one of Domingo de Leyenda's gatherings; *fashionably late* didn't exist in the Spaniard's world. As he'd said, the guests were of their own kind. No humans allowed at this party, so they'd been able to speak frankly and freely, air grievances, and generally let their real faces show.

And then it happened . . .

The doorbell sounded. Dom's butler opened the double front doors, ushering someone inside, and the host hurried forward to greet the new arrival with a kiss to her hand and an embrace.

"Dami . . ."

Damién stood with his back to the door, making trivialities, feeling out of place and wondering how long he must endure even Domingo's good intentions before he could make his escape. At the sound of his name, he turned.

"I've someone I want you to meet."

It was *déjà vu* all over again, as Domingo led the woman toward him, though there was no resemblance to fragile, blonde Alysse. This female was the most beautiful creature he had ever seen . . . midnight-black hair, alabaster skin, eyes like polished pieces of jade. Afterward, he never remembered what she was wearing or anything else about the evening except his first sight of her . . .

Taking Gabrielle Champollion's hand in his own, Damién knew he'd found the woman he'd been searching for. As her eyes met his, he realized she knew it, too.

cide, *ma douce*."

As he fell silent, he realized he was waiting anxiously for her answer.

"There's only one thing to do, I'm afraid," she said, with finality.

"Never be afraid, *amour*." Damién's heart sang. "Not where I'm concerned."

That was the extent of their courtship. The next evening, Gabrielle closed her own apartment, moving her things to Damién's. Within a week, they were back in public again, a happy couple for the entire world both Undead and mortal to see. Domingo was pleased to host the reception celebrating their *alliance d'amour*.

Who would've expected Cupid to be a nineteen hundred-year-old vampire?

Chapter 10

Liliana
Chicago, Illinois
June 25, 3527

His first conscious thought was of the coffin rolling, being flipped end over end. He was thrown against the inside of the lid, then back again as it struck something solid, rebounded and lay still. The lid bounced open and he flung his arms over his face, hissing as he braced himself for the holy light to pierce his body and spiral its way into his heart.

It didn't happen.

With a gasp, Damién lowered his arms, looking around wildly. It was moonlight, not sunshine, shining around him, reflecting off the snow and giving a pallid imitation of daytime.

Where in hell am I?

Not in *Hell*, surely—unless it was true the center of that place was frozen solid, as Dante claimed.

His last waking thought had been for the safe haven of his coffin as he eluded his pursuers, and at that time, he'd been in Chicago, Illinois. *How did I get from the Windy*

City to the Great White North?

Scrambling out of the coffin, he wavered a moment, disoriented, as the wind whipped through the trees and scattered snowflakes over the drifts.

Behind him was a snow-covered hill.

As he wrapped his jacket closer around himself, he ruefully wished it had been December when he'd been discovered, rather than June. At least he would've been more appropriately dressed. He zipped the garment closed, turning and trudging back to the hill. The ground was uneven and he slipped several times, going down on one knee before regaining his balance.

Above him on the side of the hill, there was a pile of rubble, the remnants of a building. He paused a moment, looking at the irregular outline showing through the snow, before he began to dig at its base, scrabbling in the hard-packed whiteness like a dog. Presently, he uncovered a piece of warped, frozen wood, part of a coffin, the lid torn off.

Empty.

Damién tossed it aside.

Further on, there were four more snow-covered mounds. Investigation found a second coffin, also empty, though beside this one lay the long-dead bones of its occupant's slayer.

What happened?

Some catastrophe had occurred between the time they had dragged the fourth coffin into the sunlight and come back for his. Something that had killed everyone and turned the world into a ball of ice.

He stared at the snow-covered mounds.

Michel... Andrea... Louis-Étienne... Gabrielle...

they were all gone? *Gabrielle*... his mate... after searching for so long, loving and losing so many others, he'd finally found her. *"We'll be together forever, Damién,"* she had told him. *"Por éternité, ma cher,"* and now...

...and what of Morgan, his friend? Once again reconciled, they were to have met after his concert tonight... no, that was probably centuries ago, now. Or Lucien, sardonic and aloof, but willing to unbend to one he considered an equal? Domingo, Alain, Armand...? Had any survived, were they somewhere in this freezing blankness, struggling as he was?

A single tear slid down his cheek. *The Undead have no feelings... oh, no!* Damién covered his face with his hands, shoulders shaking silently as the snow continued to fall.

He was half-buried in a drift when he raised his head with an abruptly determined shake. His companions were gone but he had survived and it was his duty to stay that way. Therefore, he had to find sustenance.

An owl flew overhead.

That meant there were rodents about, and perhaps hares and other small creatures. Well, he'd lived on such before, and Mr. Owl would learn to share or become a meal himself. As he rose and shook the snow from his shoulders, Damién took a good look at the world into which he'd awakened.

Here and there, white-covered mounds of various heights were probably the remains of buildings. He could see still intact pieces of brick and mortar protruding from the snow. There were trees everywhere, dark pines and cedars, some over fifty feet tall. One near the ruins was tilted slightly, as if its roots were pulling out of the soil. A single, massive branch lay upon the rubble. Probably the weight of the breaking branch had caused the wall of the building where he'd hidden to collapse, tossing his coffin out into what had once been the alley running behind it.

Whatever had happened had saved him. He was already hidden, caught in *Unsleep*, and it had simply kept him that way. If the mishap with the wall hadn't occurred, he'd probably be sleeping yet.

With a shrug, he decided not to worry about what was past but concentrate on the present . . . and how he was going to survive in the forest that had sprung up in the middle of Chicago, Illinois.

***

The snow hare died with a single squeak and a kick. He was surprised how quickly his ability to pursue escaping prey had returned after so many centuries of gentler hunting habits. Nearly inhaling the nourishing liquid, he drew it from the still-warm body in long sucking gasps. Not a single drop fell to the snow and afterward, he stood looking at the small carcass, thinking it was a pity to toss it aside, that if he could abide eating flesh, he would devour what was left instead of letting it go to waste.

It was then he saw the little she-wolf.

She was huddled in the shelter of a thicket across the clearing, a forlorn creature, alone and looking quite small in the surrounding shadows. He wondered where her pack was, or if she, too, was the last of her kind, if the unknown catastrophe had killed off the others. She didn't move, made no offer of violence, and he knew she wouldn't harm him.

As if to confirm this, her eyes, luminous and smoky,

I spoke too soon.

Apparently, God doesn't forgive les sans mort *as easily as he does his mortal children. I ignore the pain as I say that* Name.

My happiness lasted only twenty-seven years . . .

It took me over three thousand years to find my beloved, the woman who would make me forget my lost loves, but the wait was worth it. In Gabrielle, I found everything I wanted, a companion, a lover, a wife. I no longer considered myself accursed. Now, I was one with my fellow Men, both living and not; once more, I had what they had . . .

Someone to love.

Perhaps He with the Unspeakable Name *can forgive after all* . . .

flowed, but a chance meeting at a patron's home introduced the two and they soon discovered mutual interests transcending lineage, namely, wine, women, and occasionally a somewhat discordant song. Alphonse also cultivated François so he might claim the status of knowing someone on the way to becoming famous. François likewise ingratiated himself with the *marquis* for the other man's wealth and influence.

"Your sons are indeed handsome young men," François replied, raising the goblet and swilling down another swallow. "Even Aubert, who, I will admit is so lean he appears to have spent at least forty days in the wilderness."

Aubert was currently fifteen and in the midst of a gawky and rail-thin adolescence. Alphonse started to point out this fact.

"... in spite of that," François didn't give him a chance to speak, "neither he nor his brothers have ever known hunger or privation. My St. Jean must be one who has starved in the desert, seen angels in his delirium, heard God speak . . . his beauty should shine through his rags and filth."

"Have you looked among my servants?" his friend dared ask, somewhat mildly, but hopefully, after this grandiose speech.

"You feed your servants too well, *mon ami*." François emptied his cup and looked around at the wine steward who didn't move.

"But of course. After all, I *am* a *marquis*." Alphonse gestured for the man to pour more wine. As the steward relayed the order to a footman who hurried to do so, he continued, a little defensively, "No one will ever say Alphonse du Maurier's servants have a lean or hungry look."

". . . and so I have failed," François returned to his theme of self-pity, drawing the spotlight back to himself and away from his friend's self-praise. He took another loud swallow. "Now I must return to Aux-le-Piémont, inform the good fathers of *St. Jean-Baptiste Amélioré* of my defeat, and give back their retainer." He sighed heavily, declaring, "I'm a failure."

"Nonsense," Alphonse scoffed, slapping him on the shoulder and jarring his hand so the wine sloshed upon the tabletop. "You're François de Montaigne, the great *artiste*, creator of *Dove of the Annunciation*, *Travail of the Magi*, and other religious masterpieces."

François raised a brow. The gesture suggested that, being a minor noble, Alphonse didn't have to worry about such things as reputations or paying back money given in expectation of something in return.

The steward snapped his fingers and a second waiting footman stepped forward. Over his forearm he carried several spotless napkins and now used one to blot the spilled wine from the highly-polished tabletop. As the servant hurried back to his place, folding the soiled and red-spotted cloth and placing it under the others he held, François resumed his lament.

"I've never before not found my subject. The dove?" He refused to be consoled, waving a dismissive hand. "A simple task. It was one of a tame pair, living in a cote on the church grounds. The Magi?" He snapped his fingers. "Three priests who gladly posed for the glory of God. But this time? My reputation is ruined."

He shook his head and fell silent.

"Perhaps not," Alphonse encouraged. He took a sip

of his own wine, marveling how his friend could consume so much so quickly while he himself had his own goblet filled only once since they sat. "Take a different route as you return home," he suggested. "Why, you may meet your St Jean begging along the highroad."

"Hm." François looked glum. His head drooped, chin resting against the smocked neckline showing through the front of his doublet.

Alphonse scowled at that. He'd made François a gift of the shirt during a recent visit and already the white fabric was marred by several bright spots of wine and some older-looking grease smears. Apparently the *artiste's* manservant didn't know how to remove stains.

"In the meantime, forget your troubles for tonight and let's distract ourselves. My steward tells me a gypsy caravan has camped on the outskirts of my estate." Alphonse looked eager. "He says their *vaida*, their chief, has promised something extraordinary to entertain the *gadje* . . . that's what they call us Christians."

"Gypsies?" François raised his head.

"Refugees, I don't doubt," Alphonse confirmed. "Come escaping the ravages of that war King Louis is waging against Italy. I daresay our part of France may see a good many of their ilk, since we're so close to the mountains."

"But . . . gypsies? The church fathers allow this?"

"I suppose it's our Christian duty to allow them shelter though *I* certainly wouldn't," Alphonse answered. "So . . . we lock up our children and our valuables and the town constable has his day *and* night watches on alert, in case they're to be routed immediately. They're no danger, and are entertaining, in their own heathenish way."

Setting down his goblet, Alphonse stood. He pulled François' own cup from his hand and placed it on the table while he grasped his friend's elbow and hauled him to his feet.

"Come, we'll go there, see their dances, listen to their music, perhaps have our fortunes told by some toothless crone speaking our good French with a terrible accent. If we're lucky . . ." He cocked his head to one side and winked. "I've heard those Romany women make love like cats in heat. Perhaps we'll discover whether it's true. Maybe she'll even *transform* into a cat for us."

"That I'd like to see." François allowed himself to be persuaded. He retrieved the wine cup and gulped the remains, then set it down again, wiping his mouth with the back of his hand and adding more spatters to those on the smocking at his cuff. "Very well. Let's go."

Calling for their horses, they rode to where the caravan was camped.

***

Want to read more? Subscribe to our newsletter (www.epic-publishing.com/subscribe) for a sneak peek prior to release as well as get release announcements about this and other books like it.

darted from his face to the body in his hands. Her tongue flicked out to lick her muzzle, steel-gray and sprinkled with white spots like tiny freckles, before she looked back at his face again. The question asked was plain.

Gently, Damién placed the hare on the snow, and backed away. *"Bon appetit, mon amie."*

The wolf didn't move. He knew she wouldn't come near the body until he was well gone. Later, when he came back, the hare had disappeared, only a trail of paw prints to and from the spot where it had lain.

That went on for nights afterward. Damién would hunt and leave the remains and, though he didn't see the wolf again, always when he came back, the body would be gone.

In the meantime, he was rapidly adjusting to his new life.

It was an eerie place he had awakened to. Even in daytime, the sky was a leaden-gray, clouded so thick no sunlight could get through. He reveled in being awake during daylight hours, though when night came, the moon, possibly because it was closer to the Earth, managed to shine through the clouds, lighting the snow.

He and the wolf had come to an understanding. They trusted each other. Needed each other, in a way. Damién determined he would make the animal his companion. Since apparently none other of his kind had survived, he would feed the creature, protect and care for her, delve into her mind and discern what thoughts lay there. They would communicate, and he would no longer be alone.

Night after night, he hunted. Until the full moon waned and vanished and the pale sliver of a new moon appeared, until, at last, when he returned to check, the wolf hadn't touched his offering.

He came back the next night and the remains were gone but this time, there were human marks in the snow. Bare footprints.

Someone had stolen his wolf's food.

A storm was brewing. He had no time to search for the animal but returned to the shelter of his coffin, worried for the wolf, concerned at the presence of a human. As the snow fell outside, he dreamed of his lost friends, of Gabrielle and how she had been destroyed. *Did she scream for me as she was dragged into the sunlight?* When the oaken stake pierced her breast, blood spattering in cold, hard drops? *Did she call my name? 'Damién, help me!'*

* * *

As the coffin lid flung open, he opened his eyes, gasping.

Something dark and furry loomed above him. *His wolf?* When he saw brown eyes and a pale oval face, he knew why the animal had not returned.

The human was wearing his wolf's pelt

With a snarl, he sat up.

She didn't appear frightened. In fact, she actually smiled. She was young and pale. Looked like some kind of winter forest sprite, with the snowflakes gleaming on the dark fur, touching her eyelashes and cheeks, highlighting the smattering of freckles across her nose.

Freckles? In this sunless world?

"Oh, you're awake. Good. I was worried. You were so still."

His anger changed to puzzlement at her concern.

The liquid caused his lips to smack unpleasantly.

Isabeau hid her distaste behind her table kerchief.

"I must have walked a hundred miles. I went to everyone I knew . . . former patrons, friends, even searched among village streets, but I could find no man worthy to be my St. Jean."

Isabeau forced herself to remain silent. She might have questions, but she could see François was going to tell the story his own way, making his search seem more difficult and dramatic than it probably was.

"At last," he continued, "in my desperation, I found myself at the home of my old friend, Alphonse, *le Marquis du Maurier* . . ."

***

"I have failed, Alphonse." François moaned his lament over a goblet of the *marquis'* best vintage. "Nowhere have I found anyone who remotely resembles my St. Jean."

"Not even among my own sons?" Alphonse still smarted from François' rejection of any of his three children as his model. To the *marquis*, it seemed he was reveling in his unhappiness, though du Maurier was too polite to say so.

They were seated in the *marquis'* salon, enjoying some after-dinner wine. It was early in the evening, but Alphonse's lady wife and his sons had been given rather pointed permission to leave their presence so the two friends could speak of old times and escapades no spouse or offsprings' ears should hear.

Some might have considered it odd for a noble to be friends with someone in whose veins no patrician blood

Until now, she'd forced herself to be civil to the cook, though the feeling wasn't returned. If anything, Mathilde was as openly insolent as possible without risking her place.

The manservant's attitude wasn't much better.

Mathilde and Maxime were both closer to François' age than Isabeau's. Living on the remnants of her late grandfather's estate, they were serfs trained to be house servants in the *château* where she was born.

In Isabeau's case, familiarity truly bred contempt. Unlike the feared reverence they gave Isabeau's mother, who ran her father's household, in their minds, they owed no homage to the young woman they'd watched grow from a colicky baby into a pretty but callow girlhood.

At her marriage, Isabeau received Mathilde and Maxime as part of her dowry. They accompanied her to her new home where their status was as it had been before, receiving food and shelter in exchange for their labor. They called her *maîtresse* but it meant nothing. As far as they were concerned, François was master of the house; he was the *artiste*, the one with God-given talent, and they immediately switched their loyalty to *him*.

Not that it mattered to François if either were blatantly outright in their disrespect of his wife. As long as Mathilde continued cooking such excellent meals, and Maxime did as ordered, he didn't care how rude they acted.

His attitude was evident now, in fact. Ignoring the greasy stains on the tablecloth, and the way the cook served Isabeau, he tore off a piece of bread, sopping up the last liquid from his own bowl before he spoke.

"I've had a long and arduous search," he said through the mouthful of bread, not really answering her question.

his doublet and shirt for different ones, cleaner, much more elaborate, and newer in style. The shirt featured a wide, low neckline, its yoke decorated with smocking. The doublet was sewn tightly at the waist, its full sleeves slashed and the fabric of his shirt pulled through the cuts, making linen puffs.

Richer clothing perhaps, but inside them was the same road-dusted man greeting her on the path. A silent, deep inhalation told her François hadn't bothered to bathe or freshen with a damp cloth before changing.

Isabeau didn't ask where he'd gotten the garments she was well aware he hadn't taken with him. Doubtless more hand-me-downs from the *marquis*, his friend and occasional patron.

It was a ploy of his, to wear his poorest clothing when visiting His Lordship. Once, he'd actually torn a hole in the knee of his stocks, having Isabeau darn it so he could appear before Alphonse du Maurier in patched stockings. When the *marquis* exclaimed over this, François explained he had yet to be paid for his last painting and "one must need wear what one has, if the francs aren't forthcoming." He'd returned home with two barely-worn outfits, taken from the nobleman's own wardrobe, and his own clothing went into the rag basket, where torn garments were tossed to be resurrected as cleaning cloths. It had served its purpose and would now be used by Mathilde for dusting.

"Where did you find him?" Isabeau asked, taking her seat at the table.

Mathilde placed a bowl before her, sitting it down so roughly the stew sloshed over the rim. Isabeau ignored her as she picked up her spoon.

Someday soon, I may reveal my true opinion of that fat sloven.

François had said to chain him.

She looked around, found the chain lying in a corner and dragged it to the cot. It had a hook-and-clasp at each end.

She saw now that around his neck was a leather collar to which the rope was fastened. He didn't move as she untied the rope and let it fall. She used one of the hooks to fasten the chain to the collar. Other than a slight grunt, shoulders sagging under the weight, he didn't make a sound as Isabeau looped the other end around one of the window bars.

Without warning, he dropped onto his side, knees drawn up, head resting upon a bent arm.

"I'll see you in the morning."

Once again, she questioned speaking to the creature as if he could comprehend, but one talked to pets, even horses and cows, didn't one? She had chatted often with the bird, and it understood. At least, she thought it did, since it occasionally replied, making noises sounding like words. When it escaped, it had even sounded as if it called, "Goodbye," as it soared over the trees.

"Good night." She went to the door.

No answer, of course. What would she have done if he'd replied?

Isabeau shut the door and locked it.

By the time she entered the dining room, François was finishing a bowl of stew. From the spatters on the tabletop around his place, it wasn't his first. She thought of meals in her father's home, where no one raised a fork until all were present and seated. François never let his wife's absence keep him from a meal.

He no longer wore the same clothing. He'd exchanged

With both hands, she caught the edge of the blanket, pulling on it with such a heave she jerked it from under him. With a yelp, he rolled over. Crouching, he cowered, arms over his head.

"Here now, I'm not going to hit you. Oh . . ." Her voice rose in exasperation. Dropping the blanket onto the cot, she held out her hand.

He dodged, crouching lower.

"Shh . . . it's all right . . ." She touched the tangled hair, feeling its gritty, greasy texture against her palm.

Whimpering, he flinched, arms wrapping tighter.

"There, there . . . I won't hurt you." She made her voice soothing, the way she might talk to a puppy someone had accidentally stepped on. "It's all right. Shh."

She continued caressing that filthy hair until the trembling ceased. He lowered his arms, peeping up at her fearfully. Again, she patted the blanket.

"Come now. Up. Here."

This time, he got onto the cot . . . actually leaped onto it, making it wobble precariously . . . tried to circle, lost his balance and toppled over the side, crashing to the floor.

She was there before he could recover, catching an arm and pulling him upright, though it was more of a half-crouch, back curved in a hunch.

"Are you hurt?"

The oddest expression crossed that dirty, hairy face, what she could see of it.

Is this the first time anyone has asked that question, or shown concern?

Again, she patted the cot. Once more, he climbed back onto it. This time, he straddled it, a leg hanging over each side, watching her.

"Come in." She tugged on the rope, then thought better of it, for surely that must hurt his neck, perhaps make him resist more, even snap at her. Feeling a surge of shame, she spoke to him as she would to a dog. "Come. Good boy."

Is he dog or man? She assumed the creature was male. There simply was no feminine aspect about him. *How does one talk to a man who thinks he's a beast?*

He loped forward and stopped again, looking up at her, mouth hanging open. If he'd panted and tried to wag his nonexistent tail, she wouldn't have been surprised.

"There's the cot. You can sleep on it." She decided speaking to him as though he understood.

Perhaps he did. Her uncle's hounds learned commands. It came to her the creature was probably some poor half-brain turned out by his family and left to fend for himself. It was perhaps fortunate François came upon him.

She gestured to the cot, blanket folded neatly at its foot. He looked from her to it, cocking his head to one side.

"Sleep. Here." To emphasize her meaning, she patted the blanket.

Again, there was that unsettling stare. When he moved, it was so swiftly she startled, staggering backward.

Seizing the blanket in his teeth and dragging it to the floor, he pawed it into a rumpled heap, threw himself upon it, circled three times and dropped with a grunt. He curled his legs against his chest, body twisting so his chin rested on crossed forearms in a pose so doglike she might've laughed if it hadn't also been bizarre.

"Not that way."

It was only with the pretty girls, however. François wasn't concerned with the equally pretty boys. He might paint them but their bodies interested him only in the way they looked on his canvasses.

Privately, Isabeau thought she would've been happier if François preferred boys also, to the complete exclusion of his wife, but she couldn't be so fortunate.

***

With the key, Isabeau opened the studio and went in, tugging on the rope as the creature hesitated at the threshold. He followed reluctantly. When she unlocked the storeroom and went inside, he stopped in the doorway, pulling back on the rope with a whimper.

That made Isabeau wonder if he'd ever been inside a building before.

Where did François find this creature?

Was he running wild in some wood, like a *loup-garou*? She'd heard tales of abandoned children raised by wolves but thought them merely fictions. Had he attacked her husband and been beaten into submission? Neither appeared injured in any way, but the creature's hair was so tangled and matted with dirt, he might have sustained a hidden wound.

How could she tell?

François seemed hale enough.

Just now the beast didn't look ferocious. Squatting in the doorway, gazing about, then back at her with those unsettling eyes, he seemed more afraid. Cautiously, he stared at the wall, sniffing the boards.

Does he smell the long-ago scent of the horses once living here?

Isabeau thought it too bad he didn't do the same where his wife was concerned.

Refusing assistance from his in-laws, he and their one manservant tore out stalls and hayloft, using the boards to make a floor covering dirt and animal detritus. Part of the roof was removed, replaced with windows holding precious panes of clear glass, purchased from the glassblowers of Murano in Italy—this was before the war—and brought to the cottage *via* ship through the port of Marseilles. They'd gone without meat for two months to pay for that glass but François willingly suffered for his art and expected his household to do the same.

He also cut out most of two walls and replaced those with floor-to-ceiling windows.

It was fortunate the little building already faced north, else he probably would've shifted its foundation to catch that harsh, clear light so necessary for the artist's canvas.

The storage room was built into the back of the studio. Once where bags of grain and harness were kept, it was entered only by an inner door. There was a single panel-less and shuttered window François fitted with parallel iron bars, lest some miscreant attempt to break in, for that was where he now kept his canvases, finished paintings, and drawing supplies.

It also held a cot and blankets. When in a creative fervor, François worked late into the night, sleeping in the storeroom where he might awaken and immediately return to the canvas. Since those times generally coincided with his finding a new and pretty model, Isabeau didn't delude herself he wasn't sleeping with her, also. She decided that was one of the reasons he didn't want her coming to the studio.

"Put him in the room inside my studio." His answer was offhanded, as if every day he appeared leading a creature that might or might not be a man masquerading as a beast. "There's some chain there. Replace the rope and fasten him to one of the window-bars so he won't run away. He may be restless, being in a new place."

He took a key from his purse and lobbed it to her. François always kept the key to his studio with him. As if he didn't trust Isabeau not to snoop during his absence.

Isabeau caught the key easier than she caught the rope.

He continued to the cottage.

"François, wait . . . will he understand me?"

He didn't respond or look back.

"François?"

Together she and the creature watched him walk away, studying the swagger of his body where the fabric of his doublet stretched across his broad shoulders.

"Come on, you." Isabeau tugged on the rope.

She started for the building that was her husband's studio. Rising from his haunches, François' new pet trotted behind her with that odd, clumsy gait.

Other than *le privé*, the studio was the only outbuilding on the property, situated to the side and behind the cottage but clearly visible from the path. Originally, it had been a stable. Shortly after they moved into the cottage, François converted it into the place where he created those paintings his patrons declared masterpieces.

Isabeau had no opinion on that score. She was rarely called upon to judge her husband's talent.

With his own hands, he'd toiled in the broiling sun, sawing, nailing, and hammering to make a home for his paintings. When it came to his art, François didn't stint.

With a whimper, he thrust his head against her hand. Automatically, Isabeau's fingers stroked the filthy hair, creeping around the side of his head to one ear, over its slightly pointed tip, scratching behind it as she'd often done her uncle's dogs. He grunted with pleasure, leaning against her palm.

His tongue shot out, brushing her wrist. She forced herself not to recoil, made her fingers continue their scratching movement.

"He likes you. Good." François looked satisfied, as if *he* had something to do with the beast's acceptance of her.

She pulled her hand away. The creature stared at her. Reproachfully, she thought. He'd liked having his ear scratched.

Her hand felt greasy. She forced herself not to scrub her palm against her skirt. She hoped he didn't carry fleas or other vermin.

"I'm hungry." François' belly growled, underscoring his words. "For the past mile, all I could think of was a bowl of Mathilde's good lamb stew. Is supper ready?"

As if the cook had nothing more to do than prepare a meal to sit and spoil waiting for his return.

"It should be soon." Isabeau put reproach into her next words. "We didn't expect you."

"No reason you should."

No apology for appearing with no warning. It wasn't in François' nature to think of others or show regret at their inconvenience.

"Tend to my pet." He tossed the rope to Isabeau. She nearly missed it, scrabbling to keep it in her hands.

"What shall I do with him?" She was resentful. As she'd suspected, she was to assume care of the thing.

Frowning, she studied the creature's face. An odd countenance, no snout, no muzzle with a wet bulbous nose, though fur-covered and whiskery, as uncomfortably disturbing as its eyes.

She glanced at the creature's body, at the long coarse hair growing in a tangled mane around its neck and down its back, spreading over dirt-bespeckled shoulders. A matted pelt encircled its hips, part of its texture and color seeming the skin of another creature, the rest its own flesh, and the legs . . . hairy but relatively bare as were the feet . . . but so filthy.

With a start, she was certain she was looking not at an animal, but a man, a dirt-caked man, squatting at her husband's side, his fingers digging into the grass. A man, watching her with curious but intelligent eyes.

Oh, surely not.

As if sensing her unease, he growled, a rough, low grating, deep in the throat. Isabeau took a step backward.

"Steady," François said, but whether to her or the creature she wasn't certain. "Don't be afraid. It's only he doesn't know you. Hold out your hand."

When she didn't move, he repeated, "Hold out your hand. Let him get to know your scent."

As if he's a dog. She wanted to tell him she wasn't afraid, then thought, *Why bother?*

Her fear, or lack of it, didn't matter to François. Defiantly, as if she were dealing with one of her Uncle Étienne's hunting dogs, she offered her hand to the beast.

He sniffed at it, running his nose along her fingertips and against her palm, snuffling loudly. He barely touched her, a mere brush of flesh against flesh, but it made her skin chill slightly though she managed to hide its shiver.

She hoped it had made its way over the mountains into the warmer climes of Italy.

Now her husband stood before her again, sweaty and travel-worn, the dust of the highroad surrounding him like a cloud, begrimed into the sleeves of his linen shirt and the shoulders of his doublet.

Briefly, she was tempted to stalk back to the house, refusing him the welcome he expected he deserved, but, as usual, duty overcame anger. What would be the use of turning away? When she looked back, François would still be there and so would that dog or whatever it was.

He stopped. So did she.

The creature dropped to its haunches.

Without preamble or greeting, she said, "Did you find what you sought?"

Not that she really cared.

"Yes," he answered. "I did. I found my St. Jean."

"Where is he?" She looked past him down the track, expecting to see some beautiful boy on horseback, hurrying to catch up. It was usually the handsome son of a noble family whom he'd entranced with promises of immortality on canvas.

She saw no one. The path was empty.

"Here." He held up the rope.

Her gaze traveled its length to where it wrapped around the animal's neck, only to have her attention caught and held by the oddest eyes she'd ever seen. They were the color of molten copper, flecked with glints of bronze-patina-green, under heavy brows meeting in a single line, looking out of place in what she could see of the mud-bedaubed face.

Isabeau thought, *These are not the eyes of a beast.*

along with his sketchbooks and charcoals, she thought he was abandoning her. He swore otherwise, that he'd come back "when I've found what I'm seeking."

It had happened so many times since, she didn't worry if she awoke and her husband was gone, didn't wait in quiet distress for sight of his silhouette on the highroad. Sometimes, she hoped he wouldn't come back.

Being an abandoned wife would've been sheer heaven.

Recently, he'd been approached by *le église de Rue Jean-Baptiste Amélioré* about painting a mural depicting their sainted namesake. François accepted and set off on a quest to find the man who'd be his subject.

This time, he'd been gone so overlong she wondered if perhaps *le bon Dieu* had finally granted her unspoken wish. Then she thought, *Why should he? He never has before.*

Now, as if to underscore that belief, François was back . . . and this time, he wasn't alone.

There was a dog with him, following him at the end of a length of rope. By its size, some big lumbering brute, loping clumsily behind him. Its gait was odd, as if its forelegs were shorter than the hind ones.

Merde, Isabeau thought resentfully. *Something else for me to tend after he loses interest.*

Like the bird he bought from a Spanish sailor off a ship supposedly having sailed to the newly discovered land to the west. Or those exotic flowers that wilted and died as soon as the first cold wind blew off the mountains. Of course, he used the bird in several paintings but after that, it sat in its cage, ignored. Isabeau was the one cleaning its droppings, taking it out and letting it fly around the cottage and sit on her shoulder, until one day it flew away never to return.

Excerpt from *Path of the Wolf* by Tony-Paul de Vissage

Coming Soon from Epic Publishing

Aux-le-Piémont, France,
April, in this Year of our Lord, 1499

It was early in the spring when Isabeau de Montaigne first met the man who would become her lover.

France was at war with Italy; that very day, the country had suffered another defeat in its continuing conflict begun by their king, Louis, the twelfth of that name. It was also the day when, after an absence of three months, Isabeau's husband returned to Aux-le-Piémont.

Skirts clearing her ankles so they wouldn't brush the damp grass making up the untended meadow calling itself their front courtyard, she met François on the path joining their cottage to the highroad. If the sluggishness of her movements was any indication, she was unenthused in welcoming him home.

The first time he went away, when she woke to find him throwing a change of clothing into his knapsack

ABOUT THE AUTHOR

A Southerner of French Huguenot extraction, one of Tony-Paul de Vissage's first movie memory is of being six years old, viewing the old Universal horror flick, *Dracula's Daughter*, on television and being scared sleepless.

That may explain his lifelong interest in vampires and why he's now paying back his too-permissive parents by writing about those who walk the night.

A voracious reader whose personal library has survived following their owner more than 3,000 miles across country, Tony-Paul has read hundreds of vampire tales and viewed more than as many movies.

Readers may discover more about this author at his Facebook page: https://www.facebook.com/tonypaul.devissage or on Twitter: @tpvissage.

TRADEMARKS ACKNOWLEDGEMENT

The author acknowledges the trademarked status and trademark owners of any wordmarks mentioned in this work of fiction.

ACKNOWLEDGEMENTS

My thanks to author Linda Nightingale for allowing me the use of her characters in this novel— *Morgan D'Arcy, Tristan Lachlan,* and *Lucien St. Albans*— as well as the quote from her novel *Sinners' Opera.*

Merci, à une amie et un grand auteur.

At last, I had found the thing I'd spent millennia searching for. Now, I had a home, family, and friends. No longer the aristocratic Frenchman with a pedigree disappearing into the mists of the past, I was now the leader of a new tribe . . . a gathering of creatures of the light and the dark, coming together with their only desire the will to survive. I had lost so much, so many times over, but now, at last, what I'd always wanted, I had come to possess. I didn't question how it happened, how it took a catastrophe nearly wiping out humankind as well as my own to bring it about. Perhaps it's true we have to suffer to deserve what we receive. They say all things come to he who waits.

I no longer walk the interminable corridors of Eternity alone. I no longer walk them at all, for now I am anchored—by Liliana, by my friends, and never need wander again.

I now silently thank that Name I am no longer allowed to speak for making it happen, and hope my happiness will go on forever.

"I'm certain you're going to shoot me down in flames if I answer that the wrong way, Damién," came the wry rejoinder. "For now, I think I'll take the *Fifth*."

"Hm. That depends. Did you ever become a citizen? I don't know if a Brit can hide behind the *Fifth Amendment*."

Surprisingly, Lucien gave a short, and remarkably mirth-filled, laugh. Damién turned to survey the little group trailing behind them.

"I'm so very glad to see you all." His voice was slightly tearful and he didn't appear in the least ashamed of it. "*Bienvenue, mes amis. Bienvenue* to all of you. Welcome to my home!"

"Damién?" Liliana nudged him gently.

It was the first time she'd spoken. Morgan was enchanted by her voice. It was low, soft, and though she was a Brother's mate and therefore untouchable, stirred him in deep places. He gave a visible shudder, was startled to see Lucien whom he had always thought had the best control of them all, tremble slightly, though he wasn't certain if it was from hearing Liliana's voice or because he was still captured in the child's grasp. Briefly, he hoped their quest was over, so he could bring his wife and daughter to safety.

"Invite your friends inside. Let's offer them some refreshment." She glanced at Morgan, smiling. The perfect hostess in rabbit fur. "We have a variety of vintages ... Canadian hare, fox, or ... yes, for this special occasion, some elk. That would be appropriate, don't you think?"

"But, of course, *amour*." Again, he gave that brilliant smile. "Afterward, we can talk about why you're here." Unfastening his son's hand from Lucien's forefinger, he handed the child to his mother. "I'm certain you didn't walk this far for a social call."

With one arm across Lucien's shoulders and the other around Morgan's, he followed Liliana down another narrow tunnel. The others followed behind them as he guided his friends toward his family's living quarters deeper inside the snow-covered mountain once an office building.

"We have a few rules here," he went on. "Having both Undead and Living, we have to, but we've survived together for nearly five years now, so it seems to be working. I think all of you will fit in. We could use a little culture and elegance, don't you think, Morgan? And I'm certain under that woodman's parka, there still flourishes the heart of the *connoisseur*, eh Lucien?"

The look on Lucien's face at that statement was worth more than he'd ever imagined.

"But what is he? Vampire or werewolf?" Morgan was unable to keep from smiling as the child reached out and tugged at the straight black locks hanging over Lucien's shoulders, and attempted to stuff a handful into his mouth.

Somewhat stiffly, the former Grand Counselor caught the pudgy wrist, freeing his imprisoned hair. Immediately, his forefinger was captured by short fat fingers. There was a brief tug-of-war ending with his abruptly surrendering, his black eyes meeting dark ones in which he saw a will relatively unformed but already as determined as his own.

You and I must come to terms, my child. The message passed between them. *And soon.*

"A little of both, it seems." Lucien's father didn't appear bothered by the question, if his shrug was any indication. Out of the corner of his eye, he'd watched the exchange between Lucien and his namesake and chose to ignore it. "He shares my dietary restrictions, but can go about outside even on the brightest day we've had. His wings only appear during the full moon. That's the only transformation he makes, so far." He leaned forward, confiding in a loud whisper, to which Liliana laughed loudly, "I can hardly wait to see what puberty brings. And—"

There was a pat to the front of her rabbit-skin cloak, an embarrassingly gentle and loving caress. Touched by the gesture, Alain looked away. Next to him, Domingo smiled slightly.

"—in the Spring, we'll have another. A daughter this time, I hope." As he finished speaking, there was total silence from the little group. No one knew what to say.

tocratic features. "*Great God.* Damién, you've mated with a *lycanthrope?*"

To his credit he didn't spit on the ground as they once had when speaking that word.

Damién, however, didn't appear insulted, nor did his wife. She simply leaned closer into him, and rested her cheek against his chest, cradling the child between them. The little boy stuck his thumb into his mouth and stared back at Lucien who appeared disconcerted by the directness of those dark eyes.

"It's impossible!" Armand asserted. "Everyone knows we can't impregnate mortals."

"Oh, *oui, everyone* knows that, don't they?" Damién's interruption was sarcastic. "I imagine there are one or two among you who can put the lie to that statement." He gave Lucien a fleeting glance, then looked directly at Morgan meaningfully.

"And how is Isabeau these days? Still with you?"

Lucien shifted impatiently as Morgan gave his old friend a quiet smile. "Always. She's waiting for me to return, if we found what we were looking for."

Damién wagged a finger at Armand.

"Generally, what you say is true, *mon ami*. We are somewhat... shall I say handicapped?... in the way we can reproduce. And I don't mean just through the blood. With our own kind? No. With mortal women? Usually not. But with supernaturals such as my lovely Liliana here, who is a blending of the two? Obviously yes. *Most definitely*. What's that old saying? *Try it, you'll like it.*" He took the little boy from Liliana, hugging him tightly. "As my little Lucien—and I hope you approve his naming, Grand Counselor?—is proof."

her shoulders. There were several knowing glances exchanged and smiles. *He finally found a woman,* they seemed to say to each other. *Thank Someone for small favors in this cold world, anyway.*

What Damién said next, however, startled everyone.

"You've already met my wife and son, I see. Nearly stepped on the boy, didn't you, Lucien? Still not looking at anything under that fine Roman nose of yours? Better be more careful. Can't have my heir flattened by a mis-step."

The glances changed to looks of surprise. Lucien managed to appear a little embarrassed as well. At least, they all assumed that was what his quick glance downward meant.

"You've married a *Breather*? And haven't *turned* her?" Domingo blurted.

"And accepted her child as your own." Armand made it a statement.

"*Oui*, Liliana's my wife." Damién's laugh and the shake of his head disconcerted both of them. "But the child's mine. *Ours.*"

"That's impossible!" Domingo stated, flatly.

"I always try to accomplish two impossible things before dinner," Damién paraphrased, giving him the impish look that had always disconcerted, and sometimes angered, the Spaniard.

"How?" Armand didn't mince words.

"If there were a full moon, I wouldn't have to answer that question," Damién began, as Liliana smiled up at him. He moved his hand from her shoulder to touch her cheek gently, then lifted her chin and kissed her, in front of everyone.

"You mean, she's—" Disdain crossed Morgan's aris-

Chopin's *Three Etudes* and the *segue* into *Waltz in A Minor*, and when I finished the rendition of Beethoven's *Moonlight Sonata*—all movements, I might add—they were speechless." He made a little *moue* of irony. "I had one second of a standing ovation before the asteroid struck."

"Such is the fleeting aspect of Fame." Damién shook his head in mock sympathy.

"Fortunately, that wasn't the day the music died, though sometimes I wish it had." There was a surprisingly ironic gleam in Lucien's black eyes. "Morgan has kept the Classics alive by humming them to us while we traveled. Incessantly."

There were several agreeing snorts from the group. Morgan good-naturedly ignored that.

"You wouldn't happen to have a piano here, would you?" He raised his hands, twiddling his fingers rapidly. "I'm longing to touch the ivories again."

"No piano, I'm afraid." Damién shook his head. "However, we have a couple of carpenters among us who could possibly construct one, under your direction, though I'm afraid the keys would have no ivory in them."

"That doesn't matter," Alain spoke up quickly, as if to get a word in before the others' voices overcame his. "As long as we can hear the Masterpieces in some way other than Morgan's vocal interpretation."

That brought a laugh, even from Morgan, who loudly agreed.

"I had heard rumors there was a colony of the *Brethren* living in New York," Damién remarked, beckoning to the young woman. She came to stand beside him, still carrying the child. "Had no idea who it was, of course."

All noticed the proprietary way he put an arm across

changing to surprise. "I don't believe it. Is it—?"

Beside him, Armand laughed, and the others started whispering among themselves.

"Damién, it *is* you, isn't it?" Morgan ran to meet him as Damién stood and came down the dais' steps, throwing his arms around his brother-in-blood. There was an overjoyed smile, a flash of slender fangs. *Undead* had no need to hide them now, by either *glamour* or otherwise.

Behind him, the young woman followed.

"Well, well." Releasing Morgan, he stepped back, regarding Lucien with amusement. "Your fashion sense may have failed, old chap, but you're still better-dressed than my people are."

He indicated his own furry garments.

"I'll admit my attire isn't that I would've personally selected if I'd had a choice." Lucien's answer was dry, thinking of his long-disappeared wardrobe of *NuArmani* and *Versace-Libre* suits buried under tons of snow in London Proper. "We were fortunate to take refuge in a sporting goods store when the asteroid struck. Whenever we had to move, that was the place we always tried to find. I'm certainly glad to know *you* survived, Damién, though I had no idea it was you we were traveling to meet."

"This is truly difficult to believe," Morgan commented, looking around. "You . . . *The Master* . . . ruler of a small but growing band of Undead and mortals subsisting side-by-side. Have you come down in the world or up?"

"There's been a lot of water—or shall I say *snow?*—under the bridge since we last met," Damién laughed. "How did your concert go, by the way?"

"Fantastic." The blond vampire's eyes sparkled. "I had them on the edges of their seats with my arrangement of

"Please," Alain, ever the peacemaker, dared interrupt. He'd been snarled at so much by Lucien during their trek, he hadn't spoken in days. "Can't we just—"

"Quiet!" Behind them, Armand interrupted with a hiss. "He's coming back."

The man stood before them, looking slightly surprised.

"He says he'll see you." With a wave of a hand worthy of the most noble courtier, he gestured into the cave. "If you'll follow me?"

Silently, they trooped behind him through the narrow, dark tunnel leading into the cave. Eventually, it widened into a large, circular room roughly dug out of the rock. There were brightly burning torches driven into holes in the walls. In the center, an enormous copper brazier further illuminated the cavern, warming it.

Hands outstretched, Lucien took a step forward toward the brazier, only to draw back quickly as the man snapped, "Watch where you're putting those big vampire feet of yours!"

Lucien looked down, past the quilted and tread-soled "moon-boots" he was wearing. In front of him sat a child, a little boy of possibly five years, dressed in furs similar to the man's. Before he could say anything, a young woman was there, scooping up the child and clasping him to her fur-covered bosom, hurrying away to stand near a dais of piled rocks at the back of the cavern . . .

. . . where someone sat on a carved stone bench.

Someone who looked very familiar.

"So!" the man called out. "You've come to see the Master, have you?"

"Good God." Morgan's head came up, his frown

When he spoke, it was with severe composure. "There's no need for that."

"We mean your master no harm," Morgan interrupted. "I assure you."

The man thought about that, and made a decision. "Stay here. I'll ask if His Majesty will see you." He disappeared inside again.

"Perhaps when we get inside," Morgan turned back to Lucien who was fuming impatiently. "I should do the talking."

"Since when do I need an ombudsman?" came the angry question. "I've spoken to kings and emperors. Are you hinting I'm less than diplomatic?"

Morgan had to smile at that. *Diplomatic* was something none of them had been for several centuries now. "Your delivery of late has lacked a little . . . shall we say . . . *finesse?*"

"Shall we say *bullshit?*" Lucien shot back at him. "I've been up to my waist in snow for the past three hundred years and my balls are frozen solid. That's apt to make anyone a little crotchety. I'm sorry I haven't been sympathetic enough to suit you."

"*Certimente,*" came a tart rejoinder from behind them. "We're none of us at our best. But in your case, Lucien, that off-day has lasted about two and a quarter centuries now."

"For the love of God." Tristan, who'd been silent for the last two miles, snapped. He'd taken off his snow goggles as they came in sight of the cave and his eyes were still adjusting to the brightness. "You two have been bickering since we left New York State. Can't you let it rest for a little while?"

waving a slender hand at their surroundings. "Everything we've heard points to a cave outside what used to be Chicago, and from all I can tell, this is the one. I—"

He broke off as a figure wrapped in furs appeared, then scowled as he saw the man was human. Long-haired, bearded, he wore a neutral-colored mass of sewn-together rabbit skins. The man took a step toward them and stopped.

"Who are you?" He didn't appear afraid, merely cautious, even a little disdainful.

"We've come to see the one they call the Master," Morgan began.

"Why? What makes you think you'll be allowed to see his Lordship?" the man spoke with the superciliousness of a Royal Herald looking at a peasant. "Though I can see you're like him."

"What does that mean?" Lucien demanded.

"You're too pale," the man replied, adding as he saw a retort forming on the handsome lips, "So are we, too, but nobody's that bloodless, except the deceased." He nodded, with satisfaction. "Yes, you're as the Master, but are you his kin or his enemy?"

"Listen you—!"

At Lucien's snarl, the man gave a cheeky half-smile and raised his hands, forefingers touching each other forming a cross. Behind the vampire, some laughed while a few gasped and closed their eyes, forcing themselves not to cringe and turn away.

Lucien's anger transformed into a cold smile, a shaggy *Dark Prince* in hand-me-downs but no less dignified than in *Hugo Boss Futura*. The Grand Counselor of a no-longer-existing *régime*.

EPILOGUE

A Gathering of Equals
Chicago, Illinois
Six Years Later

The little group of travelers paused before the mouth to the cave.

"Are you certain this is it?" asked the dark-haired one, pushing back the hood of his parka to peer at the entrance.

He and the others were a motley-dressed assortment, their clothing consisting of threadbare parkas and overcoats, bodies wrapped in blankets tied at waist and neck with ropes, and camouflage coveralls so worn in places bare skin shone through. All were pale from lack of sunlight, though a few had the pallor of the severely-ill or close-to-dying.

"I'm positive, Lucien," the man standing next to him answered a little impatiently. He was tall and blond and appeared tiring of his friend's disbelief, expressed continuously during the long trek from mid-town New York City to where they now stood. Pulling off tattered mittens, he stuffed them into the neck of the poncho he was wearing,

There is one more thing I must tell—one snippet of information left to convey, a vignette, if you will, a brief glance into the future, an ending of sorts, as well as a beginning . . .

In that moment, I understood why my search was never successful. I had been looking for love in the wrong places—pardon moi *for stealing the title of an ancient song, but one always falls back on clichés, because they're always so true. I hunted among mortal women and those immortal for the affection I desired, when I should have sought someone different. Liliana combined the best of two species; as a supernatural, she understood my isolation, as a human, she mirrored my need for love. I hope she will understand it forever...*

as if expecting some miraculous transformation to take place. He felt an odd twinge inside, then it passed, and he was as he was before. A killer. Still vicious. Still a danger to humans.

"You don't understand." There was no way around it; he'd simply have to tell her, state it as a hard, cruel fact, and be done with it. "I can't stay with you Liliana, because I'm a vampire. And you're a human."

He wasn't prepared for her laugh. Nor for the force with which she flung herself into his arms, suddenly warm and dark and furry.

Luminous smoky eyes looked up into his, "Oh, Damién, my dear, it's *you* who don't understand!"

She smiled, and the smile grew and grew until the firelight shone on two-inch incisors protruding from a steel-gray muzzle dusted with white spots like tiny freckles.

Damién's arms tightened about her as he pulled her against him, his body answering her touch as he allowed the desire he had been fighting to blossom into full growth.

She was, he thought as he bent to press a kiss against the gray fur, the most beautiful werewolf he'd ever seen.

"No, it's not the coffin, Liliana. It's— I can't stay here . . . with *you*."

"Why not?" She was clearly puzzled, forehead creasing in a frown that had behind it the threat of tears.

How could he explain without frightening her? They were possibly the last of both their species and he knew if he stayed with the girl, no matter how much he craved her companionship, soon or later another, stronger desire would surface. He would hunger for the sweet liquid pulsing through her throat, would rip out that white column of flesh to obtain it.

It would be good to make her into one like himself, but for some reason, he felt it was necessary for them both to survive.

Alone.

He'd go back to the ruins, leave food for her as he did for the wolf. And if even that closeness proved too much of a temptation? He'd simply leave. He looked away, not wanting to see the stricken look on her face as she realized she would be alone again. He knew exactly how she felt.

"Is it because of what I am?" she asked.

Perhaps she *did* understand.

"In a way. It's partly because of what *you* are but it's more because of what *I* am."

"What do you mean?" She shook her head. "I thought we could set our differences aside, be together, you and I. We may be the last."

She came closer to him as she spoke, and Damién could feel the confusion within her. And something else. Something that made him lean toward her, responding not with lust or hunger but an urge to take the girl into his arms and comfort her. For an absurd moment, he waited, twisted pieces of wire.

Somewhere, his wolf still lived.

"I thought you left the food for me."

"No, it was for her. You haven't harmed her?"

"Harm the wolf?" She seemed shocked he would even think it. And a little amused. "Oh, no, Damién, I could never harm her."

"Is she still here?"

"Yes, she's here. The wolf will always be with us." She smiled and gestured to the makeshift table, picking up a bowl and offering it to him. "You must be hungry. I've saved you some food."

He looked at the bowl. It held some type of soup, thick and red. How could he tell her he couldn't eat that? Taking it from her, he stared at it a moment. It wasn't very well-prepared, was hardly cooked at all, cold now with a thick skim on its surface. He could swear he smelled . . . *blood.*

He felt his insides quiver. He set down the bowl. "I can't stay here, Liliana."

"Why not? Oh, I understand. Your box. We can go back for it once the storm stops, if it makes you feel more secure."

He'd never thought of his coffin as a security blanket.

"I certainly envy you such a thing to sleep in," she went on. "I have only the hard ground." She gestured toward a pile of ragged blankets near the fire. "Do you suppose I could share it with you? Would there be room for two?"

He found himself considering the idea. It would be good to have a companion he could actually talk to, could love.

strike the earth, sparing him and killing all the humans within its path, and turning the entire planet into a frozen ball by enveloping it in a mass of clouds too thick for the sun to penetrate.

Dubious honor in being able to say, *I told you so!*

"I mean, I know what an asteroid is," he amended his tone to sound milder. "How long ago?"

She glanced at one of the cave walls. There were lines cut into the rock, a vague attempt at a calendar, clear and symmetrical at first, soon becoming disorganized and random. She shook her head. "I don't know. I lost track after I came *here*. I think that was about five years ago. I guess it must be several hundred years now."

"How many survived?"

"Only a few. Most of them went to the equator. There's snow there, too, but it's a little warmer."

"Why didn't *you* go?"

"I tried, but they wouldn't let me. They chased me away. Said they didn't want my kind following them, as if our differences matter now."

He frowned slightly. *Her kind.* Her name was Hispanic ... "I thought that sort of prejudice died out a couple of millennia ago."

"Some intolerances never die," she replied, a trifle grimly. "Even after a catastrophe. Oh, I'm so glad I found you, Damién. You don't know how lonely I've been."

She bestowed a smile upon him he would have sworn could melt the snow outside, while at the same time, it caused dismay in his own heart.

"Is that why you stole food from my wolf?" Now that he'd gotten a better look, he could see the furs she wore were rabbit skins, clumsily fastened together with

Startled, he said the first thing coming into his mind. "Ill-met by moonlight, my proud Titania."

"More like *well*-met by moonlight, I'd say." Surprisingly, her smiled widened.

"Who are you?"

"My name's Liliana, but we can talk later." She took his hand, pulling him out of the coffin. "We have to go before the storm gets worst. My cave's near here."

* * *

He followed her to the cave, pulled along by her hand, surprised by the strength in that frail-looking limb. To a bare hole gouged out of the mountain of mortar, where a fire burned in a ring of stones.

"Put your coat near the fire," she ordered. "It'll be dry soon."

As he obeyed, he looked around. A sparsely-furnished place to be sure. A board resting upon two pieces of crumbling brick for a table . . . two cracked bowls set upon it.

"Who are you?" he asked again.

"Liliana Flores, and you're—?"

"Damién La Croix. What happened? Was there a war? Did the humans finally annihilate themselves as they've always threatened?"

"War? No, it was an asteroid."

"*Asteroid*," he repeated the word stupidly.

"Yes, you know, a rock from space."

"I know what an asteroid is." It came out sharper than he intended.

The doom-sayers had finally been right. A piece of stone hurtling through space had chosen that moment to

Printed in the USA
CPSIA information can be obtained
at www.ICGtesting.com
CBHW010330221024
16173CB00004B/165

9 781734 648669